tempted

AVA HARRISON

Tempted
Cover Design: Hang Le
Editor: Editing4Indies
Proofreader: Marla Selkow Esposito, Jaime Ryter
Formatting: Champagne Book Design

Dedicated to my team of kickass superstars that help
make my dreams come true.

'Tis one thing to be tempted, another thing to fall.
~William Shakespeare

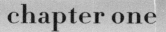

chapter one

Drew

I HAVE A LIFE MOST WOULD KILL FOR.

At twenty-eight, I own the hottest club in New York City.

There should be absolutely nothing to complain about . . .

But unfortunately, that's not the case. I do, in fact, have one problem.

Cal Loche.

The bastard won't stop calling me. I hate that little fuck, but as much as I don't want to answer, I do business with him, and it's a necessary evil.

"What do you want, man?" I hiss through the phone.

"I need a favor."

A deep breath escapes my lungs. I shouldn't have answered the call.

"And why would I do anything for you?" I pivot my chair away from my desk and lean back. This could take a while, so I might as well get comfortable.

"Word around town is you are looking at space uptown."

"Is that the word? Maybe you should check your sources."

I am looking for space, but I don't like this douche knowing anything about my plans. I'm so close to getting what I want, and I don't need him fucking it up.

"My source is just fine, and what he says is that you want to buy it."

Shit.

Even though what he says is true, I don't need anyone knowing it. I have too many competitors who would love that piece of information. They would scoop it up just to mess with me, regardless of my plans for the space.

"And why does this concern you?" My voice sounds steady and uninterested. I'm plenty interested but giving him that knowledge only plays right into whatever hand he's playing.

"Well, as it so happens, I own it."

My body jerks forward at his words. "How come I didn't know this?" I ask through gritted teeth.

"It's owned by a different holding company."

"So basically, Mommy and Daddy own it," I fire back. I probably shouldn't poke the beast, but I'm too pissed to care. This is not what I want to hear tonight. I'm dealing with enough shit.

"Doesn't matter who owns it. If you want it, you'll do me a favor."

I let out a sigh. He has me by the balls. He knows it, I know it. "And what exactly is this favor?"

"You still looking for a waitress?"

"I am."

"I have one for you."

"I'm not employing some girl you're banging."

"I'm not banging her. She's my girl's sister. She's a charity case, just the way you like them. Actually, you'll want to meet this one in particular. Trust me."

"What the hell is that supposed to mean?"

"That would be too easy. But she's exactly the kind of girl you have a soft spot for." His words have me sitting forward in my chair. Cal knows my sordid past. He knows about Alexa. He knows my weakness. How much he knows is another problem, but I keep my voice steady.

"A druggie?"

"Recovering. But still. Look her up and make your own decision, man. But if you want the property, you'll hire her."

"Name." It doesn't matter what he says, I know I'll offer her the job. My need to help, to fix, to save is too great.

"Bailey Jameson."

Placing my hand down on the computer, I start to type, and the moment her picture pops up, my hands pause, hovering over the keyword. She's gorgeous. Stunning in a girl next door sort of way. Her haunted eyes cause my stomach to turn. I don't have time to process why I've had such a reaction because what I see on the page has my attention. I pull up the article on her.

My fingers freeze on the keyboard once again.

"What do you gain from this?" I grit through clenched teeth.

"I don't need some recovering addict getting evicted and moving in with me and my girl. Her sister is a lead prosecutor with the city, and I can't have Bailey fucking that up for me. That connection is gold. Do this for me, and you'll get your property."

"Fine." I slam the phone down, knowing full well this is probably the biggest mistake of my life, but there is no going back now.

I reach across my desk and grab the decanter of scotch and pour myself a glass. The night hasn't even begun, and it's already off to a shit start. How can it get any worse?

The answer to my question walks in the door as if being summoned.

Another thorn in my side I can't get rid of.

Monica.

She is here, yet again, begging for another night of what she claims only I can provide.

Hiring her to work at my club was another bad idea—a

growing theme in the life of Drew Lawson—but at the time, I didn't anticipate a problem. Why would I? We never dated. We just fucked.

Once.

The problem is, by bringing her into my world, she now thinks it means I want more.

I don't. Never did.

Not from her. Not from anyone right now, to be honest.

For me, there is no time for a date, let alone a relationship. All of that shit isn't in the cards for me and definitely not with Monica.

I have big things on the horizon, and I can't have some indiscretion fucking that up.

She should know nothing will happen between us.

But apparently, the hints and flat-out refusals haven't been enough to break through her thick skull.

So here we are at the club, and yet again, she comes up to my office trying for more.

There's a bar full of people downstairs and a mountain of paperwork waiting for me to do. Letting this girl down easy is not something I'm in the mood for.

This might be some men's fantasy, but right now, it's my nightmare.

This gorgeous woman—I won't deny her that—is throwing herself at me, and I'm not feeling it. Her hand slips the collar of her skintight black dress down her shoulder until she's fully uncovered one breast.

"Monica," I warn, hoping my tone is enough to finally have her seeing reason. It doesn't. She slips the other side off so that she's completely topless and slides the rest of the dress down her legs.

"Get out," I say, rather lazily. She stops and stares at me.

The fact that nothing I say is getting through to her only manages to annoy the shit out of me. "I said. Get. Out."

She's a ten on any man's scale: blonde, five foot ten, long-ass legs, and a nice, tight ass. She must see some change in my expression because she throws a coy smile my way as she saunters closer and runs her fingers down my chest.

"You don't want me to go," she says without a hint of shame. "Let me make you feel good."

I can feel the bass of the system below pulsing at my feet. This was my life: the party, the music, the alcohol, the drugs. As the tempo from the club speeds up, I almost cave.

I run my hands roughly down my face before making my way out of the office.

"Where are you going?" she asks, looking at me with doe eyes as I walk past her.

"We've been over this, Monica. You've gotta go." I open the door, and the deafening noise from below filters in, nearly drowning out her next words.

"But I—"

"But you what, Mon?"

A fucking nickname. What the hell is wrong with me? I see the glimmer of hope flash in her eyes. I'm going to crush her. I have to smash all that hope because it will never happen. I don't do relationships, let alone commitments. If tonight is any indication that I've yet to make that perfectly clear, I need to rectify this situation. Might as well get it over with.

"I didn't call you. You've come into my space uninvited, and this is done."

Her head whips back as though I slapped her. "What? But you . . . What the hell, Drew!" she shouts in her high-pitched screech.

My ears sting from the sound, and I lose my patience. "We are not in a relationship. You work for me. That's it. It will never be more."

Her eyes go round as it sinks in. As she pulls her dress back up, her lips begin to quiver. You've got to be fucking kidding me. I can't handle a crying girl.

"Why? Wasn't I good enough?"

"You work for me."

"And if I didn't?" She looks at me, hopeful. As much as she drives me crazy, she's my best bartender. I can't afford to lose her.

There's the million-dollar question. What do I say to make this end? "Monica, I'm sorry. I'm just not that into you." There, I said it. Dick move quoting a movie, but fuck it. It works like a charm.

She rushes of out the room, slamming the door behind her.

That went well.

The truth is, I feel horrible.

If I had known I was going to hire her, I wouldn't have touched her.

I really am the asshole she thinks I am.

chapter two

Bailey

I WAKE WITH A START. MY BODY THRUSTS FORWARD FROM MY bed as sweat beads at my temples.

What time is it?

Groaning, I turn my head until my eyes find the alarm clock. 3:00 a.m.

Of course, it is. This is how my nights go.

Dream of the past, then wake in a state of panic. Fall back into a deep sleep and miss the alarm.

My arm starts to hurt at the thought. A phantom pain. A scar to remind me.

I look down at the now faded mark.

Most people can't tell it's there anymore, but I know, and it does its job every time I look at it.

It holds me responsible.

It holds me prisoner.

The pain, normally a dull reminder, has intensified ever since I went behind my sister's back to get a job at a nightclub. I have no business working there, but I don't have a choice. I had just received my third eviction notice, and my sister's boyfriend, Cal, was my last hope.

My only stipulation was Harper can't find out I work there.

Ever.

Given my past, she'd be livid that I'm even contemplating working in a bar.

I kick my legs over the side of the bed and pad across the hardwood floors to my small kitchen. Grabbing the Oreos and a glass of milk, I take a seat at the kitchen island. Oreos were always my dad's method of problem-solving. When he had to work out something in his head, he grabbed the cookies and milk and got busy thinking.

My eyes catch on the frame that's home to my favorite picture ever. It's of Harper, Dad, and me in front of Coney Island. He'd ditched half a day of work to take us for a spur-of-the-moment trip to the amusement park.

I stare at the picture. So much has changed, but some things remain.

I miss him.

Since his death, trouble has followed me. It's my shadow. I'm basically a cosmic tragedy. But that was before.

I'm clean now.

No pills in two years.

This time will be different. It has to be.

I dunk one more cookie into the milk, saturating it until it practically falls off my spoon.

Shoving it into my mouth, I stuff down all thoughts of my losses.

Just because I'm working at a bar doesn't mean I'll have the desire to take a pill.

My pain is gone.

But are your memories . . .

Club Silver.

I'm here even though everything inside me screams to stay

away. Perhaps it's the sheer creepiness of the place, but more likely, it's the angel on my shoulder trying desperately to win out over the devil on the other. Those two have been at war since my dad died. The devil's tallies are far greater.

Silver isn't much to look at from the outside of the building, just a typical New York City warehouse. The concrete slabs with no windows serve to make it completely frightening. It's dark and utterly ominous on the outside, but it's the inside that's home to the proverbial monsters in my closet. The depths of this carnivorous building hold a whole different world of problems for me. Problems that I've promised myself will stay buried in the past.

I have no choice. I'm all out of options.

My phone rings and I groan when I see it's my sister. The universe seriously hates me.

It's like the woman has ESP or something. I shouldn't answer, but I know Harper. She'll keep calling until I do.

"Hey, Harp. What's up?" I try my best at playing nonchalant when inside I'm quaking. I need to be inside starting my job, but I can't tell her that.

"Nothing. Just headed out to meet Cal in SoHo. There's some property he's interested in, and then he's taking me to dinner."

"That's fun. I'm headed out too," I lie, hoping she doesn't expect me to give her a play-by-play. I have less than five minutes.

"Where to and with who?" she badgers.

Harper means well, but I don't exactly have the best track record, and she's made it her personal mission to keep me on the straight and narrow.

"I have to grab some groceries and run some errands. Nothing much, but I'm catching a ride with a woman from work, and she's waiting on me."

"Hmm," she says, clearly concerned about this stranger she's yet to vet.

"Don't hmm me, Harper. She's doing me a favor."

I'm annoyed that I have to fabricate a story. The lies just keep adding up, and I hate it, but I'd hate to disappoint her more.

"Okay." She sighs. "Will you call me when you get home? I want to catch up."

Inhale. Exhale. Lie some more.

"I have a really busy day tomorrow. Can we catch up after work?" I grind my teeth, hoping she'll just go with it for once.

"Ah, all right. Tomorrow works," she assents. "I love you, Bae."

"I love you too, sis."

I disconnect and run my palms down my face, feeling extra shitty for all the deceit even though I know it can't be helped. I've learned over the years to simply keep Harper ignorant to certain aspects about my life because she just doesn't get it.

Running a hand through my brown locks, I decide it's time to move. I breathe in deeply, counting slowly to ten, and allow each breath I inhale to calm my fragile nerves. With tentative steps, I make my way inside. To think that, in a few short minutes, this barren building will become my lifeline—or my demise.

I stop in my tracks and shake my head. I can't think that way. If I get myself keyed up before I make it in the door, I'm done for. I shake it all off literally and figuratively. If anyone is watching me, they'll think I'm tripping. After one more deep breath, I begin to walk again.

With all my strength, I push open the heavy metal door. It screeches across the floor as I walk over the threshold. My eyes dart around the room and goose bumps break out on my skin. The familiarity is unnerving. I already feel myself falling back on old habits as I locate the bar.

I'm waiting for the itch to begin.

The need for a pill.

That need to feed the beast within.

It doesn't come, though, and for that, I'm relieved. There's no place for that in my new life.

I walk into the room filled with decadence and sin, clinging to the hope that I'm stronger than this. There's no temptation great enough for me to break this clean streak. Putting food on my plate and making rent are quite the motivation to stay on the straight and narrow.

My ears begin to ring as my feet carry me closer to the bar. The bass is so loud it actually shakes the room, and I can barely hear myself think. It would be easy to lose myself to the oblivion of the pulse in this familiar terrain. For this reason, I haven't stepped foot in a club or a bar since the night I attended my first NA meeting.

This feeling of wanting to drown in booze gnaws at the pit of my stomach as my eyes scan the room. I shouldn't be here, but I have no choice.

Club Silver is a white and sterile, modernistic space. Along the outskirts of the room are faintly lit alcoves for bottle service. White chiffon drapes hang from metal wires that allow the patrons to close themselves off from the outside chaos and be free to drink and party the night away.

My jaw tightens. *No.* Not going back there.

Pushing back my memories, I continue to the bar. I walk up to the stainless-steel monstrosity that takes up the whole wall, and the most beautiful man I have ever seen turns in my direction. He has short, brown hair that looks kissed by the sun and piercing blue eyes. His intense gaze causes me to flush from head to toe, and a perfect five o'clock shadow adds just a bit of ruggedness to his otherwise boyish features. This man can easily play the main character in my next fantasy. He's sheer perfection.

"Um, is something wrong?" I ask, feeling shy under his blatant staring.

"Nope. Not so much as a hair out of place." He cracks a warm smile. "You just remind me of someone I used to know. No big deal," he says, pulling down the handle of the tap and filling a glass full of amber beer. "Damn," he barks as the keg splutters, spilling the last of its contents and spraying a bit at him. "Give me one minute," he says, running toward the back.

I take my time looking over the liquors that line the wall in front of me. Top shelf and the most expensive bottles sit highest on the wall. I'm sure in a place like this, bottles even that expensive don't gather dust.

"Sorry about that," he says, wheeling in a new keg. "What's your poison?" Mr. Beautiful throws my way.

"Actually, I'm here to see Mr. Lawson. I'm Bailey Jameson."

"Your name is Bailey Jameson?" He chuckles. "Did your parents have a drinking problem or something?" he says over his shoulder as he slings the keg into place.

Oh my god, his arms are so toned and sexy. He raises his eyebrows, signaling he's waiting for me to speak.

"Um, what?" Brilliant, Bae. Now he thinks you're a moron.

"You have two liquor names. Ya know, Bailey and Jameson?"

"Oh, right. I'm pretty sure that was an unfortunate accident." I grin and continue my quest to locate my new boss. Please don't let it be a hot bartender.

"I'm supposed to be starting here tonight."

"Ah, yes. The fresh meat." He smirks.

Oh god, that smirk. My insides melt right then and there.

"Unfortunately for you, Bailey, you're stuck with me. Drew is meeting with someone in his office. I'm Carter Cass."

Carter Cass. His name is perfect . . . He's perfect.

"That's okay." Suddenly, I'm nervous at the prospect of being stuck with this guy. He leans forward across the bar, his muscles becoming more defined, and I gulp deeply as I'm sure my cheeks turn crimson. His lips tip upward as he catches my perusal. Keep your head in the game.

"You sure you want to work here? You look a little scared." His grin deepens.

My eyes widen. Shit. He's hot, but no reason to make an ass out of yourself. "I'm fine. New jobs always make me a bit uneasy."

"Well, you got nothing to fear at Silver, Bailey. Everyone is real chill, plus the tips are killer. You can't get better than this anywhere in New York." He motions around the room to prove his point. "Why don't you come back here, and I'll show you the ropes? What did Drew tell you about the job?"

"Honestly, nothing. I've never spoken to him." I shrug.

"So how did you wind up here with us?"

"A friend called in a favor. I was about to get evicted from my apartment—"

My hand clamps over my mouth. Carter lifts his head to me. He doesn't say anything, but I know he wants to ask. He's giving me time to spill, but I won't. We stand here in silence until he averts his eyes and gives me the out I desperately want.

"You don't need to say more. I get it. So, where were we?" He taps his chin with his pointer finger. "Oh yes, the ropes. Come on back. Don't be scared. I won't bite." A small dimple forms in his right cheek, and it's so cute, my whole body relaxes. It gives me the strength I need to overcome this first obstacle, remembering how I got here.

I make my way inside the bar and peer up at him as he tells me the ins and outs. With his tanned arm, he points toward the secluded banquettes lining the dance floor, showing me the way to the VIP rooms I'll be serving.

"So, Bailey, what's your story? You a struggling model too?"

"Hardly. I assume you are?"

"Model, actor, singer. Typical bartender story," he says as he pours a shot of Patrón Silver for a group of guys across the bar from us. "I can tell you're going to do great. The men will love you."

He goes about pouring more shots for another group of people. The idea of "the men" loving me isn't sitting well. Guys are another distraction I don't have time for.

"If you start to need a drink or a pick-me-up, just let me know. I've got you covered on both fronts," he whispers in my ear conspiratorially. "However, you have to be careful because the boss is a tight-ass about it. He used to be cool, but now, not so much. We find our way around it, though." Fuck, so not what I wanted to hear. "Thanks, but I'm good. I'll stick to Coca-Cola or Red Bull."

"Good for you. I respect that. Honestly, though, according to all the girls who work here, the only thing you need is a good look at Drew. Apparently, and I quote 'The man is sex on a stick.'"

"And you . . . what keeps you distracted . . ." I trail off, not knowing what to say.

"Tall, blonde bombshells who love to party." Great. The complete opposite of me. I'm not tall, have mousy brown hair, dull blue eyes, and the word "bombshell" does not apply. So much for a chance with him. Although that's probably a good thing, seeing as he does drugs. I can't be involved with someone who does.

Hours pass and I can't remember the last time I clicked so well with someone. I'm working my ass off, but at least it's fun.

A movement to my left has me leaving that thought behind. Carter is trying his hand at juggling but failing miserably. I can now add cleaning the floor of broken bottles to my list of things to do tonight. Carter passes a gorgeous smirk my way. My lip involuntarily rises into a large, goofy smile of my own. This guy is undeniably some exquisite eye candy. I must have been standing here for minutes, just staring, when I hear Carter call out to me.

"Hey, earth to Bailey. I know I'm hot, but can you please stop staring? And for the love of God, close your mouth. The drool is not attractive, love. We can't be friends if you keep looking at me like that."

Shit, was my mouth open? Lifting my hand, I go to check for drool, and Carter bursts into laughter. Great, not only am I caught gawking, but now I look like an idiot, too.

"Um, sorry, lost in thought. What did you say?"

With a wave of his hand, he manages to move into work mode. "Nothing. Can you take a bottle of Goose and the usual mixers to table three?" I must still look confused because he narrows his eyes at me and lets out an audible sigh. After a shake of his head, he resumes berating me with directions. "It's the one toward the middle of the room."

I start to head in that direction, but clearly, I'm not going the right way because I soon hear, "No, to the left. To the left. Right next to the table with the blinds closed. See the guys?" I throw my hands up to signal that he can stop now. Jeez, am I really that clueless?

Heading toward my target, I take in the scene. It reminds me of a distant memory. A memory I have no business remembering right now. My arm starts to throb, and I feel the familiar need clawing through my veins.

My first day here and I'm already jonesing to escape.

It never gets easier.

The accident changed everything.

Made everything worse.

I shake off all thoughts. I need this job, and I need the money. I can do this. I have to do this.

I make my way to the VIP table. As I step into the alcove, I notice four men in business suits conversing. They barely acknowledge my presence. Not even a glance up as they lift the empty bottle of vodka toward me and wave it around.

"We need more Goose," a handsome man slurs at me.

That's not any old bottle of vodka. That's Grey Goose Magnum, and it's a steep eight hundred dollars a bottle. One of my friends back in the day had an infinity for the stuff. These men are clearly wealthy, so I decide to play nice to hopefully garner a fat tip.

"Um, of course. Sorry, I grabbed the wrong bottle of Grey Goose." I flash my biggest smile at him only to be met with a sneer that quickly turns to something else. His face pales as it goes slack, and he blinks several times, never removing his eyes from mine. *Um. Strange.*

"Are you okay?" I ask, concerned for the man.

He shakes his head and clears his throat before slipping right back into the asshole he was to start.

"You brought us that cheap shit? Don't you know who I am, girl? I don't wait for anyone." His antics draw laughter and hoots from the other men at his table. "Go fix your error and ask Carter if Monica is available to wait on us." He dismisses me with a wave of his hand. "Monica knows what we like."

More laughter follows me out of the VIP room. *He's drunk,* I remind myself while trying to hold the anger at bay. It also felt like he was covering up whatever strange reaction he had to me by his over-the-top rudeness.

I don't need anything from those assholes. There is plenty of money to be made in the place, and if it's Monica they want, then fine. I'll find my next paycheck somewhere else in this building.

"Do you know who Monica is?" I ask the first waitress I see. She's a petite blonde with a pixie cut and enough makeup caked on to last tonight and tomorrow.

"Yeah, she's in room five right now. Probably giving the geezer a lap dance." Pixie rolls her eyes. "I'm Darla. You must be Bailey."

I nod. "Nice to meet you. And seriously? Lap dances?"

"Don't mind me. I'm jealous. Girl makes bank." She shrugs. "If you need anything, let me know," she calls over her shoulder as she walks past me.

I head to room five and practically run into Monica as she exits.

"Excuse me," she snaps, looking at me like a flea.

I ignore her. "Are you Monica?"

"Yes," she hisses, sounding equal parts annoyed and bored.

"Room three specifically asked for you."

She looks at the room and raises her perfectly manicured eyebrow. "You couldn't handle Reese? He's a big flirt, but he's harmless," she jeers. "I'll take care of him. Go. And let Carter know we're switching rooms."

I turn on my heels to leave.

On my way back to the bar, I stifle a yawn. I'm such a lightweight these days. I check my watch. It's not even 2:00 a.m., and I'm already exhausted. As I'm doing my best to stay awake, the patrons of the club are in full force party mode.

I throw my towel onto the bar and fling myself onto a stool. "Those guys were real pricks," I say, Carter raises an eyebrow and follows my gaze to the VIP room I came from. Turning back to me, he shrugs.

"Reese is an ass. Welcome to the party."

Turning my face away from Carter, I focus my attention on the table of assholes. I shouldn't continue to torture myself over what a few douchebags in overpriced loafers think of me. I take a deep cleansing breath and resolve not to give the jackasses from table three any more of my thoughts.

"I need coffee." I groan. "Or an Oreo."

"Oreo? Interesting . . ."

My brow lifts. "Why?"

"I saw you more of Sour Patch Kid kind of girl. Either way, what you need is a distraction, some eye candy."

"And how will eye candy help?"

"If you saw some, you would know. Nothing gives a pick-me-up like staring at someone hot at a bar. For me, I stare at Monica. Would never touch her, but damn, is she fun to look at."

"I've got you to stare at . . ." I stifle a yawn. "It's not working."

"Hotter."

"Hotter, like what?"

"From what the girls who work here say . . . He's behind you."

My head shifts so that I'm looking over my shoulder, but I don't see anyone who fits the image I have in my head of who Carter is talking about.

My gaze roams the room, squinting through the mass of people congregating on the dance floor. The crowd parts, and for a split second, my heart stops beating. I'm frozen in place, my hand trembling under its own weight. Directly across from me stands a divine creature.

He is tall and sculpted from head to toe. His brown hair has that just fucked appearance that makes me want to run my hands through it, and his eyes remind me of the night. An endless depth, a bottomless pool of darkness, that promises to hold secrets like the midnight sky.

He is a Greek god amongst men.

I have never seen a man this beautiful.

He's rendered me useless.

I watch him push his sleeves farther up on his arms, showcasing toned forearms, and I notice the way he seems to be clenching his jaw. He looks almost irritated as he looks out into the crowd, surveying the people. This man makes Carter look ordinary. It's ridiculous.

Carter starts to speak, but I can hardly hear him. I'm lost in a trance. Completely riveted by this man. "Who is that?" I sound breathless because I am.

"That, my dear, sweet Bailey, is what the girls like to refer to as our resident hottie," he says while pulling out a bottle of Johnny Walker Blue and pouring it into a tumbler beside me. His irritated tone gives him away. He clearly does not like sharing the spotlight. I can't help but tease him.

"And here I thought that title went to you." I bite back a laugh, and from my peripheral, I can see Carter smile.

"Oh, it does. He's just the bonus," he says, and I return my focus back to the dashing stranger. He practically glides down the stairs. I'm mesmerized.

"But who is he?" My eyes narrow, and I can feel a line forming on my forehead as I try to figure out who this man is. Everything Carter has said is completely lost on my one-track mind.

"Sweetie, by the way you're looking at men tonight, yours truly included, I'd say you really need to get laid." He chuckles. If only he knew what kind of a dry spell I was in, he wouldn't be so flippant with those comments. It's a travesty.

"Oh, shut up and just tell me who he is." I need to know.

"Turn your head to me 'cause I don't want to miss your reaction to this bit of news."

I roll my eyes blatantly at him as our gaze meets.

"That, my love, is Mr. Drew Lawson. Doesn't it just suck that you'll have to look at that every night?"

Fuck. That bit of news just made this job a bit more interesting. But, Lord, will he be a distraction at the same time. I finally pull my gaze away long enough to wipe down the bar. My rag comes across more pieces of glass from Carter's attempts at juggling bottles. I toss the shards into the trash when the hair on my neck rises. It feels like someone is staring at me. It's not a creepy feeling, just my body's realization that I'm being watched. Raising my head slowly, I'm trying to find the person responsible for eliciting such a reaction, and my gaze collides with Drew Lawson's from across the room.

I know I should avert my eyes, but I can't. It's like some force is holding my head hostage. The draw to him is innate. I can feel it in my bones. Maybe it's just his incredible looks, but my body is telling me to pay attention. He's looking at me with the same quizzical expression that implies he's more than aware of me.

It's startling.

chapter three

Drew

A S MUCH AS I LOVE THIS CLUB, THE LAST THING I WANT TO do is socialize with the patrons, so I take my sweet-ass time making my way downstairs. Silver is an upscale club. Only the elite and best looking in New York City are allowed entry, and with that comes a whole different set of problems. They can all afford the real party. I've banned the use of drugs in my club, but enforcing that rule isn't always so easy. This clientele rarely enjoys a night out without your standard line of cocaine. I despise it, and I despise them.

It wasn't always like that. I used to be the life of the party scene. Hell, that's how I ended up a club owner. But things change, and shit happens. One of my biggest regrets came at the hand of one line too many.

I shake my head, not allowing the memories to take root in my brain right now. No, instead, I ready myself to deal with the mayhem. My office is my sanctuary, but down here is my hell. People think I have the life they'd kill for. I'd kill for it all to go away.

Rolling my sleeves up to my elbows, I survey the scene. It's a packed house. Nothing new there.

I need to check in with Carter and get the hell out of here.

Too much work to do and a meeting in a few days in Napa. I'm sure he's at the bar chatting it up with the new girl.

Fucking Cal.

Typically, I would have told him to fuck off, but after reading everything I could find about her online, I knew I couldn't.

Which brings me back to the here and now and a new employee who makes me remember all the shit that haunts me.

Shaking my head, I look for Carter, and when I see him, I can't help but grin. I was right. He's his typical charming self. Women love him. Men love him. Hell, I believe my grandma would even love him. I can't see the girl's face, but she's probably eating him up. Most of the new girls do.

My eyes wander down her backside.

She's average height, with a narrow waist and hips that protrude just enough to give her the hourglass figure men fall over themselves for. Her long, brown hair falls in waves around her shoulders, but it's when she turns around that my breath literally hitches.

That face . . .

Her eyes, although I can't see the color from here, which I know from the pictures online, are blue, are also large and mesmerizing. They're wide as she takes in the mayhem that is Club Silver. And her full lips are pulled up in a smirk at something Carter says behind her.

God, she's beautiful.

I can't explain my reaction. I experience insta-lust often, but this is something different.

It's her eyes.

Her haunted eyes.

Her demons make her different.

No, it's more than that . . .

I internally groan at my own wayward thoughts.

She's clearly a siren, but I don't have time to contemplate my body's visceral call for her. I'm going to chalk it up to . . .

Yeah, I have nothing.

I shake my head to clear the fog I appear to be in and decide to forgo checking in with Carter. Instead, I look around the space and notice the curtain to Reese's table has been pulled shut.

No surprise there.

I stalk up toward the VIP section.

Reese is a fucking problem.

But he's also a problem I'm not sure how to handle. There is no love lost between us, but the part of me that will always be attached to Alexa holds me back.

Guilt is a vicious thing.

It slithers inside like a venomous snake.

You might not see it at first, might not notice its presence, but it's there, hidden beneath the grass, ready to strike.

Reese has this hold on me.

But something has got to fucking give.

I'm not in the mood for this shit, but I deal with it, nonetheless.

Swinging open the curtain, I'm met with his bright green eyes. They are glassy, and his nostrils are red.

Surprise, surprise. Seems not much has changed.

"Drew Lawson, to what do I owe the honor of your presence tonight?" he slurs.

"You need to get your shit together, or I'm going to have to ask you to leave. No drugs in my club."

"Careful there, Lawson, you act all high and mighty, but don't forget, I know everything. Wouldn't want your perfect reputation tarnished."

"Shut your mouth."

"Why? Guilty conscience?"

"I said shut the fuck up, or you'll be out of here so fast you won't know what happened to you."

"You won't throw me out."

"Try me."

"Alexa wouldn't want that . . ." He grins.

"You don't know shit about what Alexa would want."

"That's right, you do. You always knew . . . how did that work out for you?"

I bare my teeth, ready to snap, but then I calm myself. Alexa wouldn't want this. She wouldn't want me fighting with Reese, and at least I can keep an eye on him here. Make sure he doesn't get into too much trouble.

Some might say it's not my responsibility, but it is.

This is my burden. My cross to bear.

Regardless of what I want.

"I see you hired a new girl . . ." he leads, his eyes narrowing at me.

"Stay away from her," I say before I turn, leaving Reese at his table, and stalk toward the new girl.

When I'm standing in front of her, she becomes stiff with recognition.

"Did he bother you?" I grit out of clenched teeth.

Her eyes are wide in shock. "No." She shakes her head. "Nothing I can't handle."

She's much prettier up close, rocking the sweet, innocent girl-next-door look. I know the truth, though. Regardless of how innocent she looks, she's anything but.

It makes her that much more intriguing.

I shouldn't want to know more about her, but I do.

chapter four

Bailey

THE NIGHT IS FINALLY OVER, AND I CAN BARELY STAND. I'M still unnerved by my first run-in with my boss. He barely said anything. Just came over like he was willing to rip off the head of the drunk loser in room three.

I only saw him that one time, but it was enough to leave an impression. Now that the club is closed, all the adrenaline has left, and my body aches, every muscle wrung so tight that one missed step would bring me down. It's after three thirty in the morning, and thankfully, the bass is no longer hammering through my ears. However, as my gaze shifts around the room, I realize the music was the least of my problems. The VIP tables, the bar . . .

This place is a fucking mess.

The debauchery and sin still clinging to the surfaces long after the last patron has gone.

Reaching under the cabinet to grab a rag, I let out a louder groan. The sound reverberates off the walls, causing Carter to turn his whole body toward me from down the bar.

"Damn, girl. You okay?" Our eyes meet, and his eyebrow raises.

"My whole body feels like it's been hit by a freight train." I stretch my arms out toward my sides and cringe for emphasis.

"Your body will get used to it."

"Promise?" I say, and he winks at me.

"Yeah, I promise. You did good tonight. Now we just have to finish sorting the bottles, and the cleaning crew who comes in at five will handle the rest." I can't even suppress the sound coming out of my mouth. I sound like a dying animal that just wants to be put out of my misery.

A boisterous laugh leaves his mouth. "Need a drink?" he drawls out. "Maybe a pick-me-up?" His lip quirks up into a large grin as he reaches into his back pocket. As he pulls his hand out, I can see he's clutching something in his hand, hard. It doesn't take a rocket scientist to know what he's hiding.

"A small bump is just what the doctor ordered for cleanup time, and with boss man gone, no need to hide in the back storage room."

"I don't do drugs." A shiver runs down my spine, and I feel a wrinkle forming between my brows. His eyes narrow.

"That's the second time you got weird tonight. There's definitely a story here. So come on, Bailey, what's your deal?"

"I-I, um . . ." My hand lifts to pinch my nose.

"I might seem a bit flaky, but I'm trustworthy. I know we don't know each other, but I'd like to change that. If you want to talk . . ." He trails off as he gauges my reaction.

"It's too late to go there right now, and there's still way too much to clean. But maybe after?"

He nods. "Okay, how about we clean and reconvene in thirty minutes. There's a great diner down the street. It might be too late in the night to eat, but it's never too early for coffee."

I can feel my teeth gnaw on my lower lip as I think about how nice it would be to have a friend here. Someone to talk to. "Yeah, I'd like that." I turn away, but before I leave the bar, I look over my shoulder, catching his gaze one more time. "Thanks, Carter." He smiles broadly, and for the first time in forever, I feel good about the possibility of unloading my burdens on someone else.

We're sitting quietly at a small booth in a twenty-four-hour diner, and I can feel my heart leaping in my chest.

"You okay?"

Lifting my gaze to his, I start to rub at the back of my neck. "I guess I'm a bit nervous."

"No reason to be nervous." He gives me a reassuring smile. "You don't have to share anything you don't want to."

I let out a deep breath. I can do this. "I'm an addict," I blurt out. "I've been clean for two years."

His hand reaches across the table, and I pull mine away from my neck and place my hand in his. He gives me a little squeeze, and I can feel my eyes begin to mist. "I used to be . . . I was in an accident. I started to take pills for the pain. It started out just a pill here and there, and the next thing you know, I was missing school, running up debt, and well, that was just the beginning." Thinking of all the things I would do when I was high makes my stomach churn. "I did some stuff I'm not proud of, but then it got so bad. One morning, I woke up—"

"You don't have to tell me the details, Bailey."

I nod. That's as much as I'm willing to share right now.

"I know a thing or two about addictions. It's been a tough habit to kick. I don't know how you've managed to stay clean for two years, but one day, you'll have to share your secret with me." He smiles.

"You have to be ready. If you aren't, no program in the world will help."

"One day. Soon," he emphasizes. "Thank you for trusting me. I won't squander that trust."

I believe him.

"School?" he questions.

"No. Right now, I'm just trying to stay clean. It's proving to be a test of wills living in this city, especially now that I work at a club." I sigh. "I was taking classes, but I missed more than I attended. I dropped out to figure everything out. I want to go back, but I can't afford it right now. I need to get caught up with bills, and then I hope to start back up again."

"I can imagine it's tough working at the club, but Drew's rules will help. Can't drink on the job, can't do drugs on the job. And now that I know your truth, I won't try to convince you to do either behind boss man's back. I've got you."

His sincerity warms me. "I'm happy I met you."

"Me too." His mouth parts into a huge smile. "I think this is the beginning of a beautiful friendship," he says in his best Bogart impersonation, and I can't help but laugh.

"So, model and actor, eh?"

He groans. "I don't know if you can call it that when I haven't had any work in over a year."

"Why? I'd think people would be lining up for you."

"It's a hard business to break into."

I take a sip from my coffee and sigh at the bitter goodness. "How old are you?" I ask.

"A gentleman never tells."

"I'm pretty sure that's not the saying." I giggle.

"Since we're friends and all, I'll tell you my secret. I'm twenty-eight." He mock-gasps. "Another reason the agents aren't lining up at my door."

"Twenty-eight is still young," I assure him.

"Not for a struggling model. I'm well past my prime. Twenty-eight is only young to be a club owner. If only I had Drew's unlimited funds." He shakes his head.

"Drew Lawson is only twenty-eight? That is really young to own a club. How does someone come into something like that? Family business?"

"Nooooo. That's a long story, but I will say this. He was a

pretty hard party boy several years ago, and after some shit went down, he cleaned up, and he's been on the straight and narrow ever since. He's a good dude." He sips his coffee and yawns.

"I need to hit the sack. I can hardly keep my eyes open," I drawl out sleepily.

The bell on the diner door chimes, and a group of people come through, laughing animatedly. I turn to look over my shoulder, and the blood drains from my face. My head snaps forward, and my body slumps down into the booth.

"What's up?" Carter asks, frowning at my strange reaction.

My eyes close, and I blow out a deep breath. "It's my sister and her boyfriend."

His brows lower over his eyelids. "And that's a problem?"

"Yes, it's four o'clock in the morning, and seeing as I used to be an addict . . . with a prosecuting attorney for a sister, this won't look good."

He clenches his teeth and grimaces. "So, basically she's a mother hen?"

"Not usually, but that's because I rarely leave my apartment."

"Incoming," he says, alerting me to her approach.

"Don't mention the club," I hiss under my breath, and somehow, he seems to understand.

The group passes by our table without incident. I throw money on the table and go to make a mad dash, but per my luck, Harper sits on the side of the booth facing me. When her eyes meet mine, they go wide before lasering in on the back of Carter's head, then narrowing.

Fantastic. She thinks I'm up to my old habits.

"Bailey?" she questions, as though she's not sure her eyes aren't deceiving her.

I raise my hand awkwardly as three additional sets of eyes look upon me. Cal's face pales, surely deducing why I'm here at this hour.

"Hey, Harp," I call, and she stands, making her way toward us.

"What are you doing here, Bailey?" Her tone is sharp and accusatory. "Do you realize what time it is?"

"I could ask you the same question," I bite with a frown, nodding my head toward my guest, hoping she'll take the hint and not make an unnecessary scene. When her arms cross over her chest, I know she's not backing down. "This is my friend, Carter," I say, motioning to him. "I couldn't sleep, and he invited me to grab breakfast with him."

Carter stands, holding out his hand. "Nice to meet you," he says, smiling wide. Harper's frosty expression melts. She's putty in his hands. Of course.

"It's nice to meet you," she says, head tilted to the side as she takes him in. "How did you two meet?"

My stomach sours as I attempt to concoct yet another lie in my head, but Carter jumps to my rescue again.

"I live close by. We became fast friends," he says, taking a seat. "Bailey and I were just discussing her future plans. We were talking about different college options."

I kick him under the table, and he yelps, but Harper's beaming so bright, she doesn't even notice. Does he have any idea what he's done? Now, she's going to nag me until I'm back in class.

"Let's not get too ahead of ourselves," I say, through partially gritted teeth. "I need to make sure it aligns with my work schedule."

"I think it's a brilliant idea," Harper praises. "You know I'll help you if it means you're back in school."

I groan. "I don't need your help, Harp. But thank you." I nod my head toward her table. "Your friends look like they're waiting on you to order."

She looks over her shoulder. "Oh, yeah, I better go. We ended up going out tonight. We ran into Stan and Rachel in Soho, and they took us to some dive bar around the corner from here." She laughs like it's funny. "Enjoy your night. I'll call you tomorrow," she says, bending down and pulling me into her. "He's cute," she whispers, and I grin across the table at Carter.

"Talk to you tomorrow," I say, waving at her, Cal, and the other two at her table.

"That was . . ."

"A close-ass call," I mumble, leaning over the table. "If she found out I'm working at Silver, that whole interaction would've gone sideways fast. Thanks for your quick thinking."

He grins. "Women can't resist my charm."

I giggle. "Thank God for that."

"You know I get it," he says, turning serious. "She clearly loves you, Bailey. If she'd have a problem with you working at the club, it's only because she cares."

I know he's right, but it doesn't change the fact that I'm out of options. What I need is for her to believe in me. To know I'm a different person. I can do this even if I shouldn't.

"Let's get out of here. I'm exhausted," I suggest, not wanting to go down that rabbit hole. Incredibly, Carter never pushes. It's like he already understands when to let stuff go. I appreciate him more and more with every minute I spend with him.

Carter insists on paying the bill, and we say our goodbyes for the night—well, morning. Having a normal night out with a potential friend was just what I needed. I think I can do this city after all.

chapter five

Drew

MY LIFE SOMETIMES FEELS LIKE AN ENDLESS CYCLE. Every day, I spend it doing the same thing—wake up, work out, go to work. Occasionally, I indulge in other pleasantries, but ever since I've decided I wanted to branch off and open something new, do something new, I've been too busy.

So now, I eat, sleep, and work.

I've been here since around nine this morning. Most would think owning a club like mine is fun, but it's not.

I work all the goddamn time.

I'm a control freak and do everything myself.

Then there's the fact that I'm planning on opening a restaurant soon. That brings on a whole other set of problems and responsibilities. If I were smart, I'd hire someone to manage the whole process for me.

Phone calls and meetings have me sequestered in my office until well past dinner, and it's only going to get worse.

Looking at the clock, I see it's already after ten.

The club is not at capacity yet, but enough of the high-paying clients are present to have a full staff on the premises.

Give it a few hours and it doesn't matter what night it is—Silver will be packed.

As much as I'd love to stay cocooned in this office and get ahead on my paperwork, it's time to head downstairs and check out how the night is going.

I'm particularly interested in how my new employee is faring. Whether it's to ensure she's keeping clean or simply to catch sight of her, I haven't a clue. I don't even want to examine that one. She's off-limits for so many reasons.

I'm about to head over to the bar where she's currently working with Carter when I notice the room that Reese always occupies has the curtain closed.

Fucking Reese.

One of these days that guy is going to have to grow up and stop trying to ruin his life.

Switching directions, I head in the direction of the VIP section instead of the bar.

Some might ask why I indulge him.

A deep-seated sense of guilt has me wanting to protect him. I know you can't help someone who doesn't want to be helped, but at least, if he's under my roof, I know he's relatively safe.

I can't stop him from doing drugs, but if he's here, I can try to push away the devil on his shoulder.

Which is what I'm about to do now. I have a strict no-drug rule here, and Reese and his friends are the only ones who push it.

Most of the patrons of my club respect the rules because they know the alternative is being blacklisted. Nobody wants to lose access to the hottest club in town, even if the rules are strict.

Reese has always been a thorn in my side, especially on the club rules. If it's not drugs, it's harassing my waitresses.

I should kick him out, but instead, I'll open the drapes and monitor him.

I'd remove the drapes, but one of the key elements of this club is the ability for the rich and famous to have fun and drink without having to worry about pictures being leaked to TMZ. No matter how exclusive we are, a beautiful reporter posing as just someone trying to gain access, could easily slip by the bouncers. So the curtains stay to protect our customers, even if removing them would be easier than having to babysit this little shit. *Sins of the past causing problems in the present.*

When I approach and fling back the curtain, I'm not met with Reese.

Instead, leaning over the table with a rolled-up dollar in hand, is a stunning redhead. Reese moved on fast from the one he had with him the night before. *Fucking typical.*

These girls never learn. They think they're important to him, but no one is important to Reese.

Not true.

One person was important to him.

But she's long gone.

Buried in the past.

A past I can't seem to forget.

A past that haunts me even now.

"Get up," I bite out, stepping beside her.

She has to crane her neck up to see me. She looks high as a kite. No way am I letting this girl OD at my club. "Where the hell is Reese?"

When she just stares at me like I have five heads, I lean down and get right in her face.

"Did you not hear me?"

"I don't take orders from you," she slurs, barely intelligible.

"Seeing as it's my club, sweetheart, you actually do."

Bored with this whole interaction and this girl's inability to understand what the hell is going on, I reach my hand over and swipe the coke from the cocktail table. Sending it down to the ground and immediately cursing myself for creating a mess for someone else to have to clean up.

"What the hell do you think you're doing?" I hear from behind me. I stand tall and turn to see Reese approach.

He looks at me, eyes glassy but narrowed, and then looks toward the little white specks barely visible on the floor.

"What the fuck, dude? You just spilled over a grand of coke on the floor."

"Probably shouldn't have brought it into my club then. You know the damn rules, Reese."

He steps closer, trying and failing to be menacing.

"What's your problem?"

"My problem is you. You could be so much more than this."

"Like you're one to talk. You aren't so perfect."

Before I can stop myself, I'm grabbing him by the collar of his shirt. Our faces are inches apart.

"Careful there, Drew. You're not the only one who could afford a place like this, and karma is a bitch. Someone might take everything you have one day. Especially if they tell someone you roughed them up."

"You're threatening me now?" I say through gritted teeth, tightening my grip on his shirt.

"Just saying." He shrugs.

"It doesn't need to be like this." My voice is rougher than normal. It's taking everything inside me not to beat his ass for being so stupid.

"It does. You made sure of it."

His words hit their intended mark, right in my heart. After everything, he should know better. He should be better.

I'm about to say more when a movement to my left has my gaze drifting.

There, standing like a ghost in the shadows, watching everything transpire, is Bailey. Her eyes are wide, and her chest heaves with her deep inhales as she looks down at the coke and then back at the girl rubbing at her nose, strung out and clearly high out of her mind.

I let my hands drop, and Reese stumbles back, eyes landing on Bailey. The way he looks at her is unnerving, and she physically shrinks under the weight of it. *Fucking Christ.* The pull to strike him across the face and pull his attention off her is so intense I have to physically refrain from carrying it out.

"Get out of here, Reese," I bite through clenched teeth. "And don't come back if you're going to bring that shit into my club."

His head shakes as if clearing the fog that settled over him. Without saying another word, he grabs the girl he's with, and they both stumble out past the curtain and into the main part of the club. He looks back once more, and I level him with a glare that I hope conveys my thoughts. *Get your ass moving.* I know he'll be back. With my luck, probably tomorrow, but I can't think about that now. I just need him to leave tonight.

"Will you be okay?" I ask Bailey, and she bobs her head in answer. "I'll be back in a minute. I just have to make sure they leave."

She doesn't answer. Just stares at me blankly.

Her eyes are still large. Still hollow.

Then she gives me a little nod. I don't want to leave her alone. She looks a little shaken by the exchange, but I have to make sure they not only leave but have transportation. Neither of them was in their right mind, and I won't have that on my conscience.

"I'll be right back," I say once more, trying to assure she's okay before I head out. "Bailey, speak," I command, needing her to verbalize she's okay.

"Okay," she says softly. "I-I'm fine. Go."

It's my turn to nod before I spin on my heels and head out, following Reese. They stop periodically to talk to people they know. They're currently standing at a table with a reality TV star, deep in conversation. It appears all of them are inebriated enough they don't notice Reese's state. While they're preoccupied, I go to the front, motioning for my bouncer, Rob.

"I need you to get a car here right away. Reese and his guest are not to leave here under any circumstances unless they get into the car you called. Got it? If they're not out here in five minutes, send someone to escort them out."

"Yes, sir," the giant of a man says, picking up a two-way radio and getting started on his task.

"Good man," I say, clasping him on the shoulder and making my way back to the VIP room. I don't pay any attention to Reese, knowing Rob will handle him.

I'm almost calm when I get back to the room, but what I find when I pull back the curtain has my fists clenching.

There, on the cold concrete floor of the club, is Bailey, wiping away the remnants of coke. The white residue is striking against the black floors. She shouldn't have to clean this. But that's not what has me so enraged. It's the way her shoulders shake.

Lowering my body until I'm eye level with her, I place my hand over hers, stopping the erratic scrubbing.

"You don't have to do this."

"I need to clean it," she says absently, as though she's lost in thought.

"No, you don't." When she doesn't stop, I reach my hand out and turn that haunting face toward me. "Stop. I got this."

She looks up into my eyes but doesn't speak. So many feelings flood through me, and I don't know which one is most potent. Our gazes lock for what feels like an eternity as her pain bleeds out of her. My own demons reflect in her eyes, making it hard to be near her, but I don't move. I won't. Not until she breaks the connection and looks away.

I take that opportunity to stand and extend my arm out to her. When she places her delicate hand in mine, I help pull her to her feet, all the while focusing on how her hand feels so small engulfed in mine. It feels familiar. It transports me back in time to another place, one that feels like a lifetime ago.

"Thank you," she whispers, drawing me back to the here and now.

I let out the breath I was holding. "I'm sorry you had to see that."

"It's okay."

"It's not," I spit, just a bit too harshly. She recoils slightly, and I feel like an ass.

"It wasn't your fault," she says, turning before I can say something else. But what more can I say?

I'm sorry for hiring you? I'm sorry for wanting the property and putting that above what's best for you? I won't say any of that because she wouldn't understand. I hardly do. This woman is a stranger. I gave her the job because she needed it, and I needed to play nice with Cal. That's all. *Keep telling yourself that, asshole.*

The similarities between Alexa and Bailey are startling. So many things about each of these women's lives are parallel, and having her here is only another reminder of all the ways I failed Alexa. I couldn't help her, but maybe I can Bailey. Perhaps this job is the very thing that gives her purpose and keeps her clean.

Right now, she looks broken.

And it's my fault.

It's always my fault.

chapter six

Bailey

AFTER WHAT JUST HAPPENED AT WORK, CARTER IS MY saving grace. His witty banter gets me through the difficulties of trying to forget the event.

"You going to tell me what finally made you decide to sober up?" he asks out of nowhere as he wipes down the bar.

I look in every direction to verify that nobody heard him. "Jeez, Carter. Can you air any more of my secrets? Keep it down," I hiss.

"Sorry, I've just been thinking about it."

I sigh. Peering once more around the bar, I find that everyone is deep in conversation and currently good on drinks, so I decide to go for it. Maybe he just needs to know that everyone has a rock bottom, and the bottom is ugly. It may just be the ticket to getting Carter on the fast track to sobriety.

"One morning, I found myself walking through a very bad part of town. I was drunk off my ass, stumbling around on way too many pills. I must have looked like easy prey," I say, swiping at a piece of dust with my rag. "A dirty man, I think he might have been homeless, cornered me in an alley." I shudder at the memory. His fingernails were caked in dirt, hair so greasy an egg would've fried on his head under direct sunlight. His clothes tattered and stained. "He had a knife and started to close me in. I was so scared." I pause, summoning up the courage to tell him the worst part. "He pushed me to the ground and held my hands above my head. I spit in his face, and he punched me in the eye. I thought he . . . I thought he was going to rape me," I admit, goose bumps forming on my arms as I speak the words.

Carter's eyes go wide. "I—shit, Bailey. I don't know what to say. What happened after that?" he asks tentatively.

"While I wriggled in pain, screaming from the blow, he grabbed my purse and ran off with all my money." I gulp. "That morning, I went to my first NA meeting." Tears well up in my eyes at the memory. "I came so close to being badly hurt that night . . . It was the push I needed to get help, and I've been sober ever since."

Carter takes my hand in his and gently strokes it, lifting me out of the fog of my memory. He pulls me into a brotherly embrace that lets me know that I have a support system here in New York. "I can't imagine how scared you must have been," he says in my ear.

"I was, but I'd put myself in that position because of my addiction."

"Nobody should ever put their hands on another person like that, especially a woman," Carter sneers. "I would've killed him with my bare hands."

"It was traumatic, but I have to tell you, I've been through worse. I lost a friend once. Watched her die. That should've been my wake-up call, but it wasn't. It took my own life being in jeopardy to finally see the writing on the wall. Don't let that be yours, Carter. You matter. This world needs you."

"I want to get better. Will you help me one day?" Carter asks shyly.

I nod adamantly. My heart breaks for Carter, my new friend. No matter how difficult it is to remain sober, it's so much harder to get clean. The battle he has before him is one that I wouldn't wish on anyone.

———————— •• ————————

The next night is here before I know it, and I'm finally starting to get in the groove of things.

As each hour passes, the club continues to get increasingly busier. I'm waiting at the bar for a rum and Coke when I see Carter reach under the cabinet and pull something from his bag. I don't have to see it to know what it is. I'm disappointed for my friend. He can't even go a few hours without a bump. I see Carter jump up and frantically start looking around for something or someone.

"What's got you trippin', Carter?" I wince at my use of words. Brilliant, Bailey.

"Boss man's here. We better get to work." He shuffles to put the contents of his fist back into the bag. I shake my head at his obviousness. Anyone paying attention would know he's acting suspiciously paranoid.

"Carter," I say. Leaning over the bar, I try to get closer to him so nobody will hear what I'm about to say.

His eyes meet mine, and I see the trepidation. He knows full well I'm onto him, and he's right to fear me at this moment. After everything I've shared with him, I didn't expect Carter to quit cold turkey, but I had hoped.

"I'm not judging you, Carter. Never. But as your friend, I'm going to make you try harder. I won't allow you to self-sabotage. You need this job, and if Drew is here, your risky behavior is going to get you canned."

His head lowers, and for a split second, I feel bad for scolding him. Then I remember all the times that I enabled people I considered friends and vice versa . . . and where did that leave any of us?

Nowhere.

The club is too busy right now to talk more about it, so I head back to the tables with the drinks in hand. It's crazy how busy it's been. I haven't had a moment's rest.

As much as I want to complain, the tips have been phenomenal. In one night, I've managed to make enough to catch up on my rent. Every single doubt I had about working here has vanished with the last two-hundred-dollar tip I received.

I might actually consider going back to school if this continues. The smile on my face doesn't go unnoticed. Every coworker I pass looks at me as though I've lost my mind. A few smile back just as widely, probably excited about the tips too.

"Hey, Bailey. Can you help me with room two?" A waitress named Lauren calls out as she balances a tub full of dirty glasses. She seems frazzled, and that alone makes me want to make up some excuse, but around here, you get what you give, and I don't want to burn any bridges in the event I ever need help. "I've just got to run these to the back and use the restroom. It'll only be ten minutes."

"Sure. Just refills or new orders?"

"Refills. Thank you, Bae. You're the best," she says, before practically running to the back.

"Welcome," I say to her back, blowing out a loud breath.

I take two steps and stop. Drew is walking this way, and as dumb as it sounds, I want to retreat. His very presence sets me so on edge I'd rather run away with my tail tucked between my legs than get any closer. After last night, I'm not ready to see him. My reaction was embarrassing, especially since he doesn't realize why I reacted the way I did.

I was weak, and I showed him my weakness.

I spin on my heels and walk in the opposite direction of the room I'm supposed to be tending to for Lauren. I get to the bar and tap my fingers nervously.

"I thought you were helping Lauren?" Carter says, frowning in confusion. "Did you already send in the order?"

All our orders are done electronically through an app on our cell phone. They're sent directly to Carter at the bar or back to the kitchen.

"Strange. You didn't get it?" I lie, fidgeting.

Carter narrows his eyes. "What's wrong with you? You're acting strange."

"What? Me?" I say, sounding even worse and wanting to hide under the bar in total humiliation. Not a damn thing warrants my acting like a teenage girl hiding out from her crush.

"Bailey," Carter drawls, smirking from ear to ear. "Why did you not go to room two?"

I throw my head back and groan. "Drew was walking toward me."

He laughs. "You're serious? Get your ass in that room and take their orders. Lauren will kill you if you mess up her tip."

He's right. I promised, and I have my own tables to check on. I spin around, prepared to get back to work and fulfill my promise when I run smack into a firm wall.

"I'm sorry," I say, shaking off the dizzy feeling one gets from running into a solid surface.

"In a hurry?" A smooth, masculine voice pulls my eyes upward until a chilling, onyx gaze assaults my senses. Drew smirks down at me, and I melt and die in equal parts.

"Um, I . . . gotta go," I blurt out, walking around him and fleeing the scene.

Oh my god, you're an idiot.

On the entire way to room two, I replay that awkward exchange and the absolute embarrassment I felt at acting like a scared kitten. He was laughing at me. Either from the way I acted yesterday, or maybe he realizes I was avoiding him. Neither thought is comforting. *He's not laughing about yesterday.* I don't know Drew, but something tells me he's not cruel. He'd been genuinely concerned about me. He couldn't have faked that. Nope, he knows I'm avoiding him.

Walking in, I almost miss the same asshole from before. Reese, I think I heard Carter say was his name. My back straightens as I prepare for his rudeness, but it never comes. Instead, when he notices me, he smiles wide and motions me to the table.

"You again," he says, cheerfully. No evidence of disdain at all. "What's your name?" His gaze lingers far too long for my liking. My cheeks heat, and I feel my body folding in on itself.

"Um, Bailey?" It comes out as a question because this change in attitude gives me whiplash.

"Ah, Bailey. Glad to see you're back," he says, finally looking away. "Can you grab us two bottles of Goose?"

I let out the breath I was holding. "Sure. Anything else?" I ask as I key in Reese's order.

"Nope, but hurry back. I'd like to get to know you." He grins, but something about the way he gapes at me has my back going ramrod straight. It's not entirely predatory, but it's unnerving as hell.

"I'm only helping out Lauren for a minute. She'll be back soon," I say, walking toward the exit. "I'll make sure you get your Goose right away."

"Bailey," Reese calls out, and he motions me back toward him. "I want you to have this."

He holds out his hand, and as I move closer to see what it is, he pulls his arm back, hoping I'll come closer. I know this game far too well, and I'm not biting. "What? I won't bite. Well . . . not unless you want me to." He grins, and the other men at the table chuckle and hoot.

His finger moves slightly, and I see a one-hundred-dollar bill in his palm. I don't play games, but for that kind of tip for taking one order? I'll gladly take the bait. I move forward like he wants until my legs hit his knees. "Sit," he commands, pointing toward his leg. I cross my arms over my chest and pop a hip. "I'm not sure my boss would like that," I say as an excuse.

"Drew doesn't care as long as the drinks are flowing, and his customers are happy. You want to make me happy, right, chwaer?"

"What does that even mean?"

He shakes his head. "Nothing."

I roll my eyes. Tip or not, this guy is something else. I'm prepared to walk away and lose out on the money when he starts laughing.

"I like it. She's not easily won over, guys. I have to work harder," he titters, but something in the way his voice shakes tells me this is all just one giant show. He's acting out for his clown friends. Why?

"Please don't," I say, sounding more bored than anything. "It's all good. I'll get your Goose, and Lauren will be back to keep you happy," I air quote and turn to the sound of the guys hooting and hollering at my brush-off.

I come around the corner and jump, hand coming to my heart. Drew's standing there, eyes narrowed and lost in thought.

"Sorry, you scared me," I say, but he doesn't answer. "Drew? Is everything okay?"

He clears his throat as his eyes meet mine.

"Yes. Fine," he says. "You handled that well," the husky, rich voice praising me belongs to Drew Lawson, but something seems off about him.

I shrug. "Unfortunately, I have too much experience with guys like him."

His lips form a line, and his one brow quirks. "Is that so?"

I nod. "Sadly, yes. I have to get his bottles," I say, motioning toward the bar.

He lifts his chin in acknowledgment. "Nice work in there."

"Thank you," I reply and haul ass toward the bar, trying hard not to trip, shuffle my feet, or otherwise look like an imbecile. The entire way there, aside from attempting not to embarrass myself, I think about Drew and how off he just was. The man is mercurial, if nothing else.

"Here's the Goose." Carter hands me the bottles.

The expensive alcohol isn't just left lying atop the bar. The bartender has to personally pass it to us. It makes sense with the sheer number of people milling about. Not that any of them couldn't afford the liquor, but according to Carter, money doesn't equal honesty. He's right.

"How's Reese acting tonight?" he asks.

"He's better. Still a douche, but not a complete asshat tonight." Carter snorts. "Reese will always be a douche. Nothing will change that."

I smile at him. "Gotta go. My tables will be needing me too."

When I make it back to room two, Lauren is waiting at the entrance. "Thanks, Bailey. I appreciate it." She grabs the Goose and turns to walk away.

As much as I don't want to deal with the group inside, I need the money, and I need to push through it. I missed out on the tip Reese was offering up. I grit my teeth and head to my own tables. I can make that much on each of them if I make sure they're all okay. So that's what I do, and it works. For the rest of the night, I run my ass off for four high-top tables. They aren't the VIP rooms, and I won't make the kind of money the VIP girls will, but I didn't do too shabby either. Each table tipped me over three hundred dollars.

I take a load of glasses to the back room and shift through my apron looking for my tip purse. It's gone. Panic claws at my chest and works its way up my throat, bringing bile with it.

Sweat beads at my temples and my hands begin to shake.

This can't be happening.

"Drop something?" That smooth, delicious voice washes over me, momentarily setting my nerves right.

I turn hesitantly, not wanting him to see the way my mouth quivers from the exertion of staving off tears. He lifts his hand out, and that's when I see my tip purse. My entire body relaxes, shoulders slouching as I breathe easier.

He doesn't move any closer, so I step forward and reach for the purse. My hand grazes his, and electricity courses its way up my arm. A traitorous sigh escapes my lips, and his brow quirks in amusement.

My cheeks heat, and I rip the purse from his grip, then take three giant steps back.

"I believe a thank you is in order," he teases, and I frown.

"Thank you," I say a tad too snippily for having just been saved by this gorgeous man.

"I'm sorry, it has been a long night. I am grateful you found this. Truly. Thank you."

He nods. "You're welcome."

I offer a small smile and grab a rag to get back to my table.

"Bailey," he calls out, and I turn my head over my shoulders to look at him.

"I'll take care of Reese. He won't talk like that to you again."

With that, he exits the room, leaving me reeling at the intensity of his promise.

chapter seven

Drew

"GOD, THAT WAS A LONG NIGHT."

I glance sideways at Carter. He's our complainer. I usually ignore him, but tonight fucking blew, and I'm not in the mood for his bitching.

"I know thousands of people who would love to look at attractive people all night and leave with over five grand in their pocket." I don't mince words. He makes bank here, and I have a stack of résumés a mile high in my office belonging to people who would kill for his position.

"But you'd miss me."

"Wrong, but I do know several people who would. So, for now, you stay," I say, only half-serious.

"What's up with Reese and the crew these days?" Carter asks with a hint of annoyance.

"How the hell should I know? Piss them off again?" Carter doesn't like to take Reese's shit and often puts him and his friends in their place, but I know that's not it. Reese is still probably pissed because I set him straight earlier in the night.

I caught Reese eyeing Bailey as she walked past his room. Then add to that his come-ons and inappropriate suggestions, and I wanted to throw his ass out again. This is becoming a pattern I need to stop. He's so drunk, he flip-flops back and forth from staring at her like maybe he's seen her before and wanting to undress her.

Once again, I was forced to watch his table, and yet again, I called him on it. He was his typical egotistical self. He threw out a few veiled threats, and here we are again at an impasse.

His douchebag friends thought they'd get some side action. Typically, this wouldn't bother me, but knowing what I know about Bailey, that shit ain't going to fly. My conversation earlier tonight with Reese basically went like this: The new girls aren't to be fucked with, Reese. Touch them, talk to them, or even glance in their direction, and you're out.

I lost five great servers last month because of his shit. I've talked to the girl once, maybe twice, but knowing what I know, she doesn't need Reese's baggage, and she needs this job.

Her eyes are haunted. She has demons. Can't he see that? Doesn't he see what I see?

I'm not going to let Bailey be his next casualty.

"No, I really haven't seen them. They were rude to my new trainee, Bailey, when you were gone, though, and tonight, I could tell they were at it again."

I raise my brows. "Does that really surprise you?"

"No. They're a bunch of dirt bags, and have you seen that girl? She's the hottest server you have." He hoots. "Then there's the whole—"

"Yeah, I've seen her," I cut Carter off. I don't want to talk about something else. "What's her story?" I ask, trying to sound aloof. I know all about her already, but he doesn't know that. I'm intrigued, and maybe he knows something a Google search didn't find.

He looks at me for a beat too long. I can tell he has something to say, and it pisses me off that he's hesitating to share it with me. *You know exactly what he's thinking.*

"What? Out with it, Carter."

"Listen, Drew, you're my boss, and you're a cool guy, but don't mess with this one. I know you can have any girl in this club, but I can assure you, Bailey is not your type."

"What exactly would you know about my type, Carter?"

"You forget that not long ago, before you owned this place, you were just another partier hanging with us low-life wannabes, hitting the powder." I scowl to show that he's riding a thin line with this conversation, but he continues. "I know the girls you go for, and I know who you steer clear of, and I'm telling you, Bailey is one you'll want to avoid. You should avoid her, considering."

"And if I don't?"

"She isn't a money-chasing whore like Monica, and she isn't the confident A-list girls you play around with on the weekends at your galas. She's not Alexa, man."

I jerk back as though he hit me. His words clearly hit his mark and aren't wrong. I'm not sure what has me more pissed— the fact that he's right or the fact that he's brought up Alexa. But either way, it has my hands balling into fists at my side. "What the fuck do you know about Alexa?"

"I knew her. You keep forgetting that at one time you weren't my boss, Drew. She was my friend. She was hooking me up with all the agents until that night."

I see red. "Don't ever speak of that night again. Do you fucking hear me? Never," I seethe.

"I'm only saying she was my friend too. I miss her every day, and you tend to forget that part. I've gotten to know Bailey, and though she's damaged, she's a good girl. She doesn't need anyone messing with her or confusing her for someone she's not."

"I don't remember asking you for your opinion on the matter. If you want to keep your job, you'd best remember who pays your damn bills," I snap, feeling off-kilter for more reasons than just his words.

Carter throws his hands up in the air in defeat. "Okay, okay, I'm done. You make your own bed."

I contemplate his words. He hasn't told me anything I didn't already know, but I want to know the rest of her secrets. I want to know the girl behind that face.

He obviously knows them, and I want to ask, but given his reaction to everything, it's not a good idea. It's clear that they've become friends in the short time she's been working here. I've missed a lot this past week, but I definitely want to catch up where she's concerned.

"I need to have her ready to run bottle service by next weekend. Send her to my office tomorrow when she gets here. I'm going to manage her training." He looks at me warily but doesn't argue. Smart move.

I lock the door behind Carter and make my way to my office. I have a few things to finish up before I can call it a night. I sit in my chair looking over the books, but I can't think straight.

Tonight just keeps playing on a loop in my head. There is just something about her, more than the obvious fact she's gorgeous.

I feel the need to protect her. The sins of my past demand it.

This isn't the time to ponder Bailey Jameson. Cal sent over the proposal—as promised—to purchase the property, and I need to concentrate on that rather than on the beauty with demons.

The club is running the smoothest it has in some time, so now is the time to expand.

I have Carter to thank for that. He's the best general manager I've ever had. He keeps the girls and customers in line during my absence, and he's, by far, the most sought-after bartender in the city.

Maybe I should take his advice and leave well enough alone where Bailey is concerned. As long as she's not currently using and bringing that shit into my bar, we're all good. No more info needed.

chapter eight

Bailey

I WAKE THE NEXT DAY TO A BANGING ON THE DOOR. WHAT THE fuck is that? And what the hell time is it? I peek my head out from under the covers and look over at my clock illuminating the pitch-black room. Blackout shades have been the best investment in this crappy walk-up apartment. The banging continues. I stifle a groan, knowing only one person in the world would be knocking on my door at nine in the morning on a Saturday. On any morning, to be honest.

Harper.

Throwing the blanket across the bed, I jump up and pad down the hall. My feet angrily hit the wood floors with each step I take toward the door. I peer through the peephole before swinging it open. Never can be too safe, especially with where I'm living. It isn't that my apartment is in an unsafe area per se, but the safety precautions are definitely lacking in the building. Case in point, unwanted visitors being able to enter the building without me knowing. I tentatively pull the door back, not ready to meet the bubbly eyes of Harper.

No bubbles to be found, just straight anger. Shit.

Letting out a long sigh, I open the door wider and allow her in.

"What the hell, Bailey? An eviction notice?" she screeches.

"Did you at least bring coffee?" I grumble.

"Don't deflect. Tell me what's going on right now."

"There was an error with my direct deposit. I have to see the landlord to get it all straightened out. It's not a big deal."

That's one truth to all my lies. I do have the money thanks to Silver. I can't tell her that, but she can at least see that I'm not lying, evidenced by her features softening.

"Come in," I huff.

"Can you at least put a shirt on?" she replies.

I look down, and sure enough, the girls are out in full force. Shit. Must have forgotten to put a top on again in my exhaustion. Leaving her standing in the foyer, I run back into my bedroom and grab an oversized sweatshirt from the floor. Placing it to my nose, I inhale and decide it's clean. If Harper knew I just smelled a shirt off the floor, she would force me to dump my apartment in Alphabet City and move in with her and Cal in their posh apartment uptown.

Not going to happen.

This might not be the most desirable location, and most might not love that it's in a five-floor walk-up, but it's mine. My place is also a one bedroom, which is practically unheard of at this price in this neighborhood.

I saunter back out to Harper. "Better?" I place my hand on my hip defiantly.

"Much," she replies, making herself comfortable on the couch she bought me. She wasn't much of a fan of the Craigslist special I'd found in my price range. The day before I was set to have it delivered, I got a surprise delivery from Jennifer Convertibles. A Harper-approved loveseat and chair. Typical. I canceled my previous order and she was happy. She was always more of a mom to me than a sister. Growing up after Dad died, it was often just the two of us.

"Well, now that you made yourself at home, without bringing me coffee, I might add, what can I do for you?"

"You certainly are cranky in the morning."

"Jesus, Harper, I had a late night. Sorry, if I'm not bubbling with excitement to see you before I've even had my first cup of joe."

"Were you with him?" She waggles her eyebrows.

"Who?"

"Don't be coy. The hottie from the diner." She smiles.

"Oh god," I groan, not awake enough to have this conversation.

"That's all you've got for me? I'm going to need more details than that."

"If that's the case, you're going to have to wait until I make coffee. You want a cup?" I ask, my back already turned to her as I make my way into my tiny kitchen—if you could even call it a kitchen. It's a counter, a burner, and a fridge.

"That would be great."

As the coffee brews, a sweet and robust fragrance fills the air, and my mouth waters.

"So . . ." she calls through the thin walls as if I'm going to get into it right now.

"Give me a second," I yell back, waiting for the coffee to finish.

Grabbing two mugs, I fill them quickly and head back, plopping down on the chair kitty-corner from Harper.

"It's not like that."

"Why not? He's sexy as hell, Bailey. And he seemed . . . normal."

I glare at her insinuation that he's not like all the others.

"Hate to break it to you, but I'm not his type. He likes overly fake, blonde bombshells." I roll my eyes.

"Really?" She pouts. "I really hoped you were hitting that."

"Harper!" I can feel my cheeks warming from her words. "Gross."

She sits quietly. Too silent for her. When she finally speaks, I want to roll my eyes. "You know it wouldn't be a bad thing for you to date, right?" Her voice is soft as she pulls me out of my daydream. "I mean, if you're in the right headspace. What can it hurt?"

I glance up at her and notice her eyebrows creased as she takes me in. Strange. The way she says it almost sounds as though she's inquiring if I'm in the right headspace.

"He's not your sponsor, is he?"

And there it is. If he's not my boyfriend, he must be a recovering addict because that's the only type of person I attract.

"Come on, Harper, I learned my lesson. Things have changed. Can't you give me the benefit of the doubt?"

"I'm sorry," she says quickly. "I didn't mean to say that. Of course, I know you're different. You wouldn't be in this city if you weren't."

I flick on the small television, needing something besides the silence we've settled into. A local news station featuring a brunette with high cheekbones is standing outside of Silver. I turn the volume up, curious as to what's going on.

"Local club owner, Drew Lawson, is apparently shopping for commercial real estate." A photo of Drew in a tux with a stunning blonde on his arm appears in the top right corner of the screen.

His piercing eyes seem to stare right through me. "No word on what he's planning on opening, but I'm sure it will be nothing short of spectacular. This is Ava Porter. Back to you, John." The screen goes back to a middle-aged man with a widow's peak. I turn it off and whistle.

"Gross. Don't fawn over that man," Harper jeers.

"Why not? He's pretty good-looking," I retort, wondering where her hostility for Drew comes from.

"Because I've known about Drew for a while, and I can tell you, you do not want to crush on the likes of him. He's a womanizer of epic proportions." Each word is said slow and pointedly, but her words have me curious. What has Drew Lawson done to get on my sister's do-not-ever-touch-him-or-else side?

"How do you know Drew?" I ask curiously.

"Ugh, his family is friends with Cal's. Drew runs in the same circles, but they aren't close. Acquaintances really." She shrugs.

I find it interesting that she's so adamant he's no good. The guy is hot. I'm sure he can pull tons of women, and he sounds just like Cal was pre-Harper. Besides, Drew Lawson is so far out of my league, it's sad. She has nothing to worry about, aside from the fact that I work for him.

"Listen, I know I screwed up in the past—a few times. But I'm not looking for another asshole, even if he's a Greek god." Shit. Did I just say that out loud?

"Bailey!"

Yep, she heard me. I'm going to need to work on putting a filter on my mouth. "Seriously, Harper, I like it in New York. I appreciate your concern, but you don't need to worry about me. I'm not going to go screw things up. Okay?"

"Okay." She nods, and with that, my past and all talk of Drew is dropped.

The day flies by super-fast. Harper stayed to chat for another hour or so before I headed over to the laundromat down the block to do a load. My closet was slim pickings for an outfit to wear tonight to work, so I was forced to wash my clothes. I had considered buying a new outfit in my laziness, but who was I kidding? I could barely afford food, let alone new threads.

Hours later, I can hear my heels clicking against the pavement as I adjust my skirt before pulling open the door to the club. As I walk in, I see Carter waving at me with enthusiasm. After only a few days, I already love him.

"Hey, love. How was your day?"

"Oh . . . just great, if you enjoy being woken up at the butt crack of dawn in the morning."

"Well, I would flip that frown upside down and put on your biggest smile. Boss man wants to see you in his office." His lip turns up as he winks.

Shit.

"Do you have any idea what he wants?" I ask, while internally freaking out.

"Nope, and even if I do . . ." He trails off, adding a wink for emphasis. "I'm not at liberty to disclose. He gives the orders, and I don't question him."

I watch Carter closely, but he gives nothing away. "Does he do that often?"

"Nope."

"I'm not getting any more than that from you, am I?"

"Nope." He shakes his head slowly.

"Ugh. You're a pain in my ass," I say, throwing my head back in exasperation.

"Yes, and you'll have a bigger pain in your ass when my size twelve shoe meets it if you don't get moving. Go," he says, shooing me with his hands.

Carter unknowingly has my nerves calmed and my mind off what is waiting for me in that office. If nothing else good comes from working here at Silver, meeting Carter made it all worth it. I smile and head toward Drew, ready to get this meeting or whatever it is over with.

chapter nine

Drew

"WHY, DREW? I JUST DON'T GET IT! WE COULD BE GOOD together," Monica whines in her most annoying valley girl voice. And she wonders why I don't take her seriously.

I groan, running my hands down my face.

"Monica, can't you see I'm a little busy here?" I shuffle the invoices I was attempting to pay, hoping she'll get the point that this conversation is done. "Get out."

No such luck.

"You—"

She's cut off by a knock on the door. "Come in," I call out.

Bailey walks in, looking a bit awkward. It's cute. "Um, Carter said you wanted to see me?" She rocks back and forth on her toes, looking very uncomfortable.

"Yes, come in, Bailey. We were just finishing up here."

"This talk is just getting started," Monica says in her most saccharine voice. She looks at Bailey, offering a small smile laced with venom before she stalks out. She probably thinks Bailey is my new conquest. That's what I get for fucking with the help.

I have to start having a bouncer monitor who's allowed up here.

Bailey stands just inside the door, wringing her hands

together. She actually looks a bit annoyed, which is funny to me. "Am I keeping you from something, Miss . . ." I let that hang out there. Of course, I know her name.

"Jameson. My last name is Jameson, Mr. Lawson." Her tiny voice belies the strength she tries to exude, and I decide to have a little fun at Miss Jameson's expense.

"Drew. There is no 'Mr. Lawson' here."

She doesn't say a word, only nods in answer.

"Bailey? Do you understand? Use your words." I'm a condescending asshole.

"Yeah . . . Yes, I understand," she says, clearly confused and utterly petrified.

"How is Carter doing with your training?"

She tilts her head to the side, studying me. "How's my training?"

"That's what I asked." Her eyes are narrowed, not answering me. "Back to the reason you're here. I'll be shadowing you tonight, and I wanted to give you a heads-up. I'm trying to get a better feel for our current training program and how my employees interact with our guests. I've recently noticed some issues with blurring the lines between flirting and inappropriateness."

She blanches. "From me?"

"No," I correct. "I'm shadowing you because you're new and utilizing that time to monitor the others' interactions."

Her shoulders relax, and the horrified expression melts away.

"While I shadow you, you'll be training for bottle service. I need another person because we'll likely be losing someone soon."

Monica will have to go if she continues showing up in my office and begging me to take her. It's becoming a real problem. Training Bailey is imperative to have her ready, just in case I'm forced to fire her. It also helps me keep an eye on Reese. He's been frequenting the place more often these days, and something tells me it's all about the girl in front of me.

"Wow. That's . . . awesome." She smiles. "I thought it would take months before that was a possibility."

It typically would. Bottle service for the VIP rooms is a coveted position. The money is easily tenfold what she's currently making on the high-top tables and the lounge booths. The girls who work the VIP rooms typically leave with three to four grand in their pockets. Second only to the bartenders.

"We've had a few regulars put in a good word for you. Keep up the hard work, and you'll make bank. Head down to Carter and tell him you're taking Lauren's place tonight. She called in with a migraine, which is yet another reason I'm shadowing you."

That's a lie. I could easily have called in another more experienced girl and had them train her. This is purely for my own curiosity.

The night is spent mostly watching Bailey rule this position. She doesn't need training, and she certainly does not need me tailing her. She's a natural, and our VIPs seem to respect her—mostly. Some of these guys have more money than sense, making them grade A pricks. Nothing and nobody will ever make them happy unless they're responsible for their bankroll increasing.

She doesn't seem to notice the assholes of the bunch. She takes orders and ensures the glasses are always full, working the rooms with ease. In fact, I've never had a first night go this smoothly. It's a bit perplexing. It absolutely takes all reason for me shadowing her away.

"Drew," Samantha, one of the senior VIP girls, calls out. "Reese and his crew just showed up. They reserved room five, but I'm slammed with my rooms and helping out with the booths."

"Where's Amy?" I ask, wondering where my booth and high-top girl is.

"She's on break."

"Call her back early," I demand, and she levels me with a *you know that's against the law* look. "Fine. I'll have Bailey take them."

"The new girl? You're going to throw her to the wolves?"

"I'm shadowing her tonight, so I'll help out. Plus, she's already proved she can handle them."

Samantha quirks a brow and purses her lips.

"Whatever," she drawls, walking off to tend to her customers.

"What's wrong with her?" Bailey's voice startles me, and I turn to her questioning stare in Samantha's direction.

"Reese and his crew showed up, and she's slammed. She asked if you could handle it." I shrug.

"And? Is there anything I'm missing?" she asks, sounding a little self-conscious but standing tall despite it. It's likely due to my staring at her like a damn predator. "I mean, I think I've done well since I've been working here."

"You have." I nod my head. "Better than most, I must admit."

She chews on the inside of her lip, looking around the club before finally spitting out what's on her mind. "Am I taking the table or what?"

"Do you think you can handle them?"

She bristles, placing both of her hands on her hips. "I'm more than capable."

"I wasn't insinuating you aren't," I defend. "It's not your abilities that have me concerned. It's the group of men. They're . . . trouble, Bailey."

"Oh," she says, dropping her hands from her hips. "Well, I can handle them. I've done it before."

I step toward her, reaching out on instinct and placing a strand of hair behind her ears.

"W-What are you doing?" she stammers, and I smile.

"Helping."

She quirks her brow. "Touching me is helping?"

I smirk. "Bailey, you have no idea."

She blushes ten shades of red before I continue. "I like your hair down, but keeping it off your shoulders will keep from getting hair in their drinks and food. These guys won't be kind with an error like that."

"Well . . . thanks."

Outside of dealing with Reese's rowdy group, the night continues on much like the first half. With me standing over her shoulder, Reese doesn't give her a hard time. He also keeps his damn hands to himself because he knows better. I don't have to do a thing. Bailey is on top of everything like a seasoned waitress. I'm impressed.

I'm standing outside of a room, answering emails when Bailey saunters up.

"I've got everything under control if you have work to do." She motions toward my phone.

"You've done a great job for sure. I'm impressed, Bailey."

"Then why are you still following me?"

I chuckle because what the fuck. This girl just called me on my shit.

"Maybe I'm enjoying myself." I smirk. "Are you sure you want me to go?"

"I-you . . . yes," she breathes the word.

"Enjoy your night, Bailey."

chapter ten

Bailey

I STAND OUTSIDE OF THE VIP ROOM, FEELING SHAKEN. OUTSIDE of a little of what felt like flirting, nothing had happened. He didn't touch me, yet my skin is on fire as if he did. The words he spoke weren't anything earth-shattering or inappropriate, but it was the way he said them. His husky voice. He left me feeling off-kilter.

He's your boss.

Living life as a recovering addict, I'm always trying to avoid chasing highs. If it isn't pills, it's some other thrill. Having an addictive personality means I desire anything that'll make my body crave it.

Drew Lawson makes me yearn for things I haven't in a long time, and that's a serious problem.

I shake the thoughts of Drew out of my head and work my ass off the rest of the night. Anything to keep my mind preoccupied. When the place is cleared, and everything is clean, Carter and I head to what has become our booth in the little diner down the street.

"How'd you do tonight?" he asks while leafing through his money stack and counting his earnings.

"Should you do that here?" I ask, looking around the mostly empty diner. "You're going to get mugged one of these nights."

"Probably not, but I've been saving for a motorcycle, and I want to see how close I am."

"Ohh, sexy. I love a guy on a bike."

"Sorry, love. Again, not my type. You're hot and all, but you're too vanilla. Plus, to be honest, I don't shit where I eat." He smirks.

I pout my lips. "That's really too bad because you're basically my dream guy. Life is not fair." I throw a napkin across the table at my friend as he laughs.

"What was up with Drew following you around like a lapdog tonight?"

I purse my lips. "That isn't normal?"

It's a stupid question. Something about Drew tells me he typically leaves the training in other people's hands. I just didn't want to overthink things.

"Um. No. He rarely leaves his office other than to mingle with the clientele."

"Oh." It's all I say, not wanting to give anything away, but it doesn't work. By the way Carter's eyes narrow, he's onto me.

"Did something happen?"

"What? No. Why would you say that?" I ask in a rush of words, looking more guilty by the second.

"Oh, fuck," he murmurs, slapping his palm to his head. "Please tell me you haven't boned him."

"Oh. My. God. Carter!" I reprimand. "Of course not. Are you insane?"

"Shh," he says, waving his hand to signal me to lower my voice.

"There's nobody in here."

"Regardless, this isn't a conversation to scream to the city. Drew is front-page news, and if it got out that he was sleeping with his employees, it would surely be newsworthy."

"Number one, I'm not sleeping with Drew. Or anyone else

for that matter," I tack on for good measure. "For two, employees? As in plural?"

"Drew has a history with Monica . . ." His words trail off, and I wait for him to elaborate, but he doesn't.

"So, the guy slept with his waitress. So what? How is that news?"

He laughs, but it lacks humor. "Drew is one of the most eligible bachelors in New York City, Bailey. That, in and of itself, makes anything pertaining to him, news. Every woman in the tristate area would be banging on Silver's door trying to get a job. It would be mayhem."

I roll my eyes at his over-exaggeration. Women can't be that desperate.

Although, I do have to admit, he's sex on a stick. Everything from the way he walks to the man's voice is arousing. However, hearing that he slept with Monica does temper a bit of the heat I felt because that means I'm not special. My brow furrows at the thought.

"Stop," Carter commands, and I look up to his stern gaze. "Don't even let Drew's actions impact you. If he's paying you extra attention, it's because something is special about you."

It's like he took the words right from my head. He knew exactly what I was thinking and the insecurities I carry. A kindred spirit is what I feel in Carter.

"Regardless of the attention, Bailey, don't fall into his trap. He's a good guy, but he's not good for you."

I bristle at his insistence that Drew and I are not a match. I know as much, but hearing someone else say it hurts. Especially coming from my friend.

"I said he isn't good for you," he repeats. "I see that look. You're misconstruing my words. This isn't about you, Bailey. It's about Drew's lifestyle. He owns a club. He runs with the elite. He dates models out in public. Everyone else is hidden from view like a sidepiece. And even those worthy models are tossed to the side eventually because Drew Lawson doesn't do relationships."

Every reason he just named is exactly why he's right. I need to stay away from Drew.

He's nothing but trouble for me.

"Well, good thing he's just my boss, and nothing is going on."

He bites his bottom lip. "That's good to hear, Bae. I hope it stays that way."

"It will."

"Good."

"Moving on," I prompt, needing to discuss anything other than our sexy as hell boss.

Most of what he said I already knew from my sister, but hearing it from someone who knows him better than Harper just solidifies what she told me.

"Tell me more about this motorcycle," I say, waggling my eyebrows.

Carter spends the next thirty minutes talking to me about all things motorcycle. From clubs in the area to the best highways to ride, I now feel like an expert.

My hands come above my head as I stretch, and a yawn escapes my mouth.

"All right, Sleeping Beauty. It's time to get you to bed. You're about to turn into a pumpkin."

"Wrong fairy tale," I mumble through another yawn, but I nod my head eagerly. The thought of my comfy duvet and feather pillows make it nearly impossible to keep my eyes open.

Carter and I head back to Silver, where I call for an Uber.

"Sure you don't want me to wait with you?" he calls.

"No. It says it'll be here in less than five minutes. I'm good."

He pulls me into a hug. "Keep your phone on you. I don't like you being out here all alone."

"I'm fine, Dad," I mock. "This place is lit up like Fort Knox. I'll be fine."

He takes off, leaving me standing outside the front entrance. I'm mostly safe, given the area, but I don't love being out here by myself. Two minutes later, a Town Car pulls up and stops directly in front of me. I look around, wondering what the hell this is about. I called for an economy car. This is beyond luxury.

"What are you doing out here by yourself?" Drew asks from behind me, causing me to jump.

"You scared the shit out of me," I say, clutching my chest.

His eyebrows are pulled into the center of his forehead, and he doesn't look happy.

"I'm waiting for my ride."

"This late? It's dangerous for you to be out here by yourself."

"Carter just left. My Uber's coming."

He scowls, stalking toward the waiting Town Car. Now it makes sense. A moment later, he's making his way back toward me, and it's my turn to frown.

"What are you doing?" I ask as he sidles up beside me.

"Waiting for your car to get here."

I look up at his stern face. "I'm fine, Drew. You can go. Your car is waiting."

"And Stan will continue to wait until you've been safely placed into your car."

I huff indignantly. "I do not need a babysitter."

"Clearly you do if you think it's a smart idea to be waiting in the dark at this time of the morning," he barks. Then under his breath, he mumbles, "Carter's ass is going to regret this."

"This isn't Carter's fault," I snap, turning toward him while crossing my arms over my chest. "I make my own damn decisions."

"Poor decision-making then."

"God! You're infuriating," I practically yell, stomping away from Drew to stand on the other side of the club.

"Bailey," he says, his tone warning. "Get your ass back here."

"You're not my father," I toss over my shoulder, sounding like an angsty teen. I cringe at how immature I'm being at this moment, but I'm unable to stop. I'm exhausted, and his alpha attitude is annoying.

"You're coming with me, or else I'm throwing you into the back of my car and taking you home myself. You know what? That's exactly what I'll do."

He moves forward, and I'm pretty sure he is going to make good on his promise, but then he stops. "I'm only not grabbing you because I know you'll make a scene, and it's four thirty in the morning. I don't want to deal with the police."

"Good call," I seethe.

He blows out a frustrated breath. "Bailey, this is my club. You're my employee. I'm responsible for what happens to you on my property. You shouldn't be out here by yourself."

"I'm not your responsibility. I left here well over an hour ago. Carter and I grabbed breakfast, and I called for a car. It's not here yet, but it will be soon."

I look down at my phone to give him an approximate time and groan. "It's been canceled. What the hell?"

He runs a hand back through his hair roughly.

"I'm going to try another one," I say, pulling up the Lyft app.

"No," he says, sounding resigned. "I'll give you a ride."

My head shakes back and forth. "Not necessary. I'll be fine here."

"Are you going to make me throw you over my shoulder? Just get in the damn car, Bailey. It's late, and I need some sleep."

As much as I want to rebel against the idea, he's right. I'm just as exhausted, and being stranded out here isn't a good idea.

I walk toward the car, indicating I'll cooperate.

"You're welcome," he says to my back.

Thank you would imply that I think this is a good idea. It's not.

chapter eleven

Drew

WE RIDE IN SILENCE AFTER BAILEY GAVE HER ADDRESS TO Stan. The car is large enough, and we have plenty of space between us, but the pull I have to her is stifling. I've never had the urge to yank a girl on top of me like I do her right now. Especially with the cold shoulder she's giving me.

And that right there might be the answer.

I see the way her cheeks color and her body shivers when I almost touched her. Yet she barely gives me the time of day.

It's maddening.

The car pulls up to a run-down building in a shady part of town. In all fairness, it's probably not that bad. I've just been afforded the ability to live in the best neighborhoods and in the best buildings, so Bailey's apartment building looks like the slums in comparison.

"Thank you, Stan," she calls out before pushing open the door and exiting without a single word in my direction.

I groan. "Stan, give me a minute." He chuckles. I'm sure he's finding this entire situation hilarious.

He's been with me for years, and he knows damn well that I don't chase women, but here I am, throwing open my own door and running after her.

"Bailey," I call out, and she stops, twisting the top half of her body around to look at me. "What are you doing, Drew?"

"What does it look like I'm doing? I'm walking you to your door," I grate out. "Do you make it a habit of putting yourself in danger?"

I watch her jaw work before she clenches her teeth, popping one of her fists on her hip defiantly.

"Do you make it a habit of chasing after women who don't want your help?"

"Bailey," I warn, and she doesn't back down.

"Go away, Drew."

"Can you just accept my help? Is it so bad that I didn't want to allow you to walk home in the dark? At that time of night, it's unlikely you would've gotten another driver."

"It's New York City. I can always get a driver."

"Your last one canceled," I say, throwing my hands up in the air.

Frustrated, she takes a deep breath and walks toward me, shaking her head. "You're right. I'm sorry. I just . . . what's going on here?" she asks, changing tactics and throwing me off guard.

"What do you mean?" I ask, genuinely not knowing what she's talking about.

"Why are you treating me differently from everyone else? You shadowed me tonight when, according to everyone else, that's not normal behavior for you. You offer me one of the VIP slots when there are waitresses with more seniority. And here you are, giving me a ride home. Why?" she demands.

Should I tell her the truth? Fuck no.

I can't even dissect what the hell is going on here.

Carter's words filter through my mind, and I wonder again what this girl has been through, *other than the obvious.*

That thought has me taking a step back. I may be an asshole, but this girl doesn't deserve it. So I concoct the best lie I can in seconds and spill.

"You're right, it's not a common practice for me to shadow employees, but I'm trying to be more in touch with what goes on in my clubs. You're also right that I should've probably given the position to one of the other girls, but I wasn't lying when I said you have drawn the attention of our regulars. You've gotten more praise than any of the others, and I don't believe that seniority equates to being the best person for a job. I also know you need the money more than any of them."

She winces. "And how would you know that?" I've clearly struck a nerve.

"Cal told me a little bit."

She rolls her eyes. "Of course, he did."

I raise my hands palm up and shrug. "How else do you think you got the job? I'm not gonna lie, Bailey. I'm not a huge fan of your soon-to-be brother-in-law. He's a bit of a dick."

"That's one thing we can agree on," she says, and I smirk. "And the ride?" she asks, obviously wanting me to explain myself fully.

"What can I say? I have a bit of a hero complex."

She narrows her eyes, not accepting that as my answer.

"Okay, okay," I relent. "I also don't need a crime happening in front of my club to attract law enforcement. I try to run a clean ship, but that doesn't mean everything's perfect over there. I'm not about to go make problems that cause the police to sniff around, and let's face it, your sister would be all over Silver if something happened to you there."

"Fair enough," she says, accepting that. "I just . . . I've heard rumors about you too, Drew. I don't want to assume anything, but I also want to make it clear that I'm not one of those girls anymore."

My head jerks back as I try to dissect everything she's just said.

I'm not one of those girls anymore.

What the hell does that even mean? Do I even want to know? No. I don't. So I go on to the next what the fuck statement.

"What exactly have you heard about me?" I asked the question, knowing full well. Fucking Carter.

I'm gonna wring his neck tomorrow.

"That you like girls."

I huff. "I like girls?" I sneer. "What warm-blooded man doesn't?" I let out a sigh. "Listen. Whatever you've heard about me probably has some truth to it, Bailey, but not everything you hear is true."

"I understand that, which is why I'm bringing it up to you. I want to hear it from the horse's mouth, as they say," Bailey sighs. "I just want to make it clear that you're my boss, and I'm your employee. I'm not looking to garner any favors from you, and I'm not willing to give favors in exchange for privileges."

"Jesus, Bailey. Do you hear yourself? I'm not running a massage parlor for Chrissake. You've done a good job, and I needed the help. Shadowing you verifies I didn't fuck up by making that decision. I brought you home because I don't want problems at the club. That's it. That's all. End of," I say, growing more irritated with every second. "Now go inside and get some sleep because tomorrow is a new day, and it's a busy one."

She shuffles back and forth on her feet, looking unsure. Good. She should. If she were any one of my other employees, she'd be let go after essentially accusing me of quid pro quo.

Turning toward her apartment, she takes two steps before turning back around. "Thank you. And . . . I'm sorry if I upset you. I didn't mean to imply you are inappropriate. I just . . ." She stops talking, shaking her head. "I appreciate everything you've done." With those words, she leaves me there to watch her disappear through the door.

I run my hands down my face, suddenly exhausted. Much of what I said to Bailey was the truth, but so much of it was bullshit too. I have been giving her too much attention, and I have been thinking about her too much. *For all the wrong reasons.* Tonight, I need to get some sleep, and tomorrow, I need to figure out a way to work alongside Bailey without wanting more. She needs this job, and based on the work ethic I witnessed tonight, Silver needs her.

I can't fuck this up.

———————◆•◆———————

All fucking night, I thought about Bailey, despite my intentions to expel her from my mind. I didn't sleep, and now I sit at my desk wholly drained and frustrated as hell. The woman has me twisted in knots, and my head's a mess.

I've watched her all night from my one-sided tower, coming and going from room to room and expertly handling a couple of high-tops as well. Every guy in the place lusts after her, causing my blood to boil, and I want to strangle them all. That's the same reaction I want from my patrons. The better connected to their server, the more time they'll spend, which leads to more money for the girls and Silver. Yet with Bailey, I don't want a single one of their eyes roaming her body like they do.

It's infuriating. And completely foreign. I've never given a fuck about guys looking at my girls—including those on my arm. The thought of them envying me for what I had only ever made me stand taller.

I want to hide Bailey away from it all. Shelter her. Protect her.

You don't owe her this. She's just a girl.

A beautiful fucking disaster of a girl.

A girl I need to help. A girl who reminds me of someone I couldn't save.

chapter twelve

Bailey

I AVOID DREW LIKE THE PLAGUE. AFTER LAST NIGHT'S RIDE home, I'm feeling stupid. I'd all but assumed he was coming onto me. Maybe he was, but who calls out their boss like that? Thankfully, I've been busy all night, and Drew's been MIA.

Another plus? Reese and his crew of douche canoes haven't shown their faces tonight. As much as I like their tips, a night without their incessant grabbing and nasty come-ons is welcome. I rifle through my money bag and see that it was yet another great night. I check the time and sigh in relief when I see I only have an hour until last call.

"Bailey, another high-top just sat down. Two girls and a guy. I put them in your section," Monica says, smiling. Although something's off about that smile. She looks more deranged than pleasant.

"Thanks?" I say, not really sure what's up with her.

As I walk toward the section where the high-tops are positioned, my eye catches on Carter, who's waving his hands frantically in the air, eyes wide and head shaking violently. What the hell?

I lift my hand, holding up a finger to signal that I'd come see him as soon as I grabbed my new table's order. As much as I love talking to Carter, he's overly dramatic at times. The customers who sit in the bar seats all night consistently create stories for our entertainment. Carter always gets excited when he has a new one.

I chuckle at the thought as I make my way over to the table.

"Hi guys, what'll it be?" I look at my customers and my entire body goes taut.

"Bailey?" My sister's shrill voice runs down my spine, and my entire body runs cold.

"What the hell are you doing here?"

Now she is yelling, and every head within earshot turns their attention toward us, causing me to shrink in place.

"L-Let me explain," I say, holding up my hand, trying to get her to calm down and stop making a scene.

"Explain what? That you're a recovering addict working at a goddamn club? There is no explaining that," she says, motioning toward the skirt around my hips, that holds my money purse. "Oh . . . and there's the part where you bold-faced lied to me. After everything I've done for you?" she shrills.

I feel a hand at my back, and Carter leans down to whisper in my ear, "Want me to have Rob remove her?"

"You," she spits vehemently at Carter. "You did this, didn't you?"

I move toward Harper. "This has nothing to do with him. I met him once I started working here. Leave him out of this."

She throws her head back and rolls her eyes. "Of course, you've made friends with the bartender. Let me guess, he's your new drinking partner? Do you guys pop pills together too?"

Carter stiffens beside me at her accusation before he lifts a hand and signals to the bouncer, Rob. There's no rectifying this scene now. She's pissed Carter off. I want to argue with him because it's clear she's wasted, but there's no use. She's attacked him, and she's drawing too much attention.

Harper is a lightweight. Where I'm the former drunk, she rarely drinks. Maybe my past has something to do with it, but the main reason is her job. She works extremely long hours, and it doesn't leave her a lot of time for a social life. Add in the fact that Cal monopolizes the rest of her time, and drinking has never been a priority. It was another reason I never in a million years considered this run-in to be a possibility.

I start speaking really fast, trying to get out everything that needs to be said before Rob makes his way over here.

"Harper, I just started. It hasn't been long, but it's helped me get out of trouble. There were some issues with my last job that I'm not going to get into here, but I had to quit. If you knew the story, you'd agree. Drew gave me this job, and so far, it's been awesome. I'm not using, and I've already been promoted."

"Is there a problem here?" Rob's grizzly form hovers over my shoulder, and I tense as Harper's eyes widen.

"You're having me thrown out?" she accuses.

"I'm having you thrown out," Carter says, coming to my defense. "You're causing a scene and badgering my employees."

"How dare you?" she hisses at him, acting completely unlike Harper.

"Come on, ma'am, it's time for you to go," Rob chimes in.

Harper stands, shrugging off Rob's hands that have come to her arm to help escort her.

"Get your hands off of me, you big goon."

I wince. The scene just gets worse as the minutes go by. More people gather around to try to witness whatever's about to go down. If they knew my sister, they'd know she's all bark.

"What's going on?" Drew says, joining the party and drawing even more attention.

"What's going on?" Harper snarls. "Tell me, Drew. Why is my sister working here?"

Drew raises a brow. "Hello to you too, Harper. Would you like to go somewhere quiet so we can talk?"

"No. I have nothing to say to you. I can't believe you hired her," she says, leveling him with a glare that could burn this entire place to the ground. "Do you know about her past?"

It's my turn to jump in. "Harper, this is not the place," I start, but she cuts me off.

"Don't tell me what I can and cannot say," she says in what I'm sure is supposed to be a commanding voice, but it's slurred instead as she rocks back on her heels.

"How much has she had to drink?" I ask her wide-eyed friends sitting with her. Clearly, they are colleagues based on the way they're dressed, which only makes this entire thing worse. She will never forgive me for embarrassing her in front of people she works with.

"I gave her a job because Cal begged me to," Drew snaps.

I close my eyes, wanting to crawl under the table at his slip. Had Cal not told him to keep that under the radar? Based on Harper's expression—a mix of betrayal and horror—this conversation was not going to end well for Cal, and it was all my fault.

"Harper—"

"Don't say another word," she practically cries as she storms out of the bar.

"I-I'll be back," I say on the verge of my own tears. "Carter, can you help me with this table?" He nods, motioning for me to follow her. I run, trying to catch up to her, but she's on a mission to get as far away from me as possible. When I get outside, she's staggering off down the sidewalk.

"Harper," I yell out, and she swings around menacingly, stalking back toward me.

"How dare you?" she says, jabbing a finger in my chest. "How dare you humiliate me in there?"

"I didn't humiliate you," I cry. "You humiliated yourself. And me in my workplace."

"You have no business working there," she shoots back.

"That's not for you to decide, Harper. I'm an adult."

"You haven't proven that over the years."

"That isn't fair. I've been clean for two years."

"You won't be for long working in a place like that," she says, pointing toward Silver. "You know it's just a matter of time before all of the shit inside those walls has you itching for a high."

I blow out a harsh breath. What she says is harsh, but it's from years of habits. She's watched this song and dance so many times, I can't blame her for questioning it.

"I'm stronger than you think."

"You are a child," she bellows, and I flinch. "You never learn, and this time, Bailey, you've gone too far." Her voice pitches. "You've pulled the rug out from under me, and you brought Cal into it. I'm never going to forgive you." She says the last part quietly before turning and walking away.

Her anger I can handle, but the disappointment I saw reflected in her eyes was too much. Tears glide down my cheeks as my body begins to shake. All of the adrenaline rushes out of me, and the sorrow that I might've just lost my one stable relationship takes over.

"Bailey," Drew calls from directly behind me. I shake my already lowered head, signaling I couldn't talk if I wanted to.

Two muscular arms circle around my body, pulling me into Drew's chest. I sag into his embrace, knowing I shouldn't but not caring at the moment. I cry, and he lets me, periodically whispering soothing words and running his hand up and down my back.

After a while, I wipe away the last of the tears as embarrassment floods my system. Not only had the entire club witnessed our fight, but so had Drew. God, he must think I'm a mess.

"Drew, I—"

"Shh," he whispers. "Let's get you home, and we can talk about it tomorrow."

I look up and over my shoulder at him for the first time. My eyes have to be swollen, and if my past history of welts after crying is still a thing, I'm likely sporting them.

I nod my thanks and allow him to make the decisions. Minutes later, my stuff is placed into my hand as I sit in the back of his Town Car once more.

"I've got to get back in there, but Stan will get you home. We'll talk tomorrow."

With that, he shuts the door, leaving me to wonder if I'll still have a job come tomorrow.

chapter thirteen

Drew

I TAP MY PEN AS I CONSIDER WHAT I'M ABOUT TO DO. AFTER the scene last night, it was clear that Bailey can't work at the club, and I'm an asshole for not recognizing that sooner. I'm not new to addiction, and I should know better than to employ addicts, no matter where they're at in their recovery—or non-recovery in Carter's case. Regardless of a damn property agreement.

That wasn't even why I did it. When I read about what Bailey had been through online, I couldn't say no. The call to help was too powerful.

Guilt over my own past sealed the deal.

So here we are . . . I have too many addicts in my employment, and I'm not sure what to do about it.

You can't help everyone.

You couldn't help her.

I can try to help Bailey.

Carter might be another issue, though. Having those two work together is asking for trouble. He needs rehab.

I groan, thinking about Carter. He's not in any better shape to work here, but there is literally nothing else for him. Bailey, at least, has a family with means. Carter is alone. His mom bailed on him the minute she was able. It's either here or the streets because any of the other options he has wouldn't give a fuck if he were using on the clock. As long as the drinks are poured and the money is flowing, every other bar in the city lets that shit fly. In fact, some even provide it to their employees as a means to keep them going throughout the night. It's sickening.

I can't worry about him right now. Bailey's my focus.

I called down to Carter moments ago and asked him to send her my way. Sam is coming to take her place. I know Bailey is going to be pissed, but I'll make it worth it. I have to.

A knock on the door has me sitting up taller in my chair. I know who's behind that door, and I'd be lying if I said I wasn't eager to have her closer to me.

"Come in," I call out, and the door opens to a flustered Bailey.

"Carter said you needed me. Everything okay? I'm super busy tonight," she spews in one long run-on sentence.

"Everything's fine, but you won't be on the floor tonight. I'm removing you."

"What?" she squeals, not giving me time to explain. "What did I do? Is this about last night? I'm so sorry, Drew."

Her face has transformed into panic. It radiates off her, and I feel like an ass for breaking the news in such a way. It's evident she thinks she's fired.

Standing, I walk to the front of my desk and lean against it.

"You didn't do anything wrong, and you're not fired, Bailey. I have a proposal for you."

Confusion takes over as her eyebrows drop low and her lips smash in a straight line. "What . . . kind of a proposal?"

I roll my eyes at the way she says it. If I had to guess, she thinks I'm calling in that quid pro quo she accused me of the other night.

"A work proposal, Bailey. Nothing more."

Her shoulders lower a bit as she relaxes, allowing me to

continue. The action brings my attention to her neck. I imagine running kisses up the slender curve. My hands would curl around her hips, pulling her close so that we are chest to chest.

As I peruse her body, I can hear her intake of breath. I know she's affected by me.

My eyes finally meet hers. Her eyes . . . The color of blue is intoxicating, holding secrets I want to uncover. I want to know everything about this girl. With just a quick glance, they tell me everything, yet nothing at all.

By the way she shifts from one leg to the other, I've made her uncomfortable. She continues to wring her hands, and she clears her throat as if to wipe away the past few minutes. I should probably stay away from her, knowing her past, but I'm losing my internal fight.

Right now, though, I need to get back on track.

I clear my throat. "Do you have any experience in accounting?"

She looks at me skeptically. "No, I can't say that I do."

"Excellent," I say, not really worried if she even finished the first grade. I'll teach her anything she needs to learn. "I'm going to promote you to my assistant. We'll start your training tomorrow afternoon."

"What? But I just started bottle service. Surely, someone else is more qualified to be your assistant."

"Are you trying to talk me out of it?"

"No, it's just . . . Well, I'm new, and I can't imagine how I've managed to earn a promotion and a raise in the short amount of time I've been here. This won't go over well with the other employees, and I'm not looking to make enemies."

"Let me worry about that stuff, Bailey. I own Silver, and I make the decisions. You'll start tomorrow. I'll text you the time and location later." I stand and walk toward her. I'm close enough to inhale her scent. It's something fruity. I like it.

"Tomorrow," I say before turning to open the door for her to exit.

Bailey stands statue-like, hardly breathing. "But—"

"Tomorrow," I repeat. "Go home and get some rest."

After what feels like ten minutes, she nods, understanding that there's nothing more to discuss. She strides through the door. At the top of the stairs, she turns back once more, gives me a hard stare, and then disappears out of my sight.

I'm not sure what the hell this girl is doing to me, but helping her has become my new crazy obsession. Followed by the desire to kiss her. She consumes my thoughts and keeps me up at night. I'm falling apart at the hands of a girl whose presence alone could ruin me.

Yet I can't find it in me to care.

chapter fourteen

Bailey

I WALK OUT OF THE OFFICE SHAKING, MY LEGS WOBBLING beneath me. What the hell was that? I'm not even sure what just happened. I went into the office as a bottle service waitress and left as an assistant. *Drew's* assistant. What the hell am I assisting with? I guess I'll find out. The thought sends a chill down my spine. Taking a deep breath, I grab the railing and cling to it for dear life. When I hit the bottom, I stride toward Carter.

"What did boss man want?" He smirks at me, not even bothering to hide his inquisition with false pretense. He just keeps wiping the glass in his hand without a care in the world.

"I-I don't really know," I say as I bite my lip.

Carter drops the rag in his hand, then places the glass on the bar before he turns to me. His eyebrow rises as he eyes me curiously. "What do you mean you don't know?"

"It was kind of confusing. I thought he was going to fire me for last night, but then he asked if I knew accounting."

"What's so confusing about that?"

My thoughts go back to the other night and how he said I was promoted because the customers love me. So why take me off the floor if not because of the screaming match with Harper?

Why is he trying to help me, when, in truth, I should be fired? Nothing makes sense. Unless . . .

"He wants to train me as his assistant," I whisper, afraid of the reaction I'll receive.

"Assist him with what exactly?" I can see the amusement in Carter's smug face.

"Accounting?"

"Is that a question? Are you an accountant?" Carter asks.

"No, I don't know anything about accounting." I reach for a rag and start absentmindedly wiping down the counter. I need to keep my hands busy, or they'll shake from the energy coursing through my body.

"Oh, I see. Interesting." The dimple in his cheek deepens as the left side of his lip quirks up.

"What do you mean, interesting?" Placing the rag down, I furrow my brow at him.

"Well, first, he appoints you as the new bottle server, and now, he wants you as his assistant. An assistant for a skill you have no knowledge of. That's interesting," he replies.

"It's really no big deal." Even as I say the words, I don't believe them. It's a huge deal.

Not wanting Carter to continue this conversation, I turn my back and get my stuff. As much as I love Carter, I don't need him to continue his inquisition. Not because I'm nervous that he'll spill, but these walls have ears, and the last thing I need is a bunch of bullshit rumors circulating about me. Oh, there will be rumors.

I notice Carter is still staring at me, a massive grin on his face. I want to smack it right off.

"Where're you going?" The teasing nature of the question has my hackles rising.

"Home."

"Why?"

"I've been replaced so that I can prepare for my new role."

He snorts. "Of course. Because being Drew's assistant needs preparation."

"You're an ass," I tell him with little conviction.

"Someone wants a piece of yours." Carter is clearly amused.

I roll my eyes. "Lame, and totally not accurate. I have skills, and he wants to put them to work." I cringe once I've finished that sentence. I'm really not helping myself.

"Oh, I have no doubt he wants to know all about those skills. Not just know them, but test them, too. He has never once needed an assistant before you walked in the door. Drew wants you."

At that, I grab my stuff and head out the door. I won't feed into Carter's prying. My sister's warning—and Carter's too—comes to mind, and I start to panic.

I need this job. No matter how intriguing Drew Lawson may be, this job means more to me, and I can't let my hormones screw things up. This line of thinking makes me crave things I shouldn't be craving.

This is dangerous.

I blink my eyes rapidly, trying to adjust to the pitch-black room. The chime from an incoming text pulls me from sleep. When I'm just awake enough to grab my phone, I see it's from Carter. He's never texted me. Mostly because at this time of night, we're typically together.

I type in the code, unlocking the screen to view his words.

Fuck.

Based on the near incoherent garble, I know he's in bad shape. The question is, where is he? Glancing at the clock, I see it's 5:00 a.m. Well past closing. I quickly hit send, calling him.

"B-Bae," he slurs, sounding even worse than his text would've displayed.

"Carter, where are you?" I ask, trying not to sound angry.

That wouldn't help in this situation. If he's reaching out to me in this kind of shape, he's obviously looking for support. Having been in his shoes too many times, I'm more than willing to be that person for him. He's come to mean a lot to me in a short time, and if I can help pull him from his addictions, I'll do everything I can.

"A building. Work . . . tired." His words are spoken in staccato, hardly making sense, but having been an addict, it's somehow easier for me to decipher. Probably from years of reviewing my own text.

"Stay put. I'm coming for you," I say before ending the call and jumping from bed.

I pull on a pair of sweatpants and a sweatshirt, grabbing my keys and shoes on my way. I'm practically hopping on one foot as I put my tennis shoe on while shutting the door behind me. From what I could gather, he's somewhere close to work, and he's likely outside.

I hail the first taxi I can, which takes damn near ten minutes. My legs are bouncing as the adrenaline pumps through my system. The fact he could speak any words gives me some measure of relief, but I'm still nervous for my friend.

The taxi driver is none too thrilled that I am on a wild goose hunt, but when I continue to throw five-dollar bills at him, that's enough for him to comply.

"There," I say, pointing at Silver, where Carter sits hunched against the building.

I wince, knowing this place has several cameras, and Drew will likely see Carter's state. I pay the cabbie twenty extra dollars to wait for me.

"Carter?" I whisper, and his head tilts up to look at me. His eyes are glassy and unfocused. He's wearing the standard-issued Silver employee T-shirt, and my stomach drops when I see a pill container.

It feels like there is a vice around my heart and the longer I stare at it, the tighter it gets.

We need to get out of here. *I need to leave.*

As much as I don't want to touch it, I have to. I can't leave pills on the street. Once in my hand, it feels heavy.

It's not, though.

It's only my demons that taunt me.

Throwing it in my bag, I move to grab Carter. "Let's go, bud," I say, trying and failing several times to help him to his feet.

His arms flail before I'm finally able to drape the one around my shoulder. We wobble to the cab, and I help lower him into the seat.

"Is he going to get sick in here?" the crotchety man barks from the front seat.

"If he does, I'll pay to have it cleaned," I hiss before rattling off my address.

He's just coherent enough that I don't fear an overdose, but there's absolutely no way I'm deserting him tonight. His head falls limply to my shoulder, and I look down to ensure he's breathing.

"T-Thanks, Bae," he slurs.

My hand finds his, and I squeeze it in reassurance.

"We're going to figure this out, Carter. I'm going to help."

If not for Harper, I'd probably be dead. She pulled me out from the darkness and gave me light. I'll be Carter's Harper. Tonight, I'll watch over him, but tomorrow, a plan needs to be put into place because if he keeps up this toxic behavior, it'll be the death of him.

After I get Carter back to my place, I strip him down to his boxers and have him climb in under my covers. I'm snuggled into his side, listening to his steady breaths and contemplating my next move when he speaks.

"I'm sorry you had to see me like this."

"I've been there, Carter. I was taking pills and drinking myself to death. You don't have to apologize to me. I just want you to be okay."

He sighs. "Things aren't good, B. I'm blowing every paycheck on drugs. I'm about to lose my place and still . . . I dunno."

"How late are you on rent?" I ask, afraid to know the answer.

"Three months. I just got another eviction notice. I've been dodging my landlord."

I blow out a deep breath, feeling for him. I'd just been in a similar situation myself, albeit not because of addiction—for once.

"If Drew finds out, he's gonna kill me," he murmurs.

"Well, then he can't find out," I say with a sense of determination.

Carter is my lifeline at Silver. I can't lose him.

"We'll figure it out. Tonight, sleep," I instruct, and he does as I suggest.

Within minutes, he's snoring into my ear, and as annoying as that would be any other night, it's music to my ears tonight. Because that means he's alive.

I can't sleep, so I quietly exit the room and pad to the kitchen, grabbing my comfort food of Oreos and milk. Tonight has been a bit much, and I need something to calm my nerves. I dip the chocolate cookie into the chilled milk and allow it to sit for a few seconds. I count. One . . . two . . . three, finally lifting the cookie that's falling apart. My lips wrap around the spoon, and I moan at the gooey goodness.

For these few minutes, I'm not thinking about pills and addiction. I'm not worried about losing another friend too soon. In the quiet of my little place, Oreo cookies in hand, I carry out my father's and my tradition, and I'm able to escape the world. If only for a moment.

chapter fifteen

Bailey

I WAKE THE NEXT MORNING TO A TEXT FROM DREW. IT'S AN address with a simple command to be at the above location by eleven. Then another text comes through.

Drew: We will be working through lunch.

I groan. What have I gotten myself into?

I look down at Carter, who is curled in the fetal position and snoring away.

"What am I gonna do with you?" I say aloud.

It's already nine, and I need to take a shower before meeting Drew. I turn on my computer and type in the address, trying to figure out where I'm meeting him. He didn't give me any more details about where we were going, dress attire, etc.

I chew on my bottom lip when I see it's an address for an upscale restaurant that, from what I've heard, serves an amazing brunch. Well, at least I'd be treated to some good food.

I lightly shake Carter's shoulders, and he cracks open one eye.

"Where am I?" he asks, voice groggy and full of sleep.

"You're at my place. I wasn't gonna take you home. Not that you were in any condition to even tell me where home is," I bemoan.

He sits up, looking straight ahead, refusing to meet my eyes. "Listen, Bailey." He pauses as if trying to formulate his words. I think he's going to change the subject, but I see his face drop, and he continues. "I'm so sorry. You shouldn't have seen me like that."

My lips are pressed into a thin line, and I don't say a word. I wasn't going to lecture him because I am the last person who has any right, but I also don't want him to think that was okay.

He knows I'm dealing with my own shit and being thrust right into the middle of someone else's has the ability to throw any recovering addict back into the fray. At least he has the decency to look regretful. That's a start.

But at the end of the day, this isn't about me and my issues. My friend needs help. He's in bad shape, and if I don't step in, who will?

"What made you get like that?" I ask, because there's always a reason behind that type of use.

He looks away from me, but I don't miss the way his cheeks redden.

His voice is thick when he asks, "The truth?" He's staring at the ceiling and still not looking at me. I remain quiet, allowing him to speak on his terms.

"Your promotion," he finally says, and my head jerks back as if he's slapped me.

I'm the reason he used?

"How so?" My question comes out with the exact inflection to showcase my bafflement. He sighs. "I'm happy for you, Bailey. Truly. It has nothing to do with you, just the fact that you're moving ahead while I'm stuck in the same rut. I just feel like my life isn't going anywhere. I'm a middle-aged bartender with no real direction."

He runs his hands roughly down his face, finally looking at me.

"You know how hard it'll be for me to get clean working at a bar." He looks tormented, and I have the dire need to reach out and soothe away his pain.

It won't be enough.

"I'm going to die from this shit, Bae. I don't know how to stop."

A tear runs down his cheek, and my heart threatens to crack in my chest. His pain is palpable, and I feel it so acutely as if it's my own pain. Having been in his exact situation, I empathize more than most ever could. I want to help him, but he has to want to help himself before anything I do will work. His words seem like a cry for help as far as I'm concerned, so I'll offer help.

"I'll help you, Carter. I promise."

He smiles, but it's written all over his face—he doesn't believe help is possible.

My smile falls a bit at the realization, but I know it's time for me to get a move on. This conversation will have to pick up at another time if I don't want to be late for my first official day.

"Listen, I have to get going."

"Ah, first day," he says with a fake smile plastered to his face. He's trying to be supportive, but I know it's hard, considering what he just confessed. "I'll grab a cab."

I pull him into a hug and squeeze. "I'll see you later?"

He nods before I run off to shower, leaving him to pull himself together and find his way home. The conversation about getting clean will happen. I'll make sure of it.

But something else niggles at the back of my mind with everything Carter said. Why did Drew give me this job?

I'm seated at a small, round table in a back corner of some grand restaurant on the Upper East Side. The place has an old-world charm to it. White marble columns bleed into the white marble floors, and ivy vines snake their way up the posts. The entire ceiling in the section where I sit consists of windows like a greenhouse. There are trees and bushes throughout the interior, making you feel like you're in a garden and not indoors. The white tables coupled with yellow high-back chairs make everything bright and airy.

I might not know much about Drew Lawson, but this place doesn't fit his personality. The fact he chose this one of all the restaurants in this area is surprising. This place couldn't be any further in style from Silver.

My eyes wander the room when they catch on the sight of Drew. He's wearing a dark navy suit, sans tie, and the first two buttons of his white collared shirt are undone. The virility of the man is so potent, I almost choke on it. He is beautiful—in an all man sort of way. His confident gait makes my mouth water.

Get ahold of yourself.

I blow out a harsh breath, tearing my eyes away from him, hoping that the burning in my cheeks dissipates before he makes it to the table.

"Thank you, Gary," Drew says to the graying man on his right.

They shake hands, and the man walks off while Drew pulls out the chair across from me and takes a seat.

"Glad to see you made it here on time," he drawls, voice husky as though he'd just woken up.

I really need to stop thinking about all the ways in which Drew Lawson is sexy as hell. It won't fare well for me if he realizes how affected I am by his mere presence. I need this position, and if I can't be professional, it won't work out.

"Yeah, I made it," I reply, looking around the place and noticing, upon closer inspection, that it's not at all as it seems.

The wallpaper on one wall is yellowed—likely due to the

direct sunshine streaming down on it daily. It is tearing away from the wall in places too. The marble is chipped in places, and many of the chairs have torn upholstery.

For as regal as the place had seemed at first sight, it's actually falling apart, which makes me even more curious as to why we are here.

"You see what I see," Drew remarks, drawing my attention back to him.

"Huh?" I say, pulling away from my inspection and not fully hearing his words.

"The place is a wreck. It's in dire need of a facelift."

"I don't know," I muse. "It has a sort of charm to it."

"It's literally falling apart, Bailey. That's why we're here."

My eyes snap back to his. "We are? How so?"

"I'm in the process of buying it," he says flippantly, and my eyebrows rise.

"And this impacts my job as an accountant how?"

He huffs out a laugh. "You're not going to be doing my accounting."

"I'm not?" I'm starting to sound like an imbecile, and I hate feeling off-kilter in his presence.

"No. You don't have a degree in accounting. I only said that to gauge your willingness to take on challenges. You passed, by the way." He smirks. "No, you'll be my assistant. As such, you'll work with my accountants, but your job will be more evolving."

"So . . . you don't know what my job will actually be?" I challenge, starting to feel like he's messing with me. Who offers up a job they haven't already thought through? What is he playing at?

"You're going to help me with a number of jobs, Bailey. I'm branching out and buying several restaurants in the city. I need someone to help with hiring, training, managing teams of contractors, etcetera, etcetera."

My eyes widen with every additional task he adds to the list. It's sounding more and more like a real job with every word he speaks.

"No need to worry, Bailey, you'll be compensated appropriately. How does project manager sound?"

"Fancy," I deadpan, starting to feel inadequate for such a position.

"Stop it, Bailey. You can do this. I watched you handle everything that was thrown at you at Silver. This isn't brain surgery. It's simply organizing projects and people. You'll have a team to carry out the tasks. You can do this." His gray eyes bore into me, conveying that he truly does believe what he's saying. But how? He doesn't know me. Regardless, it warms me to have his absolute confidence. I only hope I don't screw it up.

chapter sixteen

Drew

I CAN SEE IT IN BAILEY'S EYES. SHE'S PETRIFIED. SHE IS IN NO way qualified for the job I'm giving her, but I don't doubt she can do it. Watching her work the other night had been eye-opening. She worked circles around my best girls without so much as a complaint. She is hungry for the money, and this position will change her life.

It will help her.

It will help you.

I'm doing this for her, not for me, not in some sick, twisted way to redeem myself from my own twisted path. But as much as I think these words, they feel shallow even to me.

Does it matter the reason or the why?

I shake the thoughts away.

Bailey will be put out of temptation's way and get paid better. Nothing else should matter.

"Good," I say, patting the table. "Now let's negotiate the terms." Her brows furrow. This part is going to be fun. Living in New York is expensive, and I know where she lives. I need her closer to the action. Somewhere safer.

I want to protect her.

"Your starting salary will be ninety-seven thousand, which is already over the average here in New York."

Her mouth drops open, and she begins to stutter. She's adorable.

"Um—" She starts, but I cut her off, loving the way I have effectively dumbfounded her.

"Fine. You drive a hard bargain. One hundred and that's the most I'll go until you've proven yourself." I dive right on to the next topic, leaving her completely speechless. "You'll need to hire a few people for your team. I'd suggest an assistant, someone with clerical experience who's good with computers. The second hire should be two people physically strong who can help with staging and can be on the jobsites overseeing the crews that come in and out. You can't be in three places at once." Things are about to get hectic. I'd already purchased two new restaurants, and I have my eyes on another. Each will be modernized but with different cuisine. I want to diversify my restaurateur portfolio.

Bailey remains silent, seemingly overwhelmed with everything I just threw at her. I need her to speak. I want to know if this makes her happy. I'm not sure why I care so much, but I do. For some reason, I want to make this woman smile.

You're in over your head, Lawson.

"Bailey, say something," I command. "Does this work for you?"

She nods, eyes still as wide as saucers. She clears her throat before finally speaking.

"I'm . . . overwhelmed."

I figured as much, but I can't help but grin as a smile spreads across her face and a single tear falls from her eye. She swipes it away, shaking her head.

"I won't let you down." Her voice is quiet and reserved, and that lack of confidence turns my own smile to a frown.

"You're going to have to believe the words you say in order to carry out that promise," I chide, hoping to break through her lack of belief in herself. At this moment, she reminds me too much of Alexa, and it makes my stomach turn.

"Do you have any ideas for your new hires?" I ask, trying to get my mind back to the present.

She blows out a breath before chewing on her lip in contemplation. Then her eyes light up, and that smile graces her beautiful face once again.

"I'll need to post an ad for my assistant, but I do have at least one person in mind for the muscle."

I quirk a brow. "Muscle?"

She nods once. "Yes. I think Carter would be the perfect person to oversee the sites. He'd be an amazing manager one day."

My nose scrunches, not in disgust but in disagreement. Carter is an amazing bartender, but his extracurricular activities—ones I've overlooked, despite my rules—won't fly in management of any of my restaurants.

Yes, I'm not ignorant. I know drugs are readily available anywhere, but my team needs to be better than that.

Bailey's face falls before I can even voice my concerns. "You don't think he'd do a good job?"

"It's not that I don't think he could do it. I know he could. It's just . . . Carter has some habits that I'm not on board with."

She stiffens in her seat, eyes flying around the room, looking anywhere but at me. She's probably thinking about her own background. The difference is, she's rehabilitated. She's sober. Her past won't prevent me from offering her this job.

When she looks back at me, there is a resolve in the depths of her blue eyes. "What if those habits went away?"

I internally groan. She doesn't know Carter like I do. He is so far gone, it would take a costly intervention to bring him around, and even then, his friendships and lifestyle would lead him right back to using. I've watched the cycle with him. He's been much better, but you have to want to quit, and I'm not sure that Carter does.

"We need someone ready to go, Bailey. I don't think Carter's our guy."

She places her hands on the top of the table. "Then I'm not either."

My head jerks back, caught off guard that she'd put one hundred thousand dollars on the line for someone she barely knows. She's either the most loyal person I've ever met or the dumbest.

"I believe that people deserve second chances, Drew. Carter is good people, and he needs this. Desperately." The sheer fierceness of her tone has me compelled to hear more.

"Go on," I urge.

She goes from determined to flustered in two seconds flat. I clearly have her confused, based on the way her eyes are narrowed, brows pinched together.

"It-it's just," she stammers, and I purse my lips to bring out the fight in her.

It works like a charm. Steel replaces uncertainty in that lovely face, and she forges on.

"These habits have been formed by feelings of inadequacy. He needs a purpose."

"He has one. He manages the club," I cut in, and in exchange, I receive a scowl, followed by a very pointed eye roll.

"A club. Do you think that's going to help his situation?"

I damn near flinch at the way she's lecturing me. It's been a very long time since someone chewed me out, and that's exactly what I feel is happening now. If I'm honest, I'm truly loving her bite.

"What do you propose, Bailey?"

"Give him something to stay . . . habit-free for."

I consider her words. Isn't that exactly what I'm doing for her? I know there is a greater chance that the stress from the position she's wanting to place him in could cause the adverse effect. He could start using more.

"Bailey, addicts turn to drugs to escape the hardships of life. His role of managing New York laborers would be rough. Don't you think we'd be throwing him to the wolves?"

"I don't need you to tell me how addicts work, Drew."

Her fire drives me crazy.

My hands lift. "I'm not trying to educate you, Bailey. I'm only trying to consider Carter. I gave him the job at Silver to get him away from the slum bar where he had been working. It was the place that caused his current habits," I offer in explanation. For some reason, at this moment, I want to level with Bailey. I want to tell her all of my secrets, and that is no good.

"Listen, I've known Carter for a very long time," I admit. "We had mutual friends, and Carter became one of mine. I watched his downward spiral and did nothing, Bailey. Silver might not be the best place for him, but it's safer than where he was. There, I can keep an eye on him. I can try to help."

Her face softens. "So, imagine how good an actual restaurant job would be for him," she says, almost pleading.

"But if he's working daytime hours, that gives him too much time at night, Bailey. That's why I try to keep him busy through the typical party hours. He's less likely to use if he's busy and tired."

She blows out a harsh breath. "True. I never thought of that." She gives a bit. "Can't we give him the chance? Maybe with a more reliable income and more responsibility, he'll have reasons not to use?"

I consider her points. Essentially, working this muscle job—as Bailey calls it—would be the perfect prelude to manager. And I have to admit, Carter would be excellent, assuming he remains sober. That would also keep him busy during the evening hours, and as far as income goes, he couldn't make that kind of money anywhere else.

"Okay. He's got one chance," I say, and she smiles wild. "But you need to get him started on his recovery before the work begins."

She nods her head. "How long do I have?"

"One month."

She reaches across the table and places her hands on top of mine.

"Thank you, Drew. This means . . . everything."

The feel of her skin on mine, coupled with the unearned reverence in her voice, has my body locking up. My eyes scan her face unabashedly, and a crimson blush sweeps across her cheeks. Her eyelashes flutter as her eyes cast downward, signaling she's embarrassed by my perusal.

"Bailey, look at me." My voice is hoarse as I try to control my basal reactions to this woman.

Her head tilts so that her azure eyes once again meet mine, and I smile.

"It's your job to make sure everything goes off without a hitch. If you truly believe he's the right person, I trust you. The best way to thank me is to make sure he doesn't screw it up."

She doesn't say anything, but I can see the brief hesitation. She knows that what she's promising means putting a lot of faith in someone she doesn't really know all that well. The fact that she's so determined speaks for the kind of person she is. Her heart is big, and she's loyal—two characteristics that mean everything.

My phone rings, and I look down to see it's my attorney, Ralph, calling.

"Excuse me for one moment," I say to Bailey.

"Ralph, what can I do for you?"

"Drew," he says by way of greeting. "That other property you've had your eye on is rumored to be hitting the market within the month. If you want this, you need to get a head start."

"Can you book me a table for two tonight?"

"Since when did I become your secretary?" Ralph chuckles.

"Since I agreed to give you double your fee if you make this happen."

"Consider it done," he says before hanging up.

"I'm afraid I need to cut our day short. I have an urgent matter to attend to. Feel free to stay and order lunch. Have them add it to my tab," I say, standing.

Bailey stands too. "Actually, I have some of my own business to attend to. Thank you anyway."

We walk side by side through the restaurant until we're out on the street.

"Allow me to call you a car," I offer, but she shakes her head.

"I'll be fine, Drew. When and where should I be next?"

A slight gust of wind blows between the buildings, and Bailey's long, dark hair flutters around her head. A stray strand whips across her face, and without thinking, I step forward, running my hand across her cheek and placing the errant strand behind her ear. Her intake of breath lets me know I'm not the only one affected.

"Apparently, this is becoming our thing," I say, smiling as I remember when I did the same thing at Silver.

Her lips part and cheeks darken, and it takes everything in me not to lean forward and capture her mouth with mine. She swallows, and my heart skips a beat.

She steps back, breaking the connection. "You better go," she says, smiling awkwardly.

Every voice in my head is screaming to let her walk away because this can only end badly. Our demons from the past would have a field day with this. But for some reason, no matter how much I know I shouldn't pursue this, pursue her, my mouth still opens.

"Tonight," I say, and she frowns. "I need you to work with

me tonight. The phone call was my attorney, and he was giving me the inside scoop that a restaurant I've been eyeing could be bought. I need to scope the place out tonight, and I'd like your help."

"Dinner?" she says skeptically. "Is that a good idea?"

"Work, but yes, we'll be having dinner."

She bites that bottom lip, and I clench my fists to keep myself from reaching out to her.

"I'll pick you up at eight. You'll want to wear a cocktail dress."

She winces. "I don't exactly have a cocktail dress."

I reach into my pocket and pull out a wad of one-hundred-dollar bills. Not bothering to count it, I extend the money to Bailey.

"I'm not taking your money," she says, appalled.

"It's a business expense, Bailey. For the job you'll have to do, you'll need a new wardrobe. My accountant will get with you on all that tomorrow with the rest of your paperwork. I'll have him add this to the mix."

She doesn't look convinced, but when she finally reaches out to take it, she stumbles. I grab her hand, and without thinking, I pull her toward me to steady her.

She squeaks as her body meets mine.

Her head tilts up so that our eyes meet, and I can see the desire there. No matter how hard she tries to deny it, it was definitely there.

I know I need to let her go now that she is steady, but with her tucked in my arms, I can't seem to.

"Drew."

The way she says my name, breathy and wanton, makes me swallow hard.

"We . . . we can't," she says, turning her head as she battles with her own emotions.

My hand goes under her chin and pulls her gaze back to mine.

Her breath hitches, and her chin quivers at our proximity. She stares at me, then takes the lead and does us both a favor by stepping backward.

I had no damn business offering anything to Bailey. She's smart to step back.

"I need to go," she says, holding her hand up to signal a cab. "I have a lot to process, and I can't think right now," she admits.

"Bailey, I—"

She cuts me off. "No. Please . . . don't say anything more, Drew. I'll see you tonight," she says, before opening the door to the cab that has just pulled up in front of her.

"I'll be there at eight."

She offers a small smile that I'm taking as an olive branch. I return it with a smile and a nod as she lowers herself into the cab and drives off, leaving me to contemplate what the hell I've just done.

chapter seventeen

Bailey

S INCE I NEVER ATE EARLIER, I DECIDE TO GRAB LUNCH FROM a corner bistro near my sister's law firm. It's a ballsy move popping in on her at work after what happened between us at the club, but I really need to see her, and this is the one place she can't really avoid me without making yet another scene.

"Hi, Bailey," Sarah, the receptionist greets pleasantly, clearly not being in the know that I'm currently on the outs with Harper. That or the girl has a future in theater. With her porcelain skin and silky brown hair, she'd be perfect. I shake my head, trying to concentrate on the reason I'm here.

"Is Harp around?" I ask, lifting the paper bags to show I brought an impromptu lunch.

She smiles. "She is, and she's currently free. Go on back."

"Thanks," I say, making my way down the hall to Harper's corner office.

I slow because as much as I tried to convince myself that everything is normal, and this is just our regular monthly lunch date, I know damn well I'm the last person she wants to see. This is going to be awkward as hell, and in truth, no matter how close I am to my sister, I'm not ready for this.

Her door is cracked, and her head is bent over her desk,

reading a document. I rap my knuckles on the door two times, and she looks up. When she realizes it's me, she frowns, and my shoulders sag.

"Can I come in?" I ask, lifting the paper bags once more. "An olive branch."

Her lips form a straight line, but she nods, giving me permission to enter. I shut the door behind me, creeping toward her desk slowly.

"What are you doing here, Bailey?"

I sigh. "I came to talk. I knew you wouldn't answer your door if I went there."

"You're right," she admits, and I want to cry.

Having my sister, who's always been my biggest supporter, not want to see me, tears me up inside.

"I needed a job, Harper. I had to quit the office."

"You said that." She sits back in her chair, crossing her arms over her chest. "But you never did say why."

I sit in the chair across from her and spill all the sordid details. When I'm done, she clucks her tongue and unfolds her arms.

"Why didn't you tell me?"

"Because I wanted to take care of myself, Harper. And you and I both know you would've wanted to press charges, and honestly, I can't handle that."

She doesn't say anything for several minutes. Her eyes never leave my face, and I begin to fidget under her intense stare.

"Why did you get Cal involved?"

I blow out a harsh breath. "I knew he had connections to Drew. I'd gotten my third eviction notice and was starting to panic. Silver is one of the hottest clubs in the city. I knew I'd be able to get back on my feet very quickly," I say, and before she can cut me off, I dive back in. "And I know I can handle it, Harper. It's been two years."

"Let's pretend you aren't an addict."

"Former," I snap.

"Semantics, Bailey, and you know it," she says, not kindly. "That still doesn't answer why you'd go behind my back and put Cal and me at odds with each other. We've already had problems, Bailey. You only made it worse."

I cringe at that knowledge. I didn't have a clue they were in a bad place.

"He was my last hope," I whisper.

"You should've come to me," she says, slamming her hands down on the desk and causing me to jump. "Dammit, Bailey," she says, running her hand through her hair roughly. "I just . . . can't do this right now, okay?"

I nod my head vigorously, trying hard to stave off the tears threatening to fall.

Harper's face softens slightly, and she says, "Give me some time."

I stand, placing her lunch on her desk and turn to leave, but she calls out.

"Bailey." I turn back toward her. "Are you still working at Silver?"

"Not exactly. As of this morning, I'm Drew's assistant. He removed me from the bar and has me managing the operations of two restaurants he's looking to open."

Her brow raises. "Are you sleeping with him?"

"No!" I snap.

"Then why the hell would he try so hard to keep you under his thumb? What other reason would he have to make you his project manager? You don't have experience with that, Bailey."

I stand taller. "Maybe he believes in me."

She scoffs. "Drew doesn't do nice things for anyone. Don't delude yourself." She shakes her head. "Look, I'm sorry. I'm really angry, but as mad as I am at you, I'm not being fair." She lowers her head. "No matter Drew's reasons, what he's done for you is huge. He's removed you from possible temptations and given you a chance to really make something of yourself. You won't even need a degree with this on your résumé. It's a gift, and as much as I don't like Drew, as long as he keeps his hands to himself, what he's done for you is a good thing."

I nod. "I won't mess it up." I walk toward the door, and before I leave, I turn my head back to my sister. "When you're ready to talk, I'll be here."

She doesn't say anything, so I let myself out.

Before leaving my sister, I texted Carter to meet me. I was pretty vague with details, but I figure once I get him to where I'm going, it'll be worth it. As I round the corner, Carter's tall and lean body comes into view. Lifting my hand, I give a little wave and pick up my pace.

"Hey." I lean up on my tiptoes and place a kiss on his stubbly cheek.

"You wanted to meet. What's going on?" His eyebrows knit together, and he points at the church behind us.

"I thought maybe you'd want to come with me."

His eyes dart back at me, the line thickening between his brow.

"What the fuck is this, Bailey?" he huffs out.

"You asked for help, Carter. I told you I would."

He lifts a hand to silence me. "I asked for help? That's not what went down."

"After what I witnessed, Carter, yes. You need help."

"God, a bit presumptuous, don't you think? It was one slip, Bailey. If I needed or wanted help, I'd ask, thank you very much." He folds his arms protectively across his chest. "I'm not an addict. I can stop. It's not like I need it."

The words ring so clear to me. It feels like ice crashing through my veins at the stark reminder of what I once was and how he doesn't see it. But I know better than anyone that until you see yourself for what you really are, and the problems you really have, you will never be open to help.

"I'm sorry. You're right. Clearly, you don't need it. I was wrong." I turn on my heels and walk toward the church, leaving him behind.

"Hey, wait," he calls out, but I don't stop.

He grabs my elbow and stops me, spinning me on my heel. I level him with my best *what can I do for you* expression.

"Stop, Bae. We need to talk about this."

"Talk about what? I misunderstood the situation, Carter. I thought you wanted to completely quit, but I see you don't have an addiction, so no need for help." I turn and take a couple of steps before turning back to him. "Drew knows you're using at the club."

His face went pale before anger took over. "You told him?" he accuses, looking as though steam is about to come out of his ears.

I frown. "You might not know me that well, Carter, but I thought we were friends. You should know I would never rat out a friend. He knows all on his own. You sneaking around isn't as undercover as you thought."

With a little shake of the head, he replaces his thin lips with a practiced smile. "I'm sorry, Bae, we're cool." He shuffles on his feet before speaking his fear out loud. "Is he going to fire me?"

I shrug. "No clue. He gave me permission to offer you a huge promotion, but it came with the stipulation you get clean first." I level him with a stare. "But since you don't think you have a problem, I don't see how that promotion is going to work. I can't hire you and have him catch you using. I have to be able to depend on whoever I appoint to this position."

"A promotion? Seriously?" he asks, looking at the ground.

"Yeah, but like I said, I'm not sure it's going to work."

He looks at the ominous church standing beside us and then peers into the city traffic.

Flashes of colors rush by as the traffic flows. Lifting his left wrist to his line of sight, he checks the time on his watch.

"I actually have some time. I have some stuff to do before work, but if you wanna go in, I'll join you."

I gnaw at my upper lip as I gauge his behavior. I hope he's not just doing this to appease me. I can't stand the idea of losing my only friend, but if he isn't ready to get help, this won't work. "You're sure that's what you want? It can't be about a promotion, Carter. It has to be because you want to change your life."

"I do. This whole thing just caught me off guard. I wasn't expecting it."

"I get that, but if I'd have told you before, would you have actually shown up?"

That's the issue. I should've told him. The bottom line, if he wasn't ready, that should've been my sign that this morning was born of the embarrassment about last night. Every addict was eventually able to shake that off and brush their behavior under the rug so that they could use another day.

"Yeah, totally."

I frown, not buying that at all. He's doing this solely for the promotion, which isn't the right reason. But he's here, and maybe attending the meeting will help convince him to finally take that leap. I can only hope the combination of a meeting and a promotion will do the trick, though it's unlikely.

"Then let's go," I say.

"Love ya, beautiful," he says as he leans in and presses a kiss to my forehead. "I promise, I'll try."

The breath I've been holding through this whole exchange is expelled. I know he will be better one day, and I will be here for him throughout that process. Today is a start.

By the time Carter and I are done talking, we're the last to arrive at the meeting. All the seats are taken except for two chairs directly in front of the coffee pot. The idea of coffee sounds appealing until I notice the black sludge inside it. The red plastic chair squeaks as the metal hits the concrete floor of the basement. I quietly sit down and try my best not to disturb anyone or call any more unwelcome attention to us.

The group leader is speaking. His words sound like a faint hum as I turn my head away from him and concentrate on the people surrounding me. Their bleak moods reflect how I used to feel and how Carter probably does feel sitting here. Completely dejected that they lack the strength to stand on their own two feet and need a room full of strangers to keep from using. It's a sobering reminder of how far I've come. I wish I didn't have to be here, but Carter needs me, and if I'm being honest with myself, the urge has become stronger since starting at the club.

My fingers nervously tap on the plastic of my seat as I hear my name called. Guess I caught his attention, after all.

"Bailey, would you like to share anything?"

Carter squeezes my hand. I stand and focus on the piece of lint by my feet, kicking it around as I find the courage to speak. "Hi, most of you know me, but for anyone who doesn't, my name is Bailey, and I'm an addict."

"Hi, Bailey," echoes through the room.

"I've been sober for two years. It feels really good to be clean, but some days are harder than others. Some days, I don't feel the pain at all, and other days, I hurt everywhere, and it feels like only a pill will fix it. I just started a new job, and it comes with a lot of temptation. I remind myself every day how far I have come and how much I have to lose. Even though I sometimes hurt so bad, I remind myself I can't go back to the person I was before. I did a lot of bad things. I almost died, so I think about how lucky I am to be alive, and that's enough to help. But I'm afraid one of these days, it won't be enough."

I sit down, my shoulders falling forward with the weight of my confession. Reflecting on my past helps me remember why I need to be here more often. The reminder of the things I did when I was addicted to pain pills will haunt me forever . . . I can't go back there. I won't.

"Thank you for sharing, Bailey. How about you? Feel like talking today?" He directs to Carter.

My eyes meet his, and I smile, giving him courage. He needs to speak for this meeting to truly work. I watch his eyes twitch and the way his body trembles, and I know how bad he's itching to use—or run. I feel for him. The memory of those first months of sobriety will always be burned into my mind. I wouldn't wish that on anyone—especially not my friend.

"H-Hi," he stammers. "My name's Carter."

"Hi, Carter," I say, along with everyone else in the room.

"Where do I even start?" He smiles, but it's forced, and eventually, he looks at the ground. "I first started drinking when I was fifteen, and it wasn't much later that it escalated. My mom . . . she had this boyfriend who used to beat her in front of me. One night, it got bad, and I gave him a taste of his own medicine. Afterward, my mom kicked me out."

My stomach turns at Carter's story. It's horrifying that a kid had to witness such a thing. Then when he acts to defend his mom, she turns her back on him. Heartbreaking.

"Anyway," he continues. "I went to this senior's party, and that's the first night I used. I was drunk, but it wasn't enough. It was only—it was pills to start," he amends, knowing that pills are the gateway to the harder stuff. "I recently had a rough night, and a friend came to my rescue. I know it's time for me to get help, so I'm here."

When he doesn't say anything else, Bill, the NA lead, takes things back over.

"Thanks for sharing, Carter. We're glad you're here."

I reach my hand over and place it on top of Carter's in re-assurance. I know that was hard for him, and the truth is, I'm proud. The challenging part will be getting him back here and keeping him on the straight and narrow. If he wants the job, he'll have to make it happen.

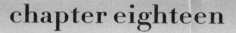

chapter eighteen

Drew

S OMETHING IS GOING ON WITH CAL.

I'm not sure what, but the man has basically disappeared. Normally, I'd be happy about that, but right now, I'm anything but.

The papers for the sale of the property should have been in my hands weeks ago. But they aren't. We made a deal, and he needs to hold up his end.

If not having the paperwork isn't bad enough, the fact the deadbeat is missing in action takes the cake.

I've tried to call.

Nothing.

One: He's too busy to speak to me, which is doubtful. The man is a lazy piece of shit who rides the coattails of his father. If not for his father's legacy, he'd be broke.

Two: He's dead.

He better hope, for his sake, it's option two because I'm losing my patience.

I grab the phone one more time, but I don't call. Instead, I shoot over a text.

Drew: What's taking so long with the papers?

I place my cell back down on the counter, not expecting an

answer. I'm pleasantly surprised when a second later, it pings. I'm even more surprised when I see it is, in fact, Cal's worthless ass.

Cal: There was a little hiccup, but don't worry, everything is okay.

Finally, a damn response. Not that it does much to ease my worry. What fucking hiccups could he have run into? His word that everything is okay doesn't settle my unease.

Drew: What hiccup?

Cal: It was more of a personal hiccup. It's all good.

Hopefully, Harper got smart and tossed his ass out.

Drew: You better hope it's only personal. Did everyone at the holding company agree to the sale?

Cal: . . .

I see the dots, signaling he's typing. They start and then they stop. *Not good.* What I want to fucking see is that everyone's on board. The length of time it's taking to say something so damn simple is alarming.

Drew: Make this happen, Cal. If not, you'll be making room in that swanky apartment of yours for your future sister-in-law.

I threaten Bailey's job, but I'd never follow through with it. The job might've been offered to her because of Cal, but not anymore. Regardless of this acquisition, Bailey's position is safe. I'd never doom her to that fate.

Cal: I told you. It's fine. I'll be in touch.

With that settled, I put my phone down and pull out the stack of proposals from all the architects competing for the job. It feels like hours go by as I sort through the overpriced bids, finally settling on one. It's not the cheapest, but I believe it's the best option.

I ring the winner, checking one thing off my list.

Thirty minutes later, the alarm chimes, signaling someone's here. I make my way downstairs to see who's in my club and stop short when I see Bailey, leaning over the bar, laughing at something on the floor on the other side.

This might be the first time I've seen her so carefree and laid-back. It's a sight to behold. At this moment, no ghosts from the past linger in the shadows. It's simply Bailey. Beautiful, relaxed Bailey. *I'm fucked.*

"Hurry up. I'm running late," she calls to who I can only assume is Carter on the other side.

"I can't find it," his voice calls back, confirming it's, in fact, Carter.

His head pops up with a goofy grin plastered across his face, and I want to smack it off. Why does he make her like this? What's so damn special about Carter Cass that every fucking woman in New York caves at his smile? More importantly, why do I fucking care?

"I'm going to check in the back. I probably left it in the stockroom. Be back."

"Hurry your ass up," she calls, laughing all the while.

I could sit here in the shadows and watch the woman driving me crazy.

Without a second thought, I step up behind her. I must startle her because she steps back and squeaks when her body becomes flush against my chest. "What are you doing here, Bailey?"

She slowly turns so that we're face-to-face. Her cheeks are stained pink, and her lips are parted. Her tongue darts out, tracing a line across her bottom lip. It's nothing like the way Monica would do such things to elicit a reaction from men. This is innocent. All Bailey.

Our gaze is locked. We're so close I can practically feel her breath.

There is an electric energy coursing between us. A current I can't comprehend. I want to cross the distance, but I know I shouldn't.

I can't go there with her.

"Drew . . . I—" She shakes her head as if to pull herself together. "I'm here with Carter. He left his tip bag here, and we're heading out to shop. I still need to get my dress." She lowers her head as if embarrassed.

Before I know what I'm doing, my hand goes to her chin, and I tilt her head so she's looking into my eyes. She inhales, biting her lip.

I take a step closer so that our mouths are mere inches apart. It would be so easy to touch her, to kiss her right now, but I know I can't, so I take a step back, putting much-needed distance between us.

Bailey's eyes remain wide, and she doesn't stop staring at me. She's flustered and worked up.

So am I.

But I'm doing the right thing for both of us.

"Ready, Bae?" Carter says, coming around the corner, stopping when he sees us in our stare off. "Um . . . everything okay?"

Never taking my eyes off Bailey, I say, "Have fun shopping."

With that, I turn and walk back to my office, adjusting myself the entire way.

Whatever the fuck that was, I'll need a cold-ass shower if I want to get anything accomplished the rest of the day. Bailey is doing things to me that nobody has in a very long time, simply by being in the same room as me. I'm not sure this arrangement is a good idea, but fuck if I'm going to change anything.

chapter nineteen

Bailey

MY BODY IS STILL QUAKING FROM DREW'S PROXIMITY earlier. The intense stare, the way he looked at me . . . I've never in my life wanted to kiss someone so badly. And that scares the hell out of me for so many reasons. I'm lost in thought, fingering the money Drew had given me earlier, when Carter's voice breaks through my wayward thoughts.

"He gave you how much for the dress?"

I quickly count the wad of cash and quickly count again because there's no way I counted correctly. Yet . . . I did.

"Two thousand," I say, stupefied. "He didn't count it."

"Because he doesn't have to." Carter rolls his eyes. "The man's loaded."

"Yeah, how did he come into so much money?"

Carter shrugs. "I've heard rumors, but who knows?"

"What were the rumors?" I press, wanting to know everything about Drew Lawson, despite my better judgment.

"There have been so many contradicting stories that I don't know what's actually true," he admits. "I've heard he comes from money. Then there was the rumor that he was a pimp." He raises his hand. "Oh, and then there was the rumor that he works with the cartel. I don't believe that one, though."

"Why not?" I ask.

"He's so adamantly against drug use, and there isn't an easy way to stop working with the cartel. If he was and quit, he'd be dead. If he were still working with them, drugs would be circulating through Silver more than the drinks we serve. There's no way the cartel wouldn't be using the club to run their drugs."

I couldn't disagree there. Drew was definitely against drug usage, given how hard I had to work to get Carter his new job. If only he knew about my past.

And knowing plenty of drug dealers, if they owned a club, they would undoubtedly be using that high-end clientele to push their stash. Silver would be a hotbed for designer drugs. Drew could be lining his pockets, but he wasn't. I was sure of that. So, what does that leave? Pimp? I mean, the man is fifty shades of sexy. He could probably talk a girl into doing an assortment of things for him. That's why he's dangerous.

"Regardless, the man works his ass off now. His fortune, at this point, has been more than earned. Drew is a workaholic," Carter supplies, pulling me out of my wayward thoughts. "So, where is he taking you?"

"I have no clue. He just said it was another restaurant he was looking to buy, and that I'd need a cocktail dress."

Carter eyes me up and down. "I know just the place. My ex used to drag me there all the time."

An hour later, I'm standing in front of a floor-length mirror wearing the most beautiful dress I've worn to date. With a high neckline and cap sleeves, the dress is equal parts sexy and modest. The lace overlay works throughout the dress, giving it a bold texture that my fingers can't stop running over. The skirt has a column silhouette and finishes with a modest hem that brings attention to my toned and tanned legs.

"Stunning," Carter muses, scratching his chin with his hand. "Drew is going to eat you alive in that dress."

My mouth drops open, and I glare at him through the mirror. "I'm not trying to draw Drew's attention. It's just a dress. I'm dressing up," I mutter, just managing to repeat myself like an idiot. "Riiiiight," he draws out. "And that must be why your cheeks are ten shades of red right now." He chuckles.

"Ass," I mumble. "But seriously, I want to impress him but only in a professional manner. I don't have any interest in being one of his conquests."

He purses his lips. "You might have all the intentions in the world of keeping things professional, but Drew doesn't have that same goal, Bailey. You have to know that by now."

"How do you figure?"

"He's been asking about you and your past. Given the way he's been acting around you, he's aiming for something. I've known him for a long time, and he's not asking because he thinks you're a killer waitress."

I frown, and he quickly jumps in.

"I'm not saying you're not, Bae. I'm just saying to him, waitresses are a dime a dozen. The guy has stacks of résumés a mile high, most having more experience than either of us have, combined."

"Great, so I'm another floozy he's trying to bone."

Carter grunts. "You're no floozy, and I don't think that's what's happening here." He sighs. "Listen, as I said, I've known Drew for a long time. For some reason, he really wants to help you, and I'm not sure why. Maybe it's because he's interested in you, or maybe it's something else . . ." He trails off, blowing out a hard breath and running a hand through his thick hair.

"So why is he going to so much effort?"

He levels me with a *come on, you're smarter than that* expression.

"It's obvious he wants to help you, Bailey. Maybe it's because you remind him of his own past? I'm not sure."

I huff. "Great, so I'm a damn charity case."

"Do you want to be more?" he asks, raising a questioning brow.

"Well . . . no, but—"

"Then take the help and don't look a gift horse in the horseshoe."

"It's don't look a gift horse in the mouth."

"That's dumb. I'm changing it."

I laugh because only Carter can manage to turn an awkward conversation to giggles.

"So take his help," I say, looking at myself once more in the mirror.

"Damn straight."

What have I gotten myself into?

Since Drew picked me up, he hasn't stopped staring. And as a result, I can't stop fidgeting. My cheeks are warm, and my knees wobbly. The three-inch stilettos that Carter insisted on aren't helping. Serves me right for taking fashion advice from a man who clearly only dates Barbies.

Drew and I are being ushered through a dimly lit, swanky Italian restaurant on the Upper East Side, right down the street from the brunch place. This place screams three-star Michelin, and I feel out of place even in this exceptional dress.

As if he read my mind, he lowers his lips to my ear, and whispers, "You look incredible."

I shiver. Whether from his words or his touch, I haven't a clue. Maybe it's the ambiance of the place. Romantic above reason. Or maybe it's all the thoughts roaming my brain this afternoon.

When I went to the beauty bar and the woman fixed my hair and makeup, Carter's words played on a loop.

Drew wants to help you. He cares.

But why?

Why is he hell-bent on it?

Does he have a savior complex?

Is it what Carter said? Is it because I remind him of his own twisted past?

Is he righting a wrong with me?

Or is it something else?

That last part is my mind's way of toying with me. Drew is not good for me. Especially with my tendency to get hooked.

But I can't deny I'm attracted to him.

I can't deny that the attention he gives me makes me weak in the knees. He's the guy a girl could easily fall in love with. And in that devilish grin that turns me to mush and . . . fuck.

He's already pulled me under his spell.

"Bailey," Drew calls from across the table.

We've been sitting here for who knows how long. My mind has been elsewhere for the greater part of the past few minutes. Everything he's said is completely lost on me.

"Hmm?" I murmur, reluctantly bringing my eyes to meet his.

I don't want to look at him. The truth is, I'm not sure if this pull I'm feeling is the real deal or yet another symptom of my addictive personality. Am I lusting after him for the right reasons? Or am I concocting falsities in my head based on something another addict has said? I hate that my mind categorizes Carter as such, but it's the truth. I have to be careful not to allow others to get into my head.

"You're far away," Drew says, cocking his head to the side to watch me.

"I have a lot on my mind," I say, tearing my eyes from his and toying with the napkin for something to preoccupy me.

"Bailey." He says my name like a command. "Look at me."

I do, and the way the glow of the lamps hanging from the walls around us casts shadows across his face makes him all the more mysterious . . . and beautiful.

"I was just thinking, I don't know much about you," I say, trying to change the subject.

He bites the inside of his cheek. "What's to know? I work hard, and I don't have a lot of time for a social life outside of my club. I'm looking to branch out so that can change."

"You want a social life?"

"Why not? Life's short, and I've spent the better half of mine working," he muses.

"What would you do if you had more time?"

He shrugs, placing his napkin on his own lap. "I guess I'd buy a boat."

I smirk. "Captain Drew?"

He chuckles. "Sure."

"Hmm." I consider the options. "I don't know much about boats, but I love the ones with the open bow."

"Interesting," he says. "I can see it, you know."

I purse my lips. "See what, exactly?"

"You. Seated, leaning back on the front of the boat, the wind blowing through your hair. Not a care in the world."

As he paints the picture, I can see it too. I smile. "Sounds amazing."

"Yeah. A boat for sure," he says with a smile in his voice.

"What else would you do?"

He appears to ponder that for a moment. "I guess I'd buy a lake house. Somewhere away from the city, where I could just relax."

"You said you wanted a social life. What you're explaining sounds more like solitude."

"I'd invite people to visit."

"What people?" I challenge, leaning over the table and grinning.

"You, for starters."

"Employees?" I raise my brow.

"No, Bailey. Just you."

I sit back, cheeks heating at the intensity of his stare. The feeling akin to being stripped bare.

chapter twenty

Bailey

THE REST OF THE DINNER GOES WELL. WE TALK ABOUT mundane topics, nothing too personal and nothing to do with Silver or his future business dealings. Why we are here, outside of his having mentioned he wanted to buy the place, is besides me. We haven't so much as discussed any of that.

As our dinner plates are removed, I decide to broach the topic. "So, why did we come here? Are we testing the cuisine, or are you looking to renovate the place?"

He shakes his head. "Neither."

I raise a brow. "Neither?"

"Neither," he repeats, smiling. "I wanted to celebrate your promotion."

I blink. What? He brought me to one of the fanciest restaurants in the city for . . . me?

"Celebrate?" I say, voice thick with emotion.

"Has anyone else taken you to dinner? You got a huge job, Bailey. Someone needs to celebrate it with you."

My eyes lower to the table as I admit, "I don't really have any friends around here."

I feel stupid voicing that out loud. It sounds childish and pathetic, even to me.

"I know the feeling," he says, and I frown. "Just because I know a lot of people who call me their friend doesn't mean I actually have friends, Bailey. People will say whatever they want if it'll benefit them in some way. It doesn't have to be the truth. I have a lot of acquaintances but very few real friends."

An insane feeling of sadness washes through me. Despite whatever's been said about Drew, every interaction I've had with him has been pleasant. More than. He truly seems to be a good guy with a good heart. Not once has he said anything that's led me to believe his thoughtfulness comes with expectations. He's been nothing but a gentleman.

It makes me sad that he seems to feel mostly alone. How horrible it must feel to constantly be used. I know exactly how that feels.

"A long time ago, I hung with a pretty eclectic crowd," I admit. "Some of them came from very little, and it wasn't until much later into our 'friendship,'" I use air quotes on the word, "that I realized they were using me for my parents' money. They wanted access to . . . stuff I could afford, and they couldn't."

"They befriended you for the access?" he parrots, looking as though he knows that feeling far too well. "What happened? They left when you finally figured it out?"

I laughed but without humor. "When I realized I had to change, they left. They only wanted to be friends with me for what my money could buy."

His eyes narrow, but thankfully, he doesn't pry. I'm not ready to talk about my past.

Especially not tonight. Not here in this luxurious restaurant, surrounded by the New York elite. For one night, I want to feel like something other than a failure. Something more than my sister's ward and my mother's dirty secret.

"If you could do anything or be anyone, what would you choose?" Drew asks me, seeming truly curious.

"Honestly? I'd choose me as I am now. It took me a long time to get here, and I still have a way to go, but I think that our past helps mold our future. I've been through some really dark times, but I know that with this opportunity you've given me, all my dreams are finally at my fingertips. Thank you."

"You don't have to thank me, Bailey. I see potential in you, and I want to give you this chance. In the short time you've been employed by Silver, you've worked circles around the other girls. I wouldn't trust any one of them with this project."

I don't have a chance to react to Drew's words because our waiter is back, placing a plate full of mini desserts and a bottle of champagne on the table. He pours two glasses, setting one in front of me and one in front of Drew.

"Thank you," Drew says to the man, who bows slightly and walks away.

"What's this?" I say, smiling.

"Sorry about that." He reaches out and moves the glass away from in front of me. "I told them it was a celebration, so they must have assumed . . . Now that I fucked that up, let's move to the second part of the celebration," he says, holding up his spoon. "Congratulations, Bailey. May this be the beginning of a successful career with Lawson Enterprises."

I lift my spoon and smile even wider. "Thank you," I say, clinking the metal utensil with his before looking down at the plate. "What do we have here?" I ask, inspecting the various confections.

There are glazed donuts with a side of what appears to be chocolate and caramel glazes, mini tarts, and a small chocolate lava cake.

I put a sampling of each on my plate and dig into the lava cake first. When my lips wrap around the spoon and taste the delicious cake, I moan around the first bite. When my eyes open, I catch Drew swallowing down something that looks a lot like desire. His eyes blaze as he's focused on my mouth.

I stare back through my lashes, trying not to get too caught up in the moment. Everything from the candlelit room to the gorgeous man sitting across from me makes me feel like I'm the only woman in the room, and it has this evening feeling like anything but a professional work relationship.

We both enjoy the rest of the dessert in a heightened silence. I'm focused on calming down the building desire while also attempting to quiet the voices that keep going between *stop lusting after your boss* and *go for it.*

"Are you ready?" Drew's husky voice pulls my attention back to him. "Stan has the car out front."

"Don't we have to pay?"

He quirks a brow. "It's already been taken care of."

"Oh." It's all I can manage. My brain feels like mush.

My body's on fire, and my head is screaming to throw all caution out the window and act on my desires as he ushers me out of the restaurant with his hand on the small of my back— creating goose bumps and butterflies with that simple touch.

We reach the Town Car waiting for us outside the restaurant when I stop short. Drew must not notice because he crashes into me. His body pins my chest to the car door.

"I'm sorry," he whispers, and all sanity leaves me.

I turn, finding my back against the car, body still trapped by Drew's arms.

Our mouths are now inches apart as the energy crackles between us.

"Kiss me." My voice is low and soft. Unsure, but desperate.

His eyes fly back and forth between mine, trying to work out if I really mean it, but seeing the look of concern coming from him is the push I need. He always puts my needs first, so now it's my turn to take what I want, and what I want is his lips on mine. What I need is to kiss him.

Leaning up on my tiptoes, I bring my mouth to his. His lips

are soft yet firm against mine. I have a moment's hesitation when he doesn't take things further, so I draw back, searching his face. His eyes darken. "Fuck it," he growls before slamming his mouth against mine, forcing my lips to part to allow his tongue entry. I moan around the expert way he massages my tongue with his. Pulling me into his chest firmly, he doesn't relent, kissing me with abandon alongside a busy New York street for everyone to see.

I'm lost in his kiss when a horn blares behind us, and Drew pulls back to glare at the offending driver. He opens the door, and I take a seat.

"Stan, you know where to go," he commands, lifting the partition with a click of a remote.

Not even a second later, his hands are all over me. Touching. Feeling. Caressing. My head's thrown back, allowing him access to my neck. He trails kisses up the curve, biting my earlobe when he reaches it.

"Tell me this is okay, Bailey. I'll stop if it's not," he says breathily.

"Please don't stop," I groan.

His hand trails up my leg, lifting the hem of my dress as he goes.

"This fucking dress," he growls, "kills me."

His tongue licks a line across my lower lip before his tongue is back to massaging. His fingers play at the lacy corner of my panties, and I'm about to lose it. It's been so long since anyone has touched me, and Drew . . . well, he does it better than anyone ever has.

He removes his lips and leans his forehead against mine.

"As much as I want to take this farther, it's not happening here in the car with Stan on the other side of that partition," he says, blowing out a harsh breath. "I want you to think about this and make sure this is what you want."

All the lust I was feeling moments ago evaporates at the knowledge that this isn't happening tonight. It's a sobering feeling to go from all in to hesitant.

"Think about it," he says, opening the door and stepping out. I hadn't even realized we'd stopped.

He extends his hand to help pull me from the car. My knees are a bit shaky, so he pulls me into him, allowing me to adjust. He places a small kiss on my lips.

"You look beautiful tonight, Bailey."

I have no words. Nothing I say at this moment would be intelligible.

He walks me to my door. "Get some rest. Think about things. I'll see you tomorrow. We'll get your paperwork filled out."

I nod, and he places a chaste kiss on my cheek and turns to head back to his car.

The entire process of getting ready for bed is done in a daze. I consider everything that we did and everything that was said. He's offering me this job with or without a fling. Carter said as much. Then there's Harper's opinion on him. In all fairness, he has basically said the same things. I'm not sure what else he can offer me other than a fling.

Can I really do that? Is it a good idea?

No. It's a horrible idea. But I can't deny I want to.

A therapist would say I can't handle the fallout. That I'd surely fall so deep into my addiction that I'd confuse lust for love like every time before. They would surely tell me I am playing with fire. They wouldn't be wrong, but this time, I welcome the burn.

Maybe if I got it out of my system, it would make working around the man easier?

Not a chance in hell.

chapter twenty-one

Bailey

For the whole day, I'm on edge. My lips still feel swollen from Drew's kisses. Everything about last night feels like a dream. From the overly romantic restaurant to the way he felt pressed against my body . . . a girl could easily get caught up in the fantasy.

Drew is not my Prince Charming, though. I'm under no false hope that I'm the girl for him. Maybe I could have been. Maybe if my dad didn't die, maybe if I didn't turn to booze to hide the pain, maybe if the accident never happened that changed my life . . .

I push the thoughts away of how much I ruined my life and go back to how I feel about what happened with Drew. I want him. Regardless of the fact that it probably won't go anywhere, I still want him.

This could set you back.

I push down the insecurities. I've already made up my mind, so there's no sense in beating myself up over it. Whatever Drew's offering, I'm taking. Despite everyone's warning against it. That thought makes me think of my sister. I miss her.

Grabbing my phone, I pull up Harper's phone number, and my finger hovers over the call button. She said she wanted time.

She hasn't reached out to me yet, which means she's not ready to talk. I know her. She'll send me to voicemail, and then I'll worry about that all day. I blow out a harsh breath and decide to clean. Anything to take my mind off Drew and Harper.

When my place sparkles, I realize it's time to get ready for work. After last night, I have the need to take a little extra care at getting ready. I'm no longer waitressing, but a skirt is completely acceptable, right?

Standing in front of the floor-length mirror, I groan. My outfit screams that I'm trying too hard, and that's not what I'm going for. I pull out a white blouse that's a little more professional and finally feel ready. My hands shake at my sides as nervous energy pulses through me.

It's not just about seeing Drew again but starting this new position. There's still so much to learn, and I'm only hoping I don't disappoint.

I arrive at work a little after three the next day. I might have gotten a promotion, but technically, my hours haven't changed yet.

Throwing my bag under the bar, I go in search of Drew, but when I turn the corner, he's there. And staring right through me. It's unnerving. He's leaning against the banister above me, running his hand slowly over the railing. His gaze penetrates me. It lights me on fire yet again.

I spent the entire night thinking up every reason I should avoid this attraction like the plague. There were a million good reasons, but none good enough to stop the inevitability that I would have him. Even if only for a short time.

Hot lust radiates off me. He looks primal, and I burn for him. I turn away to hide my feelings. He doesn't need to know how badly I want him. I'm mortified at the thought of him knowing. But as much as I try, I can't stop the assault of sexual thoughts.

I imagine what his hands would feel like running up my body, how they would feel pushing me forward and teasing my skin. My body aches to be touched. I need to calm down and get myself in check. Working with him here in this empty bar will be torturous or dangerous, depending on my actions.

I feel a presence behind me, and my breath catches in my chest. I attempt to mask my want. "Turn around," he commands.

I obey, saying, "I've made up my mind."

"Is that so?" He grins.

He steps forward, caging me in. I'm in so much trouble. I'm nearly panting with need, and he can see it. It's all over my face. He's so close I can feel his breath. I don't know what to say, so I go with the one thing that might stop this madness. "My sister warned me about you."

He doesn't flinch. "I don't care what your sister said," he says in a low, husky voice. "What did you decide?"

I answer the only way I know how. Grabbing him, I slam my body into his, and all thoughts about stopping this are gone.

chapter twenty-two

Drew

GOD, THIS WOMAN ...

She's maddening. She literally attacked me, and I roll with it. I tried to fight this attraction for so long, but now that I had a taste, I can't resist her anymore. Her sudden urgency only serves to make me happy with my decision not to try to stop this from happening. Now with that settled, all I want to do is fuck her right here in the middle of the club.

And I will have her today. There is no doubt about that.

I push her back into the bar, effectively pinning her. She's not getting away. She's like a cornered cat. I don't know if she'll succumb to the pleasure of being stroked or claw my eyes out to escape. She can do her worst. I like it rough.

I lift her by her hips and place her onto the bar. Her skirt rides up, giving me an up close and personal view of her black thong. Her breath comes in short pants, her desire only serving to fuel mine.

"This is your last opportunity to stop this." I nearly growl.

"I'm done trying to stop it, Drew."

This isn't where I want this to happen, but I've lost my mind where Bailey's concerned. I'm not thinking about anything but having some piece of her. Before I talk myself out of it, I act.

With one quick tug, I tear her underwear. One more yank, and they are off. Without fanfare, I dip my head to run my nose up the inside of her leg, nipping as I go. She lets out a whimper as my head meets the juncture of her hip. My eyes meet hers, silently asking for permission. Wrapping her legs around my head, she answers. I'm ravenous for her.

My tongue swipes up, and she bucks under me. Inserting one finger and then another, I pump in and out, which isn't necessary as Bailey is more than ready for me. She pants and mewls, begging for more. I oblige, continuing to lap at her. Her back arches off the bar, and I feel her quiver, signaling her orgasm is near. I want to get her there. I need to.

I nip and suck at a punishing pace. I've never been inclined to take my time with foreplay. It's always just been a means to an end. A quick prelude to my ultimate pleasure.

But Bailey is a different story.

I want to please this damaged girl lying spread open for me on my bar.

After a few more strokes of my tongue, she seizes up. She goes limp on the bar, and I know my work is done, but hers is just beginning.

I reach to pull her down when I hear the front door slam open. I look up in time to see Bailey's eyes go wide. She scrambles off the bar backward, fixing her clothes as she goes. She disappears from sight just as Carter comes strolling around the corner. I lazily wipe the remnants of Bailey from my mouth, scowling in his direction.

"What the fuck are you doing here this early? It's a quarter to four."

I can't help the venom spewing from my lips. I was so close to having her.

"Dude, I have to get the bar stocked. We ran out of everything last night. If I don't start now, I'll never be ready for opening." He doesn't seem fazed by my mood, which is a good thing. I have to get him out of here, or he's going to find Bailey hiding behind the bar, naked from the waist down.

"Can you come to my office quickly? I want to go over a couple of the parties we have in the VIP rooms tonight."

He looks at me skeptically. "Um, sure, I guess my shit can wait. Let me throw my bag behind the bar. See, isn't it good I came early?" He winks at me before bending his knees to lean down. I go to stop him when up pops Bailey.

"Uh, hey, Bae . . . What the heck are you doing down there?" Carter looks a little smug, and I have the sudden urge to punch him.

"Oh, hey, Carter. I was just clearing out the empty liquor bottles from under here. I was going to take them down to the art center. I figured we could donate them. I hear there's a local artist who makes really cool lamps out of them." She doesn't miss a beat, and I'm impressed.

She looks up at me, and I see her cheeks turn a shade of pink. I can't imagine Carter missed it, but he doesn't say anything.

"Good work today, Bailey. We'll pick up where we left off tomorrow. Same time. Oh, and Carter, forget meeting now . . . something else just came up." I don't wait for either of them to respond. Turning on my heels, I haul ass to my office. I have one hour before our staff meeting, and if I don't pull myself together, I'll be miserable all night.

I slam my door shut and lock it. Throwing myself into my chair, I recall the image of Bailey from moments ago. Just thinking about the sounds of her whimpers and moans cause me to adjust myself. Fuck.

I take several deep breaths and think of anything but Bailey. Puppies. Babies. Sunshine. I give myself a minute to get under control. When I look down at my pants, I see I'm still hard.

I call down to the bar.

Carter answers. "Yeah, boss man?"

"Is Bailey still here?"

"Uh, yeah."

"Can you hand her the phone, please?"

"Sure, hold."

There's silence on the other line for about thirty seconds when I hear her voice. "Hello?"

"Bailey, can you please head up to the office? I need your help with an urgent matter."

"Okay, I'll be right there."

Hearing her voice has my blood pumping again. The things this girl does to me. I might just have to take advantage of the alone time with her.

Round two is about to happen right on this desk.

chapter twenty-three

Bailey

FUCK. FUCK. FUCK.

What the hell did I just allow, and how the hell am I going to face him after he just had his face buried in my—

Fuck.

I should quit immediately.

How can I ever look at Carter again? Surely, he knows something happened.

To think I just let Drew do that to me in public.

Is it possible to die from mortification?

Who lets a guy they barely know do that to them on top of a bar, in public, during broad daylight for anyone to see?

Drew is my own personal kryptonite, and even after being humiliated, I'm itching for another hit.

I start walking toward the stairs and realize I have no panties on. *Oh god*, I groan to myself. Shit. This is bad. My day keeps getting worse and worse. What the hell is wrong with me? One minute alone with Drew Lawson and I was sprawled naked on the bar. Sure, I was the one who kissed him first, but I didn't think it would go that far. What the hell am I going to do alone in his office?

Breathe.

With my luck, this man will have me crawling on all fours within five minutes. Heat pools in my belly at the thought, and my hands cover my face as I reach the banister. Shaking my head, I try to right myself. I'm acting like a bitch in heat. No more. I need to go in there, see what he wants, and then get the hell out. We didn't even do a damn thing associated with work today. Why did I even come in? "Get in. Get out. Go home," I say under my breath, prepping myself for this run-in.

No distractions.

As soon as I walk into his office, I'm frozen in place. My eyes bulge as my breath catches.

Standing in front of his desk is Drew. If I thought he was attractive before, it has nothing on how hot he looks eyeing me like this. This man is drop-dead gorgeous. His smoldering gaze lights me on fire. He's my every fantasy come to life.

"You, um, you wanted me?" I stutter.

He looks up at me, his eyes perusing my body. Slowly.

His lips curve upward into a wicked smirk. "Come closer." He starts to walk toward me until he circles around me, and I turn to meet him. His eyes are dark. Dangerous.

"We were interrupted, Bailey," he draws out. "Turn around," he orders, and I have no choice but to comply.

Turning slowly, I can feel his presence behind me. His hands find my hips and lightly stroke me. I take a step closer to the desk, trying to get some distance. After one step, my front is flush with the cool metal, and I have nowhere else to escape to. My hand skims over the surface nervously as he closes in on me. Drew pushes my back forward, and I place my palms flat against the desk to steady myself, biting my lip in anticipation.

He slides his hand up my thigh, his warm fingers hiking my skirt up to expose me. The cold air hits me, and my body shivers. My legs are pushed apart, and my mouth falls open to release a soft moan. Wrapping his hands in my hair, he pulls my head back, his mouth slamming onto mine. Our tongues move in sync until I feel the sharp bite of his teeth against my lower lip as he pulls away. His breath is ragged as his hand moves between my thighs. His finger dips inside me, teasing me. I spread my legs farther apart, shamelessly panting.

He moves away, and I miss his presence immediately, my body pulsating with need. I push my hips into his, rolling them against his body and feeling his hard cock against my ass. I'm burning up, and I need him to alleviate the pain.

"Do you want me to fuck you, Bailey?" His voice is low as he presses harder against me.

I groan in response.

"Words."

"Yes!" I cry out.

He pulls back, and this time, I hear the sound of a condom wrapper tearing. "Fuck," he growls as he nudges at my entrance.

I'm dizzy with want, and I might die if he doesn't take me now. Just when I think I might pass out, he thrusts deep inside me, and I bite back my scream as he fills me completely.

I could die happy right here, right now.

chapter twenty-four

Drew

GOD, SHE FEELS EVEN BETTER THAN I IMAGINED. HER CHEST is flat on the desk, so she's bent at a perfect ninety degrees as I pump her from behind. I tilt her up just enough so I can grab her palm-sized tits and squeeze. There's nothing romantic about this. It's filthy, raw, and utterly fucking fantastic.

She is fantastic.

Bailey arches into my hands and throws her head back in pure pleasure.

I don't want to pull out, but I need to switch positions. I want to feel every part of her. I direct her behind my desk. "I want you to ride me, Bailey." She moans at my words as I take a seat in my chair.

Bailey turns to face me. I grab her hips and help to impale her harder onto my length. Bailey pulses all around me, and the sounds coming from her mouth have me rock hard. Despite my best efforts, I won't last long at this rate. One pump, two pumps . . .

I don't make it to the third.

She goes slack against me, panting through the shocks still wracking her body. Her skin is damp, and the smell of sex permeates the room. If anyone walked in right now, they'd get an

eyeful. Not that it matters, since Bailey's moans did not go unheard. Carter more than likely had a free soundtrack complete
with erotic blasphemy, and I couldn't care the fuck less. I chuckle
at the thought.

Bailey tenses, and just like before, she springs to her feet and
starts collecting herself. She's ten shades of red, and I find it hysterical, if not a bit insulting.

"No, 'Thank you, Drew. That was amazing, Drew.' I get nothing?" I tilt my head to the side, waiting for her reply.

It never comes.

"You can't be serious. You're going all bashful on me?" I can't
help but laugh at her obvious embarrassment.

"I . . . um, this shouldn't have happened. I, we . . . We can't
do this again." She hangs her head low, and I can tell she's having
some inner battle.

It's bullshit.

"Fuck it. I'm not begging you for anything, Bailey."

I know I sound like a dick, but it's kind of late for her to
change her mind after what we just did. She looks like she could
cry. Christ. What's with fucking women crying all the damn
time? Jumping up from my chair, I tuck myself back into my
briefs. I put my fingers under her chin, lifting her eyes to mine.

"What's going on in there? Tell me why you're so hell-bent
on running."

She considers this for a second. "I feel cheap. Who lets their
boss do the things I just let you do to me? I'd be a whore if I didn't
feel this way."

This whole scene is ridiculous. One minute, Bailey is this
tough as nails, I-don't-have-a-care-in-the-world girl, and the
next, she looks utterly broken and small. What the hell?

"Stop, Bailey. You're not a whore, and I won't let you talk
about yourself that way. We're both consenting adults. This is
fun, right?" She gives me a small nod. "There's no reason to be

shy, feel embarrassed, or make this something it's not. I'm not going to tell anybody. This can be our little secret."

She goes from wounded to pissed in point two seconds.

"Go to hell, Drew. I'm not your call girl, and I'm definitely not your dirty little secret. I've been there and done that, and I'm not interested!"

"Calm down, killer." I go to grab her, and she smacks my hand away. I don't even have a chance to say another word before she's out the door.

Fuck.

I stay in my office the entire night stewing over what happened. Carter had to run the employee meeting before opening. Thankfully, he can run the place just as well as I can. As luck would have it, things ran smoothly, and I went uninterrupted. Carter called up to the office at 4:45 a.m. to inform me he had everything cleaned up and was leaving.

"Did Bailey already leave?"

"She left right after leaving your office. Didn't even stay for the meeting. She stormed off in a bit of a huff. I'm not even going to ask what you said to piss her off."

"Smart move. Go on and get out of here."

I hang up the phone and sigh. I'm too tired to drive home, so I make my rounds, checking that everything is locked up and the lights are off, then head back to my office to sleep. The couch is comfortable and has been my bed for many nights.

Bailey enters my mind, and I immediately shut her out. I don't have the patience to solve that riddle tonight. My eyes grow heavy, and I succumb to sleep.

I awake to something or someone touching my thigh. What. The. Fuck? I open my eyes to find Monica on her knees, leaning over me. "Monica, what the hell are you doing here? Better yet, how the fuck did you get in?" I glance at the clock. It's a little after 5:00 a.m.

She doesn't stop trailing her hand up higher on my leg. A traitorous moan gives her the wrong idea. "Stop," I say while grabbing her hands. She looks puzzled. I know it must be a shock.

"I still have my key from when I opened the bar for Carter a month ago. I waited for him to leave, and I came in. He stood on the corner forever, talking to someone on the phone." She smiles a huge Cheshire cat smile. She clearly is impressed with herself. I, on the other hand, am not. I'm still tired. I just want to go home, shower, and then fall into my own bed for a couple of hours.

"Monica, you've got to go. This isn't happening."

She huffs but finally gets to her feet. "I'm not leaving. I stayed out all night waiting for him to leave so we could have alone time," she whines.

"I didn't ask you to do that. Get the fuck out. I'm tired, and you're pissing me off," I grate through my teeth. She holds her hands up in surrender.

"Okay, I'll leave, but I'm going to be looking for a rain check soon, lover."

I roll my eyes. "Whatever you say. Out. Now." I point toward the staircase.

Monica runs her red nails down my chest before kissing my cheek and sauntering off. She makes a display of swaying her ass as she goes. Typical Monica, never getting the hints that this won't happen again. She's already down the stairs when I realize I didn't get my key back.

I yell down the stairs, "Monica, I want my key back!"
Silence.

I hear the door slam. She heard me, but she didn't listen. I have to remember to get that key.

A worry for another time.

chapter twenty-five

Bailey

I RAN OUT OF THERE SO QUICKLY IT WAS LIKE MY ASS WAS ON fire. Well, in my case, it kind of was. Hours later and I can still feel him inside me, stroking the orgasm out of me. My body pulsating around him. My cheeks flush. God, I'm a hot mess. My boss had me lying flat on my stomach as he fucked me within an inch of my life, and I'm already craving more. I'm already daydreaming of when and where.

I need help.

My phone beeps in my purse.

Carter: Where the hell are you? Is everything okay?

Me: Everything is okay. I'll text you later. I'm sorry.

I toss the phone back into my purse.

I've been walking the streets of New York since I hightailed it out of there. My legs are killing me, but I needed lots of air so I could think. I left the club a little after 4:00 p.m. without even notifying Drew or giving Carter any reason for my departure. I won't have to quit. I'm going to get fired for that. I'm missing the first employee meeting since I was promoted. Not that it's official. The paperwork I was supposed to do today? Yeah, that didn't happen.

Internally panicking at the thought, I pick up my pace. Whether I quit or get fired, it will undoubtedly mean the end of my days in the city. I am out of options. Going home means dealing with my mother. The thought makes me ill.

I had sex . . . with my boss. Great sex. But seriously, how did I think that was going to end? Not with me running out like a chickenshit. I groan, feeling like such an idiot.

As I'm walking through Union Square, about to get to Park Avenue, I see someone waving to me and shouting my name. My initial thought is to put my head down and get my ass home.

"Bailey." The voice and my name together have me stopping dead in my tracks.

Shit.

"Wow. How long's it been?"

The answer came quickly. I knew exactly how long it had been. Two years. I have not bumped into Jet since the night I got mugged. I was partying with him, we got into a fight, and he left me. I ended up walking the streets alone. . . It was the wake-up call I needed.

"Two years." I nod, scanning the area to plan my escape.

"What the fuck are you doing here? I swear I thought you died. One day you were there and the next day poof. Gone."

Hiding from you.

"Yeah, I just needed to lie low. After everything that happened, I needed a change."

"Damn, girl, it really is good to see you."

My skin crawls as his gaze runs up my body. I feel dirty. I don't want to think about what's running through Jet's mind. None of my memories from the time we spent together are good. They're the very thing I run from. Just being this close to him makes me cringe. He's everything from my past I want to forget. He's the pain I want to forget. But as if being transported back in time, my scar starts to throb, and the need to take a pill fills me.

"Good to see you too," I say, but I can't hide the disdain in my voice.

"Where you off to? Any crazy parties to hit up?"

"Nah. I was just taking a walk after work before heading home. I don't party anymore," I say, letting him know my days of being reckless are over.

"Where do you work?" I cringe at his question.

Telling him will only make it seem as though I'm back to my old habits. He's like a parasite. He'll try to find a way to breach his way into my life. Back in the day, it worked. I'd be doing well only to have him enter my life again, and soon I'd be spiraling out of control.

Looking at him now, he has no control over me.

He raises his brow, and I spit it out.

"Club Silver."

"Oh shit, I hear that place is hot. I totally need to go. Do you think you can get me and a few of my buddies in? After work, you can come over . . ." He winks.

My palms grow sweaty, and my heart rate accelerates. "Not interested, but thank you," I reply quickly, my voice shaking as I speak. I knew it. I fucking knew he'd try to worm his way in. Typical fucking Jet.

"But I miss you."

Nothing about hanging with Jet and his friends sounds appealing right now. I won't let my guard down, but I actually smile because I truly feel in control for the first time ever where Jet is concerned.

"Nah, sorry, Jet. My boss is strict. He's very protective of who he allows into his club. If I let you in, and you're not on the list, I could get fired."

"Come on, Bae. You owe me." His voice cuts through me like a knife.

"No, Jet. It's not happening. Stay away from Silver."

Without another word, I turn and head toward my place. I'm walking slower than normal as a million thoughts run through my head. The strength I just showed with Jet. The way I just turned my back to him and drowned out the insults he hurled at my back.

I look at my phone to see what time it is, and I notice a missed text from Harper from earlier in the night. I'm nervous to read it.

Harper: I'm sorry it's taken me so long. I was just hurt that you were keeping stuff from me. I just want you to know I'm proud of you for already being promoted and no longer waitressing. I just want you to be okay.

Harper finally texting feels more like a punch to the gut. She's finally come around to the idea of me working for Drew in a different capacity—proud even—and here I am, contemplating a way out. All because I gave in and gave him my body.

What the hell was I thinking?

Typical irresponsible Bailey at her finest. I cringe at the low point I find myself in. I've come so damn far only to crush it with one slip with Drew. Then add to it the unwanted run-in with Jet, and I know what I need to do.

Reaching into my pocket, I pull out my old sponsor's card that I keep in my wallet in case of an emergency and dial quickly, hoping he's still awake.

Ring.

Ring.

Ring.

"Hello," Jeff says, and it's quickly followed by a yawn.

"Hey, Jeff, it's me, Bailey. I'm so sorry for waking you."

"It's okay. I was just falling asleep. What's going on? I haven't heard from you since you moved to New York."

"I'm freaking out."

"What happened?" he quizzes.

"I-I fucked up."

"Shh. Breathe, Bailey. How did you fuck up?" I stay silent even though I called him for help. "Talk to me."

"I did something stupid. Okay, I did a lot of stupid, actually."

"Start from the beginning."

"I got a job at a nightclub." I cringe as I say it, knowing what he must be thinking.

Idiot.

"Bailey, you know that's not okay for you. That has trigger written all over it. Why'd you put yourself in a situation with that much temptation? What else happened to set you off?"

"It was a bad move, but I had no choice. I was about to get evicted, and there were no other options for me. But I already got promoted and won't be working in the actual club anymore," I try to explain.

"All right, so the promotion is good. What else happened?"

"I slept with my boss," I spit out, knowing he can't help if I don't come clean.

He blows out a harsh breath. "That's not healthy, Bailey. Addictions come in different forms."

"I know, Jeff, and I've been handling things. I know it's not the preferred way, but it's the only way that works for me," I say defensively. "I haven't slept with anyone since I stopped taking the pills."

"If you feel like this is different, why are you calling me?"

"I bumped into Jet."

"Bailey, don't let your past control you. You've done so well. I'm proud of you."

His scripted reply makes me cringe. "I know all of this, Jeff. What should I do?"

He sighs. "First things first, prioritize you. You need this job, right?"

"Yeah," I admit.

"Then don't let one mistake take that away from you. You set boundaries, and if your boss can't honor them, you find another job."

"He might allow me to keep working at the club so I'm not working one on one with him."

He sighs. "You haven't been sober long enough for that. Two years might seem like a long time, but if you're constantly tempted with issues, you could fall backward. Baby steps, Bailey."

He's right, and I know it. "You're right. I won't go backward."

"Remember, you can do this," he coaches.

"Thank you. I'm going to let you get back to sleep. I'm sorry for waking you again."

"I'm always here for you. Remember that."

"I will. Thanks again. Good night," I say as I hang up the phone. I finally let out the breath I was holding, and my shoulders slouch forward as the feeling of dread passes. Tomorrow, I will set boundaries.

No more temptation.

No more Drew.

Once I get back home, I throw myself into bed, hoping to forget the events of tonight. Sleep comes easier than I thought it would.

chapter twenty-six

Bailey

I WAKE THE NEXT MORNING WITH A NEW RESOLVE. NO MORE distractions. This job is my lifeline, and I can't allow anything to get in my way. After bailing on work last night, I'm sure some groveling will need to take place. I'm prepared.

Calling isn't the mature way to handle this, and I don't want to be unprofessional. I need to face Drew and secure my position as the project manager. It's time we discuss business.

I walk in and square my shoulders. Standing extra tall, I see Drew standing by the bar in front of the register. Does this man ever look bad? Focus, Bailey.

"Drew, can we talk?"

He looks up and nods toward his office upstairs. Without another word, I take off with him following close. When the door shuts, he doesn't make a move to come near me, and I appreciate it.

"About yesterday . . ." I pause for him to interrupt or say something, but he doesn't. He waits for me to continue. "What happened between us shouldn't have. I'm not blaming you because I wanted it, but I really need this job. I can't have sex getting in the way of that."

He purses his lips but remains quiet.

"I left because I didn't know how to handle what we'd just done. I was embarrassed. I felt . . . cheap."

He blanches as he pops one fist on his hip and runs his other hand through his hair. "I'm sorry, Bailey. I never wanted to make you feel cheap."

"It wasn't you. It was the way I acted. It . . . it reminded me of my past," I admit, lowering my gaze to the floor.

He takes a step toward me, and I take a step back. He grits his teeth. "I don't know who's hurt you in your past, but I'm not them, Bailey. What happened here yesterday was two consenting adults. Nothing cheap about it."

"Like I said, it wasn't you who made me feel that way," I say, getting flustered. "But that's beside the point. What matters here is that we need to be professional moving forward. I need this job."

"And as I said, I didn't offer you the job with any expectations of sex. I'm not going to lie and say I don't want it to happen again, Bailey. But I understand where you're coming from. You want professional? I'll treat you like every other girl who works for Silver."

I wince at his harsh tone. If he's going to go from hot to cold over my insistence of professionalism, then how the hell is this going to work?

His hard stare evaporates, and he rubs at his temples. "The job is still yours. What happened yesterday doesn't impact that at all. If you want a strictly business relationship, I'll respect that."

My shoulders relax at those words. "Thank you. I appreciate the opportunity, and I just don't want to do anything to make you change your mind."

"Do a good job, and you have nothing to worry about," he says.

I nod. "I intend to."

"The club's going to be opening soon, but I have some paperwork for you." He motions to the chair. "Take a seat."

I do as I'm instructed as he walks around, taking a seat across from me at his large desk. He pulls out a folder from the drawer on his right and sets it on the top, sliding it toward me.

"All the paperwork you need to fill out is in there. That would be the first step," he explains. "The acquisition hasn't been completed yet, so until we're able to get into the site, I'd like you to begin shadowing everyone here at the club."

He starts up his computer and pecks away at the keys before moving on to the next topic.

"Although the restaurants will run differently, a lot of these positions will correlate. You'll need to know how the waitstaff works with the kitchen and how the kitchen works with the bar. Find the problem areas and start thinking about ways to fix them. Ask the staff for suggestions."

I pull up my notes in my phone and make a list of things to do.

"As soon as the sale is complete, our next step will be the hiring process. I have a stack of resumes over in that corner," he says, motioning to an enormous stack. "I'll need you to go through them and begin conducting interviews. You'll want to bring Carter in on that since he'll be managing Le Blanc."

"Has he been replaced here?"

"Not yet. I'm working that out this week," he says flippantly, like he has no interest in talking to me about anything more. "Take the paperwork and head home. You can drop it off tomorrow around three and plan to shadow Carter tomorrow night."

I bite my lower lip, trying to rein in my temper. He's been so cold since I voiced my demands. What do you expect? I have to get over it. I can't have my cake and eat it too. It'll take a bit for this awkwardness to subside. I chose this, so I need to be okay with the small—and hopefully temporary—fallout.

I pull the file toward me and stand. "Thank you, Drew. I'll see you tomorrow."

I make it three steps before he stops me. "Bailey."

I turn my head to look at him over my shoulder. "Don't run out on me again. If we're going to work together closely, we need to be honest with each other, and running away isn't how we're going to handle things."

My body pivots to look him head-on.

"No more running," I agree.

Now if we can get back to normal, that would be great too. Though things were never normal between us.

chapter twenty-seven

Drew

THIS NIGHT WON'T END. I HAVE A HEADACHE FROM HELL, and Bailey is just about to send me over the edge. She strolled in this afternoon all pissed off, ready for a fight. Not only did she demand that things stay professional between us, but she also compared our moment to one from her past. One she clearly doesn't want to remember.

I know a little about her past. I know about the accident, but what I don't know is what happened after that.

From what I gathered, nothing good.

My stomach tightens at the implication.

I don't know how to feel about the thoughts running through my head right now.

Guilt that I made her feel that way. Sadness for the past I don't even know the half off.

I can't deal with the things I'm thinking, so I do what any grown man would do.

I avoid her like the plague by sending her home.

I'm making my rounds in the VIP rooms, rubbing elbows with the high rolling regulars. I grew up with a lot of these people in New York high society. A bunch of spoiled-ass pricks. Not that I have room to talk. The only difference between them and me is I actually like to work for my money. These guys live off their cushy trusts.

Take Edward Wright. His dad is worth hundreds of millions. He started some direct sales company that peddles smoothies. Now you see them sold in malls and kiosks all over the United States. Eddie was a sophomore in college when Daddy hit it big. He immediately dropped his business degree and took up residence on the family yacht. He's done literally nothing with his life since.

The second room contains a pop princess and an NBA basketball bench warmer. They were all cozied up. Since the paps aren't allowed in my club, Ms. Bubblegum probably brought her second-rate ballplayer here so nobody knows she's slumming it.

I approach Reese's room for the night. The curtains are drawn, so I decide against stopping in. God only knows what I'd walk in on. As I pass, I hear some girl hacking up a lung. I pull back the curtain to see if she's all right, and the scene that unfolds in front of me renders me speechless.

Reese is bent over the table snorting lines. I'm immediately transported to another time. One I've tried to forget every day for the last two years.

"Drew, come play with me," Alexa calls to me from the other room. Her whiny drawl grates on my nerves. I'm drunk and don't want to deal with her. "Do you have any blow?" The girl is out of her mind. I'm fucked beyond belief, but even I know my limits.

"Alexa, I'm out."

"But—"

"No." I know she won't let this drop, so I reach in my pocket and throw her the little baggy I bought but haven't opened yet. "Here. Take it. I need to sleep sometime tonight." I can hear her sigh in resignation.

"You're no fun."

I should tell her to come to bed with me. I should insist that she does. But instead, I watch her take the bag I gave her and throw some on the table. I walk around the corner in time to see her take a bump.

I shake myself back to the present. "What the fuck!" I scream, trembling from being so fucking pissed. "What did I tell you last time?"

Reese slowly looks up, completely unfazed by my outburst. "Lighten up, man. Nobody saw us," Reese says with a lazy smile. I want to beat the fuck out of him.

"You're fucking kidding me. We have been over this a million times. Come on. What the hell would Alexa say if she were here?"

His face goes pale at the mention of Alexa, and his eyes narrow on me.

"You're one to talk," he snaps back, and I take a step closer, making him crane his neck to see me better.

"What the fuck does that mean?"

"You act all high and mighty. But don't forget I was there. You gave her those drugs . . ."

The drugs that killed her.

The drugs that hurt so many people.

It's all my fault.

It feels like a knife is stabbing me in the heart. Then twisting slowly to inflict the most pain.

The day she died will always be burned into my brain. I can't escape it because it was my fault.

"Fuck you, Lawson. You didn't even give a flying fuck about her." His words are slurred and barely understandable. "And if you're not careful, I'll make sure everyone knows your part in her death."

"You don't know what the fuck you're talking about." I look at the chick next to him. "Do you want to die?"

She looks at me without a care in her miserable world. "It was only one line," she slurs out.

"Get the fuck out of here," I say to the skank. She grabs her jacket and scurries out. I turn back to Reese. "Clean yourself up, Reese. Go home." He doesn't move. "Now!"

He just stares at me, and I continue to glare at him. He finally gets the hint that I'm not changing my mind on this.

"All right, I'm out. Fuck this place." He walks out, barreling into my shoulder on his way. "And fuck you."

I go to work cleaning up their shit. I can't have anyone else seeing this because I've done my best to rid my life of drugs. This club was reinvented after Alexa's death. I fired the staff who notoriously sold the contraband, made it increasingly harder to get in, and renamed the club Silver after Alexa Silver as a constant reminder.

In a rage, my hands swipe over the table, knocking everything to the floor. With all the force I can conjure, I throw the table over.

"Fuck!"

Slamming my fists into the wall of the room, I finally calm myself down, focusing on breathing. This whole night has me in a tailspin—first Bailey and now the reminder of Alexa. I'm not sure what has me angrier.

I'm just calming down when Carter comes barreling in. "What the fuck, man? I just got a complaint from room four that there was banging on the wall and shouting. What's going on?"

"Nothing I can't handle. Get back to the bar." I don't give him a chance to speak. I turn and leave the room, desperate to escape to the safety of my office.

I can't deal with one more thing tonight.

chapter twenty-eight

Bailey

A FEW DAYS PASS AND DREW IS MISSING IN ACTION. I'VE been working with Carter all night, taking notes on ways we can run the bar at the new restaurant once it opens. I have to admit, bartending seems fun. Carter is having a blast, and although I'm standing back and watching, I'm having fun watching him.

The night has practically flown by. I haven't even caught sight of Drew, and I have to admit, I'm thankful for that. I'm trying very hard to stick to my own demands.

Spoke too soon.

Not even a moment after I'd thought about not seeing him, he's walking through the door with some beautiful model on his arm. The woman is at least five nine and has on a short cocktail dress that shows off her killer legs. Gorgeous doesn't even begin to describe her.

"Huh. That's . . . interesting," Carter mutters from next to me.

"What's interesting?"

"Drew broke things off with Juliette months ago. I wonder when that started back up."

A glass slips from my hands and breaks at the mention of

this having been a former Drew fling. So what? He screws me and moves on all in a matter of days? Why should I care? I'm the one who made the decision. I can't be mad. Right? Right.

I'm pissed.

I understand I'm not a model, but to flaunt your next fling in my face seems a bit ridiculous. Callous. Bastard.

This is exactly what Harper warned me about. It's my own damn fault I didn't listen.

"What's with the face?" Carter asks, grinning ear to ear.

"What face?"

"The one in which you look like you ate something sour."

"I did," I lie.

"Right. Since you broke things off with Drew, I guess you would be pissed he's moved on so quick."

"What?" I snap. "I didn't break off anything. There was nothing to break."

"Bae. I know you weren't behind that bar the other day because of your humanitarian activism. Plus, half the block could hear you two."

I cover my eyes with my hands, groaning. "It wasn't like that."

"Girl, I don't care what it was like. You sounded very happy to be right where you were."

My head lolls back on my shoulders. "I'm trying to forget."

"Why?" he asks, looking horrified. "That man is not someone you forget."

I hate Carter. Why the hell does he need to talk about this now when I'm trying my hardest to forget and move on.

"Listen," he says conspiratorially. "Give him a taste of his own medicine. No way is he going to like it if you seem unaffected. Look at nine o'clock," he says, motioning with his head toward two guys sitting at the side of the bar. "Blondie is the opposite of Drew but still fine as hell. Go flirt it up."

"I don't want to play games, Carter. I'm here to work."

"Fine." He shrugs. "Let Drew win."

My eyes catch on Drew, whose hand is on the model's lower back. It might make me childish, but I won't let him get to me. What's the harm in flirting it up with a cute guy at the bar? *You're playing with fire.*

For the better part of an hour, I flirt shamelessly with the blond at the bar. At some point, I forget why because I'm enjoying myself. No part of me wants things to go anywhere with this stranger, but it's just nice to be seen. Scott—at least I think that's his name—owns a car dealership in the 'burbs. He's in town visiting his friend who works on Wall Street. They're having drinks at Silver because they've heard so much about the place. First-timers who clearly have connections.

"Bailey," Scott calls out, gaining my attention. I smile wide, playing up the interested card.

"I'd like to see you again," he says, placing his card on the bar top and sliding it toward me. I smile wider.

Over Scott's shoulder, I see Drew approaching. He's shooting daggers at me, and internally, I celebrate that he's witnessed the exchange.

"Gentlemen," Drew says, slapping the dark-haired friend of Rob's on the back in a friendly manner. "Glad to see you made it."

"Thanks for the in," the one with dark hair says. "This place is great, and the service has been top-notch."

"I'm glad to hear it, Glenn. Listen, I need to borrow Bailey for a moment, but Carter will take care of you in her absence."

They shake hands, and he motions with his head for me to make my way to his office. What the hell? I was just doing my job. Carter makes mad money by entertaining the bar patrons. I wasn't doing anything different. He doesn't get to hound me when he has a model on his arm.

We make it to his office, and he slams the door behind us, whirling around and bearing down on me.

"What are you doing?" he snarls.

"I don't know what you mean?" I play coy.

"Oh, you don't? Do you?"

"No."

"What did you say?" He pulls me toward him, his arms wrapping around my torso.

My breath hitches.

"I asked you a question," he growls. "You tell me nothing can happen between us, and then you practically throw yourself at someone else in my bar?"

My hands fly up. "First of all, I didn't throw myself at him. Secondly, you don't get to decide who or what I do, Drew. I didn't say I don't want you. I said it wasn't a good idea. You're my boss."

"I don't give a fuck."

"I do!" I yell. "This is the first chance I have at making something of myself, and no matter how much I love the way you make me feel, I can't take that risk."

"You're being dramatic," he says flippantly. "I would never fire you just because whatever this is ends. I'm a lot of things, Bailey, but I'm not a bastard. I know how much this job means to you."

"Tell me how we could have a sex-only relationship?"

"We're adults, Bailey. It's that simple."

"It's not for me," I stress. "I can't promise to shut off my feelings."

"Is that so? You'd walk away out of fear?" His voice is vacant of all warmth.

"That's exactly what I'm saying, Drew." I watch as he takes deep, shallow breaths, a cold knot forming in my stomach.

Fuck.

He seems pissed at my answer, and I think I see hurt there too.

I know I shouldn't care. That I should just walk away while I still have the chance. Yet I can't help but want to comfort him, help heal the pain behind those dark, endless eyes. I know what it's like to be that lost, and maybe, just maybe, I might help him find peace, if only for a minute.

"Are you okay?" I whisper.

"Just leave," he snaps. My pulse begins to beat erratically as I step closer to him. My hand reaches for his, my fingers trembling as I make contact.

"I said leave, Bailey." A tense silence fills the room.

I contemplate everything he's said and done. He's as broken as I am. I don't know why, but I can see it as plain as day. Maybe two broken people can heal each other? Could he be right? Am I turning my back out of fear? I'm no coward.

"No," I finally say, my voice firm.

"First, you say no because you want to leave. Now you say no because you don't. Make up your fucking mind, little girl. Because if you stay"—he grabs me roughly by the waist—"I'm fucking you, hard."

I feel like my breath is cut off, my mind fluttering around in a million directions. Against my better judgment, I want to submit to him. I want to be what he needs, and if this is what he desires, then I can't help but want to give it to him. I lift my hand and lightly stroke his jaw. His body stills, his eyes narrowing.

"Bend over, Bailey." His words come out thick and hoarse, and the rich timbre sends a chill down my spine. "Hold the desk." I walk toward it. With each step I take, I shimmy my panties off. When I finally place my hand on his desk, I'm fully exposed, the cold air hitting my core.

Peeking over my shoulder, I see him standing there stoically, and a tingling in the pit of my stomach forms. A delightful shiver of desire runs through me.

His pupils dilate, sending an electric flare of heat through my body. Stepping toward me, he quickly unzips his fly and begins stroking his length slowly.

Painfully slow.

Deliberately teasing me.

His other hand reaches into his back pocket and pulls out a condom, ripping it open with his teeth and running it down his thick length.

"Turn your head back toward the wall," he commands, and I do, my vision focusing on the painting hanging above his desk. The slow torture of waiting for him to touch me makes me dizzy, and I try to concentrate on something else. Anything to stop my heart from thrumming so hard that I think it might implode. Just when I think I can't take another second of waiting, he grabs my hips so tight I'm sure there will be a bruise there tomorrow. A moan escapes my lips, and I bite down to silence myself.

"No need to fight it. No one will hear you over the bass," he growls out, his lips teasing the curve of my ear. He slides against my core before entering me roughly. Drew thrusts in and out, barely allowing me to adjust to him. The pace speeds up, drawing a moan from my lips.

"I fucking love the sounds you make. Tell me you want more. Tell me, Bailey."

I moan once more. "God, yes, I want more. Please," I beg, raising my hips to meet him thrust for thrust. His strokes are hard and deep as he reaches around me and starts stroking me, causing me to spasm around him. My release comes quickly after. He pushes forward a few more times before his body collapses onto my back. Fully sated, we simultaneously sigh.

I peer around my shoulder, and his eyes are shut as his breathing calms. As he opens them, his eyes find mine, slanting slightly as he takes me in. But it's not Drew staring back at me, it's Jet.

Memories from the past assault me, and Jet is in the lead, always hurting me.

"Fuck, Bailey. Did I hurt you?" he asks as he examines my bare hips.

"I'm okay." My voice is only a whisper, suddenly feeling sick. Drew didn't do anything wrong, but my mind is messing with me.

"Fuck," he mumbles again as he pulls out of me and readjusts himself. He moves away, disposing of the evidence of what we just did.

"I—Here, let me help you." His hand reaches for mine, and he helps pull me upright. "Listen, I'm sorr—"

I cut him off, shaking my head. "No need." I can't take his apology right now. It's not him. I'm the one continuing to allow the past to rule my present.

"It's not you—"

"Please, don't."

Tears of shame threaten to expel. I need to get out of here before he sees me fall apart.

chapter twenty-nine

Drew

I T'S BEEN THREE DAYS SINCE BAILEY WAS LAST HERE. SHE RAN out of my office like she was on fire. I know I screwed up by being rough, but I thought she wanted it. She was practically begging me to fuck her. Carter told me that she called in the past three days because she's sick, but I'm not buying it.

As I look through tonight's list of VIPs, my head starts to pound. I've never cared about how things were left with any girl, but something about my last time with Bailey doesn't sit right with me. I'm sitting here contemplating sending her flowers when my phone rings.

"Drew Lawson."

"Hi, Mr. Lawson. My name is Amanda Canelli, and I'm calling from Andrew Kors's office. He asked me to reach out to you because we have been interviewing a potential candidate currently employed by you. Mr. Kors is ready to extend an offer of employment, but he wanted to give you a courtesy call before he does."

Andrew Kors and my father have been business associates for a long time. I appreciate his reaching out, but there isn't an employee in this club I would be sad to lose to him. This is a steppingstone. It shouldn't be a lifetime career.

"Hi, Amanda. Thanks for the heads-up. Please tell Andrew I appreciate the call, but he's free to hire anyone he pleases." I'm bored with the conversation and I need to get shit done.

"Thank you, Mr. Lawson. We believe Miss Jameson will be a great fit for us here."

That name is a punch to the gut. Immediately, I'm pissed. It might have just been sex, but her attitude is bullshit.

"You know, on second thought, Amanda, I don't know if Bailey would be a good fit after all. She is notoriously late to work, and her performance has been subpar to say the least." I'm going too far, but I can't help it. I've never played fair.

"Oh, I'm sorry to hear that. She seemed like such a great candidate. I will relay this information to Mr. Kors. Thank you for the heads-up. Have a nice day, Mr. Lawson."

"You too, Amanda. Good luck in your search." At that, I push end, and the line goes silent.

I'm not letting her off this easy.

When I pull up to Bailey's apartment, I'm angrier than I was before. I can't fathom why she'd want to trade the promotion I've offered her for some low-paying runner job. Does she really want to be a coffee girl for some overpaid middle-aged executive? I know what they're hiring for. It wasn't hard to find the job listing. I'm not going at her half-cocked. Fuck that.

I stalk up to her door, banging without consideration to whom I may be disturbing. I hear shuffling on the other side of this paper-thin door before it opens. Bailey stands there with a look of shock on her face.

"Drew. What are you doing here?"

I push past her and walk right into her apartment. Going straight to her couch, I make myself at home and sit.

"Have a seat," she groans in irritation.

"Well, since you decided to call out 'sick,'" I say with air quotes, "I decided to come call you on your bullshit. You'll never guess, Bailey. I got a call today about a reference for you. The funny thing is, I don't remember receiving a two-week notice." I'm trying really hard not to lose my cool, but I'm failing miserably. With each word I speak, my voice gets louder and more furious.

"Drew, please. Just calm down. I don't need you making a scene."

"Fuck, Bailey. You said you wouldn't run. Then the next thing I know, you're doing just that. Running out of my office and calling out sick. Then I find out you're leaving through someone else."

"Drew, I have to." Her voice is low.

"The fuck you do. What you need is to grow up, Bailey. You need to be mature and talk to people about what's going on. I told you no more running, and here we are again."

"I can't," she snaps, raising her voice. "I can't, Drew. There are some things I just can't talk about."

"Like what? Did I hurt you? Did I make you feel bad? Because I have to tell you, Bailey, it sure the fuck looked like you were enjoying everything I was giving."

"You didn't hurt me, and I did enjoy it. Then when it was over, it felt too much like my past."

I feel sick at her words.

At the missing pieces of the puzzle of what she went through.

Her hands are shaking, and she's trying hard to hide it by wringing them together.

"Come here. Come sit down and talk to me. Tell me what's going on in that head of yours."

She looks my way, contemplating what I'm suggesting. Finally, she makes her way to the love seat and takes a seat across from me. Then Bailey starts to cry. I'm baffled and completely caught off guard. I am in no way prepared to handle this.

"I'm pretty sure you already know from the outburst with my sister that night, but I'm an addict. A recovering one, but an addict, nonetheless."

I know this, and so much more, but I school my features. I'm finally getting her to open up to me for a change, and I won't fuck that up. "Go on," I prompt.

"I've been sober for two years. When I was younger, my father died. I started drinking back then, but—" A tear rolls down her face. I reach my hand out and swipe it.

"It's okay, Bailey, if you don't want to talk about it." As much as I want to hear the next part, I don't. The pain in my chest intensifies with each piece of the puzzle that falls into place.

"One night, there was an accident. I lost someone else. First my dad, and then my best friend, Emily. That's when I started to take the pills." She looks off into the empty space beside me, lost in the memory. Her hand touches her arm, absently rubbing it. "It got bad after that. Really bad. I got clean eventually, but it's a constant struggle, and the club is just a horrible temptation. I can't go back to those days, Drew. Lately, I feel like I've been drowning. Then there's you and me and whatever we've been doing, and it's like I'm one step away from relapsing."

I listen to what she's saying, and I can't help but remember the days when I too struggled with the need to lose myself in booze. Losing Alexa was what finally made me realize I needed to make a change. I was the lucky one. I was able to walk away with my life, even if I'm haunted by the ghosts of my past. Bailey making them rise to the surface.

"Bailey, I'm sorry."

"Oh my god, Drew, it's not your fault. You've given me hope." A sob escapes her throat, and it's my undoing. I jump up from the couch and grab her in my arms, holding her while she cries into my shoulder. Stroking her hair and telling her it's all right has me realizing how strange this situation is.

I grab her shoulders and bring her to look at me. Tipping her chin up with my right hand, I force her to look into my eyes. "I'll help you, Bailey. Whatever you need. If you have to get another job, I'll help you. Please let me help you."

Her eyes are so bright. She searches my face, and I see the moment her entire body relaxes. The moment she decides to put her trust in me. It's an aphrodisiac. The urge to kiss her has never been greater.

So I do.

chapter thirty

Bailey

H IS GAZE SEARS ME. HE'S TELLING THE TRUTH. I MIGHT NOT really know Drew Lawson that well, but looking into those eyes right now, I know he would do anything to help me.

My shoulders slump forward, and the tension leaves my body. I lean against his chest, listening to the steady beat of his heart, and it further relaxes me. I run my hand down his firm chest, and his heart beats faster. Pulling back, we lock eyes. The lust is evident, but there is something else. Something breaking through the lust and morphing into a haunted stare. I've seen that look before, but not in him . . .

In me.

My eyebrow rises slightly. I need to know why he wants to help me so bad. It's clear that there's more to his offer, and it has me on edge.

"Why, Drew?" My voice quakes. I know I don't have the right to ask, but I can't help but want to know more about this man who, beneath his tough and indifferent exterior, would do anything to keep me safe. "Why do you want to help me so bad?"

"I—"

A look of regret and loathing crosses his face. It's enough for me to wish I hadn't asked after all. I lift my hand to stop him from speaking. "Forget it. You don't need to tell me. I'm sorry." I turn my head down and look away, staring at my hands resting in my lap. Staring at anything to stop me from looking at him.

Warm fingers slowly caress my jaw, turning my face upward to meet his. "Things weren't always the way they are now at Silver. Actually, it wasn't even called that in the beginning. I was a very different man from who I am now." He blows out a harsh breath. "Before you ask, yes, I was just as much of an asshole." He laughs, but his smile doesn't meet his eyes. I can tell it's forced and fake. "Back then, I dated a girl named Alexa. She was adventurous and beautiful . . . she had the world in the palm of her hands. She could've been anything." He closes his eyes, pain etched in the creases in the corner of his eyes. When he opens them, the pain is even more evident. "She—died. I lost her." I swallow the lump in my throat at that knowledge. Looking at me with conviction, he goes on. "I will help you."

I lean forward and place my head gently on his heart that's in the right place. "Thank you." I want to erase the pain, so I turn my head up and place a gentle kiss on his lips. He responds eagerly, his tongue begging for entrance. I give in to his demanding kiss, wanting to help him chase away the ghosts of the past. I understand too much. I've lost people too.

Pulling away, he buries his face into my neck, tickling me gently with his lips. "Enough of this heavy shit. I'm starving. Get dressed. I'm taking you out."

My eyes widen and my mouth hangs open. "Um, like on a—"

"Like for lunch, Bailey."

"Lunch?" I pucker my lips at him. *Is he asking me out?*

"You know the meal after breakfast but before dinner?"

God, I sound dumb. "Oh, okay."

Drew leans forward and brushes a gentle kiss on my lips. "Yes, Bailey. Like a date."

I can't help the smile that forms. A date with Drew Lawson? I walk into my bedroom and peer at myself in the mirror. I'm a mess. My eyes are sunken, and my hair looks like a bird's nest sitting on the top of my head. Fuck, what the hell am I wearing? I can't believe he saw me like this. I can't go in public with him looking like this.

"Drew?" I shout through the walls.

"Yeah?"

"Where are we going?" I want to ask what I should wear, but that just seems pathetic.

"There's a great little sushi restaurant I know a few blocks away. How about we go there?"

"Okay."

I rummage through my closet. Pulling out a white cotton eyelet dress, I quickly undress and slip it on, then head into the bathroom and attempt to apply makeup and brush my hair.

Fifteen minutes later, I step out of the bathroom a new woman. The look in Drew's eyes sends a shiver down my body. I can clearly see his hunger from across the room.

"Okay, you want to eat?" I say, grabbing my purse off the side table next to where he's now standing. His eyes roam up and down my body, and his lips turn up slightly. It pulls more on the right side and causes a small dimple to form. The look he's giving me makes me melt.

"You have no idea," he states in a silky voice that causes my knees to buckle.

The sexual innuendo isn't lost on me. Desire pools in my stomach as I try to regulate my breathing. He steps forward and clasps our hands together, then pulls me closer to him.

His breath fans my neck as he whispers into my ear, "After lunch . . ." He pauses, and his tongue trails down the curve of my neck. "You're dessert."

Yes, please.

I wish we didn't have to eat at all. Being here with him in my apartment is surreal. It's crazy and strange and I want to stay in this private bubble a little longer. I take a step away from him because if I don't, we'll never leave.

Maybe that's a good thing.

My face heats as I remember him going down on me in the bar and bending me over his desk and—goddammit, Drew notices because his eyes narrow and his dimple shows again.

"What are you thinking about over there?" He smirks.

"I'm not about to contribute to your already enlarged ego, Mr. Lawson. So I'll just say that you know how to please a lady." I giggle at the word *lady*.

"Lady, huh? Well, I think we should skip lunch and give it another go. We'll see just how much of a lady you are." There is mischief in his eyes.

"Wh-what are you doing? Drew Lawson, don't come any closer. Lunch. You said we need to eat lunch." His grin is ear to ear.

"Fuck lunch." His eyes smolder.

The next thing I know, he has me up over his shoulders and carries me to the bed. He sets me down, tickling my sides.

"Stop. Oh my god, Drew. Stop!" I screech.

"Say please," he taunts.

"Never."

"Say please, Bailey, or we'll be doing this all day."

"Okay, please. Please! I'm begging." My side hurts from laughing.

When he finally stops, he's laughing so hard he's holding his side. He looks so young and carefree at this moment. He leans down, capturing my lips in a searing kiss.

But this kiss is different. There is a level of passion behind it that has never been there before. It has me questioning if he could be feeling what I'm feeling.

His hands cup my cheeks. Pulling away, he stares into my eyes before running his hand through my hair.

"I want you, Bailey," he whispers.

"Take me then."

He bends down once more, kissing me softly. "I promised you a date, and you deserve that. I want you to know that this is turning into more for me." His eyes penetrate my soul. "It's not just about sex."

I melt at his words. "It's more to me too." My words come out shy and vulnerable. He smiles.

"Let's go eat."

chapter thirty-one

Drew

"**W**HAT THE FUCK DO YOU MEAN I GOT OUTBID?" I SHOUT as I walk into Cal's office. His eyes dart to me. At least he has the decency to look unsettled by my unannounced appearance in his office.

"What are you doing here?" he asks, his eyes shifting around the room.

Good. The bastard should be scared. I have a mind to strangle the sonofabitch.

"Did you really think after the text you just sent me, I wouldn't show up?"

"Hoped . . ." he mumbles under his breath.

"You obviously don't know me as well as you thought you did if you think I am going to let this fly."

"What do you want me to say? I'm sorry. This is business, Drew. You, of all people, should know this is how stuff goes."

"I fucking hired your girl's sister to get this property. I was assured it was a done deal."

I hate speaking about Bailey like this, but I have to play the game that Cal would. He doesn't care about anyone but himself, not even Harper.

"Don't pretend you haven't enjoyed every minute of having her in your club. I know all about you and your side action."

"What the fuck is that supposed to mean?" I see red. This guy is asking for me to end him.

"Nothing, bro. Just that she's hot. That's all. Listen, I had no choice."

I stalk forward, menacingly, baring my teeth. "Don't ever speak about Bailey like that again. Do you fucking read me?"

His hands fly up. "Calm the fuck down. I was just saying."

"You don't speak about her," I yell.

"All right. Fine. Are we done here?" he asks, eyes finding the door behind me.

"Not even close. We had an agreement."

"Never on paper."

I slam my hands down on the desk, and the fucking coward jumps. "That's not good enough. The papers were being signed, according to you."

He gulps. "I'm sorry. I am. You did me a solid, but I had no choice."

"You had a choice, Cal. You made the wrong one, and you know it." I grate the last part through my teeth.

"It's not like that. This time, I didn't. He had me by my balls." His face is ruddy, and I have to wonder what this mystery buyer has on him. "There was no other choice."

"Who bought the property?" I say, low and threateningly.

He grimaces. "You know I can't tell you that."

I lean over the desk until our faces are only inches from each other. "I'll ask one more time. Who. Bought. The. Property?"

He looks down, fidgeting with his hands.

"The name, Cal. I won't ask you again."

When his eyes lift to mine, I'm caught off guard by the concern in Cal's expression. "Listen, before I tell you, I need you to promise not to kill him. He's fucked up, man."

He doesn't need to say the name for me to know who he's talking about. Reese. He'd threatened as much.

"Say it," I demand, needing to verify that my assumption is correct.

"He still hasn't gotten over her death. He's hung up on you for some reason. Always talking about you and her."

"Say it!" I bellow, and he jumps yet again.

"It was Reese."

Fucking Christ. Will my past ever stop fucking with me? Will I ever be able to bury my sins and move ahead?

"Why?" It comes out pathetic. Broken.

No matter how many times Reese has pissed me off, I feel his pain. I know he's beyond help. I feel powerless, and that's not something I feel often.

"What do you mean, why?" Cal huffs a humorous laugh. "Isn't it obvious? You wanted it, so he took it."

"Did he say anything else?"

He blows out a breath. "Yeah. He mumbled that you'll get what's coming to you. Dude, he's unhinged. I don't know if it's the drugs or what, but he's lost his fucking mind."

"I'll handle him."

"If you mean you'll get him help, good. But as far as the property, it's a done deal. Nothing can be changed now."

I pick up a picture frame from his desk and smash it against the wall. "Don't ask me for another favor. You and I? We're fucking done, Cal."

"You don't understand . . ."

"Don't give a shit," I say, walking out and leaving a simpering Cal to ponder all the ways I could ruin his life.

I won't bother. There are other locations. Yes, this is a setback, but I've dealt with worse.

The first thing I need to do is calm the fuck down. Then I need to deal with Reese.

I know he blames me. Shit. I blame myself, but messing with my life and my livelihood needs to stop. He needs to get help.

I indulged him by allowing him entrance to my club. In a weird way, I thought if he was in my space, I could watch over him, make sure he didn't go overboard, but I've only enabled his behavior. Those days are over. He's gone too far.

I'm on a mission to locate Reese. Any feelings of sympathy I harbored for him disappeared the moment that little shit went after my business.

I'm not sure what he's up to. Knowing him, he doesn't have a plan. He just wants to mess with me. I should be impressed that he stopped snorting coke long enough to make the deal happen.

Point to him. He's won this round.

But I won't let this indiscretion go unnoticed.

When I arrive at his apartment, I knock on the door. I don't need to be rung up because my name is on the list. It's been there for years. Back when Alexa and I would crash at his place after a night of partying. When we were actually friends.

This is not my first time stopping by unannounced. Just goes to show how gone he is if he hasn't had me removed. He can't be bothered to make a change like that, but he can organize a multimillion-dollar real estate deal. Fucking bullshit.

This will be my last time here. After this, I'll have my own goddamn name removed.

I knock on the door, and when he doesn't answer, I resort to banging my fist against the wood. "Open the fucking door, Reese!" I yell. He's probably passed out in his own vomit somewhere and can't hear me.

"I'll break down this fucking door." My fist raps on the door a few more times before I hear footsteps behind it. Then the door swings open.

Reese, as per usual, looks hungover. Actually, he seems like he's still high.

His nostrils are flared and red-rimmed, but it's the lockjaw that confirms he's been snorting coke and probably still is.

That's probably what took him so long to get to the door.

I should leave because there's no point in talking to him right now, but the part of me who still cares about him and misses Alexa as much as he does wants to attempt to get through to him.

He doesn't say a word as he lets me pass through the doorframe. He turns on his heels and walks toward his living room. I'm quick to follow and not at all surprised by the scene in front of me.

On the glass table is an open bag of coke and a few lines already set up beside it. He sits on the couch while I remain standing with my arms crossed at my chest.

Reese reaches forward and grabs the rolled-up dollar bill.

"Want a line? For old times' sake?" he practically slurs, indicating he's already had way too much.

"You need to stop that shit."

"You're no fun."

"It's going to kill you."

"You mean like it did her?" I blanch at the mention of Alexa. I shouldn't be surprised, but it's still jarring. "Are you here to be my dad? Spoiler alert: I already have one of those."

"He's not doing a very good job."

"You're not telling me something I don't know."

Despite me being here, he leans forward and then inhales.

"Why are you here?" he asks as he wipes the remnants away from his nose.

"You know why."

His brow lifts until understanding hits him because his lips tip up into a smirk.

"Doesn't feel good to have something you care about be taken away from you."

"It's a fucking building, Reese. I'll find another." I shrug, knowing there are greater issues at hand. "You need to stop. I get it, you miss her." I point at my chest. "I miss her too, but it's got to stop. Snorting another line . . . buying a building out from under me . . . It isn't going to bring her back."

"But replacing her will?"

My hands ball into fists. But I don't play into his jab because he's high.

There is no reasoning with him when he's like this.

"I'm out of here. I'm not gonna watch you kill yourself."

"Because you care."

"I do. Regardless of all this shit, I do. But I'm done, Reese. What you did? Not cool. I get you're in pain, but going after my business . . . I'm done. I don't want to see you again. Don't come to my club anymore."

"You can't keep me out."

"Try. You won't be allowed access."

He starts setting up another line, and I know if he keeps going, he will actually kill himself. I step forward, pushing him back onto the couch. He's so damn high he doesn't even put up a fight. After I round every last bag of coke I can locate, I head to the bathroom and flush it down the toilet. I don't bother checking on him again, leaving him alone to do whatever he'll do. The chances he has more hidden are high, but it can't be my problem. I could stay, but I refuse to watch another person die.

chapter thirty-two

Bailey

THE DOOR FLIES OPEN TO DREW'S OFFICE, AND IN WALKS what can only be described as a very pissed off Drew. His face is hard, and his body tense. He looks scary.

I narrow my eyes at him, trying to gauge what went wrong since the last time I saw him. It gets even more confusing when he walks to where I'm sitting at his desk, reaches forward, grabs the stack of sketches, and tears them up.

"Um. Something the matter with the drawings?" My brows rise, sky-high.

"You can say that." He doesn't clarify what he means. Instead, he scoffs all the way to his chair and sits down.

He doesn't waste any time reaching for the decanter and pouring himself a drink. He knows better than to offer me any because I don't drink. Regardless of the fact that the idea of having one at this moment—to tame the anxious feeling rolling inside me—is looking better and better.

Instead, I think of milk and Oreos and my father's laughter, and my heart rate finally begins to slow.

"Okay, so now that you've had your drink, do you want to tell me what's going on?"

"The property for the restaurant is gone."

I gasp. "What do you mean, gone? How can it be gone?"

He opens his mouth to say something but must change his mind. Instead, he shakes his head.

"It doesn't matter how. It just is."

I lean forward in my chair, placing my elbows on the desk.

"So then let's come up with a plan. Just because the property is gone doesn't mean we have to give up. This is New York City. There have to be plenty of properties that fit the bill."

He nods his head as he places the glass next to his lips and takes another swig of the amber liquid.

But even though he's in agreement with me, he still doesn't speak. He's lost in thought a million miles away, and I'm not sure how to bring him back to the here and now. What the hell happened to have him so despondent? Instead of bringing up what is obviously a sore subject, I trudge forward with work. It's the best I can do.

"Tell me what you're looking for. This is why you hired me. Let me help you."

He mulls over my words, all the while watching me with an intensity that has me shrinking under the pressure of it. I'm not sure what finally has the hard edges on his face relaxing and the tension from moments ago dissipating, but I'm grateful.

"Okay." He places the glass down and opens his desk drawer. He passes me a sheet of paper. On the paper are the specs from the original building. The square footage, not just for the whole space, but also broken down by how much space he would need for the kitchen, dining area, and then the lounge he wants to set up.

The next thing he pulls out is a business card.

"This is my realtor." It's all he offers.

"I'll take care of all this. You relax and let me do my job." A look passes through his eyes, and it's filled with an emotion I can't quite gauge.

"Thank you," he finally says before going back to his drink.

I grab the stack of papers and make my way into the adjacent office to make the calls.

It's about an hour later when I finally make my way back into Drew's office. When I sit across the table from him, I slide over the papers I printed for him to look at.

"What's this?"

"These are all the properties we are going to see today."

"Today?"

"Yep. So take one last moment to sulk, and then get up and come with me."

He looks down at the sheets, and one by one, he nods his head in approval.

"Good job."

"That's why you pay me the big bucks." I wink.

He laughs, and the sound warms my heart. "Thank you for doing this for me. I'm sorry you had to see me like that."

"It's okay. We all have bad days. I'm here for you, Drew."

Before I can say anything else, he stands from his chair and holds his hand out for me to take. I place my hand in his, allowing him to pull me toward him. He places a kiss on my lips, and I melt into it.

"Thank you," he says again, this time against my mouth. His breath tickling my skin. "You're . . ."

"I'm what?"

I pull back and look into his eyes.

"I was just going to say you're special, Bailey."

My heart starts to beat frantically at his words.

"When I first saw you . . ." He stops and shakes his head. "I felt drawn to you . . ." He smiles. But this smile is different; it's soft and sincere. "You're so much more than I even imagined."

Tingles race up and down my arms at the reverence of his words and the look of wonder in his expression. The heartfelt way he talks about our first meeting, makes me wish for things I haven't dared. Drew is cementing himself into my heart, and it's scary as hell.

Not knowing what to say, and out of fear I'll botch the moment, I lean forward and place my lips on his one more time, then turn to walk toward the door.

"You ready?"

"I am."

Whatever Drew's going through, I'll help him. I won't allow anyone or anything to ruin this day. I'll do what it takes to keep that smile on his face. As much as he's helped me, I can do the same for him. I'll be his lifeline when he needs it. And today appears to be one of those days.

chapter thirty-three

Bailey

THE WEEKS PASS QUICKLY. DREW AND I HAVE SPENT A LOT OF time together. During the day, we work side by side, and at night, we explore each other. We've still yet to make anything official, which is what's best. I don't want anyone at Silver to know about us. The thought of people thinking I slept my way to this position makes me cringe. I've worked my ass off, and nothing was happening between us when he offered it to me. We're focusing on getting to know each other. Slow is a good thing. Slow is something I've never done before. We're building a true relationship.

"What are you smiling about?" Drew asks, his lip quirking in a knowing grin.

I tap his shoulder with mine. "You. This. Us." I shrug, and he chuckles, squeezing my hand.

With every day that goes by, I learn more and feel more for him. He's pretty spectacular. Aside from the glitz and glamor that comes with being with Drew, he's funny. He's intelligent. He's absolutely amazing with what he can do to my body.

"What about us?"

It's my turn to chuckle. "Oh, you know . . . just how we've been secretly spending time together for over a month, and I'm having a hard time wrapping my head around it."

He looks down at me, eyebrow raised. "You can't wrap your head around what?" There's a hint of apprehension in his tone that I don't want to examine right now. Not when everything is going so perfect.

"Only because it feels like yesterday. As cliché as it sounds, time truly does fly when you're having fun." I smile, and he grins back at me.

And I truly mean it. Every day with Drew is just that . . . fun.

Today, we're going on yet another date. Every Monday night during the summer, Bryant Park comes alive. In the center of the lawn, a large screen is erected, and a classic movie is played. It's equal parts romantic and entertaining. Tonight, it's a romantic comedy.

"My favorite," I say out loud, not meaning to.

"What's your favorite?" Drew asks, steering us toward the street.

"Romantic comedies. I can't wait to watch this one."

"Women," he remarks, a smile in his voice.

As we walk across the street, I can't help but smile. This date is pretty perfect, and it hasn't even started yet. Once we find a clear spot on the grass, Drew spreads out a blanket he packed in the bag he put together. He pulls out a bottle of lemonade with two plastic cups next. Sneaky man. Then he opens a to-go bag and takes out the sushi, and I just about melt. Another favorite of mine. He's always so thoughtful, and that never ceases to amaze me. I've never had someone put so much care into pleasing me, but Drew goes above and beyond.

Once we're settled, we begin telling stories from our childhood. I share memories of my father with him, and with a mouth full of food, he tells me stories of his youth. I can't help but fall even more for this man.

"So, Bailey, be honest. How did you like working at Silver?" He flashes me a wicked smile.

"Honestly?"

"Yes, of course. Just because I own it doesn't mean you have to lie to me."

I sigh.

"When I worked VIP . . . Well, I kind of hated it. All the people who go to your club kind of suck, Drew." He bursts out laughing, and I follow suit. "I'm ready to move into the project management side of things."

He smiles at me, his gaze lifting to the left in thought. "It's funny how we've spent so much time together these past few weeks, yet we've never actually talked about the dumb stuff normal people talk about on dates."

"We've talked about other things, though," I say defensively.

"Yeah, of course, but I want to know more." His brow raises.

"What are you getting at?" I probe.

"For instance, I know you hate working VIP, but I still don't know what your favorite color is or where you went to college."

I drop my gaze to my plastic cup filled with lemonade. "I dropped out," I mumble, not lifting my eyes to meet his. I'm too embarrassed to see the judgment in his eyes.

"Bailey, look at me."

I tilt my head up until our eyes meet again, and I see no judgment at all.

"There's nothing to be embarrassed about."

"I just . . . I couldn't hack it. It was too expensive, and I really didn't know what I wanted to do. It was a big waste of time and money."

"Do you want to go back to school?"

I ponder his question. "Yes. When it's the right time."

"Well, things are good now, right?" I nod. "So why not consider going? I'll adjust your schedule if I have to."

"It's not that, Drew. I had to take this job just to avoid being homeless. What I'm making now is only keeping me afloat. I can't afford school yet." His lip turns up into the most beautiful smile I have ever seen.

"I guess you need that raise effective immediately."

I shake my head. "You're not giving me the raise early. Not until I start. I haven't done anything to warrant it."

"You're going to more than earn it."

"Even with the raise, I have so much to get caught up on. I'm not sure it's a great idea."

"There are other options, Bailey. You could apply for loans. You could even take out enough to pay your bills if needed. I wouldn't suggest that, though. You'll be paying loans back forever that way."

"Really? You think I could get loans for school?" I ask excitedly.

"Yeah, really. I can help you if you need it."

"You'd do that for me?"

"Of course. I just don't understand why your family hasn't helped you with this."

My face reddens in embarrassment. "My mom could afford to pay for school. She just won't."

"We all make mistakes, Bailey. At least you are a big enough person to recognize yours. Your mom, however, she sounds like a bitch."

"She is," I whisper. "The worst."

He doesn't say anything more, and I'm thankful. I don't want to talk about my mom.

As scary as it is to start the process of going back to school, I know it's time to move forward and start planning my future. If Drew can help me find ways to do it without putting myself in a bad situation financially, then I'm ready to do it.

"Okay." I take a gulp of my drink and turn my head toward the large projector screen.

The movie begins to play, and Drew moves closer to me,

laying his hand gently on my thigh and tracing circles on me. I smile up at him, and he leans forward, placing a gentle kiss on my lips. My eyes flutter closed, and I bask in his warmth. Our bodies are so close that I can feel his heat radiating off him and through me.

Opening my eyes, I peer up into his. "This was a great idea, Drew. Thank you."

"My pleasure," he says as he drops another kiss to my lips.

chapter thirty-four

Drew

THE PAST MONTH WITH BAILEY HAS BEEN AMAZING. Scratch that. It's been sublime. Every time I'm with her, she tears down one more wall I've built. She chases away the demons, allowing me to be happy for the first time in years.

She has helped me more than she'll ever know.

Without her, the restaurant would have died with Cal and Reese's betrayal. But not with Bailey on my side. She jumped in, rolled up her sleeves, and got to work. Her tenacity floors me. I've never met a woman like her. Ever.

She's picked up all the broken pieces of the past and helped me put it back together for a much brighter future.

Now it's my turn to help her the way she's helped me.

Taking her to the park last week and helping her realize she had to do something more with her life was a start. It meant everything to me that she opened up the way she did.

I would be lying if I didn't admit that a small part of me is still holding back because of the fact that she's a recovering addict. I swore I would never go there again.

But it's different with her.

Bailey's strong, and I'll be right here to help her.

This is our second chance.

My redemption.

Now I just need her to open up to me more. I need her to help me understand the best ways I can help.

As much time as we have spent together this past month, it's almost always when we are working. On the rare occurrence we don't have to be at the club, we get lost in each other. I want to spend some uninterrupted time with her.

No work.

No interference.

Just us.

A plan springs forth in my mind. I pull out my phone and start to work on it.

We are pulling into the luxury hotel I booked a few hours later. A very excited Bailey has her leg bouncing up and down as we turn into the circle drive.

"I've never been to Boston before." Her soft voice echoes through the car as I put it in park. I turn to face her.

She looks beautiful. That's not to say she doesn't always look beautiful. But today, she looks like a kid in a candy store.

Without the real-world looming overhead, she's different.

Full of life.

Here, with the hotel in front of us, it's like all her worries have faded away.

The only thing looking back at me is happiness.

"Come on. There's so much to see, and we only have a few days."

I fling open the door, and she does so too.

As soon as I step out, a valet steps forward to take the car, and the porter unloads the luggage we have.

Reaching out, I take Bailey's hand in mine and start to walk toward the doors that will lead us to the lobby.

Together, we walk to the front desk where a young woman about the same age as Bailey greets us with a warm smile.

"Good afternoon. Welcome to The Berkley Hotel."

"Hello. How are you today?" I say in response, realizing immediately how ridiculously happy I sound. I don't consider myself an asshole, but this is next-level excitement. To have Bailey all to myself overwhelms me in the best way.

"Very well. Thank you for asking. How can I be of service?"

"We have a reservation under the name Lawson."

The young woman looks down at the computer and starts to type. "Yes, I have you right here, Mr. Lawson. Two nights. Presidential suite, is that correct?"

"Yes." I nod.

I don't need to look at Bailey to know she is staring at me. Her sharp intake of breath gave away her surprise.

"I will have a bellman escort you to your suite. If you need anything, a reservation or help planning an activity, please do not hesitate to contact me. It would be my pleasure to assist you." She walks around the desk and speaks to the bellman.

Together, we follow him through the hotel until he's opening the door to the suite on the top floor.

I finally peer over at Bailey to see her eyes are opened wide. As much as she knows about me, I don't think she understands just how much money I come from. It's refreshing to see that she doesn't. It validates what I've known all along. She likes me for me and not my money.

I know she's here with me for the right reasons.

As soon as the bellman puts our suitcases down and leaves, Bailey turns to me.

"Holy crap, Drew. This place is insane."

My lips spread into a broad smile.

"Thought you would like it."

"Like it? I love it. But this is too much."

I step up to her, slide my thumb along her jaw and bring her face up so she looks at me. "Nothing is too much." And before she can say another word, I silence her with my mouth.

With our lips still touching, I lift her into my arms and walk us out of the foyer, through the living room, and into the bedroom. Once inside, we make our way to the bed, never separating.

Holding her tight, I lean forward and place her down in front of it, and only then do I stop kissing her.

"Undress," I rasp out, making quick work of removing my own clothes.

Once naked, I crawl up between her spread legs until I'm hovering above her. A shudder runs through her body as I settle on top of her.

I take the second to meet her gaze, and the look in her eyes makes me want to thrust inside her. Her chest heaves, and her eyes are glassy with desire. I watch her with hungry eyes, like a predator stalking his prey and waiting for the perfect moment to pounce.

Time stands still as I align myself with her core.

She lifts her pelvis in invitation, an invitation I'm not going to turn down, so I thrust.

A soft sigh escapes her mouth once I'm fully seated. Holding still, I reach my hand around to cup her face, and then with our eyes locked, I start to thrust.

I move inside her.

In and out.

Never breaking eye contact.

In and out.

Never once looking away.

It feels different right now. Watching her watch me is different, and for some reason, it makes me push harder, move deeper. Claim her in a way I've never claimed her before.

She doesn't break the stare. Not when she clenches around me. Not when she shudders with bliss. Not when she comes undone.

Never.

And when I follow her over the edge, I'm still looking into her eyes.

Owning her.

Body. Mind.

Soul.

Only then do I stop. Only then do I burrow in the crook of her neck, panting as we catch our breaths.

A few minutes pass as we both come down from our high. I lean up and kiss her on the lips before separating us.

I leave her sated in the bed and walk over to the bathroom. Turning the faucet on, I wet a washcloth and return to clean up the mess we made.

"Ready to get out of here and see the city?" I ask.

She laughs—a perfect laugh with a wide, happy smile.

After we get up from the bed, we head into the shower. Once we are done, we both grab clothes from our suitcases before we unpack. Neither of us brought much. I'm actually pleasantly surprised by how low maintenance Bailey is.

Once she's dressed, I walk up to her and lean down and kiss the top of her head. Normally, Bailey wears heels, so I never really noticed how much shorter she is than me. It's cute. I pull back and kiss her hard on the lips.

"What was that for?" She giggles.

"Just wanted to."

"Um . . ." She turns around to face me. "Okay. What's the plan?"

"Like I'm going to tell you." I laugh.

There are no big plans. I just want to hold her hand and walk around a different city with her. Somewhere we can just be us. Without work. Without hiding from the staff at Silver.

I'm okay with everyone knowing we are dating. It's been over a month. It's time. But Bailey, on the other hand, I don't think she's ready for that. I understand. She doesn't want the rumors to spoil what we have. Nobody needs to believe she got the job because she's sleeping with the boss. Especially as it's simply not the case. I don't want anyone to demean the hard work she's done to earn her position.

However, being here in Boston and having the ability to freely kiss her in public is a change of pace I could get used to.

We walk the streets hand in hand, taking in the sights and just enjoying ourselves. When we finally arrive at our destination, a restaurant well-known for not only its fantastic food but also the vibe, we head inside and head to the reception desk. We don't make it before I see someone I know.

"Cavendish. What are you doing here?" I say to my old friend. I haven't seen him since college. He's a good guy and trustworthy, which is hard to come by in the circles I've run. Money muddies the water but not with Charles.

"Good to see you, mate. I'm on holiday. What brings you to Boston?"

"Needed the break. You know how it is." I smile, looking down at Bailey. "Charles, this is my girlfriend, Bailey. Bailey, this is an old friend of mine, Charles Cavendish."

I don't even realize what I've said until I've said it. Bailey's cheeks are pink, and her eyes are wide. I smother the smirk that threatens to take over my face at her reaction.

"Nice to meet you," Bailey finally says, and the charming bastard Charles takes her hand.

"The pleasure is all mine." He moves to kiss her hand.

"Kiss her, and I'll have to kill you," I warn.

"You always were a brut. Don't mind him, dear, Andrew doesn't like to share."

She smiles at him when he calls me by my full given name. One I refuse to go by, seeing as it's my father's name, and I want nothing to do with that man.

"What brings you all the way to Boston?" I say, changing the topic.

"It's not *all the way* anymore." He grins.

I cock my head. That's news to me. "You live here?"

"I've moved to New York."

"Really?" I say, happy to hear the news. It'll be nice having a true friend around.

"Yes, I'm opening an office there."

"Advertising, right?"

"Yes. New York could use some new blood." He smirks, and I laugh.

"I might be needing you soon."

"For the club?"

"No, I have plans to open a couple of restaurants."

"Nice." He reaches into his pocket and hands me a card. "Ring me."

"I will. Good seeing you." We shake hands as he smiles and says goodbye to Bailey.

"We have a reservation under Lawson," I say when we finally make it to the hostess.

"Table for two. Follow me."

I turn back to take Bailey's hand as we follow the hostess to our table.

It's an intimate table tucked away from the crowds. Just how I like it.

"Who was Charles?" she asks once we are seated.

"An old buddy from college," I say, picking up the menu and perusing the selection.

"He's from England," she muses, and I laugh.

"What gave it away?"

"Probably the accent." She smiles wide, joining me in laughter.

Once we order, I turn to look at her. She's lost in thought, browsing the menu. The pensive way her eyebrows meet between her eyes is adorable.

I want to know more about this amazing woman.

I want to know everything.

She's an enigma I want to uncover. In more ways than one. I hope being relaxed and away Bailey will feel like she can open up to me.

"Tell me about your family," I say, breaking the silence between us.

She places the menu down, looking at me with a frown. "What? Other than my sister likes to yell at nightclubs, what do you want to know?" She laughs, but it's an uncomfortable noise. One that tells me she doesn't want to go down this path of conversation. Too bad.

"Seriously, Bailey. I want to get to know you."

"Fine." She sighs. "I'll tell you all about my boring family." She rolls her eyes in a funny way before she settles into her chair, but I know what she's doing. She's downplaying her life in order to make herself more comfortable. I've done it myself for years.

"Getting comfortable?" I voice my thoughts, and she looks at me skeptically.

"This could take a while." Her lips thin, and she takes a deep breath. "Where do I start . . . hmm." She taps her chin, continuing to stall. I level her with a look that says she's not getting out of this, and she finally blows out a breath. "I guess the main thing you should know is that Harper and I couldn't be more different." She shrugs. "She's blonde and fair-skinned like our mother, and I'm dark and brooding like our father—was."

She looks away for a second, obviously still feeling the pain from his loss, but then she smiles back up at me. The smile warms her face. Hell, her smile could warm the whole room.

"I'm sure you know, but she's one of the top prosecuting attorneys in New York City, and until you hired me, I was unemployed."

"Bailey . . ." I start, but she shrugs me off.

"What? You asked. Seriously, the comparison of light versus dark or good versus evil comes to mind." She chuckles. "It describes Harper and me to a T, but it couldn't be any more different to describe our parents." She forges on, and I wonder if I shouldn't stop her. The self-deprecating way she's discussing herself makes my blood boil. But she changes to talk of her parents, so I let it go. "Our father doted on us, loved us. Our mother only cared about status and whatever the next big event would be. While he had us out playing for the day, she was probably off spending his money on herself."

As little information as she's given, it's enough to paint a picture of what life for Bailey must've been like after losing her father. No wonder she's struggled. Who wouldn't?

"Your mother sounds like a lot of people I know."

"Right." She frowns. "My father was the one who didn't fit in. He was too good. Too caring."

The way she talks about her father warms me. Knowing she had someone who loved her, and she loved just as much in return makes me feel better about Bailey's childhood.

"When did your father pass away?"

She swallows, and I instantly regret asking that question ahead of all the others I could've asked. "He died of a heart attack when I was a senior in high school. It was likely caused by strenuous hours in stressful environments—both in the office and at home." Her eyes well up with tears, and the need to comfort her is almost more than I can take. I reach out and grab her hands, lending the support I can manage from across the table. "When he died, I don't think our mother cared about anything other than the payout from his life insurance. She collected and practically deserted us for a life in the city. She blew through our inheritance before finding another willing victim to sidle up to and drain of money."

I want to hunt down her mother and strangle her for deserting Bailey. She doesn't deserve to have a daughter like her. And if I ever get the chance, I'll tell her as much.

"She's back and forth between our small town of Hudson, New York, and the city, pretending she's royalty."

"I'm familiar with Hudson. It's a great town."

She nods. "I love it there. If only she were gone, I'd go back more often. She's a leech, and someone I only half tolerate."

"I'm sorry you had to deal with that."

"I didn't really deal with it," she says, lowering her eyes to the table.

I frown, trying to work out the meaning behind her words. I don't have to ask because she forges on as though she needs to purge the past from her subconscious.

"I got drunk and partied, eventually screwing up my life. Things got bad." Her eyes seem far away and hollow as she looks down at her arm and rubs at the small scar. "I was in an accident in college." We both grow quiet at the admission. "I-I . . ."

"You don't need to tell me more," I offer, not wanting to ruin this day by forcing her to relive painful events from the past. But a part of me wants to know. Needs to. It's the only way I'll know how to help her.

"I want to."

"But it doesn't have to be here, Bailey. We can do this somewhere private."

"If I don't tell you now, I'm not sure I ever will." I nod, signaling for her to go on. "My best friend and I were drinking . . .

I was too drunk to drive. Hell, she was too. But I pressured her to take us to another party . . ." Her words trail off, the meaning clear.

The guilt and self-loathing present in her tone. I don't have to hear more to know what she's going to say. I know this story.

Bailey was the only one who walked away from the accident. The guilt was her burden to bear.

We both sit in silence until Bailey lets out a deep audible breath, releases my hands, and then reaches for her water. After she takes a sip, she stares at me.

"And that's my story."

"And that's how you ended up in my club. Something I'm happy about, by the way. Your path was rough, but it got you to where you are now, Bailey. Our pasts don't have to define our future."

"I basically screwed up my life, Drew. No degree, a string of bad jobs, and an empty résumé, I had no choice. No offense. Silver is a great place, but it wasn't the best place for me to work. It was the only place." She places her hands on her lap and looks at me. "My rent was due, so as the saying goes, beggars can't be choosers. The job paid well, and it was a lot better than my last position."

"What was wrong with your last employer?" There's an edge in my voice because when she said it, she stiffened. There's a bigger story there, and I want to know it.

"Nothing, forget I said anything." Her eyes shift around the room, and now I'm growing angry. Not at her, but at whatever has her trying to avoid the conversation.

"I'm not going to forget."

Taking a deep breath, she relays the story. "My last employer was handsy, and I finally quit when I realized he wouldn't stop. I didn't tell Harper because she would've tried to prosecute him, and what my sister fails to realize is New York City is one big boys club. She can fight the injustices all she wants, but I'm not getting dragged into it."

I see red.

"Who was it? I want his name, Bailey."

She sighs. "And this is the reason I didn't tell Harper."

"She would have helped you. Like I'm going to," I grit through my teeth.

"I don't want her pity. And I don't want yours. I made mistakes. Now I have to live with them."

"Everyone makes mistakes, Bailey, but that doesn't give any man the right to touch you."

"I know," she says, peering deep into my eyes. "But it's done, and I'll never go back there. You've given me that opportunity."

I take a deep breath, trying to calm my nerves. She's right. She's no longer in that position, and I'll make damn sure she never is again.

"Now enough of this heavy stuff," she says. "Let's enjoy dinner."

With that, even though I'm seething at the thought of someone touching Bailey without her permission, we settle into a comfortable silence as we eat.

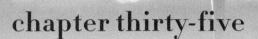

chapter thirty-five

Drew

GUILT SETTLES IN MY CHEST.

Bailey opened up to me while I have been less than forthcoming with my own past. I'm not ready to tell her everything, but I need to tell her something. "Are you okay?" she mutters, her voice laced with worry.

Without thinking it through, I blurt out the words. "Remember how I told you I lost someone too?" She nods. "Her name was Alexa."

Her eyes widen, fully awake now. "Do you want to talk about it?" she asks tentatively, her voice low and soft.

"No," I say, quickly changing my answer. "Yes. I don't know. I feel like we should," I admit.

"Tell me about her," she prompts, and I do.

"She was gorgeous and fun, and it was easy." I look off across the room as if lost in a memory, and it makes my throat tighten as my heart beats rapidly in my chest. "We dated on and off for years." I confess.

"Keep going," she encourages, so I do.

"She was a talented model, but that career has a short lifespan. She was aging out, so to speak, and was looking for her next move. Both of us had more money than we knew what to do with, and owning a club seemed like the answer." I huff. "It seemed like a brilliant plan at the time. We came up with it one night when we were high off our asses. It was typical for us."

"What was?" she asked, eyes wide as though the scene were playing out in front of her.

"Taking bumps under the table. Chasing our next high." I sigh. "We were young and stupid."

"What happened to her?" Bailey's voice is small, scared even. It's as though she knows exactly what happened but is hoping for a different outcome. One I can't provide.

"One night, shit just got out of hand, and I wasn't able to save her."

She nods her head like she knows exactly what that's like. And she does. I know she does. We're kindred spirits in the worst way possible, having experienced loss and heartbreak too young. I wish I could erase that past for her. For us both.

"Did you love her?" she asks, pulling my attention back to her face. She bites her lower lip as she waits for my response. As much as I don't want to say it, I know I need to be honest.

"Yes." My voice cracks. "I did. I'd known her since we were kids. We were all friends growing up, and one thing led to another with us."

A small tear falls down her beautiful face. Not because of my admission to loving Alexa, but for my heartbreak. Of that, I'm sure. There's no jealousy at this moment. Only shared misery.

"That night . . . that night was my fault, Bailey. I was fucking stressed and needed to escape. I didn't have shit on me, so I bought a bag from a new guy at the club. It wasn't pure. I'm not sure what it was cut with because I never ended up taking any of it . . ." I run my hands through my hair as her eyes meet mine. "But she did."

Bailey stands, leaning across the table. Her hands reach out to touch my face. "It's not your fault." I lean into her touch, whispering the words I hate to speak more than anything else.

"It is."

I turn my face into her hand, placing a kiss on her palm. She smiles sadly, before sitting back down and leaving me cold once again. Her warmth is what I need at this moment, and I curse myself for allowing us to have this conversation here in this restaurant of all places. It isn't crowded, but it's not private enough for such heaviness.

"Believe me when I tell you, you can't hold this in your heart. Nothing good will come of it," she says, pulling me back to her. "Maybe you gave her the drugs, but you didn't make her take them. If she didn't get it from you, she would have found a way."

"She wouldn't have died."

"You have no way of knowing that," she says. "I don't know much, but what I know is for years I harbored the guilt over my friend Emily's death. After the accident, it was easier to take pills for the pain than to grieve properly. Soon the physical pain faded because my wounds had healed." She lifts her arm and turns it over to point out a very faint scar. "But the wounds inside me were still there. The pain was still there. I tried to dull it with pills, but that never helped. I needed to forgive myself."

"It's not that easy, though, is it?" I say, knowing she feels the same way.

"It's not always easy, you're right. Yes, sometimes I want to reach for a pill. But instead, I look at my scar to remind me of why the pain is there in the first place. It won't bring Emily back, but it could cause me to join her. I don't want to die. I want to live."

"I do too," I croak out the words, emotion welling in my throat.

"Then live . . . with me," she implores. "Allow me to help you heal your scars." She stands, coming around and taking a seat next to me. She leans forward and places her lips on mine. Kissing me. Caring for me. Making me feel I'm not to blame for a moment.

chapter thirty-six

Drew

"WHAT'S WITH THE PERMA-SMILE?"
I look over to see Carter watching me closely.
Fucking Carter never misses anything. "None of your business.
Get back to work." Hopefully, he doesn't ask where I went this
past weekend. There will be no way I can lie to him.

"Okay, okay." He throws his hands up in mock surrender.
"I'll leave it be."

The front door swings open and in strides Monica. Fucking
Monica.

"Hey, cowboy. Wanna ride?" I wince at her innuendo. I glare
at Carter for forgetting to get his key back despite my insisting
several times.

"What are you doing here, Monica? Your shift doesn't start
until nine."

She shimmies her hips as she strides toward me. Running
her tongue across her lips, she eyes me with predatory aggres-
sion, and I back up to avoid her defilement. "I thought I'd come
help you work off some tension before my shift."

Carter grunts in the background, reminding me that he is
still here and can save me from the impending assault . . . but he
doesn't come to my aid.

"I know you want it," Monica drawls. "Stop acting like you don't think about the things I've done to you."

"You're clueless. I don't think about you, and I most definitely do not want anything you're offering. Where do you even get these ideas? I haven't given you any reasons to think that," I grate.

Carter clears his throat loudly and rather grotesquely. This does the trick. Her head snaps in his direction, and she retreats a step. "Oh, hey, Carter. Didn't know you were here."

"Yep, you know me. I'm always around." Whistling, he goes about slinging barstools down off the bar. His movements are exaggerated and obnoxious, but I might just give him a raise for saving my ass.

"You know, Drew, I could use some help lugging bottles from the cellar. Do you mind if Monica sticks around and helps me out?"

As much as I just want her gone, I appreciate Carter's tactics. "Sure, whatever." I make haste to my office. Releasing the breath I had been holding, I slink into my chair. I have to do something about Monica. She's becoming an issue.

My mind drifts to thoughts of Bailey. The girl has me wrapped up in her. It's not only about sex. I like simply talking to Bailey. She's easy to be around. It's refreshing.

My phone rings, and I see my mother's face light up the screen. She's beautiful, if bitch is your type. I love her, but she's a high-society snob. "Hello, Mother."

"Darling, Andrew," she purrs through the speaker. "What is my favorite son up to? You aren't at that filthy club, are you?"

"I actually just finished shoveling manure off the floor. Now I'm going to begin my afternoon of plunging vomit from the toilets." My sarcasm never bodes well with Alta Lawson.

"Not funny," she huffs.

"To what do I owe this pleasure, Mom?"

"I want to invite you to dinner tomorrow night. We're having filet, your favorite."

It's not, but I won't correct her. Despite my mother's bitchiness to the world, she has always doted on me. She cared for me as much as she could without breaking her well-manicured nails. I haven't spent much time with her since Alexa's death. Alexa's mother and mine are extremely close friends, and I can't help but feel like my mother blames me and the club for what happened to Alexa. I know her family does. If only they knew that Alexa was into cocaine way before we ever hooked up.

"Can't. I'll be at the club."

"You own the club, Drew. You can take the night off."

I sigh. I know there's no use fighting it. "Okay. I'll see you tomorrow."

I'm ready to move forward with my life. Perhaps enduring a night with my mother will be a step in the right direction.

chapter thirty-seven

Bailey

I'VE BEEN AT SILVER FOR AN HOUR, AND THERE'S BEEN NO sign of Drew. I've kept busy by looking at the proposal sent today by his architect for the new space we found. I might not be the best person to look them over, but even with my limited knowledge of the topic, I can already see some tweaks we'll have to make to the sketches. All the extra time I've spent at the club has paid off.

I can't wait for Drew to get here so we can discuss what I found. As pathetic as it sounds, I'm practically bouncing with excitement to see him. Not just to tell him about this, but also because I miss him.

The past few months have been the best of my life, and after our trip last weekend, I can't help but feel as though we've turned a corner.

The thought has me scared out of my mind. I didn't want this, but he makes me wish for things I have no business wishing for. This is the type of thing that can hurl me right down the rabbit hole and back into the world of kaleidoscope vision.

"What the hell has gotten into you, Chipper Charlie?" I raise my brow at Carter.

"Chipper Charlie? What the heck is that?" I tease.

"Don't dodge my question, missy. Spill it."

"Keep this on the down-low, and it's not a big thing, but Drew and I have been . . . seeing each other."

He frowns, causing my eyes to shoot up in question. "Just be careful, Bailey."

I blanch. "Wow. No congrats, I'm happy for you, Bae?"

"Are you in a relationship? Does he call you his girlfriend?" It's my turn to frown at Carter.

"I'm sorry. Just forget I said anything. I care about you, and I want to make sure you're okay, is all." I smile at my friend.

"I know, and I love you for it, but Carter, I am so happy. I want to live in my bubble for as long as possible." He nods.

"It's not the bubble I'm worried about. It's what happens after that bubble bursts," he says warily. "But hey, it might not, so let's go with that." I bite my lip at his words.

At that moment, Drew walks by, winking in my direction. My insides melt and all talk of this not being anything goes to the wayside. I'm back on cloud nine.

"Hey. I know you have a fancy job . . ."

"Spit it out, Carter. You know I'm here to help."

"Since you offered . . ." He laughs because clearly, I walked into a trap. "Can you head to VIP three and clean it up?" Carter requests, and I oblige. Even though I don't have to anymore, I still help out around the floor and bartend when Carter needs me. Might as well until the deal with the restaurant is finally done.

As I wipe at a spot on a table in VIP room three, I hear voices right outside, giggling about something. This place is full of waitresses gossiping about their trysts with high-end clients. Apparently, they didn't get the memo that it only makes them sound like high-end prostitutes. I move closer to the doorframe to eavesdrop on their conversation. I'm interested in what has them giggling like schoolgirls.

"He doesn't want anyone to know." The hushed voice is hard to hear, but it sounds like Monica's whiny vocals.

"How long has it been going on?" another voice chimes in. I recognize it as Ashley's.

"Just about three months. I have a key to get in here at any time. We've christened this entire place."

This information has me ramrod straight. She can't be talking about this place, right? The only person who would have access to another key around here would be Carter.

"I came in early today to help him relax. Drew is insatiable."

I round the corner, ready for blood. This is total bullshit. "Monica, you are delusional. There is no way Drew is sleeping with you," I say tersely. She straightens at the sound of my voice and turns to me, a wide grin taking over her entire face.

"What's got your panties in a twist, Bailey?"

"You spreading lies about Drew, that's what," I seethe.

"You're new here, so let me clue you in. Drew is a playboy, and he happens to love playing with me." She looks at Ashley and giggles again.

"That's a lie," I say through clenched teeth.

"You obviously don't know how our fearless leader is. I have him so tied up he won't even look in anyone else's direction. You're safe from him, Bailey." She grins, and Ashley chuckles.

Her smug face has me on the edge of losing it, and tears begin to flow without my permission. This, right here, is exactly why any type of relationship, sexual or otherwise, is bad news for me.

"Are you okay, Bailey?" Ashley asks. Clearly, she has no idea why I'd be acting so irrational.

I shoulder past her, trying to make my escape. I need fresh air. I'm not paying attention when I run straight into a hard chest. I know without looking who it belongs to. The one person I really don't want to see at this point.

He grabs my shoulder to steady me. "Whoa, Bailey." He chuckles. I will myself to look up at him, and the smile immediately leaves his face. "Baby, what's wrong?" he whispers so only I can hear.

How convenient. The fact that he's trying to hide what we are from Monica stings. "Don't call me that. Get your hands off me."

"Calm down. Come to my office." He looks panicked. Good. He should.

"I'm not going anywhere with you. How was your rendezvous with Monica today?"

The asshole looks confused. "What are you talking about? I wasn't with Monica." I watch as his face turns from confusion to realization to . . . amusement? "Bailey Jameson, are you jealous?"

He's laughing at me. The dickhead is actually laughing.

"Fuck you, Drew," I spit in his direction.

"Come to my office and take a breather. I don't know what you heard from Monica, but I absolutely did not touch her. You can ask Carter. She ambushed me, and he came to my rescue."

I consider what he's saying. It does sound like something that slut would do because she isn't exactly subtle in her ways. I brush his hands off me and stalk toward his office. I pass Monica on the way and watch as she takes in the scene, but I have a one-track path straight to my answers. However, what Drew says has me stopping in my tracks.

"Monica, have you met my girlfriend, Bailey?"

My heart skips a beat. Did he just say that?

"What?" Her tone is cold. Deadly.

"Bailey and I are dating." Monica's face is red in anger. "Come on, baby. We have stuff to do." He grabs my hand and walks away from a gaping Ashley.

I'm walking on air at this point. When we reach the office, I hear the door shut and lock behind me.

"We won't be interrupted."

"Girlfriend? Since when are we labeling this?"

"What? I thought you'd like that touch. Did you see her face? She got exactly what she deserved," he says vehemently.

"Tell me what your history with her is?"

His back straightens. "Bailey, I don't think you want to know everything about my past."

"Um, yes. Yes, I do. If it involves you sleeping with half the staff I work with, I absolutely want to know. It's not fair that I have to listen to this shit, Drew. We may not technically be in a relationship, but I don't share. If you're sleeping with other people, then you aren't sleeping with me. Period."

He smiles. I want to wipe it off his face. "Since the moment I met you, I haven't touched another woman."

He walks to me, taking me into his embrace, and his touch sends heat directly to my center, turning me molten. I see the corner of his lip raise into a grin, and it literally makes my knees go weak.

"Does that make you hot? Do you want me to prove that you're the only girl I'm fucking? I will. Right here on this desk, I'll show you there hasn't been anyone else."

I need him to show me I'm the only one.

My hand moves to touch him. He's practically bursting at the seams. I stroke his length through his pants, eliciting a groan from his lips. I'm feeling brave. I need to show him that he doesn't need anyone else. I can be everything he needs.

"Do you like that, Drew? Do you want me on my knees?"

"God, yes. On your knees, Bailey."

I drag my hands down his sides as I slowly drop to my knees in front of him. Looking up through my lashes, I lick my lips. Gradually, I pull the zipper down, allowing him to spring free from his confinements. I lean in and run my tongue along the tip. He moans, which only encourages me to go further.

When he's done, he sighs in contentment. I take my mouth off him and gently wipe my lips.

"Come here."

"No, tonight was for you. I have work to do."

"Your work is up here now." He quirks his eyebrow in confusion as to where I'm going.

"I know I'm not supposed to help downstairs, but Drew, I can't leave Carter on his own without a backup bartender." He chuckles at my defiance. "But later, I want to go over the sketches. Pencil me in." I wink.

I stand on my feet and make my way out of the office. As the door opens, Monica is on the other side with her hand raised, ready to knock. I look back toward Drew and see he's zipping his pants. He doesn't even try to hide what we were just doing from Monica. It gives me a sense of possessiveness, but at the same time, I pity her. Up until his declaration, Monica was unaware of our relationship. I decide at this moment to give her the benefit of the doubt.

I turn back to Monica. "I'm sorry if you feel like I took him from you. I didn't know you two had any sort of a relationship. I hope you can respect the fact that I'm with him now."

I look back at Drew, smiling to show that I'm not concerned. As I make my way down the stairs, I hear the door close behind me and know that Monica is stalking in my direction. With nothing more to say to her, I keep walking. She doesn't stop as she rushes past me and out the door. I feel bad, but he's mine now. There's no room for someone else in our relationship. She'll find the right person someday.

chapter thirty-eight

Drew

THIS THING WITH BAILEY IS GETTING SERIOUS. NOW WE ARE officially in a relationship, and I'm out of my element.

After the shit with Monica tonight, I need Bailey to know how genuine I am about giving this relationship thing a try. With my focus entirely on her tonight, Monica is never mentioned again. Thank fuck.

I listen to Bailey breathe. It's so melodic and peaceful. If I lie here and listen to her for a while, it might lull me to sleep as well.

"What are you doing, Mr. Lawson?"

I'm caught. "Just thinking. Go back to sleep."

"What are you thinking about?"

What should I say? I'm not about to tell her because then I'd sound like a fucking pussy. So, I say the next thing that comes to mind. "I have dinner tonight at my mom's, and I'm dreading it."

"Oh? Why's that?"

"My mother can be a bit much at times. I've been avoiding her."

"I could go with you if that would help."

I appreciate the offer, but I wouldn't put her in that awkward position. My mother would eat her alive. "Thanks, but I don't think that's a good idea." I feel her deflate beside me. Clearly,

I've said the wrong thing. "Bailey, what's going on in that head of yours?"

"I guess I'm just wondering what we are."

"What we are?" I repeat.

"I'm not trying to put a label to it, Drew. I'm just not sure what's going on. You told Monica I'm your girlfriend."

"We are sleeping together."

Wrong answer. She flies out of bed and begins throwing on her clothes.

"Wait, what are you doing?"

"We're sleeping together? So, I'm just like Monica?"

Oh fuck, here we go. "No, no. I just mean we're not sleeping with anyone else. We're exclusive in that sense."

"Fabulous, so I'm your plaything then."

It's not a question. She's throwing her skirt over her legs, and not gracefully, I might add.

"Stop, Bailey. We are exclusive, period. Do you want me to say you're my girlfriend? Fine, you're my girlfriend. Is that better?"

She stops and looks at me. "You don't have to classify me as anything, Drew. I'm sorry I put you on the spot." She looks defeated, and I feel like an ass.

I practically crawl across the bed to her. Grabbing her by the hips, I bring her back into my arms. "I want you to be my girlfriend. I haven't said that to a girl in a long time, and I didn't know if I would ever say that. But I do. I want you to be mine."

She melts into my arms, and I feel the tension leave her body. She grabs the sides of my head and kisses me with abandon. When we finally come up for air, we sink back into the bed.

"Drew, now that I'm your girlfriend, can I meet your mom?"

Fuck. Me.

"Bailey, we just got over one fight. Can we not do this?" I'm whining like a fucking girl.

"Are you embarrassed by me?" Her voice is small.

"No, baby, I'm not embarrassed by you at all. My mom is just . . . difficult. We're so new that I don't want her scaring you off. I think we need time to grow in our relationship before you have to endure a dinner with her."

"Oh. Okay."

I sigh with relief.

"I'm going to go shower. Is that all right?"

"Want me to join you?" I smirk.

"As amazing as that sounds, I don't think I'd actually get clean, and I need to get going. I have some errands to run. I also want to catch a meeting."

I nod my head and let her get up from the bed, watching as she sways toward the bathroom. I look at the clock. 10:40 a.m. I should probably get up as well. I grab my phone and see I've missed a call from the devil herself. I decide to call her quickly to see what she wants. If I'm lucky, she's calling to cancel dinner.

"Drew, darling. Are you among the living, or have I caught you in bed?"

"I'm up, Mother. What's going on?"

"I was calling to remind you about dinner since we know how flaky you can be at times."

I cringe. "No, Mother, I haven't forgotten."

"See you soon." She hangs up before I can even respond.

Hours later, I'm walking into my childhood home. It's more like a museum filled with antiques, priceless paintings, and stiff furniture adorning every corner of the pretentious estate.

"Drew," my mother croons as she waltzes into the room. A beautiful blonde follows closely behind. I have no idea who she is, but she peruses my body boldly.

"Drew, you remember Allison Estep. Her parents are Susan

and Allister Estep." Her brows rise as if to indicate that I should absolutely know who these people are, and I do—old money with trusts to rival the Hiltons.

"Yes, of course. Allison, it's nice to see you." I smile.

Allison gives me a sheepish grin. She knows what my mother is saying, and she enjoys the praise her family name brings. My mother is obviously up to her matchmaking.

"Mother. A word, please."

She looks from me to Allison and frowns. "Drew, that's rude. Can we at least eat first?"

I don't give her a second to continue. I walk briskly out of the room with my mother right on my heels.

"What's the meaning of this, Drew Lawson?"

"I don't know what you're up to, but I won't be a pawn in your games. I'm not interested."

"It's time for you to start thinking about your future."

"What if I am, Mom? What if I like my life?"

She scoffs. "Your life is a train wreck. You live at the club pining over a girl who died of a drug overdose."

The mention of Alexa has my blood running cold. "You don't know what you're talking about."

"You blame yourself for that girl's death. It wasn't your fault that she was an addict. Her parents are to blame."

"It was my fault." I stress the last word.

"I just want you to be happy."

Her sad eyes have me softening. "I am, Mom. I promise."

"Will you at least talk to Allison? She's such a pretty girl and from such a well-respected family."

"No, I have places to be."

Without another word, I walk out.

chapter thirty-nine

Bailey

I'M MILDLY HURT THAT DREW DIDN'T WANT TO TAKE ME TO meet his mother, but I understand. I need to proceed slowly with this. Going too fast isn't good for either of us. To keep my mind off Drew, I call up Harper and invite her over for sushi. She was the one to extend the olive branch, but I haven't seen her since. It's time we have some sister time.

"This is nice," Harper says around a mouthful of California roll.

"Mmm," I say in return.

"So, what's new with your job?"

I avert my eyes. I don't want to have this conversation with Harper. I know how she feels about Drew, and she can't know about us right now. "Everything is good. Still waiting on the restaurant closing to begin. How is Cal?" I ask, despite the fact I don't care. He's not my favorite person, but I'd never tell Harper. She loves him, and that's good enough for me. I think he's a pompous ass. Something about him is slimy. Harper is happy, though, so I put up with him.

"He's Cal. He's always working," she says dejectedly.

"I can imagine."

"What's that supposed to mean, Bailey?"

"Nothing. I just mean with his job . . ."

"It's hard. We've been struggling lately."

"Because of me?" I ask, knowing that the position I put him in is likely at the top of their struggles.

"Not just that. I just . . . don't trust him, Bailey."

"What? What do you mean you don't trust him?"

She blinks a couple of times. "I think he's cheating."

I jerk back. "Are you serious? Have you caught him doing something?"

She shakes her head vehemently. "No. Nothing concrete. He's just been extra shifty lately. Working really late. Not coming home a few nights a week."

"You need to end things," I snap. I'd always questioned Cal's loyalty. My sister's intuition is typically spot-on. If she thinks he's up to no good, he's likely up to no good.

"Bailey. Please stop."

I put my hands up in surrender.

"Fine. But listen to your gut, Harp. Get to the bottom of it."

She looks at me expectantly. "Will you help me spy?"

"What?" I giggle, finding the question absurd coming from Harper.

"I need you to spy on him with me. We can try to break into his Facebook or something."

As much as I think this is a bad idea, I can't let her down. I nod in affirmation.

For the rest of the night, there's no more talk of Cal. We laugh, eat, and talk about everything we've missed these past few weeks until my phone beeps, and I look down.

Drew: Get your ass to my place. I need you.

I look up at Harper's baffled face.

"What's with the goof-troop grin?"

"Just a friend." I shrug.

"A guy friend? Spill it."

"Nope, nothing to spill. It's Carter. You met him at the diner. Then he kicked you out of the bar," I remind her, and she grimaces.

"I should get going. Cal wants me to meet him." She grabs her stuff and makes her way toward the door. Leaning over, she smothers me in an embrace. "Thanks for tonight. I miss you."

I squeeze her back. "Me too, Harp."

When I get to Drew's, I can tell he is tense. "What's wrong?" I ask, concerned.

"My mother can be very difficult at times." He rolls his eyes. "Come here," he says, bringing me to his chest. "You smell like fish."

I laugh at his tone. It's cute. "Harper and I had sushi."

"Harper, eh? Did you tell her about us?"

I stiffen in his embrace. "Tonight wasn't the right time. She asked me to help her spy on Cal."

"She's still marrying the douche?"

I laugh. "Yep. There's nothing I can do about it. I just have to support her."

"You don't have to support your sister making the biggest mistake of her life, Bailey."

"What am I supposed to do? I don't have anything on him. She's spying. If she finds something, she'll walk."

He kisses my forehead. "Let's take a shower."

He leads me to the bathroom, stripping me along the way. When the warm water hits my skin, I sigh in contentment. Drew takes care of me, washing my hair and massaging my scalp, and I am putty in this man's hands. For the first time since we've been intimate, he doesn't initiate sex. He simply pampers me. I don't know what to think, so I don't. I just enjoy all he offers me.

chapter forty

Drew

THERE ARE A FEW HOURS TO SPARE BEFORE I HAVE TO MEET Bailey at her apartment to pick her up. I decided to give us both a day off today. However, even though I won't be working, I should probably stop by to check on things and make sure everything is running smoothly. With the new restaurants' openings looming in the distance, I can't have anything going awry.

When I walk in the door, it's still early. The club doesn't officially open for another hour. But that doesn't stop it from being crowded. Most of the staff is here already. A private party before the main club opens was booked in the VIP room tonight, so some of the bartenders are here, making sure the bottles and mixers are ready.

When I see Carter, I give a little wave before heading over to the stairs that lead to my office.

Before I hit the landing, though, I hear a noise and giggling from the storage room. Normally, I wouldn't stop, but I don't need employees distracted tonight.

Stopping my pace, I turn around and move toward the door, swinging it open.

What I see hits me in the chest.

In front of me is Lauren and Darla. Lauren is kneeling over an extra table that isn't set on the floor. She's got a rolled-up dollar bill to her nose.

My hand clenches into a fist, but I take a deep breath before I speak.

They both look up from the table, eyes wide.

"Drew..." Lauren starts but then stops, clearly unnerved and not knowing what else to say. She puts down the bill and tries to cover the powdery white mess. "I didn't think you were coming in today."

"Clearly." I look from her to the pile of coke. "Both of you, clean that shit up and then head to the VIP room. I'm holding a mandatory meeting right now."

Without waiting for either of them to say another word, I walk out the door, stalking to where Carter stands behind the main bar.

"Boss man?"

"I want everyone in the VIP room in five minutes."

"Um. Okay."

Needing to get my head under control, I step outside. It's nearly impossible to push down the thoughts I'm having.

This has gone far enough.

Things need to change, and they need to change now.

After taking a few more calming breaths, I head to the VIP room where I'm met with my whole staff minus Bailey. But that's okay because she no longer works in the bar.

"First things first... and let this be a lesson to everyone here." I turn toward Darla and Lauren. "You are both fired."

"But—" Lauren starts to say, and I hold up my hand.

"Don't give a fuck that you weren't the one doing blow at the particular minute I walked in. You were next in line. Get your shit and leave."

Each of the girls' eyes go wide, but they at least have the decency not to object.

Now that I'm done with that, I turn back to the remaining faces of my employees, and I see the look in Carter's eyes. He wants to object, or at the very least tell me not to be so hot-headed and let them work their shift tonight. But fuck that.

He knows what today is.

Today is the anniversary of Alexa's death.

I am not going to allow drugs in my club anymore.

My rules were clear, and now I'm going to enforce them.

"From here on out. No drugs. I know I have said this before, but now I'm going to make myself real clear. If I catch you doing drugs . . ."

A few of the resident druggies don't look too fazed, and I know why. It's because even though I have said this over the past few years, I have never done shit about it.

I lock eyes with Carter. This will get my point across. "Zero tolerance. This has been the rule for some time, and I really hope you all fucking listen because starting this week, I will be implementing random drug tests. It's your choice if you want to work here. But let me say one thing, this is the hottest club in New York City, so I won't have a problem replacing you." I study the crowd one last time before I go to make my departure. "For all your sakes, I hope you didn't use recently." And with that, I leave.

It's a few days later, and I've been so busy I haven't been able to spend time with Bailey. The whole threatening the staff talk just managed to create more work for me. It was necessary, but damn. It's the last thing I have time for.

While I've been playing babysitter and testing the staff, Bailey's been working her ass off. I have her running around the city, sorting shit for the restaurant. There's so much to do, and if I'm being honest, I've loved watching Bailey step into her role. I'm proud of the way she's taken charge.

I'm about to head to her place when my phone chimes with a message from Monica, of all people. I groan but stop short when I read her message.

Monica: Fire alarm is going off, and Carter needs you.

Fuck. Her timing is always impeccable. It's as though she knew damn well I was heading to Bailey's and is doing her best to cock block.

"Changes of plans," I tell Stan. "Take me to the club."

I then fire a text to Bailey, hating to disappoint her.

Me: Something came up at club, and I'm needed there now. Call you later.

It's not even ten minutes later when I'm pulling up and heading inside.

"Dude, what took you so fucking long?" Carter is behind the bar wiping down bottles.

"I was on my way to Bailey's. What the fuck is happening here that I had to stand her up?" I'm livid that this shit couldn't be dealt with without me.

"The fire department came, checked everything out, and shut the alarm off. Some idiot was smoking in the bathroom, and it set off the alarms."

"You've got to be fucking kidding me. You called me out here for that? What the hell do I pay you to run the club for?"

Carter throws his hands up in the air. "I didn't call you, man. I said we could handle it. Monica insisted the alarm company called you and said you insisted on coming. I thought you'd be here way before this, or I would've called you and told you not to bother."

Fucking Monica. She called me and said Carter had instructed her to. My jaw clenches.

"What did they say?"

"Who?"

"The fire department." It's taking all my control to rein in my temper—incompetent asshats.

"They fined the club for the smoking. The fine and paper-work are in your office."

I huff out in frustration and stalk to my office. I'm grabbing this shit and getting back to Bailey. We're going to forget this entire night once I'm buried inside her.

I throw my office door open and stop dead in my tracks. Sitting on my desk in nothing but thigh highs and fuck-me heels is Monica.

What. The. Fuck?

"Where have you been? I've been sitting here waiting for-ever, lover." Monica's whiny voice grates on my already fragile nerves. Once upon a time, this scene would have been enough to make my cock throb. Tonight, I just want her to get the fuck out of my office.

"Monica, get the fuck off my desk and get dressed." I go to grab her clothes off the floor, and the next thing I know, she has her legs wrapped around my head. I drop to my knees in front of my desk with this skank's legs literally choking me, her bare skin staring me in the face.

I remove her legs from around my shoulders and stand, lifting her off my desk to save my papers from any more contamination.

"Drew. Play with me." She runs her long red nails down my arm, and I shudder.

"I'm tired, and this isn't happening. It's never happening. Get dressed, leave your key, and get the hell out of my office. I'm done. I tried to fucking be the bigger man because I know you need the money, but I am fucking done. You're fired. After your shift tonight, I never want to see you again." I know I should tell her to leave now, but we are seriously short-staffed right now, and I need someone at the bar in VIP.

I go to step back and make for the door when she grabs me and slams her mouth to mine. At the same time I'm registering what the hell is happening, I hear someone gasp behind me. My body locks up. I know that sound. I know all her sounds.

Bailey.

I push Monica back and whirl around to chase after Bailey as she makes her way hastily down the stairs. The club is packed. Even if I did call out her name, she wouldn't hear me over the commotion. I'm ready to commit murder.

"Get. The. Fuck. Out." I annunciate each word nice and clear so there is no question as to the seriousness of my words. By the glower on her face, I see that she's getting the memo.

"I don't get you, Drew. You used to be so much fun, and now that little bitch has you wrapped around her finger. Lame."

I throw her dress at her. "Leave the key. After your shift, you come around here again, and I'll have a restraining order on your ass so fast."

She pouts the whole time she's getting dressed. I have my back turned to her, but I'm not leaving this office until I know she's gone for good. Finally, she pushes past me and flies down the stairs. Once again, she leaves with the key. Fuck. I'll call the locksmith in the morning. I don't trust that she hasn't made copies. She's that crazy.

I lock up and head out of the club doors to find Bailey. Hopefully, she's back at her place so we won't have an unnecessary scene.

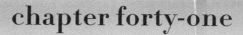

chapter forty-one

Bailey

I CAN'T BREATHE. I TRUSTED HIM, AND HE BROKE ME. I KNEW he would, but I let him anyway.

Monica wasn't lying. I'm such an idiot. I shake with the need to escape. A part of me long since buried the cravings to lose myself for the night. But tonight, those cravings call to me.

I crave the euphoric burn only a drink will bring.

I need one shot. Just one. The taste will make everything around me—all the betrayal—fade away. The devil on my right shoulder fights with the angel on my left.

My head shakes back and forth.

No.

I'm not that person anymore. It won't solve anything to drink. As much as I want it, I'm better than that.

But still . . .

Just one.

I need to forget what I saw, even if only for now. Tomorrow I can move past it, but tonight, I need to forget.

I need a drink. If I can find someone to drink with, maybe I can pace myself.

Lies.

As if I conjured him, Reese appears out of nowhere.

His eyes blink when he sees me. "Chwaer?" There's a look in his eyes I know too well. He looks lost in his own nightmare too. His pain is palpable, like mine.

"Are you okay?" I ask, realizing the irony that I, of all people, might need to help him forget something.

"No," he says, shaking his head. "What are you doing?"

"Not a damn thing." I step closer to him. "I'm having a bad night . . ." I meet his dark gaze. "Honestly, I need to get drunk, and I don't want to do it alone." My voice dips with emotions I don't want to purge in front of him. "Please." I grab his hand. He's shaking his head vehemently. "I don't want to drink alone."

A line creases his forehead, and his mouth opens. "Not here." He looks around the space. "This is his place, and I'm not even supposed to be here. One of the bouncers let me in."

"Trust me when I say, Drew is too busy to care." Disdain drips from my words. "But just in case you're still worried, we can drink in the back VIP room. No one will be in there. Certainly not Drew. He never goes in there."

He contemplates it and then shrugs. "Fine. Lead the way." He gestures for me to walk first. I start to head toward the private bar in the VIP room.

"Bailey, where are you two going?" Carter's voice sears through me.

"This isn't your concern. Leave it alone."

"You shouldn't be going anywhere with him." Carter's voice is hard, but Reese seems nonplused by the whole thing. "Who let you in here?" Carter barks.

"We're not doing anything wrong. You didn't see us. Get back to work," I warn.

"Bailey, please. Listen to me. I'm your friend. You look upset. Let's go somewhere and talk. Don't hang out with him. He's trouble." I wave him off.

"I'm trouble." I grab Reese's hand and take off. "Let's drink."

I pull him deeper into the room, away from all prying eyes. We take a few steps, and then we both turn toward the bar that's in the corner only to find a very smug Monica staring back at me.

Of all the people to be working the VIP room, it has to be her.

She gives me a coy smile before purposely adjusting the top of her dress. Making it very clear what she was just doing and with whom.

A part of me wants to turn around and run out of here, but I refuse to show her that I'm hurting. I refuse to let her know she's won. A childish, irrational part wants to lose my worries at the bottom of the bottle and leave the aftermath right here for her and Drew to clean up. I want him to know what he caused me to do. *Your choice. Not his.*

I brush off the pesky voice of reason and give Monica my own fake smile. Looking her straight in the eyes, I say, "Two shots of tequila. Make them extra chilled."

She stares at me for a beat, probably wondering what I'm thinking, but instead of waiting for her to speak, I turn to face Reese. "You drink tequila, right?"

"I'll drink anything," he answers.

"Good. Then let's celebrate."

His eyebrow lifts at my declaration. "And what are we celebrating?"

"New fabulous beginnings, of course." My voice is loud, and it hits its desired mark when from behind me, where Monica is, I hear her scoff, but I pay her no mind. Instead, I concentrate all my attention on Reese as Monica prepares our drinks.

A few seconds pass before I hear the sound of the shot glasses being set down on the glass bar.

With that, I finally turn to face her. Her lips spread across her face, and now her smile seems wicked. "To new beginnings." She winks.

Her words feel like a stab in the gut.

I reach my arm out, and my hands shake as I grab the glass from the bar and lift it to my mouth.

As soon as the liquid hits my lips, I feel the burn. It goes down my throat roughly, but it does its job. When it pools in my stomach, it's like a magic wand has been waved, and my shoulders almost instantly relax a little bit.

However, even now, once the drink settles, I can feel the pain in my heart. It feels like a hand wrapped around the organ. Each time I try to breathe, it tightens.

This is hell.

Agonizing hell.

One shot isn't enough.

I square my shoulders and look back at Monica as I place my glass back down in front of her and then turn my head to Reese. "Another?"

"Hell, yeah," he responds, laughing. "To old times," he cheers.

I'm not sure what he's talking about, but I hardly care at this moment. I'm trying too hard to get to the point of not caring.

"To old times," I repeat for shits and giggles. I don't need to look at Monica to know she's beyond annoyed as she makes her way over to the bar behind me and grabs the glasses.

She's huffing and puffing, making it clear she doesn't want to do this, but Reese is my free pass. He's important, and she can't say no to him. Thus, she has no choice but to serve me too.

I hate that she is the bartender on duty, but at the same time, I need to show her that she didn't hurt me. As much as it's a lie, I don't want her to see my pain, and it's a bonus by doing that, I'm also taking the edge off.

I also need to pretend I don't care about anything.

Turning back around, I stare at her as she moves back in front of Reese and me with two newly filled shot glasses.

My own lips spread across my face. Still fake, but I don't care. It's the illusion I need to portray.

tempted

I take the glass, and this time when I shoot it, it goes down smooth. The euphoric feeling hits me again.

We stand there a few minutes, taking shot after shot.

Each one makes me looser. Each one working its magic.

With the sixth drink, it finally works. My head is no longer spinning with the images of Drew and Monica. Now, it's replaced with a feeling I haven't felt for a long time, one only present in my once favorite vice. It feels like I'm floating. Like my head is no longer a part of my body.

I'm light, and nothing can possibly bother me right now. It's as if I'm living in a dream world.

I welcome it.

My eyes close, and then when I open them, I throw my head back and start to laugh when I see the way Monica looks at me.

But it doesn't matter how she stares. This laughter is not a fake one for the crowds. No, this is a real one.

It makes me laugh harder.

I must be drunker than I thought because I can't stop. Not even when from the far corner of the room, I can see into the club's main part, and I can see him.

He hasn't spotted me yet, but he's speaking adamantly to someone. My angle isn't ideal, but then when he looks toward the VIP section where I'm currently drinking, I know he must have been speaking to Carter.

Traitor.

I need to get out of here unless I want him to see me here, which I don't. I have no desire to ever speak to him.

Nor do I want that bastard to see the pain I'm in.

My hand reaches out, and I grab Reese. From the corner of my eye, I watch as Reese follows my gaze. He must notice what has me pissed because his face splits into a wide smile as he looks in the direction of where Drew is watching us.

"Let's go," I say, pulling his attention back to me.

"Where?" he asks.

"Anywhere." I stand from the barstool and start to walk away, pulling him along with me.

It feels like I'm floating out of my body. I stumble forward, my feet having a hard time keeping me steady, but Reese grabs me tighter and does the steadying for me. He pulls me into the curtained alcove out of Drew's sight line.

chapter forty-two

Drew

AS MY FEET HIT THE LAST STEP, I LOOK AROUND FRANTICALLY for Bailey. I thought maybe I could find her upstairs in one of the offices, but my search came up fruitless. She's probably long gone, having walked in on what she did.

"Fuck!" I yell, drawing the attention of a few customers in earshot. "Sorry." I wave it off, continuing my search, hoping like hell I'm wrong, and she's still here. I grab my phone and try to call her, but it goes to voicemail.

Fuck.

Where is she?

The first place I head is to the door that leads to the front of the club.

I find Tony standing there. His arms are crossed at his chest, and he's shaking his head at some dude. Obviously, he doesn't deem him worthy of my club.

When he sees me, he turns and gives the poor fool his back. He's been discarded.

"What's up, boss?" he asks.

"Have you seen Bailey?"

"Not since she arrived a while back. I thought she was looking for you."

"She didn't leave?" I say, ignoring his comment.

Bailey did look for me, and Monica . . .

Doesn't matter. I need to find her, and I need to explain.

If she didn't leave out the front door, she probably went out the back. I start to stalk in that direction when I feel two hands shove me before it registers that Carter is in my face looking like he wants to pummel me.

"What the fuck did you do to her, man?" Carter screams at me.

"Whoa, you better get your hands off me if you still want a job."

"Fuck your job. I told you not to hurt her, Drew." His hands fly to the top of his head, worry etching lines in his forehead. "The way she looked . . . it was almost like . . . fuck, man! Tell me you didn't. Tell me I'm wrong and you didn't fuck that slut, Monica."

My tongue feels heavy as I try to find the words to explain. "I'm going to excuse everything you've just said to me because I know you're only looking out for Bailey. I know you care, and because of that, this is the only time I'm going to allow you to speak to me like this." I take a deep breath, trying to calm down.

Carter means well, and he doesn't deserve my wrath. What Bailey saw didn't look good, and his defending her is noble.

"She ambushed me in my office. I didn't touch her. I wouldn't, Carter." I run my hands down my face. "Fuck," I yell. "I'm in love with her, Carter. I need to find her."

There, I said it. God, I do. I'm in love with her, and this whole damn scene drives that home. I can't lose her to a fucking misunderstanding staged by the likes of Monica.

"About damn time you admit that," he bites. "She's a wreck. She just walked off with Reese, man. I tried to stop her, but she wouldn't listen to a fucking word I said. She's going to get drunk, and then who the fuck knows what she will do. You

need to find her. She's a recovering addict. One drink is one too
many . . ."

His words hang in the air, not finished and ominous. He's
right. There is no telling what she will do.

One drink will lead to two, then with her inhibitions down,
it's only a matter of time before Reese is offering her coke.

Fuck. Fuuuuck.

"Which way did they go?" I yell over my shoulder.

"They're in the VIP room drinking."

I turn toward the glass that separates the rooms, and I see
her and Reese, shots in hand, drinking. Her gaze meets mine.
Carter grabs me.

"Let go, man," I say through gritted teeth.

"You have to calm down." His hand drops, and I turn back to
go get her, but when I do, I notice the space is empty.

"They left."

Without another word, I run, pushing through the doors to
the bar.

"Where did they go?" I bark at Monica, who is staring at me
from behind the bar.

"Probably to his table to fuck," she answers, her hand reaching across the bar to touch me. My entire body goes rigid. "Oh,
come on, Drew. She's obviously going to get high with Reese
then hook up. This is pretty cliché if you ask me. You can do so
much better."

"Shut the fuck up, Monica," I grit through my teeth.

"Let it happen, baby. I'll take care of you." I jump out of her
grip, baring my teeth.

"I'm only going to say this one time, Monica. Get the fuck
out of my club."

"But—"

I don't wait for her to say anything else. Instead, I push past
her.

"Get her out of my club," I tell Carter as I storm past him. I'm so keyed up that I vaguely register his nod of acknowledgment.

Why the fuck is Reese in my club after I warned him not to be, and how in the fuck did Bailey, of all people, end up with him? My biggest nightmare come to life is happening somewhere in my fucking club.

When I reach Reese's typical room, I throw open the curtain and freeze. Bailey is lying on the floor with Reese next to her, her pale face in his lap. I fall to my knees on the other side. She's not moving. My hands fly to her neck, checking for a pulse. It's barely there.

"What did you give her!" I scream.

"N-Nothing," he stammers. "I gave her nothing." His hands are squeezing hers, "Please, chwaer, wake up. Please don't die." A silent sob leaves his mouth as he tries to shake her.

"Move, Reese."

"I can't. She can't leave me. Chwaer, you can't leave me." His eyes are crazy, Lost in a memory. Lost in a horror. One that I'm all too familiar with.

I'm having déjà vu. I feel like I'm in a nightmare reliving the night Alexa died. Except this isn't Alexa. It's Bailey. My Bailey. The girl I'm falling for, and it's my fault. I let this happen.

I fumble with my phone and dial 911.

"Help. I need an ambulance." Carter takes the phone from me, and I continue to hold her.

I vaguely recall being pushed out of the way, and Bailey being torn from my arms. The paramedics whisk her out of the room, and I just sit here. I'm paralyzed to the spot. This can't be happening. I promised I'd take care of her.

A sob breaks from my chest. I sit on the cold floor with my head in my hands and sob. I feel someone place their hand on my shoulder and give it a gentle squeeze.

"You've got to go to her, Drew. She needs you at the hospital."

I look up into Carter's sympathetic gaze. I don't deserve his pity. "She wouldn't want me there. I've failed her."

"You haven't failed anyone. She made her own choices. Piss-poor choices at that. It was a misunderstanding, and instead of being an adult and talking it out, she made a terrible decision. That's on her, Drew, not you."

I'm looking at Carter for what feels like the first time. His stone-faced features tell me everything I need to know. He doesn't blame me.

"Is she . . . Is she . . . ?" I can't even bring myself to say the words.

"I honestly don't know, man. She looked pretty bad, but from what I could gather, she was stable. Go to her."

I don't give myself another second to think. I run out the door to her.

chapter forty-three

Drew

I RUSH INTO THE EMERGENCY ROOM WAITING AREA, AND I immediately see Harper pacing. Carter must have called her. Or maybe she's listed as the next of kin for Bailey. It feels like I am being stabbed in the chest as I move closer to her. She sees me approach, and her face goes red with anger.

"What the hell are you doing here, Drew?" Her hands start pounding into my chest. I allow her to take her fear and anger out on me. I deserve that, and so much more.

"What did you do to her?" Harper is yelling through her sobs. "Isn't it enough you ruined some other girl's life . . . Now you ruined my sister's."

"How do you know about that?" It's not the right time to interrogate her, but I can't help it.

"Cal told me." Her eyes are narrowed on me. I nod.

"I'm sorry, Harper. It was a misun—"

"Stop." She holds her hand up in front of my face. "Stop right there. I do not want to hear any of your excuses. I don't care what happened. All I know is my baby sister is in the hospital, and I know it's because of you. Sure, Bailey has made mistakes in the past, but this . . . she was clean. I'm betting it's you. So, don't fucking tell me you're sorry. I trusted you to take care of her," she screeches.

I wrap her in my arms and console her the only way I can. "Shh. I would never intentionally do anything to hurt her, Harper. I know you don't want to believe me. She was gone before I could stop her. By the time I found her, it was too late."

She stiffens.

"When she gets better, and she will get better . . . just please . . . understand, what she thinks happened isn't true. Everything will be okay."

She relaxes in my arms, and I let her cry.

I know she blames this on me, and she's right, but it's obvious she needs support and doesn't care where she gets it from.

Her mother comes rushing into the ER and immediately starts barreling Harper with questions. I try my hardest to stay out of sight. I've never met Mrs. Jameson, and I certainly didn't want the first time to be in a hospital under such shitty circumstances. I sit in my chair, furtively bouncing my knee. If the goddamn doctors don't come out with some news soon, I'm going to tear this place down.

"How is she? Can we see her?" Her mom asks before turning to me, looking at me questioningly. "Who the hell are you?"

"Mom, this is Drew Lawson. He's the owner of the club. He was there . . ."

I hate how that one sentence minimizes what I am to Bailey. She's everything and I'm tired of hiding it.

"I'm her boyfriend."

Harper gasps at my declaration.

Her mom's eyes widen, but she quickly rights herself, standing taller.

"Then you better stay to hear this," she says, turning back toward Harper. "They said she was having a seizure. Do you know what happened?"

"They haven't said much," Harper answers, looking at me out of the corner of her eye.

I step forward, my tongue heavy, but I swallow and force myself to speak. "Bailey was upset—" I take a deep breath. "She was drinking at my bar. I don't know much more than that."

"Why was she upset? Why was my baby drinking?" her mother cries. Then she stops herself, narrowing her eyes and pointing a finger at me. "You did this." Mrs. Jameson doesn't ask, she accuses. "You and that god-awful club did this to my baby girl." She looks ready to commit murder, which is different from what I expected after Bailey told me about her.

In truth, if Bailey wasn't in that hospital bed, I'd tell this woman just where to go. I'd blame her for it all. If she weren't so damn consumed with herself and money, maybe her daughter never would've turned to drugs to begin with.

No matter how badly she needs to hear that, I don't say a word of it. It's not the time or the place. Not while Bailey is possibly fighting for her life.

"Mom, stop. His club happens to be one of the cleanest clubs in the city. He doesn't condone drug use. This has nothing to do with him." Her lies feel like sharp daggers stabbing into my gut.

With nothing more to say, I start to pace.

My feet pound the linoleum as I walk back and forth through the small waiting room.

I'm not sure how much time has passed before the door across the room opens. All of us stop.

Hell, time might have stopped too.

I can feel how my pulse accelerates as a man, who appears in scrubs, walks toward Harper.

"Mrs. Jameson?"

"Yes. This is Bailey's mother."

"I'm Dr. Bell, I treated your daughter. Would you like to go to a more comfortable place to talk?"

Mrs. Jameson looks warily in my direction and then at the doctor. "Please. Tell us she's going to be all right."

"She's stable."

"Can we see her?"

"Right now, she's being observed. As I'm sure you know, Bailey came in under the influence." The doctor looks toward me, and I'm sure this is when they kick me out.

"What aren't you telling us?"

"We ran her bloodwork. Along with alcohol, there was an array of drugs found in her system."

"Drugs . . . ?"

"We found—" The doctor talks, but it feels like I'm stuck in quicksand, or maybe like I'm drowning in an ocean. I can hear the words, but they sound muffled. I knew she went to find Reese to get drunk, but I never thought Bailey would revert to drugs. It hurts to breathe, knowing that I pushed her. That I broke her. I shake my head. It wasn't you. She made her choice. She decided to do drugs. Maybe I was the catalyst, but this rests on her. No matter what she thought.

"She has a long road ahead of her. She's sleeping, and we want it to stay that way, so for right now, we want her visitors limited to two at a time and family only. You won't be permitted to stay in her room for more than ten minutes. I'll have my nurse get you when it's a good time."

"Thank you, Dr. Bell."

I head back to my seat and resume bouncing my knee. It's the only comfort I have at this moment.

I feel sick.

I didn't stop Alexa that night, and because of my actions, another person I care about is fighting for their lives. I've tried my hardest to keep my club clean, but it's a club. Drugs and nightclubs go hand in hand, despite my best efforts, and that's never going to change.

I hear someone sit beside me, but I don't bother looking up.

"You can go home, you know. You won't be able to see her

anytime soon. You stink. Go take a shower." Harper tries to lighten the mood, but I just can't.

"I'm not going anywhere. I'll sit in this damn waiting room until she's released." I look up to find her studying me.

"You care about her." It's not a question.

"I love her." I don't say more because what more is there to say. I haven't even wrapped my head around my own feelings yet, but I know Bailey is my world.

"What really happened tonight? Why do I feel like you aren't telling me everything?"

I look at her long and hard. She's the opposite of Bailey, yet I can see the love in her eyes. It makes my heart hurt.

"As much as I want to tell you, Harper, I need to tell Bailey first. However, that being said, I heard what the doctor said. She had drugs in her system. The first sign of trouble, and she reverted back to her old habits. You need to be ready. When she gets better, you need to be prepared to send her somewhere. I know you know about her past, but as someone who has lost someone important to them, she needs help. No matter what she says, she won't get better on her own. Don't let this happen again."

She looks like I've slapped her.

"What do I tell my mother? How do I tell her I knew but never told anyone?"

She clearly only knew the surface of her sister's habits. Bailey said as much, but I assumed her family would have at least suspected. How the hell had she kept something like that a secret from her mother?

"I'm scared, Drew. I can't lose her." She begins to cry.

I grab her hand to offer a semblance of support. "I'll help. I'll get you the information on the best inpatient facility around. She's going to get better. But I have to tell you that this is partially my fault. She walked in on something that looked bad. It wasn't what she thought, but she didn't give me the chance to explain." She gives me a wary look.

"I swear to you, Harper, I would never hurt Bailey. I was ambushed by an employee, and Bailey walked in at the worst time possible. I love her." As soon as I say the words, I know they are true. I feel them in my soul. "I'm not sure how it happened, but she's changed my world."

She gives my hand a squeeze, then gives me a very stern look. "I don't blame you for this, Drew, but I can tell you blame yourself regardless of what you're saying. You've been through so much and now this. I just . . . Ugh. I don't know what I'm trying to say, but I do know that Bailey has to get better."

"She will, Harper. For now, you should get some rest. You smell a little too." She giggles. "Where's Cal?" I ask, noticing his absence. She lowers her gaze to the floor.

"He's stuck in a meeting out of town. He said he'll try to make it here this evening."

Fucking asshat.

"I know it's not my place, but I think that's bullshit. There isn't anything more important than being here for you. If he loves you, he'd be here." She stiffens.

"He does love me. I told him to take care of his stuff," she says defensively. I throw my hands up in surrender.

"I'm just saying. You need support, and he should be here." A tear slides down her cheek. I reach out and wipe it away. "Go get some rest, Harper. There isn't anything you can do for her right now either. She'd want you to take care of yourself."

"Okay," she whimpers.

I release her hand and stand.

"Where are you going?" she questions.

I throw her the best smirk I can manage. "I'm going to take that shower you said I need. Then I'm going to make some calls and get some things lined up for Bailey."

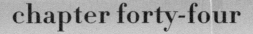

chapter forty-four

Bailey

MY EYELIDS FLUTTER. I'M FIGHTING WITH EVERY OUNCE OF strength I have to open them. Hazy light filters in through the barely visible crack. But the exertion is too much, and darkness descends yet again.

Where am I? How did I get here?

Soft muffles scratch at my subconscious, but I can't make out words or decipher who the voice belongs to. My brain flips through a series of memories like flashes of light.

Standing in my apartment.

Heading to the club.

Drew.

Monica . . .

Monica. That's why I'm here.

Memories crash down upon me. Suffocate me. Seeing Drew with Monica, finding Reese . . .

Drinking.

Drinking until I forgot.

Then what?

My memory is hazy. It hurts too much to think.

I saw Reese . . .

He took me to the bar. The private one in the VIP section.

Monica was there.

My back muscles tense as my fists clench.

She poured us drinks.

Lots and lots of drinks. And then it did its job. It faded. Everything faded.

Did I pass out? Is that why I'm here? No. There's more . . .

Think, Bailey.

What happened after you drank?

You saw Drew coming. Yes, that's what happened. I saw him looking for me. Reese led me to his private table.

My eyes flutter open, every part of my body quivers.

Am I hurt? I try to move my arms, but they feel too heavy to lift.

The door opens, and I see a doctor walking in.

"Hello, Ms. Jameson, I'm Dr. Bell."

"Is everything okay?" I croak out.

"How are you feeling?" he asks, approaching my bed with a clipboard.

"I'm fine. What's going on?"

"Due to the tox report we ran, there might be some questions that need to be asked."

Tox screen?

"What do you mean, tox report?" I know I drank, but this man's words make no sense. "Why would I need to have a tox screen run?"

"When you came in, you weren't responsive. Your alcohol level was three times the normal limit, but it was the drugs that had us worried."

"The drugs?"

"Yes, we found cocaine as well as narcotic painkillers in your system."

"I don't understand," I croak out, because I truly don't. I didn't do drugs.

I wouldn't have done them.

Would I?

chapter forty-five

Drew

I SIT QUIETLY IN THIS CHAIR, WAITING FOR MY TURN TO SEE her. We've been told she can have visitors for a short period. At first, I wasn't going to be allowed in as I'm not family, but since I'm fronting the hefty bill for the rehab facility in Arizona, her sister pulled some strings and put me on the list.

I have no idea what I'm going to say to her. The question of why comes to mind, but I know why. Monica. Well, in all fairness, what she walked in on probably looked like I was a willing participant. Regardless, there is no reason big enough to ever be in this position. As much as I care about her, and I do, very much, I can't have something like this happen ever again.

"Drew."

I look up to see Harper standing above me. She looks conflicted. I cock my head to study her.

"What's up?"

She continues to stare at me. The look of contemplation on her face has me anxious.

"She doesn't want to see you."

The truth of those words hurts more than if she'd slapped me across the face.

"I don't know why she's being so stubborn. I told her it

wasn't your fault and she needs to hear you out. I don't feel like it's my place to set her straight. She needs to hear it from you. I—"

I cut her off. She's rambling, and as much as I appreciate her struggle to make me feel better, I don't need her to soften the blow. The damage has been done, and it was served on a silver platter courtesy of Bailey.

"It's fine, Harper. If she doesn't want to talk to me, it's okay. As long as she's going to be all right, I'll survive." I get up to head out, but Harper stops me.

"Drew, don't go. She'll come around. I think she just doesn't want you to see her like this. She's mortified. She says she doesn't remember taking drugs. She swears she didn't, but the tests don't lie, and now she's finally starting to understand that. She's embarrassed."

"I'm okay. Hopefully, she'll come around. For now, I'm going to get going. I have some more arrangements to make for her relocation to Serenity Vista. Call if anything happens?"

"Of course." She gives me a sobering stare. "Thank you so much for saving my sister." She rushes forward and envelops me in a hug. I squeeze her back.

As soon as I hit the highway, I dial the club. Carter answers on the second ring. "Silver, how can I help you?"

"Carter, it's Drew."

"Man, how is she? I've been a wreck over here."

"She's doing all right. You'll be able to see her tomorrow if you want."

"Of course, I want to see her. I'm freaking out," Carter barks.

"I know. Listen, can you do me a favor and hold down the fort tonight? I need to take a personal day."

"You're the boss. I've got everything under control over here. Some guy named Mathis called about an hour ago. He said he was returning your call."

Shit. I hope that's all he said. I haven't had a chance to tell anyone my plans. He was supposed to call my cell.

Mathis is a guy I met in boarding school. I heard around town he was shopping buildings, looking to start a new club. He owns clubs around the world, so I reached out to him about buying Silver. The place is a money horse, and it would be a waste to sell to anyone else. There is no need for Mathis to have competition when I just want out. He's a decent guy, and that's what Silver needs.

He will pay top dollar, and the transaction will happen quickly and without hassle. The best part is that he has already agreed to keep all my staff. It's a no-brainer. We just have some last-minute details to work out.

"Anything else?" I ask, hoping for a big no.

"That's all. Oh, and Drew? Monica put in her resignation."

I laugh at the pure audacity of that girl. "She was fired, Carter. There is no resignation. Can you make sure that if anyone calls for a reference for that girl, you tell them to call me directly?"

"Sure thing. Take it easy and kiss my girl for me."

I hang up, completely wiped out. I'm so tired, but I have a lot of work to do. But first there is someone I need to see.

———— •◦• ————

I pull up to the gated community of Long Cove. The attendant asks for my pass in which I advise him why I'm here.

"Name please?"

"Drew Lawson," I say, knowing that my name is still on that list. Nobody ever updates their permanent visitor list unless there's a stalking situation.

"Have a good day, Mr. Lawson."

I drive up the road until I find 1680 Romalade Drive. It's been some time since I've been here, and it was under very similar circumstances. This time, I plan to leave with a very different outcome.

Marla answers the door with a look of shock marring her face. "Drew. What can I do for you?"

"Hello, Marla. Can I come in?" My voice is not pleasant. This woman won't even care what I have come for. She's too concerned about herself to bother worrying about Reese.

"I just wanted to talk to you about Reese and getting him help."

She just stares at me with a look of boredom.

"Why would you want to waste your time talking about something so pointless? Reese will never give up his drinking and drugs."

The look of disgust must be evident on my face because she scoffs. "Come on, Drew. This is Reese we're talking about. If Alexa's death wasn't enough to wake him up, he's a lost cause," she says flippantly.

"I think he needs help."

"And what do you think I can do about it?"

God, I hate this wretched woman. I can understand why Reese is so fucked up. But as much as I want to tell her to go fuck herself, it's not worth it.

"Well, I just thought you should know . . . He was involved—"

"I don't care. I'm done with this conversation. We're heading out to the Cayman Islands in two days. I have too much to do to worry about Reese."

I shake my head. Her son could be the one lying in the hospital from a drug overdose, and she wouldn't care. It's sick. They are sick. I have nothing left to say, so I turn and walk out.

chapter forty-six

Bailey

I'M STARING OUT THE WINDOW, WATCHING THE RAIN TRICKLE down the windowpane, when I hear a low cough reverberate around the room. Pulling my focus away from the outside, I sweep my gaze over to the door where the sound is coming from. Harper stands there. Her body is stiff, unmoving, and I can see her chest vibrating through deep breaths.

"Can I come in?" she asks. She doesn't wait for me to answer as she inches her way farther into the room.

"Hi." My words come out sheepish. My teeth gnaw at my lower lip as I think of something to say, but I don't know where to start. We spoke earlier today, but now, as every second passes, I'm at a loss for words.

"I-I'm sorry. I should have told you about Drew and me. I should have come to you instead of drinking. Instead of taking . . ." My words dry on my tongue. They feel heavy. It's as though I have rocks in my mouth and can't speak the words. "I'm just sorry."

I apologized before, but there are not enough ways to say sorry to make up for what I have done. For what I have put her through, for what I've put my mom through. Even though I can't remember, Harper was right; a test doesn't lie.

If the test says I did drugs, then I did, regardless of whether I was too drunk to remember.

The night is a blur.

I was hurt, angry, and worse, wasted. I made not one but two awful decisions that night.

I can barely remember being with Reese, let alone doing drugs with him at his VIP table, but I'm sure that's where it happened.

I feel sick to my stomach.

Regret sits heavy in my heart. As much as I try, I can't remember, and it's making me tremble with fear.

What if I had waited at home for Drew?

What if I never went to check on him that night?

I shake my head back and forth, refusing to let myself think about it. It didn't happen.

Regardless of how hard I try to push the thoughts away, the damage is done.

Tears prick the backs of my eyelids and then slowly trail down my cheeks. My cold finger swipes across my face, wiping away the moisture that has collected.

Harper takes a seat in the metal chair adjacent to my bed and places her hand on my arm. "You okay, Bae? We need to tal—"

I start to shake my head because I don't want to talk about it. Not now. Not when it's still fresh. Not when it feels like a serrated knife has cut through my skin and pulled me apart, leaving me open and bleeding all over the floor.

"Bailey." Her voice comes out more forceful than before, and I know we have to do this. "I think you need to hear him out."

"I can't . . ." Tears begin to come in earnest as I envision his body pressed against Monica.

"Bailey, it's not what you think."

"I know what I saw. I can't look at him right now, let alone talk to him. I just can't."

"Listen to me. I'm not one to defend Drew, but he explained what happened."

"He explained that he was about to have sex with Monica?" I bite out.

"That's not what happened. She came on to him. She ambushed him, Bae. You just walked in—"

"I can't believe you believed him. God, Harper. I saw her. I saw her naked!"

Harper's eyes widen, her surprise evident. Guess he forgot to mention that tiny piece of information.

"Oh, did he not tell you that Monica the whore was butt-ass naked while kissing him?"

"No, Bailey. He told me he loves you, and you misunderstood."

My heart starts to pound in my chest at her words. I shake off the feelings threatening to rise. "He doesn't love me." He doesn't. "He cheated on me." He did. I keep repeating those words in my head, trying to hold on to my anger. Anger is easier to handle. With anger, it's easier to walk away, and I need to get as far away from Drew and his club as I can.

"I think you should hear him out."

"No, absolutely not. I don't care what you say. He doesn't love me, so there's no reason to see him."

"If he didn't love you, if he didn't care, why is he paying for your—" She stops herself mid-sentence, placing her hand across her mouth to silence her words.

"Paying for my what?" Her hand quivers, but she doesn't speak. "My what, Harper?"

She drops her hands, placing them on her hips, her chin turned up. "Your rehab, Bailey. Drew is paying for your rehab."

My stomach drops as I let out a soft gasp. "He's-he's paying for my rehab?" I stutter out, shock flying through me. I'm caught completely off guard by this. Why would he do that? Guilt? Was he paying because of guilt?

"Why would he pay, Harper? Is it because he feels guilty?" I search her face for the answers I'm scared to find.

"No. Trust me, I would never lie to you. I saw his face. I saw his eyes. He loves you. There was no lie." Her voice fades into a hushed stillness. I can see unshed tears glistening in her eyes. "He loves you."

"He loves me?" I ask softly, my voice rough with emotion.

"Yeah." She nods while grabbing my hand and giving me a sad smile. "He does."

"What do I do? Do I speak to him?" My eyes close, and after taking a deep breath, I reopen them and look into Harper's eyes. Her gaze is soft and full of emotion.

"I think you need rest. To heal more. As much as I know you should talk to him, he's not here right now. He left to take care of some things. Truth? I don't think you are strong enough at the moment anyway. I think just before you're discharged might be better, so I say you rest now. Clear your head a bit more, and then you can say goodbye."

I can feel my heart break. It breaks into a million tiny pieces for everything I have done and for the pain I must have caused everyone. The familiar itch spreads through my limbs, and I realize Harper's right. I'm not strong enough to see him today. I'm not sure when I will be. Right now, I need to take care of me. I need to heal. When I'm ready, he will be there.

"Okay. You're right. I agree. When do I leave?"

"As soon as the doctors say you're free to go. Everything's already been taken care of." She squeezes my hand in hers. "We'll get through this. Okay? Together. No more secrets. I love you, and I'm here for you."

I smile a tight smile back and then close my eyes. I can do this.

A knock on the door has my eyelids opening. My mother stands in the doorway, looking like hell.

"Hi, Mom," I say weakly.

My mother rushes to the side of my bed, sobbing. Harper walks around, placing her arms over our mom's shoulders in comfort. "I-I was so scared. Why? Why would you do this, Bailey?"

Alta Jameson is the coldest woman I know. Seeing her cry is breaking me even more. She's never shown this much affection for me in all my years.

"I-I've struggled with pills before." My words cause her to cry harder. "I don't remember taking the drugs . . . It doesn't matter because I did. And that fact alone means I need more help than NA can give me."

That's the truth. I might not remember taking the drugs, but regardless, I did. It has always been my crutch. When things got bad, I used. It seems all it took was a few shots, and I fell.

"I don't understand. How could we not know? How?"

"It was hidden well. I moved away to hide all the trouble I was in. You were busy. You couldn't have known." I try to reassure her, but my words seem to only upset her more.

"It's my fault. I didn't spend enough time with you. I was always . . ." She stops herself as she sobs into my sister's shoulder.

I study my mother's face, the lines of aging evident and deep right now. The harsh lines of years of hard work have me feeling ashamed.

"I'm sorry," I whisper. She looks at me long and hard.

"I'm sorry I failed you. I should've known what was going on. You are our number one priority along with your sister, and I failed you." Her eyes well up, and I can't handle it.

I place my hand on her arm, squeezing lightly.

"Things were hard for all of us after Dad died. I don't blame you, Mom. I just fell into the wrong crowd, and then I got into the accident . . ."

"But I should've noticed!" she bellows, causing my sister to lift her head and scowl at her.

"Shh, you'll get us kicked out," she scolds.

"We should've known," she repeats.

"It's over. I need you to be here for me and help me get better. That's all I want."

"We'll be here. We aren't leaving you," she promises. I take in my mother and my sister. Even though we may be broken and battered, it feels like we could be a mighty force coming together to fight for one another.

chapter forty-seven

Drew

I'M PACING YET AGAIN.

Time seems to be standing still as I wait for word on Bailey. I'm supposed to be working, but I can't. She's all I can think of. All I see when I close my eyes.

As if conjured by my thoughts, my phone rings.

I swipe the screen once I see who it is.

"She's ready to see you," Harper says through the line.

It's been a week since I saw her. Harper had asked that I give Bailey space, so I've stayed away. I've called every day for an update, and today she's finally ready. The doctors say her concussion is gone, and she's now strong enough to be moved to the facility in Arizona for rehab.

"Okay. Should I come to the hospital?"

"No, she's being discharged within the hour. Why don't you come to my house and sit with her while I run out and get some last-minute things for our trip?"

"Just text me when you're there, and I'll head that way. I have some errands to run, but everything is set at Serenity Vista. You'll have to sign her in and finish the paperwork, but all the financials have been taken care of. She should have the best of everything there."

"Thank you, Drew. Seriously. You don't know how much this means to us." I hear her sniffles on the other line. The emotion in her voice is a testament to how much she loves Bailey. It makes me happy to know she has the support system she's going to need to get better.

"Anytime, Harper. Take care of her."

"Always." I hear the phone click. No goodbyes necessary.

I have grown to admire Harper in ways I never would have imagined. She's a great sister and not a bad person. I think her dickhead fiancé brings out the worst in her. He never made it to the hospital. Fucking jackass couldn't even support Harper during a family crisis.

I swing by the club to quickly do some paperwork. We're in the final closing stages for the club, and it's time I start telling the employees what's going down. Not that it fucking matters. They all have their jobs firmly secured.

Three hours later, I get a text summoning me to Harper's. I sit in the back of my Town Car with frayed nerves paralyzing me. I don't know what to say to Bailey. How will she look? Frail? Ghostly? Or will she be my Bailey?

I rap on the door twice before it swings open, revealing a very eager-looking Harper. "What took you so long?" she questions.

"I got here as soon as I could. Go do your errands. Where is she?"

"She's in the far room watching Netflix. She's good, Drew. You don't have to look so nervous." She chuckles, and I scoff.

"I'm not nervous."

She gives me the "oh, really" look.

"Okay. I'm petrified, but don't say a word."

She laughs lightly. "Just be honest with her. Tell her how you feel. She needs to hear how scared you were. She needs to know you're angry because, Drew, you have every right to be. I'm angry. Her actions affected all of us, but you finding her like that. I can't imagine what that's done to you." She shakes off the images that I'm sure are filtering through her mind.

"Go. You have stuff to do, and I can't keep delaying the inevitable."

She pats me on the shoulder and walks out, throwing, "Good luck," over her shoulder.

I walk slowly down the hallway. When I come to the opening of the family room, I silently peer around the corner to see Bailey sitting peacefully, watching some god-awful vampire show. She looks good, all things considered. I take a moment to watch her. She doesn't know I'm here, and it allows me a few seconds to just see her. This very second, she's the girl I fell in love with, and she's alive.

Thank God, she's alive.

She throws her head back and laughs at something said on the show, but I have no clue what it was. My entire focus is on her and her alone. God, she's gorgeous. Breathtakingly fucking beautiful. I want to wrap her in my arms and take her out of here. I want to forget all the shit and just go live, but I can't. We can't go back. Everything is different now.

I love her but I can't have her.

I came here tonight not knowing what I was going to say, but it's clear now. I'm here to let her go. They say if you love something, set it free, right? I guess that fucking saying is about to have a whole new meaning for me, and it's already breaking me.

chapter forty-eight

Bailey

A SOFT NOISE PULLS ME FROM THE SHOW I'M WATCHING. I turn my gaze to the side of the room and see Drew standing by the doorframe. His lean, sculpted body is resting against the wood. One foot is propped behind him, and his arms are crossed against his chest. A smoldering gaze locks with mine. My lips tighten, offering him a timid smile.

"What are you doing here?" I ask. I'm not sure why I ask since I did tell Harper I wanted to see him and say goodbye. "I mean . . . I mean . . ." God, why am I so nervous? "What are you doing here so soon? I wasn't expecting you for a few hours."

His gaze continues to unnerve me, my heart pounding in my chest, waiting for him to speak.

"As soon as I could get away from what I was doing, I came. Hope that's okay?" His eyes bore into mine. It unnerves me.

"Yeah, of course." I bite down on my lower lip. "Thank you for coming."

"Of course, Bailey. I told you, if you needed me, I'd be here."

"I know. I just—"

He raises his hand to stop me from speaking. "You didn't think after what went down, I would still come? Of course, I would, Bailey. I love you."

His admission knocks the wind out of my lungs. Breathing becomes more difficult as I try to think of a response.

"I know things happened. I know you don't know what to believe. I get it. I know it's no secret I slept around, and even that I once fooled around with Monica. I wasn't looking for anything before I met you, and I haven't been with anyone since we've been together. What you saw was Monica throwing herself on me. I know your sister told you this, but I wanted you to hear it from me. I love you, Bailey, and I would never do that to you."

"I know. I know that now." A tear falls down my cheek. "Drew, I'm so sorry. I'm so sorry for not trusting you, for finding Reese . . ." Dampness continues to slide down my cheek, and I swipe away at it, drying my face. "I can't remember why. I don't remember anything . . . but, god, I'm so sorry for hurting you and making you relive . . ."

A fine line forms between his brows as he gathers his thoughts. His left hand runs through his hair, then he pulls his hand away and covers his eyes.

"Yes, Bailey, and that's why, as much as I love you, I can't do this anymore. I wanted to save you, but I will always fail if you can't save yourself."

My eyes blink rapidly as I think about what he just said. Sadness courses through my veins, killing any joy I had moments ago. What does this mean? Have I lost him forever? Will he ever want to try again? But no matter what I feel and how miserable these unknowns make me, I know he's right. I might not remember taking the drugs, but I did.

Regardless if it was a drunken mistake, I made that mistake. Everything he says is right. If all it takes is a few shots to make me go backward, I need more help. I need to get the help I should have gotten a long time ago.

Rehab is the best place for me right now.

I inhale deeply, and after a series of breaths, I finally gather the strength to speak.

"I understand that now. I know I need to get better." I look up and find him looking intently at me. "I'll get better for you."

"No, Bailey. Get better for you. If you do this for me, you're only setting yourself up for failure. Setting yourself up to relapse again. Only for you, okay?"

"Okay, Drew. You're right. I'll get healthy for me. But then what? If-when I get better?"

"I don't know, Bae. I really don't know."

The uncertainty in his voice is my undoing, and I burst into sobs. He crosses the room quickly and takes me in his arms.

"Shh. It's going to be okay. You're going to be okay."

I want to plead with him not to let me go. To stay with me. That I love him, but I hold it all in. Drew has already done so much for me. I can't burden him with any more. I have to leave and heal myself, and this is the moment when I'll start. This is the moment I will change my life.

His hand reaches under my eyes and collects the wetness gathering with his fingertips. My gaze focuses on the ceiling, willing the tears to stop falling. When I know no more will fall, I cast my eyes back to his. His gaze is hollow and raw. This is not the same man I met that first day at the club. I need to be strong for him.

No.

I need to be strong for me.

After a few minutes of Drew holding me, I feel him place a gentle kiss on the top of my head and pull away.

"I have to go, Bae. You can do this. I know you're strong enough."

"Bye, Drew," I whisper. My mouth is dry from the emotions choking me.

"Goodbye, Bailey."

I watch as he gets up.

I watch as he walks toward the door and walks out of my life.

chapter forty-nine

Drew

Broken.

I feel completely, utterly, fucking broken. Saying good-bye, whether it be for the short term or the long haul, was the hardest thing I've had to do in a long time.

As much as I'd like to say I was being selfless, that's a fucking lie. I was being the most selfish bastard I've ever known.

I can't do it. I can't be around while she tries to get better. I can't save her, and I feel helpless, which means I can't do it anymore.

I get into the car and pound my fists into the steering wheel. A growl breaks through my throat as I release frustration like I've never felt before. Agony that I didn't know could exist.

I love her. I am one hundred percent in love with that girl, and not to be able to have her is excruciating.

I pull myself together and drive to the club. I have business to attend to. My life has to move forward, and the steps I've put into place are just the beginning.

As I walk through the door of the club, the realization that this will likely be one of the last times I do so hits me hard. It's not that I will miss the nightclub. It's the fact that everything changes.

I see my staff sitting around and can only imagine the

speculation circulating through the place. They were told that an emergency mandatory meeting was being held, and that if they didn't make it, not to come back. It's no secret about what went down with Bailey and Reese. Everyone knows. I've heard some of the rumors, and I know everyone is scared.

"Relax," I say with a smile. I'm hoping this helps to ease everyone's worries. When I see a few shoulders sag in relief, I know it worked.

"I can see you all know something is brewing. Let me just tell you, it's not bad. In fact, I believe the coming changes will make Silver better. I also know these changes will benefit all of you." The silence is so thick it's palpable, but I continue.

"I'm selling the club. Silver will be under the ownership of a world-renowned club owner named Mathis."

There is a collective gasp, and the room fills with murmurings and panic. I raise my hands to hush the crowd.

"You guys, give me a minute to finish."

The room slowly quiets, and all eyes turn to me, beckoning me to continue.

"Mathis is a private investor, and he has been seeking out space to branch out in the city with his own nightclub. Guys, he's savvy and has unlimited funds. The money he's looking to invest is leaps and bounds above what I possess. If we were to go toe to toe with his club, we'd go under or, at the very least, feel a significant cut in business. By making a deal with him and selling this club, I saved all your jobs and prevented competition."

Hands fly into the air. Everyone has questions, which I anticipated, but this level is beyond my scope. This is a club. These jobs should be steppingstones. Looking out into the faces of my employees, I see that this is so much more to them.

I point at one girl. "Yes, Amanda?"

"When you say you saved our jobs, do you mean we won't be let go?"

"Yes, that's what I said. Mathis and I negotiated the terms that every single one of you will keep your current jobs at the current pay rate. As long as you do your job well, you won't be going anywhere. Fuck up and you'll be out. It's as simple as that. Mathis isn't where he is today by being a pushover, but he's fair."

Hands begin to lower as the elephant in the room has been addressed. I answer a few more questions, mainly involving working conditions, etc. until Carter's hand goes up.

"Are you going to be okay, Drew?"

I contemplate how to answer his question. "Honestly, I'm not sure." I take a breath. It's now or never. "That's not true. For some time, I've needed a change, I'll be fine." It feels good to get that out in the open, to finally be able to start the next chapter of my life.

But when I look out at the club I've built from the ground up, the sentimentality hits me. This is it. It all ends tonight. The more I think about that reality, the lighter my chest becomes. It's strange. It's as if I can feel the weight of each brick slowly release me from the spot they've had me pinned to. This place wasn't what I really ever wanted. It was a prison sentence I imposed upon myself. It was the constant reminder of what I allowed to happen to Alexa. But after everything with Bailey, I now realize it wasn't my fault. I can't be held responsible for the decisions they made. With that realization, I feel free.

I smile a genuine smile, which elicits a confused look from Carter. "It's going to be epic."

I stick around to receive well wishes and answer any lingering questions before heading to my office to finish clearing it out.

This place holds such a battery of mixed emotions for me, but one thing's for sure. At the end of the day, I won't miss it. The cold, stark walls of this place hold nothing for me anymore.

For the first time, I'm in love, and fuck I can't have the one thing I want more than life. Bailey makes me feel and I'm actually afraid that no matter how strong our love is, we can't be together now and possibly not ever.

I finish packing the last of my stuff and head down to elicit some help from the barbacks. When I get to the bar, Carter and Austin are going on about something.

"What's up, guys?"

"Not much. Just don't go into room four. They are definitely fucking. I walked in and right back out." Carter is nonplused, but I'm majorly disgusted. Doesn't surprise me, though. I've been there, done that in another life.

"Jesus, well make sure to sterilize the shit out of that room before tomorrow." Shaking my head, I look at room four just in time to see the culprits walk out while adjusting their clothes. It takes a second for everything to register, but when it does, I see red.

Cal Loche, Harper's fiancé, is the culprit along with someone other than Harper. I don't even think. I just stalk toward him and grab the collar of his shirt. I'm up in his face before he can even register me.

"What the fuck, Drew? Get your fucking hands off me."

"You son of a bitch. Harper's off taking her sister, who almost died, to rehab, and you're out fucking around? You're a piece of shit."

"Like I care about her druggy sister. I'd have left her to die in the club."

My arm flies up, and my fist connects with his nose, sending blood splattering all over the whore who is just standing there idly watching. She screams as the first drops hit her.

"What the fuck, Drew? You fucking hit me!"

"If you ever talk about Bailey like that again, you won't walk. Are we clear?" He doesn't say anything. "Are. We. Clear?"

"You have some balls, man. I'll press charges."

"Good luck."

The girl finally speaks. "Excuse me, but you owe me money. I did my job, now I want to go home."

"Shut the fuck up, slut. I'll pay you when I'm good and ready. You'll stay put until I tell you otherwise."

"You've got to be fucking kidding me." He's spending his time with a prostitute.

At those words, Cal's head jerks to me with eyes wide as saucers. "Drew, man, you can't say anything. My parents, they'll cut off my trust if they find out."

"Break it off. I don't care what you need to say, but you and Harper are officially done. You get back together, and this whole interaction will be plastered on every tabloid in New York. You feel me?"

"Drew. I-I can't. I love Harper. I just need to switch it up sometimes. I'll change. I'll be good to her. I can't break off our engagement." He's hysterical at this point, and I love being in control.

"Take it or leave it. Mommy and Daddy take the trust, or you man up and let Harper be happy with someone who deserves her. Your call, but you better make it quick." I pull out my phone and act like I'm dialing.

"Okay-wait. Fine. I'll-I'll do it. Shit. This is going to break her."

"You should've thought about that before you fucked around with a whore."

"Hey, I'm right here," the prostitute says from the side.

"Get out of here, and if I see you again, I'll call the police and turn your skank ass in myself."

She huffs off leaving me with the sniveling Cal. With his head hung low, he groans, "Fuck this call to Harper is going to be a shitstorm."

I watch him slug off in satisfaction. Harper may hurt for a while, but she'll be much better off in the long run.

chapter fifty

Bailey

HARPER AND I ARRIVE IN ARIZONA ON FRIDAY AFTERNOON. The heat is sweltering, and I hope to God that this place has air-conditioning.

As we pull up, I see that Drew spared no expense. I can tell this place is amazing, and I haven't even walked inside yet. He clearly forgot I am a commoner. It looks like it was made for Hollywood royalty. I can't imagine many people could afford the opulence of Serenity Vista.

"Wow," Harper says beside me. "He hooked you up."

"He sure did. This place is incredible." My gaze lingers across what will be my home for the next thirty days. A large terra cotta house spans the distance, stretching out against the Arizona horizon. Cactuses and flowers that I imagine are indigenous to the locale are scattered across the property to make up the peaceful ambiance.

Harper squeezes my hand lightly. "Come on, let's see what this paradise has to offer."

And that's just what this is—paradise. Paradise hopefully not hiding the hell I imagine rehab should be.

We begin to push open the dark mahogany door when a friendly man offers to take my bag. This place really seems more like a fancy spa. Walking through the door, we are instantly greeted with a serene and calming atmosphere. Candles line the walls, and soft classical music plays over the surround sound.

As we walk farther into the lobby, a tall, lithe blonde gracefully strides over to us. "Hello, you must be Bailey. My name is Harmony."

Of course it is. She's probably the holistic life coach on staff. I want to roll my eyes, but I refrain. I need to be here. So instead, I lift my hand to meet her already extended hand.

"Hi, Harmony. This is my sister, Harper." I step back, allowing Harper to reach out with her hand.

"It's a pleasure meeting you as well, Harper. I'll be giving you both the tour of the property, and then I'll show Bailey to her room." She walks toward a set of double doors that must hold the treatment facilities.

"At Serenity Vista, we have a much different approach to healing. We treat the underlying issues that lead to your addiction, rather than just the substance that brought you to us. Ultimately, our goal while you are here is to find the root of the problem and focus there." Her lip turns upward, and her eyes crinkle as she smiles.

"That makes complete sense. It's pretty pointless just to put a Band-Aid on it," Harper agrees as she nods repeatedly. Harmony points at a room on the right as we continue our way down the hall.

"That way is our state-of-the-art spa. Inside, you will find every amenity your heart could desire, as well as a full staff including estheticians and a masseuse. Anything you need is at your disposal."

My mouth drops open. Wow. Drew really spared no expense. My heart tightens in my chest about how wrong I was. How I had let a misconception crush me. How I didn't have enough trust in him to seek the truth before I succumbed to my usual self-destructive tendencies.

"If you would like to see the spa now, it would be my pleasure." I shake my head, so we continue our path. "Right over here is the art studio. We find art is a great outlet for our guests' emotions."

She pushes open a large glass door, and we step inside. The room is spacious. There is a scattering of easels facing the glass retracting walls that face the outside patio. Through the glass, I can see more easels with an unobscured view of the mountain in the distance. It really is perfect.

Harmony leads us out onto the patio. In the distance, I see a group of women doing yoga. "We also hold daily workout classes outside, as well as meditation sessions. We have a full gym off the spa. We highly suggest that every guest takes a meditation session every day."

"That sounds wonderful. Doesn't it, Bae?"

I just nod, not able to voice my words as I'm too overcome with emotions. I still don't understand what I did to deserve this. If anything, Drew should have written me off completely and told me to fuck off. But instead, he has given me all the tools to heal myself, and for that, I will be forever grateful.

"How about therapy? Also, is Bailey allowed to call me?" Harper asks as we walk back inside to continue our tour.

"Each day, you will have one group session as well as a one on one. They are held in whichever location you feel the most comfortable. We feel that being connected to the outside world is essential to having long-lasting success, so we allow and encourage it. So yes, to answer your question, there are phone privileges. We find that if a problem arises, we are here to help. If we keep the guest cocooned in a bubble, the moment they reenter reality, they are often not equipped to handle the new pressure and have a tendency to regress."

"Perfect. That makes complete sense."

We continue our tour of the facility, and I'm floored by how perfect it is. Once we arrive in my private suite, my shoulders have finally loosened. This is going to be good.

"I'll give you a chance to say goodbye, and I'll return in an hour to see how you're adjusting. It was a pleasure meeting both of you." Harmony steps out of the room, and Harper turns to me.

"Wow. That's all I can say." She laughs.

"I know, right? This is crazy nice. I feel like I don't—"

Harper lifts her hand to cut me off. "Stop that thought right there. You need this, and no questioning anything past that, okay?"

"Okay."

"Need some help unpacking?" She starts toward my suitcase when her cell rings. She pulls it out of her purse and sends it to voicemail. One second later, it begins to ring again.

"Do you mind?" she asks, a fine line forming between her brows. "It's Cal. He's been trying to call me since last night. I had forty missed calls from him. He never calls me this much. Must be important." Her voice is tense.

"Why haven't you called him back?" I probe.

"I've been pretty busy trying to help my sister get to rehab. His stuff can wait," she says, irritated.

"Right now might be a good time to see what's going on." I press.

"Yeah, I better, or else he's going to keep blowing up my phone. I have to go anyway."

Walking over to me, Harper places a kiss on my forehead. "I'll see you soon." I nod. She smiles, heading toward the door to exit. Her phone begins to blare once more. "Cal, hold one second, okay?" She looks back at me. "I will call you the moment I'm back in New York. If you need anything, Bae, don't hesitate. I'll always be there for you. I love you."

"I know, and I love you, too. Thank you for everything. For

bringing me here for . . ." Tears begin to fall down my cheek, and I swipe them away. "Thank you, Harper."

Harper's lip turns upward, and she nods before placing the phone back to her ear. "Hey, sorry about that, baby. I miss you. I'm heading back home now." She grows quiet for a minute and then steps out of the room. I lie in my bed, and I think I can hear Harper's voice change when she says the words, "I don't understand," but before I can register the rest of the conversation, her voice fades into the distance.

chapter fifty-one

Bailey

THE FIRST NIGHT IS HARDER THAN I THOUGHT IT WOULD BE. I'm alone in my room, and without someone to distract me, I have too much time to think.

I know I shouldn't be thinking of that night, but I can't stop myself.

Drew says what I saw was wrong, and I didn't even let him explain.

Instead, I ran off.

Got drunk.

And high.

That's the part I keep getting tripped up on.

I don't remember getting high.

I've never resorted to drugs before.

How and why had I escalated, and if I don't remember, how will I ever train myself not to resort to it again?

I know the answer should be simple—don't drink.

Find another outlet. I plan to do that, but while I'm here, I also want to figure out my catalyst. If the going gets tough again, will I fail?

Even though I try to push the thoughts away, it consumes me. I pace the room for a while, and finally when the walls start to go blurry, I realize I'm ready to crash.

The next morning comes before I know it. As my lids flutter open, I sit up with a start. For a second, I forget where I am. Why I'm here.

But eventually, it all comes back to me. Every last twisted detail.

I had given in to the sinful temptation only drugs can have. I was weak.

But now regardless of everything, I'm going to get strong. I had tried on my own . . .

But I wasn't strong enough.

Now I am.

It's only a few hours later when I'm sitting in front of Dr. Roberts, the resident therapist. This is my first time talking to one. I'm not sure what to expect.

When she leans forward to the table and grabs a little recorder, my back tightens.

"Don't worry, Bailey, no one will hear this but me." It does nothing to ease the tension that is coiled inside me.

It's like a venomous snake ready to extend its neck and snap.

"Bailey, would you like to tell me why you're here?" she asks.

"You know why I'm here."

She places the recorder down but not before she flips it off. Then she leans back in her chair. Getting comfortable. Relaxed, the way she holds her body is as if she's my friend. Just someone who wants to chitchat.

"I do, and it's important you know why as well as what your expectations from treatment will be."

Her voice drops sugary sweet. Like a strawberry syrup one would put on a sundae. If I didn't know better, I'd think we were friends. My shoulders drop.

Her lax attitude penetrates my own uptight one, like a strange case of psychological osmosis.

"I fucked up. I thought I had it under control," I mutter out, embarrassed on how weak I was.

"And?"

"I didn't," I admit on a sigh.

"So why don't you start from the beginning then."

This place is nothing like I imagined, but it's exactly what I need.

It's not like all the rehab facilities you see on TV. Nope, not at all. Here, there are no crazy celebrities fighting and seducing each other.

No, this is very different.

This place reminds me of a luxury spa, and yes, there might be therapists on staff, but they act more like friends you would drink coffee with.

I spend my day getting massages, painting, reading, and yes, talking to the doctor.

But today we don't meet in her office. Instead, we are having herbal tea on the terrace.

The temperature is perfect. There is a light breeze in the air, and under the canopy where we sit, we have the perfect view of the gardens without the blaring sun beating down on us.

Dr. Roberts lifts her cup and takes a seat, and then she smiles. Yesterday, I told her my story. Today is when it will get harder.

Recounting facts is never the issue. It's the root of the problem that is.

Like a dead tree, you don't just cut the leaves. The whole thing must go, roots uplifted, that way you can plant something new.

I'm that tree. The work in progress, but hopefully, after I'm done here, I'll be able to grow.

"Tell me the way you felt that night. Tell me the way you felt all the nights."

"You can't possibly want me to go over every night I ever got drunk."

She lets out a chuckle. "Not every night, but how about the ones that stand out."

I lean forward in my chair, hands on the teacup. My fingers warm, and I continue to hold them there despite the heat.

A night that stands out . . .

Other than the obvious, I try to remember how I felt the last time I got high before.

"Helpless." I close my eyes. "Less than. A failure." My eyes open. "Not good enough. Rejected."

"And the night of the incident?" she asks.

"Helpless. Less than. A failure. Not good enough. Rejected," I repeat.

"I think we found your catalyst. Now to work on these feelings. To find the root . . ."

"The thing is, other than feeling those things, I don't remember why I decided to do drugs. Why I needed more to make me numb that time. In the past it was always pills. Never cocaine . . ."

"It could have been the alcohol."

"Wouldn't I remember now?" I ask.

"The mind is a complex place, sometimes we protect ourselves."

"You think not remembering taking drugs is a coping method?"

"It could be. You could have blacked it out for many reasons. Or"—she shrugs—"you were too impaired to remember. Either way, it doesn't matter. Without the proper tools, sobriety will be a lifelong battle."

I nod my head. I'm not sure what else to say. I sit back, not speaking. Time does pass, but it passes in an uncomfortable silence I wouldn't wish on anyone.

I don't have to stay silent for long because she starts firing off questions about my family. It's easy to talk about them. Much easier than talking about me.

At first, the days go by rather slow, but before I know it, a week has passed. For the first time in a long time, I feel refreshed. It's funny that it would take a stint in rehab to make me feel like this. But it's true, nonetheless. I feel like a new person.

Each day I work out. Each day I do yoga. I've learned how to meditate. Old Bailey would've laughed at all the stuff I've done. Making pottery would've been something I would've only done drunk with friends. But now I see that painting can be therapeutic.

New Bailey. Sober and clean Bailey has a better outlook on life.

It's only been one week, but it's as if my depleted battery is finally starting to charge and I can thank Drew for pushing me toward this.

With my therapist this past week, we reflected so much on my childhood.

We reflected on the fact that my catalyst stems from there. That I believe I'm worthless because of my mom. How after my father died, I felt I had no one. She was absent in my life, and instead of understanding it was her way of grieving, I thought it meant she didn't love me. That was why I started drinking. The pills followed next, after the accident. The blame I unfairly put on myself.

Rationally, I know it's true, but irrationally I'm still working hard to believe it wasn't my fault.

I am still trying to forgive myself for my part in it.

chapter fifty-two

Drew

TIME HAS MOVED REALLY FUCKING SLOWLY SINCE BAILEY has left.

I try to keep myself busy and with the impending sale of Silver, it shouldn't be hard, but it actually is.

Her presence is missing. Not just in my bed. Or in the club.

It's missing everywhere.

As much as I never want to walk into the club again, I have to. The paperwork is still being finalized. To make sure it doesn't fall through, I have to go in. I'm up earlier than normal today. It's only six. Normally, this would be the time that I'd be closing down the club and coming home, but a lot changed when I became involved with Bailey. Now, I'm up for the day.

First, I remove myself from my bed and head over to the bathroom. I turn the water on scalding hot.

This shit will need to burn me to make me feel anything.

As the water barrels down on me, I realize nothing will help. Not a shower.

Not the club.

There's a void from where Bailey should be.

Once I'm dressed, I leave my apartment and head to the club. Hours have passed, and there shouldn't be anyone there, just the people who work in the office. Maybe Carter. It only takes me about thirty minutes to get there, and when I do, the main room is empty. When I walk up the stairs, I hear voices.

"She was acting all cagey when I asked what she meant," one voice says.

"Cagey how?"

"She said she deserved it . . . but when I said *what,* all she said was it was her fall from grace, whatever that means."

"Do you think she was talking about Bailey . . . ?"

With that, I push the door open and storm into the room. They both are staring at me when I barge in. Their mouths are open, and their eyes are wide. They didn't expect me here today, clearly. When neither of them speaks, I step closer. I narrow my eyes and drill them with my stare.

"Who exactly said what? And what does this have to do with Bailey?"

It's Carter who speaks first. Stepping closer so I can see his face.

"Monica apparently made a comment . . ."

"Monica can talk all she wants. Nothing happened."

"Not about that," he says.

I cock my head. "Then what exactly did she say about Bailey?"

"She implied that the bitch got what was coming to her, and it was karma."

"Karma?"

"That's the thing that doesn't make sense. When Amanda asked what she meant, she didn't answer but was talking cryptically about Bailey's much-deserved fall from grace."

"She's a bitch, but I don't understand why you are talking about this."

Amanda steps forward. "It wasn't what she said . . . it's how she said it."

I step closer, standing right in front of her. "And how exactly did she say it?"

"As if she knew something I didn't."

I nod my head and then leave them to their gossip. Heading back down to the bar, I walk over to the VIP room. This is the first time I've been here since the night of Bailey and Reese's accident. It brings back too many awful memories. While I was upstairs, she was down here drinking. Why hadn't I followed her right away?

Because I thought she left. It never dawned on me that she would be here drinking.

The words Amanda said keep turning over in my mind. I'm not sure what to make of them.

With a shake of the head, I head into the room with the security cameras. I fire them up for that day.

I watch as Bailey storms down the stairs, then finds Reese and pulls him to the bar.

I switch to the VIP camera and watch as she proceeds to get drunk. Nothing on any of my cameras shows Bailey getting high or taking anything else.

Too bad I don't have any cameras behind the curtains of the VIP private rooms.

I rewind the camera, looking for anything from Reese.

Anything at all.

But I still see nothing.

The only thing I notice in the video is Monica's smug face. She looks like the cat that ate the canary.

I zoom in.

Watching her as she smiles a cool smile at Bailey. She's gloating. She's feeding into Bailey's insecurity, and with every smile, Bailey drinks more.

I continue to watch over and over again.

Torturing myself, I watch as Monica goads Bailey until Bailey can hardly walk.

As much as I want to be angry with Bailey for getting drunk and succumbing to the pressure from Reese, I can see that this is also my fault as well as Monica's.

On my fifth or sixth pass on the video, I notice something I never saw before.

Fuck.

I press stop.

I didn't just see what I thought I did.

Did I? My fist clenches.

I press record on the computer and then send the information to my email address.

Once it's completed recording, I storm out of the room.

There is only one person who can explain to me what the fuck is going on.

Monica.

chapter fifty-three

Drew

I DON'T WASTE ANY TIME GOING TO THE ADDRESS WE HAVE IN her file, and before I know it, my fist is banging on the door.

"Hold on," Monica shouts from inside. I expect her to say more as I hear her approach, but she swings the door open. "Drew." She smiles at me.

The smile is a seductive one. She thinks I'm here for her, but I'm only here for answers.

Answers only she can give.

"Come in," she coos.

I'm still standing in the hallway, but I know I won't get her to answer shit from here, so when she steps back, I enter.

I walk into her apartment, and I hear the door shut behind me.

My shoes echo on the wood floors until I'm standing in a tiny living room.

She looks around the space. It's not clean. It's actually a fucking mess.

"Sorry about—" She gestures to the pile of clothes on the couch. "If I knew you were coming . . ." She trails off.

"I'm not here to talk about clothes."

She places her hand on her hip, her posture going rigid at the sound of my voice.

"Why are you here, Drew?" she asks, taking a step back.

"Why don't you tell me why you think I'm here?"

Her eyes are wide. She's shocked, but when her mouth trembles, I know I was right.

"I-I don't know what you mean," she stutters.

"Now that's funny. Because I think you know exactly what I mean."

Her face grows pale, and I use that moment to whip out my phone from my back pocket.

Now it's my turn to approach her. She at least has the decency to appear scared. I would never hurt a girl, but ruin her . . . ?

That I can certainly do.

"I told you, you were done. To stay out of my life."

"Drew—"

I lift my hand to silence her. "Do not speak." I start to scroll through my phone, and then I hand it to her. "Watch this video, and then and only then, think long and hard on how you are going to respond."

Reluctantly, she takes my phone in her hand. When she sees the video I have filmed, her hand begins to shake. She is quick to rein in her reaction, though.

"I don't know what you think this is. Your drug addict girlfriend wanted to get drunk . . . I did exactly what she asked for."

I nod my head and take my phone from her hand. "So that's how you want to play it? Okay." I move to turn.

"Where are you going?"

"To the police."

"What?"

"Well, according to this video, a crime took place at my club, and since you have nothing to say . . ." I turn and walk toward the door.

"Wait."

I don't turn around. She still is speaking to my back.

"It—I—She deserved it!" she shouts, and that makes me finally look at her.

I lift the phone toward her. The image on the screen zoomed in. It's clear as day the exact moment it happens.

The moment in which Monica drugged her.

I smile at her. A sardonic smile. She blanches, her mouth opening and shutting to figure out what to say. She's trying to come up with a plausible excuse for what is depicted on the video as clear as day.

On the video, she slips drugs into both the drinks. It's not clear what she puts inside it, but I know its cocaine and pain killers from the tox report.

Now to figure out what to do about her.

Was she trying to kill Bailey and Reese?

"You slipped drugs in their drinks . . ." At my words, she does something I don't expect. She stands up straighter, taller, and she places her hands on her hips.

"I did." Her answer shocks me, and her lack of remorse even more.

"Very well, I'll be handing over the tapes to the authorities."

"Don't you want to know why?" She smirks.

"I can't give a flying fuck why."

"She took you from me." She looks delusional. How had I not seen how crazy she was. "Then, like fate, you gave me the perfect out. You said you would test every employee. I knew this was my shot to get rid of her for good. It was like all the stars aligned in the sky. I was finally going to be able to get rid of her. You were the prize. That night, I knew it was a losing battle, so I upped my game." She smirks.

"You could have killed them."

"Hardly. Death was never the endgame. My goal was to

ruin her. For you to see her for what she was. Then, once you fired her, I could have you all to myself again."

"Well, it didn't work."

"Didn't it?" She lifts her brow. "You shipped her off. She's gone."

"But what you don't know about Bailey is that she is the strongest person I know. Much stronger than you or even me. She will come out of this on top, and guess what? I'll be there waiting for her. Because I love her."

And with that, phone in hand, I walk out of her apartment.

chapter fifty-four

Drew

I'M A MAN POSSESSED.

I don't even stop to talk to the police or anything, instead I send the incriminating evidence to my attorney and tell him to handle it. This isn't about me anymore. It's time I do what I should have done a week ago and talk to her.

It doesn't take me long to get on my family's plane and head to the treatment center. When I arrive, I don't even bother to check if I can see her. She needs to know the truth, and I need to grovel.

It feels like forever since I've held her. As soon as I park the rental car, I head into the building and straight to the front desk. I walk with purpose. I'm not one to be trifled with.

"Can I help you, sir?" asks a woman behind a desk.

"I'm here to see Bailey Jameson."

"Visiting hours—"

I hold my hand up and cut her off. What this woman doesn't realize is my donations to this place keep it running. I have spent a fortune to make this the sanctuary what it is after Alexa died.

"I'm here to speak to Dr. Roberts."

"Do you have an appointment?"

I take a deep breath. This woman has done nothing to me other than prolong my seeing Bailey, but that's not her fault. She's only doing her job. The truth is, I should have called first.

"Please tell her Drew Lawson is here to speak with her."

Her eyes narrow, but she nods as she picks up the phone.

"Dr. Roberts, there is a Drew Lawson who wishes to speak to you." She's quiet for a minute before her head bobs. "Yes, yes. I understand. Very well. Of course, ma'am."

When she hangs up the phone, she looks up at me. "Dr. Roberts is ready to speak with you if you can follow me." She stands and walks around from behind the desk.

Her heels click on the marble floor as she leads us through a door and into another room. This room I have been to before. It's floor-to-ceiling glass and faces the gardens.

"If you can just take a seat, she will be right in."

I nod before sitting. "Thank you," I say, as she walks out the door.

In silence now, I try to figure out what I will say to Bailey. The sound of the door opening stops my train of thought.

I turn to see Dr. Roberts approaching. "Mr. Lawson. I wasn't expecting you."

"I know. I'm here to see Bailey."

Her eyes go wide. "That's not possible. She's only been here for a week. Although she is allowed visitors—"

"Please," I say. I lift my hand and run it through my hair. "I wouldn't ask this if it wasn't imperative."

She looks at me. My appearance must be alarming because she inclines her head. "I will see what I can do. I will ask her if she wants to see you." She turns to leave.

I stand when she's out the door and start to pace.

My feet stalk back and forth across the space. I start to count my steps before I hear the door open a few minutes later.

I expect to see Bailey, but when I see the nurse, my heart drops.

"I'll take you to see her." She smiles at me. I let out the breath I didn't even realize I'm holding.

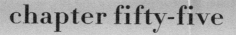

chapter fifty-five

Bailey

THE DOOR TO MY ROOM OPENS, AND DR. ROBERTS WALKS IN. I'm instantly on edge. I'm not sure why, but something seems different about her posture.

"Bailey, this is highly unorthodox, and I understand if you say no, but . . ." She pauses, which makes my stomach tighten. "Drew Lawson is here to speak with you."

Drew.

Drew is here to talk to me.

My heart hammers in my chest. It feels like it will explode. The doctor is speaking to me, but I can't hear her words.

I take a deep breath. It's one of the things I have been learning to do since coming here, and once I'm present again, I address the doctor.

"I'll see him."

I'm not sure what he has to say, but it must be important.

"Would you like to follow me?" she asks.

"Lead the way." I try to joke, making light of the situation. Maybe then it wouldn't feel like I was drowning in nerves.

Inhaling deeply, I will myself to calm, and when she finally leads me to an outdoor patio, I think I might faint when I see his back.

He's facing the grounds, but when I open the door and step outside, he turns to face me.

He looks the same, but different.

Handsome as always, but now he looks almost unkept. Disheveled. He looks tired too. Dark circles and shadows adorn his eyes. His five o'clock shadow is almost a beard. It looks like he hasn't slept in days, either.

"Drew." I step closer. "What are you doing here?"

I don't mean to come off aggressive, but he said goodbye. I said goodbye.

"I needed to talk to you." He looks rattled, and I can't help the way my heart squeezes.

He gestures to the table, and I make my way closer and sit.

He sits across from me, which feels too close right now. I'm a live, exposed wire.

"I'm sorry."

I shake my head, not understanding. He already explained what happened with Monica . . . unless…

"What? I don't—"

"I'm sorry for doubting you. I'm sorry for everything."

"You're making no sense."

He stands and starts pacing. Now I'm even more on edge.

"I-fuck—I don't even know how to say this . . . You didn't do anything wrong."

"Drew—"

"No, listen. You didn't do anything wrong, Bailey. You didn't get high."

"But my tox—"

"You were drugged," he blurts out.

Everything around me goes numb. The sounds start to fade in and out. If I wasn't sitting, I would be afraid I'd pass out.

That makes no sense.

Why would anyone . . . ? No, Drew is wrong.

"Bailey, Monica drugged you."

His words stab me. "I—" I stop myself, not able to form words.

"She wanted to get back at you. She said it was your fault."

"What was my fault?"

"She-she thought you took me away from her. This was my fault for hiring her. I didn't realize how unhinged she was. When I announced the mandatory drug test, she thought she could finally get rid of you. She decided to spike your drink, knowing full well would I not only fire you, but I would also dump you."

My whole body starts to shake, and I'm not sure what to think about this.

"Bailey, do you understand what I'm saying? You didn't do drugs. Not willingly, at least. You don't need to be here."

He walks toward me. His hand reaches out and touches mine. "You can come home with me."

I stare at where our hands are touching. It would be so easy. But all my life, I have been doing easy.

There is only one answer I can give him.

"No."

"You don't want to see me, I understand. I didn't believe in you."

"It's not that, Drew." I move my hand away from his. Then I take a step back. "I want to go home with you. I want it so badly. I wish I could."

"But don't you understand? You can."

"I can't. I might not have taken the drugs, but it doesn't change anything. I got drunk. I'm an addict who got drunk, and it's only a matter of time before it escalates. That is on me. I made a reckless decision. On me again. Sure, maybe I didn't take the coke or the Vicodin, but it was only a matter of time. When you hurt me, I searched out a high. I've taken the easy way out all my life, but it's time I get the help I need. The help I should have gotten a long time ago. It's time I put myself first and heal."

He looks at me with large, sad eyes, but he nods his understanding.

"I'm proud of you." He moves closer and wraps his arms around me. "I hope this isn't goodbye."

"It is for now."

I kiss him on the lips and turn and walk away. A heavy weight is lifted, but it's not enough. I still have a lot to heal inside me.

But I need to do that alone.

And I'm finally ready to.

chapter fifty-six

Bailey
Three weeks later . . .

I ANXIOUSLY WATCH THE DOOR, TAPPING MY TOE AGAINST the ceramic tile floor. The sound ricochets off the walls as I wait for Harper to arrive. Thirty days. I can't believe thirty days have passed so quickly. I told her I didn't need her to fly to Arizona to pick me up. We flew out here to have time to be alone and talk, but she wants to get here and get me home this time. I think it's silly, as I can fly home myself. I'm a big girl, but in usual Harper fashion, she insisted, and I love her for it. As strong as I am, I still welcome the comfort and strength her presence grants me.

I hear the faint sound of the wood from the door creak, and I jump up and run forward, leaping into Harper's arms. God, I hope it's her, or I just made a huge ass of myself.

"Wow, Bae. Excited to see me?" She laughs, and the sound warms my heart. I didn't realize how much I missed her until this very moment.

"You have no idea, Harp. You have no idea." I hold her to me, not ready to let her go.

"Well, you look great," she says as she pulls back. Her gaze trails up the length of me, from my shoes up to my eyes. Her nose scrunches, and she lifts her eyebrow up at me. "I was a bit concerned," she admits as her lip turns up into a smile, and I can't help but laugh. I could always count on Harper to be honest. It was the lawyer in her.

"Are you ready to get out of here?"

"Lead the way," I say, motioning toward the door.

She grabs my hand in hers, and we start to head outside. As we walk out of the sanctuary that has been my home, my eyes squint against the early morning sun peeking out from behind the clouds. Streams of light glisten in the distance of the desert, causing a haze to form and take shape into a mirage.

Harper lets go of my hand and links her arm with mine. Turning my head up so our eyes can meet, I see her eyes glisten with unshed tears. "You okay?" she mumbles, and I give her a small smile as my head nods.

"Yeah, I am, Harper. I really am."

She lets out an audible sigh. The last thirty days were a real eye-opener for me, but they were also essential for my healing. I learned so much about myself, and for the first time, I believe I have a shot at happiness. I'm going to be just fine. It took me a long time to get here, but I'm stronger than I ever was before. I'm finally able to love myself. That's the most important thing I've learned during this whole ordeal. That if I don't love myself, I'll never be capable of loving anyone else. I might have thought I loved Drew, but now that I've begun the process of healing, I realize all of what we had before was built on false truths and lies. I'd only showed him half of who I really was, but now I'm ready to give him every part of me.

I just hope he's willing to accept me for who I am.

Hours later, we land at La Guardia Airport. Harper has arranged a car service to take us back to the city, but as the car drives toward uptown instead of downtown where my apartment is, I turn toward her with a puzzled expression on my face.

"Where are we going? I thought you were taking me home?" I ask.

"We are," she responds, and I raise my eyebrows at her until she continues. "We're going to my place first. Don't be mad, but there are a few people who wanted to see you before you went home. Namely, Mom," she blurts out and gives me the biggest pair of puppy dog eyes.

I groan and feign annoyance, but I can't hide the smile that plays on my face. "I'm not mad."

My time in rehab has helped me make peace with Mom.

A little over thirty minutes later, we pull up to Harper's apartment. Or what I assume is Harper's apartment because it's not where she lived with Cal.

"When were you going to tell me you got a new place?"

"I was more concerned about you getting healthy than burdening you with my problems."

"I refuse to get out of the car until you do."

"We broke up."

I lift my brow. "That much is obvious."

"He was exactly what we thought he was . . . a lying, cheating, bastard."

I reach my hand across the space that divides us. "I'm sorry."

"It's okay. This isn't about me. This is about you. I'm proud of you. You have come so far."

"I love you, sis."

"I love you, too. Now get out."

I step out of the car and make my way into the building. Together, in silence, we ride up the elevator until we are on the ninth floor, and she leads me to the apartment.

As I open the door and glance around the room, I notice it's filled with people who love me, who I now see have always loved me.

My mom, Carter, my sister, and Drew.

I finally understand everything they taught me at rehab. It's not about where you are or what you have. It's not about others and their opinions of you. All it's really about is loving yourself, and the rest will follow. If you don't love yourself, you will never believe or see the love that surrounds you. I never saw the love pouring out at me in the past. Before, I'd believed my memories were scars marring my skin. I saw them on my exposed surfaces and got high to hide them from others and myself. I'd clung to those memories of everything I'd done wrong like someone who was drowning would cling to a life preserver, and now I know it's time to move on.

Making my way farther into the apartment, I greet my mom with a giant hug. "Mom, I missed you so much."

"Oh, Bailey," my mom cries, burying herself deeper into my neck. Her wet tears are running across my skin. "We love you so much. We're so happy you've come back to us." We continue to embrace until the tears dry up.

My gaze wanders around the room. Carter beams from the corner, waving frantically. I wave back, smiling widely at my friend.

Standing on the other side of the room is Drew. His tall, lean frame comes into focus. I take him in, and I can see creases fan out along the side of his eyes. He looks tired and worn as though the past month hasn't been good to him.

Our eyes lock, and his pain is evident. His pupils dilate, and I can see his shoulders tense. I can't help but wonder if he still loves me. My chest caves in with the thought that he might have moved on. Tears begin to pool in my eyes. The rhythmic beat of my heart echoes through my ears. But instead of sinking back into my own despair, I remember what my therapist taught me in my private sessions.

"With every obstacle you encounter, if you take it one step at a time, you'll never get stuck."

Squaring my shoulders, I set on my path. My pulse races so fast it feels as though the ground under me might give way. My body won't stop until I'm with him.

I lean forward on my tiptoes and place an awkward kiss on his cheek. Pulling back, he stops my retreat, placing his hand to cover mine completely. We look down at our hands, now interlocked. Neither one of us is able to speak. But the silence doesn't last long as I suck in a loud breath to calm my racing heart.

"Are you okay? Why are you shaking?"

My eyes dart back and forth across the room to where my family and Carter are gathered. "Everyone is staring at me."

"They are. They're so proud of how far you've come. You're incredible."

His words wash over me. He's right. I have come far. My time at rehab has proven that I have what it takes to fight. It gives me the strength I need to have and hope that I'll only go farther on this journey of soberness.

"I've missed you," he says.

"Me too. It feels like forever. I'm sorry I never returned your calls. I needed—" I take a deep breath. "I needed to find me. Do you hate me?"

"I love you. I could never hate you." His lips hover over mine. "I missed you." He places a soft kiss on my lips. "Every day you were gone, I craved you, your body, your heart, but most importantly, your soul. Because that's what you are to me, Bae. You're my soul."

His lips descend, showing me just how much he loves me. Showing me every emotion he couldn't say with words.

Merging my soul with his.

A bond that could never break.

Wrapping my arms around him, I deepen the kiss. And without words, I pour my heart out to him. At this moment, I finally feel home.

chapter fifty-seven

Bailey

IT'S GOOD TO BE HOME. AT FIRST, THERE WAS AN ADJUSTMENT period, but now, weeks later, I'm getting back into the swing of things. It was hard at first, having to talk to the police about what Monica did to me, but Harper, being Harper, is handling everything. She is going after Monica for second degree assault. A part of me wishes I can put the whole mess behind me, but I know this is for the best, even if going to court brings up terrible memories, I'm stronger than that. My time at Serenity Vista gave me the tools I need to weather any storm that might come my way.

I'm no longer working at Silver at all. The sale is almost final, so I have relocated my desk into an office space Drew has rented for us. He comes and goes, keeping busy. It's definitely a change. It's quiet, but I like it.

We spend every night together. Mostly at his place.

"Knock, knock," Harper calls from the door, pulling my eyes away from the document I've been staring at.

"Hey! What are you doing here?"

She holds up her hand, clutching a bag from our favorite deli. "I come bearing gifts. Thought you probably needed some-one to force you to eat."

tempted

At that very moment, my stomach growls. "You know me too well." I smile.

She takes a seat across from me, unpacking the food and arranging it between us. We dig in, not saying a word for the first several minutes as both of us are clearly starved.

"How are things going?" I say, breaking the silence. She sighs, and for the first time since she arrived, I see the bags under her eyes. A sign she's struggling. "Cal?" I prompt, and she shrugs.

"I know I acted all tough about it, but it's hard. I don't like being alone."

"So date," I say, popping a chip in my mouth.

She groans. "It's not that easy. In a city this big, it shouldn't be so hard, but it is. The men I meet are either weak and annoying or intimidated by my success."

"You are pretty badass."

We both chuckle.

"I'm going to be single forever," she cries, and I set down my food and take a long look at my gorgeous, intelligent sister.

"I promise you won't. The right guy will come along. Be patient."

"Like he did for you?" she says, grinning.

"Exactly."

"Have you met the mom yet?"

"No," I say, defeated. "I can't help but feel like he's holding back."

"He loves you, Bailey. Give it time."

"I know he does. It's just . . . I can't help but wonder if he's embarrassed to introduce me to her."

"Stop, Bailey. You can't think like that. You're a great girl. Maybe he's more afraid of his mom than you."

I sigh. "You might be right."

"Might be right about what?" Drew asks, walking through

the door with a handful of beautiful white roses.

"Hi, Harper," he calls, making a beeline straight for me. He leans down, kissing the side of my cheek. "For you," he says, holding out the bouquet.

"These are beautiful. Thank you, Drew."

"You're beautiful."

"Barf," Harper says, mock vomiting. "On that note, I'll be leaving." She stands, and I follow, coming around and pulling her into my chest.

"Thanks for lunch, Harp. Love you."

"Anytime. Love you more."

We get one final squeeze in, and she heads out, leaving Drew and me to ourselves.

Drew pulls me into him. "God, you smell good," he says into the crook of my neck. I squirm under him. "I thought she'd never leave."

"You just got here." I giggle, sounding like a teenager.

"And still . . . she couldn't have left soon enough. I want some time with my girl."

"And what do you plan to do with that time, Mr. Lawson?"

"I have some ideas," he says, stepping back and looking around the room. "For starters, that desk would work really nice."

"Nice for what?" I ask coyly, playing into this game.

He taps his chin. "Let me think."

"Chess?" I say, batting my eyelashes.

"Definitely not chess." He grins. "I've already captured the queen."

"Oh, you think so, do you?"

"You disagree?" he says, and I back up, preparing to say something contradictory. "Perhaps I need to be more aggressive and solidify my win." He jumps forward, capturing me in his embrace. I squeal, but it's lost as his mouth fuses to mine.

I melt in his arms, opening up to allow his tongue entry into my mouth. The expert way in which he kisses me only manages to make me want every part of him. Right now. In this office.

I pull away. "You're right," I say, and he quirks a brow, a grin forming on his lips. "This desk will work perfectly."

"Checkmate."

I'd lose to him every time if it leads to this.

chapter fifty-eight

Drew

MY PHONE RINGS. I IGNORE IT, BUT IT STARTS RINGING again.

I answer. "Yes, Mother?"

I haven't spoken to her in over a month. Not since the last time when she did what she did. At first, I was avoiding her. Then I was dealing with the club, then Monica and Bailey. I can't avoid her forever.

"I'm sorry, Drew. I shouldn't have ambushed you with Allison last month." I stay quiet. "I know you're still angry, but will you consider coming tomorrow for dinner? Let me make it up to you," she says, her tone hopeful.

"I'll have to get back to you."

"But, Drew," she whines. "Gretchen Long is in town from London and would love to catch up with you. She's such a beautiful girl, and her parents—"

Unbelievable. She should save her apologies since she clearly isn't sorry. "No. Mother, you are ridiculous." I look over at Bailey, whose eyes are wide in question.

"Then just come for dinner. No girls. No setups. I promise."

I want to say no. I should just tell her to go to hell, but then I have an idea. "I'll come, but I'm bringing a date."

"Oh? A date! Fabulous. Who is it?" she says excitedly.

"A girl I've been dating. She's a nice girl, Mom. Please, don't frighten her."

Bailey's eyes go even wider as she mouths, "What?"

"I wouldn't. Do I know her? Who are her parents? Are they members of the club?"

And so it begins.

"No, Mother. You do not, and no, they are not members of the club. I like this one. Please be cordial."

Bailey smiles her big, beautiful smile. I can tell she's thrilled with this.

"Drew Lawson, you insult me. I would never. I'm excited. I'll see you both tomorrow."

I hear the click on the other line, and I look up at Bailey.

"Going to see your mom?"

I nod. "Yep. Hope you're ready." I chuckle.

chapter fifty-nine

Bailey

HOLY. SHIT.

I'm meeting his mother.

Now what am I supposed to do? I'm so not ready for this. Drew Lawson is in a class of his own, and I'm petrified of the woman who birthed him. I can only imagine what she'll be like. Perfect, that's for sure. Skinny. No flaws. She definitely has never worked a day in her life.

I groan as my fingers start clawing at the skin on my arm. In the past, there was only one thing that could fix the anxiety coursing through me. Thank God I found a meeting for tomorrow morning, or I don't know how I would ever survive this.

I dress quickly for bed and only give Drew a small kiss on the lips. It's soft and sweet, and even though our lips barely touch, it's filled with passion. It knocks the breath out of my lungs. How can something so trivial affect me so much? I got it bad for him. We both fall asleep quickly.

The next morning, when I finally walk out of his loft, I make my way west to the church I regularly go to now for a meeting when I stay at his place. The meeting starts at eight, so I pick up my pace. I debate finding a cab, but the truth is, although I can afford it, I need to save money to go back to school. That's one of the things I have been working on since leaving rehab. Looking into a school I can go to in the city to get a degree while I work.

Fifteen minutes later, and with only a few seconds to spare, I make it. A light sweat has broken against my brow from the exertion of trying to make it here on time, and my breath is coming out in short bursts. I lean against the brick and wait for my heartbeat to regulate.

Pulling the door back, I enter and head down the stairs to the basement where the meeting is being held. My gaze scans the room as I take in the ensemble of people gathering to find strength. Just being here calms my frazzled nerves.

"Hello, my name is Thomas, and I'm an addict. Welcome. Can we open this meeting with a moment of silence for the addict who still suffers, followed by the WE version of the Serenity Prayer?" He takes a slight pause before his eyes shut, and his head bows as he repeats the familiar words. My eyes flutter closed, and silently I repeat his words.

When the session ends, I am one of the first to stand. Facing the back, I'm ready to leave when the air leaves my lungs as I see Carter quickly exiting.

He came.

I told him about how much I liked this meeting and that he should come, and he did.

A sense of pride washes over me for my friend. I hope it's the beginning of a life change for him. Should I call him? The more I contemplate it, the more it becomes clear. I need to leave this one alone. It's his fight, and he has to do it his way. If he needs me, he'll find me.

An hour later, I feel rejuvenated. A huge weight is lifted off me as the craving has passed. As long as I keep up with my meetings, I think everything will be okay. No slipups.

I head back to my apartment, and I stare blankly at my closet once there. Holy hell. What does one wear to dinner with one's brand spanking new, wealthier than God boyfriend? And worse, what does one wear when meeting his pretentious mother? Because if it's one thing I'm sure of, this woman is going to be a spoiled witch. Why did I push for this?

Bailey, Bailey, Bailey . . .

You really are an idiot.

I feel like my blood pressure is climbing. I take deep breaths and silently repeat the serenity prayer.

Inhale.

Exhale.

Inhale.

Exhale.

I got this.

I see a baby blue wrap dress that falls just to my knees. It's nothing fancy and certainly not high-end, but it will work. Paired with a nude peep toe and simple makeup, it will probably look good, but not good enough for his socialite mother. Oh, there you go again. Freaking out. Shaking my head back and forth, I dismiss all doubt that I won't be accepted and proceed to the bathroom to redo my hair and makeup from this morning. Luckily, I don't have to shampoo and rinse it, but I need to run a brush through it.

As I'm putting the final layer of lip-gloss on, my cell phone rings. "Hey, Harper, what's going on?"

"Where have you been?"

My forehead creases. "What do you mean? I haven't been anywhere."

"I stopped by your office."

"Wow, checking up on me . . ." I laugh, poking fun.

"Why are you giggling? What are you up to? You know if you don't check in every morning, I start to get worried."

"God, Mom," I tease. "I'm fine. Just stopped at a meeting this morning."

"Oh, really? Are you okay? Is something happening? Is Drew treating you okay?" she asks.

"Yes, he's treating me perfectly." If she only knew just how perfect.

"Okay, good. I was kind of worried. But that doesn't answer the question. Why the meeting?"

I'd love to tell her I have a lot of work to do, and I can't get into it now.

"Listen, Harp. I'm running late because of the meeting, so I can't talk now, but can I call you tomorrow?"

"A dinner tonight?"

"Not tonight, but tomorrow. Promise."

"You sure you're okay?"

"Yeah, but I really need to run. Love you." I don't wait for her to say goodbye before I hang up. I'm not trying to be rude, but I am running late, and I need to be perfect for his mother.

chapter sixty

Drew

WHEN I PICK BAILEY UP, SHE LITERALLY STEALS MY breath away. She didn't even give me the chance to walk to her door like a proper gentleman. She came flying out the door as though someone was chasing her. Other than her adorably flustered look, everything else from head to toe is perfection.

I snap myself out of the trance I'm in just in time to fly around the car to open the door for her.

Leaning in, she whispers, "You smell so good." She reaches up on her tiptoes and places a kiss on my cheek. Instinctually, I inhale her. If I smell good, then she smells divine.

"Did you just sniff me?" she asks.

"That sounds like something I've heard in a movie." I chuckle. "Yes, yes I did just sniff you. It's your fault for wearing whatever that is. It's intoxicating, devil woman."

She laughs. "Devil woman? What pray tell have I done to warrant that moniker?"

I stare at her for a few moments and take in the delicate angles of her face. Making my way back to her almond eyes, I smile.

"You have entranced me, Bailey, and I'm not sure what to do with it."

She only smiles as she finally sits in my Jaguar.

The drive to my mother's is silent. It's a direct contrast to the excitement of seeing each other a few minutes ago.

"What's going on in that head of yours?"

Tilting her head to the side, Bailey says, "I'm petrified." She bites her lip, obviously afraid of my response.

"I could lie and tell you everything will be all right, but honestly, I have no idea what to expect. My mother and I . . . Well, we haven't had the best relationship over the past few years. She's always been a very strong force. I wouldn't say she was an absent mother, but she was authoritative and very busy. She wasn't nurturing, but she wasn't always cold either. I know I'm not making sense."

I'm getting flustered. Explaining my conundrum of a mom is a challenge. Half the time, I don't know where we stand or what her motives are. I've always felt loved by her, but I wouldn't say we've ever been close.

Bailey shakes her head. "No, I get it."

Such simple words and if they had come from anyone else, I'd have passed them off as words to placate me, but somehow, I know Bailey truly does get it.

"My father was a workaholic. But he loved my sister and me dearly. My mother, on the other hand, was too preoccupied with herself. I know now she did love me; she just didn't know how to show it. Certainly not with words and cuddling." She shrugs.

I want to make a joke at the cuddle mention, but she is so vulnerable at this moment. I don't want her to take my jest the wrong way. So I just say, "Exactly. I wish I could prepare you for my mom, but who knows what we'll get. She has always been very adamant about me dating someone from our country club or another trust fund girl."

I cringe that I even mentioned it, and I see her face fall. She's white as a ghost, and I know I've fucked it up.

"No, no, Bailey. It doesn't matter what she wants. I want you. Just be yourself, and she'll love you."

Grabbing her hand in mine, I bring it to my lips. When she finally smiles, I give her hand one final squeeze of reassurance as we pull up to the front gate of the Lawson Estate. Looking at Bailey, I watch as her eyes go wide. I probably should have prepared her a little more for just how wealthy we are.

"What the hell? You didn't say your father is Daddy Warbucks."

I snicker at the reference. Not quite, but close. No need to petrify her further.

I take her up the stairs and pray I'm not walking her into a fire. I grab the handle, but the door flings open. Mother is standing on the other side in a pair of leggings and a long tunic. What. The. Actual fuck? My mother never dresses down. Never. I haven't seen this woman in less than her Sunday best in my twenty-eight years of life.

"Drew. I'm so glad to see you." Her smile is warm, and she looks sincere. It's startling.

"Mother, are you feeling well?" I cock my eyebrow up in question. Perhaps she meant to cancel and forgot.

"Silly boy. I'm fantastic. I'm so glad you came. Don't be rude. Come in, come in, and introduce me to this beautiful girl you have on your arm."

Bailey smiles a hesitant smile and looks back and forth between the two of us. She has no idea what to make of this. That makes two of us. I just shrug. Not helpful, I know, but I think we are both out of our element today.

"Mother, this is Bailey Jameson. Bailey, my mother, Cynthia."

"Drew Lawson, stop being so proper. It's pretentious. I'm Mom." She rolls her eyes at me. She actually rolls her damn eyes. I'm about to call Dr. Palmer. I think she's having a stroke or started the downward spiral into Alzheimer's. Either way, it isn't good.

"Okay, Mom . . . Are you all right?"

She smooths down her chestnut hair. "Heavens, yes. Stop looking at me like that and get out of the foyer. Bailey doesn't want to stand all day. Jeez, have you lost your mind?"

I might have.

In all honesty, I'm kind of feeling like Alice being thrust down a rabbit hole after ingesting a handful of whatever shrooms the creator of that story was on. Bailey looks at my dumbfounded face and laughs, and her laughter makes me laugh, which in turn has my mom laughing. What the fuck we're laughing at is beyond me, but hell, it's better than screaming.

"Bailey, come on in and have a seat. Would you like a glass of wine?"

"No, thank you, Mrs. Lawson, but I'd love a glass of water if I may."

"Please, call me Cynthia."

The evening continued with my mother fawning all over Bailey. We had a dinner of steaks and potatoes, nothing fancy. It was surreal and really nice if I'm being honest. I'm relaxed, and this is the first time I've been relaxed in my parents' home in years.

The conversation is so easy between my mother and Bailey. I would have never guessed it in a million years. Bailey is one of a kind, but she's not my mother's kind. My mom pawned me off on girls like Alexa: rich, beautiful, and worldly. Bailey is beautiful and unique, and everything all of those girls weren't, and I'm feeling like I've grossly misjudged my mom all these years.

They talk for what feels like hours about New Jersey, of

all things. Leggings, music, cosmetics—you name it, they discussed it. I'd usually be bored out of my mind by now, but I'm not. I feel at peace. I'm completely captivated by both of the women sitting before me. For the first time, I can envision a life beyond the club, and it doesn't scare the fuck out of me.

"Can you point me in the direction of a powder room?"

"Of course, dear. It's down the hall and to your left three doors down."

I jump up to pull her chair out for her, and my mother beams. She's clearly proud. Bailey walks out of the room, and I prepare myself for the disappointment.

"She's lovely. I adore her."

"What's going on, Mother? This whole thing . . . What's your angle?"

"There's no angle. I sincerely like her. She's beautiful, funny, intelligent, but most importantly, I can tell you genuinely care for her. It's the first time you've ever looked at a girl that way. She's special."

"She is. I do care for her. I love her."

"Take it slow and make sure because I truly see a future with you two. She reminds me a lot of myself."

I snort.

"I'm serious, Drew. There's a lot you don't know about me. I wasn't always a wealthy heiress. I don't think now's the time to discuss it, but soon I'd like to tell you my history. It might help you understand more about me."

"Did I miss any fun stories?" Bailey strolls in, completely oblivious to the revelations of my mother and my conversation.

"No, dear, I was just about to remind Drew of our annual gala. It's a fundraiser that we do every year. I was hoping you'd accompany him?"

"I believe you just stole my thunder, Mom." I chuckle at her enthusiasm. "But yes, Bailey, I'd love for you to be my date." I give her my most charming smile and watch as the blush creeps across her cheeks. It's time for me to get Miss Jameson home before I do things to her that would embarrass us both right here in front of my mother. This night just solidified in my mind that Bailey Jameson is mine.

chapter sixty-one

Bailey

AS MY EYES FLUTTER OPEN, MY THOUGHTS FILTER BACK TO dinner last night. Mrs. Lawson—Cynthia—is nothing at all like I expected. She was funny and warm and, most of all, not pretentious. I could see in Drew's eyes that he was just as shocked by her behavior, and a warm feeling weaved its way through my body. Drew's mom liked me.

I remember how his keen eyes were, probing hers all through dinner, waiting for her to slip but then how relaxed they seemed after I returned from the bathroom. I'm not dumb enough to think they didn't talk about me while I was gone, but whatever was said obviously put him at ease, and that put me at ease.

When we arrived back at his apartment, I began to muse about it, but he quickly shut me up the way Drew always does with his filthy, domineering ways. And, god, was he filthy last night. The way he's in tune to my body should be illegal. He had me screaming within five minutes of walking in the door.

I stretch my arms above my head as I yawn, wringing out every last bit of sleep I have left in my body. Moving my right foot off the bed, I go to stand, but as my foot feels the cold wood floors, two strong arms envelop my waist, pulling me back.

"Where do you think you're going?" His husky voice tickles the back of my neck as he pulls my back flush with his chest.

"Bathroom," I whisper. My breathing becomes shallow as I feel his tongue gently lick the shell of my ear. My heart pounds rhythmically against the walls of my chest.

"I don't think so, Bailey."

The authoritative way he says my name sends a chill down my spine. Slowly, I feel one hand unwrap from behind me and begin his descent downward, skimming my waist then my taut stomach all the way to my pelvic bone. My body is a live wire, sparking with each move he makes.

His hands burn my tingling skin, causing me to tremble all over. Drew's fingers feel like the soft whisper of a feather, and I can barely breathe by the time they find their destination, the place I need him most. He dips one long finger inside me, and I'm so wound up, I gasp with ecstasy. The pleasure is pure and explosive, but it's not enough. Not nearly enough to sate the hunger inside me.

Reaching my hand behind me, I find him hard and ready. He throbs in my hand, and in response, I tilt my hips up so I can feel him pressing against my ass. Swinging one leg over his hip, I open myself up to him, then guide the tip to where I need him most. As I welcome him into my body, I moan softly, adjusting slowly to the delicious intrusion. My world spins on its axis as he thrusts hard and deep inside. His hand still between us, he begins to rub in earnest, each stroke of his dick and fingers working together in a perfect symphony. I feel myself become tense with the need for release, my body arching closer to his.

Panting.

Throbbing.

Exploding.

I come undone as he jerks inside me.

Once our breathing regulates, I feel him leave my body as he turns to lie on his back. I miss the feeling instantly but quickly forget as his arms pull me around to lie on his chest with my head resting over his heart.

"Wow," he says with an audible exhale. "I want to wake up every morning like this." His hand reaches across and down to my chin. He turns my head up, causing my neck to strain, but it's worth it just to see the look in his eyes. They drink me in, sated and dilated, but something else flashes there, and it makes me feel all warm inside.

By the time my phone rings, I've showered, dressed, and eaten. I look at the screen, and it's Harper. I'd called her before showering, but now she's ringing me back.

"Hey," I say into the phone as I take a seat next to Drew on the couch. His leg is propped up on the coffee table, his laptop on his lap.

"Hey, what's going on? Everything all right?"

"Yeah, of course, why?" I lean across the coffee table and reach for the coffee cup Drew had placed on it for me.

"Well, you don't often call me so early in the morning, and after yesterday, I just assumed you—"

I cut her off before she can go on. I'm in a good mood, and I don't want to hear one of her motherly lectures. "I'm fine. All good here. I just wanted to know if you wanted to go shopping with me. I need a dress, and that's more your thing."

She doesn't respond right away. Maybe she thinks I need her money? I don't. I might not have a lot, but I have a few bucks saved, so I'm sure I can find something that would work.

"I would—I would love that." Her voice cracks, and I realize she's not pissed I asked her. She's moved.

"Okay, so how about we meet in thirty minutes? Let's say we meet at . . ." I trail off as I mentally think about what area has a lot of options. "Outside Macy's."

"Sounds great. Thanks for thinking of me."

I hang up the phone with a huge smile on my face and peer over at Drew sitting next to me. He lifts his eyes from the screen in front of him and turns his attention toward me. His eyebrows rise.

"What's going on in your head?" he questions, and I run my hand through my hair.

"I'm meeting Harper to shop."

He closes the laptop and places it back on the coffee table. "And this is a problem because?"

"It's not. But she's always such a mother hen. Sometimes it's overwhelming."

"She loves you. It's kind of cute," he says as he leans forward, placing a soft kiss on my lips.

Standing on the corner of Thirty-Fourth Street in front of Macy's, I wait. My foot taps nervously, and I pull my phone out to check the time. The party isn't until tonight, but I'm starting to freak out about it. From the corner of my eye, I see Harper strolling toward me, her hips swaying with each step. Her lips turn up when she notices me, and she waves.

"Hey, Harper," I say as she approaches.

She smiles brightly. "Look at you. You look so good. I feel like I haven't seen you in forever." She hugs me tightly.

"It's only been a few days. I've been so busy."

"What's keeping you tied up?"

I chuckle at the image those words bring forth. She cocks her eyebrow at me in question, but she doesn't say any more.

"I've been looking into schools, and I think I'm going to apply for classes in the fall."

"Bailey. Oh my god, I'm so proud of you! What are you going to do?"

"Whoa, slow down." I laugh at her enthusiasm.

"I'm just so excited. You seem to really be getting your stuff together." I see tears in her eyes, and I move toward her.

"Harper, is everything okay?"

"Everything is great. I just really miss you, and I mean it, Bae, I'm so proud." Her words melt my iced-over heart. We may not have grown up close, but she has more than proven that there is nothing better than a sister.

"Don't give me too much credit. I'm starting undeclared because I'm not sure what I want to do yet."

She wipes her eyes. "You have time for that. What are you interested in?"

I contemplate her question. "I'm really enjoying helping Drew with the business side of the restaurant, so I'm thinking business, but we'll see."

She nods in agreement. "Whatever you do, I know you'll be great. Is that why you wanted to meet?"

"Drew invited me to a fundraiser." I pretend to rummage through my purse so she doesn't see my eyes.

"Drew Lawson invited you to the Night of Hope Gala?" Her eyes widen with disbelief.

"And I met his mother." My words are fast.

"You met his mother?"

I swear she could catch a fly in her mouth. It's hanging so far open I'm afraid she might hurt herself.

"Yeah, why?"

"Bailey, no one meets his mother. This is huge!"

No one meets his mother. The notion makes me giddy inside. He did say he loved me.

"Wow, you met his mother," she repeats, and I nod.

"So, can you help me find an outfit to wear?"

"For tonight? Oh god, Bailey. There's no way anything will be fancy enough here."

"I-I have nothing to wear." My mouth tightens, spreading into a thin line.

Harper lets out a sigh, and I peek up at her as her eyes soften.

"Let's go find you the perfect dress. I know just the place—my treat." She winks.

"I don't expect—"

She waves a hand, cutting me off. "I know, sweetie." And with that, she grabs my hand and pulls me down the street.

We walk about fifteen blocks before Harper slows her pace. As we stand at the corner of Fifth and Forty-Ninth, I allow my gaze to skate across the distance. A truck stopped at the light obscures my line of sight as I try to figure out just where Harper is taking me. She steps forward and, as the traffic clears, I can see where she is pointing.

"Saks, Harper? I can't afford a pair of socks there, let alone a dress."

"Will you let me worry about that?"

With a soft nudge of the shoulder, she walks by me and begins to cross the street. I quickly follow, not wanting to be left behind.

"Bailey, what are you doing in these parts?" A familiar voice says from behind me. I whirl around to see Carter, who, before I can figure out what's happening, has me wrapped in his arms.

"Carter!" I squeal.

"Hi, Carter," my sister says from beside us.

In true Carter Cass fashion, he lets me go and moves on to my sister, where he forgoes the handshake and crushes Harper into a hug. "Nice to see you again."

She laughs. "You too."

He smiles. "What are you two ladies doing?" he questions.

"Bailey has been invited to a gala and needs a dress. Oh, and she met Drew's mother."

Carter's eyes flip to mine. His are wide.

317

I giggle.

"That's amazing! We need to catch up and talk. I would love to stick around, but I'm meeting a friend down the street." He waggles his eyes suggestively. I smirk.

"Well, we wouldn't want you to be late, Casanova."

He grins.

I wave goodbye to him and then grab Harper's hand to continue our shopping adventure. When we arrive at the department store, Harper steps forward and opens the door. The door must be heavy as the muscles in her arms flex with the exertion.

The first thing I see is money. Not actual money, but you can just tell right off the bat that I don't belong here. This place is dripping with fancy designers and expensive pieces. This place is more Harper's scene. Harper was always more into this stuff than me.

"This way," Harper says as she pulls me through the cosmetic section and toward the ornate gold elevators along the back wall of the room. It's shocking how chaotic the space is. I'm not sure how so many people have the time or the inclination to go shopping. I can think of a million things I would rather be doing right now. The truth be told, I'm so nervous about this gala that I would rather have a root canal than be shopping for a dress.

I look over to see Harper rummaging through a rack of dresses. She's definitely on a mission. The first dress she pulls out is god-awful. It's pink and frilly, and I think it might even have rhinestones on it. I shake my head adamantly at her, then mouth the words, "HELL NO."

Next, she pulls out a long black and nude dress that dips so low in the front I'm not sure how she thinks the "girls" will stay in place. I don't even need to veto this one as her eyes look like they may pop out of her face as she replaces it. She then eyes a white chiffon dress across the room and makes a beeline to grab it. Once standing in front of the dress, I see her scrunch her nose and turn to look me up and down. Pulling the hanger off the rack, she thrusts it at me.

"Try this on," she orders, and I throw my hands in the air while shaking my head back and forth again.

"God, no. I'm not wearing that."

"Why not? It would look amazing on your skin tone."

"I'm not wearing white. Next." My hands go to my hips as I stand my ground.

"You're impossible. You know what? I'm going to grab some help. Stay here. Do. Not. Leave."

I let my eyes roll back. "Fine, Mom."

She sticks her tongue out at me and laughs as she turns the corner and goes in search of a sales associate. I pull my phone out of my bag and check my messages. One from Drew. My lips part into a huge smile.

Drew: My bed is lonely without you.

Me: You're still in bed!!! Must be nice. Harper has me all over the city shopping—it's torture!

Drew: I'm sure it's not that bad.

Me: It's pretty much like waterboarding.

Drew: Being a bit dramatic, are we?

Me: Shut it!

Drew: God, I love that mouth of yours.

Me: Shit, I see her coming back.

Drew: Let the waterboarding resume.

Me: You're no help.

Drew: Sorry, babe, I'll see you tonight and make it all better. And I'm sure no matter what you buy, you will look stunning.

My cheeks flush. God, I adore him. He has this way of making everything all right. Placing my phone back in my bag, I turn my head to Harper, who is quickly approaching with a tall, willowy blonde. When they are standing directly in front of me, the blonde reaches out her perfectly manicured hand.

"I'm Claudette. Your sister tells me you need a gown for the Night of Hope Gala. We won't find anything in this section that's appropriate, so I'm going to set you up in our private fitting room and pull a few dresses that will be perfect. Follow me."

She flashes me a smile so bright I might go blind before taking us to probably the most beautiful fitting rooms I have ever seen. A gorgeous Louis XVI French sofa sits in the back of the room. It's an exquisite shade of plum with hand-carved mahogany arms.

"Would either of you like a glass of champagne while you wait?"

"Would you mind if I had one?" Harper asks, softly.

"Of course not. Drink away." I laugh at my sister and then turn to Claudette. "I'll just have water, thank you."

"Great! Let me grab both your drinks, and I'll be right back." She shuts the door, and Harper sits down on the couch.

"Pretty fabulous, right?"

"Yeah, it's amazing. Not sure I belong here, though," I say as I take a seat next to her. Her hand reaches across the couch and pats my knee.

"Of course you do, Bae. You deserve this and so much more." My eyes mist, and I turn my attention away from her to halt the onslaught of emotions threatening to expel.

We sit in quiet until the door swings open and we are given our drinks.

Within ten minutes, a giant moveable rack of gowns is placed before us. All long and made with different fabrics. I look them over, and then one jumps out at me. A sheer, floral pattern, black lace gown. It's the most beautiful dress I have ever seen. With the help of Claudette, I step into the gown, and Harper's mouth drops.

"Wow, Bae! You look amazing," she says, her eyes huge.

"Really? You think?"

"I don't think, I know. Turn around and look at yourself."

My breath leaves my body. If I thought the dress looked good on the hanger, it's nothing compared to how it looks on me. It molds perfectly to every curve on my body. Pulling out the price tag from under my arm, I begin to choke.

"Oh my god, that can't be right. Shit, Harp . . . This dress is—"

She holds her hand up to me. "Stop right there. This is my gift to you, and before you utter another word, don't. I want you to have it. I'm so proud of you, and it would mean everything to me to give this to you."

Tears well in my eyes, and I throw my arms around her neck. "Thank you. I love you."

"I'm so proud of the woman you are becoming, Bae."

A lone tear trails down my cheek. Her words mean everything to me. I hope I never let her down again.

chapter sixty-two

Drew

AFTER BAILEY SKIPS OUT ON ME TO GO SHOPPING, I PONDER what my mom said the other night at dinner. What could she possibly be hiding? The whole thing is so strange. It's utterly shocking in the best way possible, but I want to get to know the rest, so I jump out of bed and into the shower. I can still smell Bailey all over me. I could sit in her scent all day, but my mother would not appreciate it. They seem to have gotten off to a good start—no reason to mess up a good thing.

When I pulled into my parents' driveway an hour later, I notice two things right away. My dad's BMW is sitting in the driveway, which is strange because typically, he'd be on the golf course on a Saturday or out of town. No fail. Secondly, an attractive younger woman is sitting in the passenger seat who is not my mother.

It's no secret that my father is a philanderer, but he has never blatantly rubbed it in my mom's face. This is downright tasteless. I've gone from zero to fucking pissed in less than .01 seconds. He better hope he manages to sneak by me because I want blood. Luckily for him, he doesn't even see me and remains in the car.

I tear out of my car, stalking toward the front door without even a second glance at that woman. I yank open the front door with a jerk and yell for my mom. Barreling down the hallway, ripping open door after door, I continue to call for my mother. I see her frazzled face as she turns the corner, hauling ass in my direction, clearly concerned.

"What in God's name, Drew? We could hear you all the way on the other end of the house. What's the matter?" She looks horrified, if not dumbstruck.

"What the hell is Dad doing here with another woman?" I'm seething.

Her face softens, and she pats my hand. "Oh, come now. That's only Sarah, his financial advisor. She accompanies him on most golf outings." She rolls her eyes. "Nothing new there."

"Golf outings, my ass," I say under my breath, but my mom throws a stern look my way. "I don't care who she is. It's disrespectful to bring his whores here."

"Drew, calm down. Nothing is going on between those two. Sarah is actually a very nice girl. In fact, I think she'd run in the opposite direction from your father if she could. She's very young and bright. She's just doing what's expected of her by him. I'm quite fond of her. You can relax."

"Why is he even here? He hasn't been around the past several times I've stopped in. I thought we were finally rid of him."

She frowns. "Despite any issues your father and I have, you should respect him."

I scoff. "I can't respect someone who has given me every reason to be disrespectful toward them."

"Please don't carry this hate for him on my behalf. I allow most of what occurs in this house." She lowers her head, looking ashamed.

That may be the case, but my mother shouldn't have to allow that sort of behavior. He's an adult and knows right from wrong. He's a world-class prick, and most days, knowing I'm his offspring makes me cringe.

"I just don't get why you stay with him."

She laughs. "Where would I go, huh? Would I come live with you? Your father isn't giving up his sprawling estate, and I organize the charities. This world would not be kind to me if I tried to start over. I came to terms with my fate a long time ago, Drew, and I wouldn't change a second because I had you."

For the first time in maybe my whole life, looking at my mom feels comforting. This is what a mother should be. Why wasn't it always like this?

"Why, Mother? Why the coldness all those years?"

She sighs, resigned to have this conversation. She knows I won't back down until I have the answers.

"I'm sorry you felt I was cold. It was never my intention. I put a wall around myself, but I never knew it affected you. For many years, I tried to build my own empire. I worked so hard to network and build a brand in myself so that eventually, when I had the resources, I could take you and we could leave. I tried to get out from under your father's thumb, but I failed."

"I can understand that, Mother, but where did it all go wrong? Between you and Dad, I mean."

"I know you think you know what my life has been, but there are a lot of things you don't know. Your grandma and grandpa were not my birth parents." My mouth drops open, and creases form between my brows. My mother continues.

"My birth parents were drug addicts. I was placed in foster care at the age of five, and that's when your grandma found me and took me in. They couldn't conceive on their own. I don't remember much from those first five years, but no child should ever have to live through what I do remember. Your grandparents saved me in so many ways. They gave me things I would've never experienced. They were great people."

I have so many questions, but I can tell she isn't finished.

"I met your father through the usual social channels. I always knew I wanted to marry someone like your grandfather—strong, hardworking, loving—and I got the first two. I thought your father loved me, but soon after we married, the charade dropped, and it became obvious I was just another step to his world dominance. Ha. My trust was quite large, and it helped to get his empire started as opposed to mine. I was a fool. His family had money, but nothing like mine. He wiped my trust clean and made sure I wouldn't receive a dime of his as a part of our prenuptial agreement."

I hate my father and all that he stands for. What he's done to my mother is unforgivable.

"I don't want you to worry about me, Drew. I'll be fine. We have a gala to get ready for." She smiles. "I want you to have something." She walks out of the room and returns shortly.

"Here, open it."

I open a box to find a ring. It looks antique with a large diamond encased in smaller ones.

"What's this for?"

"This is the ring your grandfather gave your grandmother. You remind me a lot of him. He was a reckless young man who grew into a strong, powerful, loving man. He may not have been our blood, but he was every bit my father from the day he adopted me. Seeing you with Bailey made me happy because I can see that you're finally happy. I believe she's helping you to find the man you were meant to be. I want you to have this. Maybe one day . . . you will give this to her."

Is it that obvious? Can everyone see what this girl is doing to me? I don't like feeling vulnerable, and that's exactly what I feel right now.

"You're more like him than you are your father. Stay that way, Drew. Promise me you won't lose that kindness I see in you. Take care of Bailey, too. I can tell she's had a rough go of things, but she's a good girl."

I don't even realize it until the first tear slides down my cheek, but my mother's praise means more to me than anything in this world.

chapter sixty-three

Bailey

A S I MAKE MY WAY DOWN THE HALL TO WHERE DREW IS, I watch as he takes me in. His eyes go wide and sweep from my head to my toes. As I move closer, his breath hitches, and his Adam's apple bobs. Leaning toward me, he brushes his lips lightly against mine.

"You are breathtaking, Bailey. I've never—" He chokes up, and I smile at his reaction. "I've never been prouder to have a woman on my arm." I peck his cheek, eliciting a smile from him. "You ready?" he asks, his words tickling my mouth. It feels like the soft petals of a flower, and I lean into him once more, never wanting to break away. A laugh escapes me at the sensation.

"Come on, we're late." He grins.

He pulls away, and my mouth immediately misses him. Our fingers entwine, and we walk into Cipriani on Forty-Second Street. As we make our way inside, I can't muffle the gasp that leaves my body. The room is breathtaking. Large marble columns rise toward the soaring ceilings as delicate trees of orchard branches climb out from the tables lit only by candlelight. I've never seen anything so magnificent in my life. A waiter with a tray of tall flutes of champagne walks past us, and Drew lifts an eyebrow to me. I shake my head, and he grabs one for himself.

I beam up at him, and he smiles down at me. He looks so incredibly handsome in his slim-cut black tuxedo, I can barely stop staring at him. He must know it too because his lip quirks up, and he leans in.

"I can't wait to get out of here and see what you have on under that dress."

Not much.

Drew trails his hands up and down my skin, sending shivers and goose bumps all over me. He lifts his eyebrow with a smirk.

"Cold?"

"Hardly," I choke out, my eyes dilating.

"Let's find my mother, dance a little, and then get the fuck out of here. It's been way too long since I've been inside you."

And, god, has it. It feels like an eternity since this morning.

I nod as he places his glass on an empty tray when another waiter walks by. The dance floor is alive and vibrant with a twelve-piece orchestra playing on the stage. On the edge of the dance floor, I see Cynthia. She looks lovely with her chestnut hair pulled back into a chignon and sparkles of diamonds across her neck reflecting glimmers of light. She throws her head back in laughter, and my own smile comes. She truly is a remarkable lady.

"There she is, Drew," I say, pointing over in her direction, and we walk across the dance floor, weaving our way through dancing guests.

"Drew, darling," she says as she places a kiss on his cheek, then beams up at me.

"Mother," he responds.

"Bailey, such a pleasure to have you here tonight. You look stunning. I can see why my son is so smitten."

My face heats, and I'm sure I'm blushing. "Thank you so much for having me, Mrs. Lawson. This is magnificent. I have never seen anything so beautiful in my life."

"Cynthia, dear. And I'm so happy you think so. This event means so much to me." We all stand silently for a minute, taking in the activity around us before I feel Drew's hand make contact with the small of my back again. I love and hate this dress. Every time he touches me, I want to beg him to take me right here on the dance floor. And seeing as that's not an option . . .

I hate the dress.

"Please excuse me. I see someone I need to speak to. Take Bailey for a dance, Drew. Enjoy yourself." I watch as she gracefully glides away, and I turn to Drew.

"Are you going to take me dancing, or what?" I wink at him.

The corners of his eyes crinkle as his mouth curves into a wicked smirk. "You sure you want to dance, Bailey? I can think of something better to do." His pupils are huge as he speaks, and I'm sure that if I gave him the word, he would whisk me right out of here without a backward glance. But being here, looking at the dance floor, I want to dance with him.

More than anything.

"No way, Drew. I want to see all the moves you have."

With that, he pulls me along with him onto the dance floor. When his hands wrap around me, an electrifying shudder reverberates throughout my body. We sway together in perfect synchrony, so close it's as if we've fused our bodies together. Soft fingers tilt my chin up until our eyes meet. He gleams brilliantly at me, shimmering flashes of an azure fire. I'm completely entranced by him.

He studies me closely. His steady gaze is boring into me as he tilts his head down to capture my mouth. The kiss is gentle, but it's the way he looks at me that's different. As if we've crossed an invisible line, and neither one of us is turning back. Pulling away, he whispers against my lips.

"You're delicious." Then he reclaims my mouth again. Shivers of emotions radiate through me. I'm falling for this man and fast.

"Well, well, well, Drew, what do we got here? You two are dating now," he grits out through clenched teeth.

Pulling away from Drew, I look up to see Reese. I haven't seen him since that night. He's staring at me, scrutinizing my every move. My posture tightens, and suddenly I feel like I'm back in the bar drinking with him.

Crossing my arms in front of my body, I turn closer into Drew's arms. He squeezes me into him protectively, and the muscles in my back loosen.

"Reese, I guess it was too much to ask not to have to see you again." His words are curt as he places a gentle kiss on my forehead. Reese's eyes widen as his brow knits together.

"So are you guys a thing now. Really, Drew? A cocktail waitress? I know you have no standards, but isn't even that beneath you? But I guess you don't care about that." His eyes bore into me, anger glowing from them. "It's how she looks that matters to you."

Then he lifts his hand and swipes at his nose. Narrowing my eyes, I can see a slight film of white residue surrounding his nostril. He's high as a kite, that much is obvious.

"Let's go." Drew takes my hand in his and turns to Reese. "I'll talk to you when you're not fucked up out of your mind." Then he pulls us away.

He continues to drag me with him until we're in a dimly lit alcove behind a marble column. Drew is taking deep, ragged breaths, his body shaking from the effort and the anger rolling off him in waves.

Gently, my fingers caress his. "It's okay, Drew. I know he was high."

"It's not okay. His—"

I lean up and place a soft kiss on his lips. "Not everyone wants to be saved, Drew."

His mouth opens against mine, his tongue seeking entry. When he pulls back, he smirks.

"What?" I ask.

"You're good for me, Bae. You calm me. You make me less angry. You make me happy."

"I-You make—"

He stops me mid-sentence, silencing me with an earth-shattering kiss. When he finally pulls back, I stand there in utter euphoria. I don't want to ever come down from this high. This feeling, whatever it is, is more potent than any drug.

He grabs my hand and tilts his chin up, motioning in the direction of the dance floor. "Let's not let Reese ruin our night. I believe my girl wanted to see my moves."

We head back out and continue to dance the night away. We must have been twirling around the floor for some time before we realized we needed a break.

"I'll go grab us some waters if you want to go have a seat."

I send a grateful smile his way. I am parched. I watch him as he gracefully weaves through the throngs of people, artfully dodging the many people eagerly vying for his attention. Heading back to our table, I take a seat, sighing at the relief my feet feel from giving them a rest.

I turn in my seat to see Cynthia beaming down at me. "Drew hasn't brought a girl around me, you know. Not since Alexa. But the way he looks at you? He never looked at her that way, even with all the similarities. I feel awful saying that *here*, but it's true."

Similarities. "Here?"

"The gala," she clarifies.

"I don't understand."

"He didn't tell you . . ." Her brow furrows.

"Tell me what?" Dread pools in my stomach, and I'm not even sure why.

"The reason for the gala of course." She turns, her head moving back and forth as though she's looking for something. Two men wheel a large golden frame into the room, taking extra care to remove it from the cart and set it on a large easel. "Finally," she says, and I look back at her. "I've been wondering when they were going to put that out." She rolls her eyes. "The gala is for her." She points back toward the easel, and when my eyes land on it, I freeze. "I had this commissioned especially for tonight."

There, looking back at me is a young woman, eerily resembling me. The likeness is so great it's like looking in a mirror. My heart lurches in my chest, and my stomach drops.

"W-Who is that?" I stammer, completely entranced by the doppelgänger.

"Alexa Silver, of course," she says softly. "Drew's ex."

Silver. Like the club. The club named after a woman that could be my twin.

I gasp. "Darling, are you all right? I thought you knew about her," Cynthia asks, but I can't speak. I need to get out of here. I jump from my seat and run, paying no attention to the scene I'm causing.

chapter sixty-four

Bailey

"**C**HWAER." I HEAR A FAMILIAR VOICE SAY AND TURN TO find Reese, but I ignore him, making my way to the exit. "We need to talk," Reese says, grabbing my arm and spinning me to look at him.

"There is nothing for us to talk about." I yank my arm out of his grasp.

"You'll want to hear what I have to say. Drew certainly won't tell you the truth. It's written all over your face. You saw Alexa's picture."

I'm too confused about what I saw to even answer him. What more could Reese possibly know? Better yet, what the fuck is Drew still hiding?

She looks like you.

No . . . you look like her.

I stumble forward, and Reese catches me.

"I got you." He continues, "Let me take you away from here. We can talk, and I can fill in the gaps that Drew obviously won't."

Too numb to react or make decisions for myself, I allow him to lead me down the street until we are standing in front of what must be his car.

"Your car?"

"How else do you expect me to get to the Hamptons?" He chuckles. "I guess I could take the helicopter."

My eyes roll.

"What was that for?" he asks, grinning from ear to ear.

"I forget you rich boys have all the toys."

"It's a rough life," he says, trying to sound funny, but even in my current state, I can hear the bite to his words. "Get in."

"Can you even drive?"

"I'm not drunk, but if you stay here, I give Drew about two more seconds before he finds you. Something tells me he's the last person you want to see, chwaer."

"Why do you always call me that?"

He stands up taller. "Just get in," he commands, not at all friendly. The sting in his tone should have me thinking twice, but right now, he's the lesser of two evils.

With that, I swing open the door, pulling my body into the car and sitting in the lush leather seats. "Nice car," I murmur.

"Of course it is," he says, sounding a million miles away. "You picked it out."

My head snaps to him, brows furrowed in confusion.

"Bailey!" I hear Drew yell. His voice is too close for my liking.

"We need to go." My legs quake as my nerves build. I don't want Drew to catch me leaving with Reese. Not right now. I need to escape. To think. To allow Reese to tell me the things that Drew hasn't. A large part of me knows this isn't a good idea and that I should probably get out of the car. But instead, I turn to put my seat belt on. Reese is right. Drew will want to talk to me, but I'm not in the right headspace right now to deal with it.

It still feels like my heart is being ripped from my chest from what I saw in the picture. Was I just a replacement for his dead love? It sure the hell feels like it. I've never seen another person who looked so much like me and the parallels to our lives. Now that I think back on what Drew has told me . . . I can't help but feel like we're the same person.

It doesn't take more than a few seconds before the driver's side door is opening, and Reese is getting into the car.

"Where to?" I ask him as he stabs the ignition button beside the wheel. The fancy car comes to life with a rev of the engine.

"Someplace where I can tell you a story." A chill runs down my spine at the alarming way he says this. But nothing can prepare me for what comes next. His head turns to me. "Somewhere we can be together, chwaer."

"W-What does that mean? Chwaer?"

He peels out of the spot, speeding away from the gala and leaving my stomach behind. He's cutting corners and driving like a lunatic. "Reese, slow down!" I yell, but he doesn't respond. His eyes are locked forward with a vacant look to them. My nerves intensify tenfold—the dread from earlier at a fever pitch.

The light ahead turns red, and I'm momentarily relieved as the car slows to stop. Reese reaches his hand to open the glove compartment, and a picture falls out.

Alexa.

The picture is the same one from the gala.

"Why do you have this?" I ask, picking it up and waving it in the air.

"She's my chwaer."

"What does that mean?" I yell again.

He doesn't answer me but starts mumbling crazy talk.

"You were taken from me. He took you from me!" he screams, slamming his hand on the steering wheel. "It means sister. You're my fucking sister!" The light turns green, and the tires squeal as he slams down on the accelerator. "He took you from me. Drew poisoned you, and now we're going to be together. You and me." His head turns toward me, and what I see petrifies me. Chills run up the back of my neck.

He's manic, and he's going to kill us.

"Pull over!" I yell at him, but his maniacal laughter drowns out my pleas. "Let me the fuck out of this car, Reese." My hand flies to the door handle, and I try and fail to open the car door. It's locked, pinning me in with this crazy person.

My heart pounds in my chest.

I need to get out of here.

"I'm not going to let you leave me again. This time, I'm coming with you."

"Help!" I scream, but there's nobody to hear me. "Please. I'm not Alexa. I'm not your sister!" I pound on the door, willing it to give. My fist collides with the metal, over and over again until my skin burns like it's being ripped off my bones.

If I don't escape this car, he's going to kill me. I know it.

"Help!" My pleas and screams fall on deaf ears. He's lost his mind. All sensibility long gone. My terror mounts as I try to find an escape.

There won't be one.

As the realization sinks in, everything slows. My body jerks, and my ears start to ring. Somewhere in the distance, I hear the screech of the tires.

Time moves in slow motion.

The humming in my ears intensifies, and the car lurches forward. Reese slams on the brakes, but it's too late.

I brace for impact, but I'm not prepared for the sudden force as we collide.

My head pitches forward, connecting with something hard.

The airbag deploys.

The sound of metal crashing echoes around me.

And then quiet.

A bone-chilling silence as my eyes blink to focus.

The world is spinning, but I'm no longer moving.

A wave of nausea erupts inside me, and the thought that I need to get out of the car floats through my hazy subconscious.

"Don't move." I hear as I try to reach my hand to take my seat belt off, but that's when I feel it. Excruciating pain.

It feels like a knife is stabbing me.

I listen to the voice and stop trying to free myself.

Sirens blare in the distance, but I worry they won't make it in time.

My vision goes blurry.

The sirens become muffled.

And then nothing.

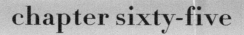

chapter sixty-five

Drew

WHERE DID SHE GO? I NEED TO TALK TO HER. I NEED TO explain. I run out of the building and down the street.

A few feet away, Reese's car peels out of the spot, and I take off after them. "Stop!" I yell at the top of my lungs, but it's no use.

"Throw me a set of keys," I scream at the valet.

"Which ones?"

"Just give me a set of goddamn keys," I bellow, and the poor kid jumps into gear. He hurls a set of keys into the air.

"The white car," he says, pointing at a beat-up Honda that must be his. I don't have time to think. My feet stomp the pavement in the direction of the Honda. In the distance, I can see Reese's car. The stoplight up ahead is red.

I feel crazed.

Out of control, I dash into the compact car. I start the engine and hit the gas, leaving the parking space on what feels like two wheels. I don't give a shit about anything other than getting to Bailey.

The light turns green before I make it to them, and the car swerves. "Fuck," I yell, wanting to bash Reese's face in for driving so out of control. Bailey's in that fucking car. *Because of your actions.*

I have the pedal to the floor, but Reese's car is too fast. A car pulls out in front of me, and I slam down on the horn, swerving to miss it. When I get around the red Ford, I see Reese up ahead and what occurs next plays out like a slow-motion picture in front of me. As he's pulling up to the next intersection, the light turns yellow, and he must think he can make it because he drives right through it, crossing into the intersection, and then my heart stops.

The tires screech.

The bone-shattering sound of crashing metal beats against my temples.

The two cars collide.

I stop the car and jump out, running as fast as I can to get to her.

"Bailey." The word blasts from my chest through my lungs, leaving my eardrums vibrating and my throat raw. I drop to my knees, my body physically unable to move as I take in the wreckage.

Bailey's inside what used to be Reese's car. Now it looks like meat after it's been through a grinder. Mangled and unrecognizable.

My heart pounds in my chest as I try to stand. I need to get to her. I'll crawl if I have to. A sturdy pair of hands come under my arms, helping me to stand. I look to the side to see a burly-looking man saying something that I can't hear. He points at a truck beside us, but I couldn't care less what he's saying until I hear his next words. "Go!"

Somehow, I manage to get my feet to work. When I make it to the car, I frantically try to open the door, but it's impossible. Through the broken glass, I see her damaged body. I know I can't touch or move her, but I need her to know I'm here.

Before I can think about anything other than her, I'm pulling the metal.

It doesn't move at first. The burly man from earlier runs up with a crowbar, and I step out of the way, allowing him to try. It gives a little, but not enough to open, not enough to even touch her.

"Bailey!" I shout through the crack. "Open your eyes," I plead. She doesn't, though. She doesn't move at all. My heart pounds in my chest as I yell at bystanders to call the paramedics.

The girl I love is in there, and it's my fault. I let this happen.

Things happen fast from that point on.

It's all a blurry haze.

I vaguely recall being pushed out of the way and Bailey being taken from the car. The paramedics whisk her away, and I just sit there on the pavement, paralyzed to the spot. This can't be happening. I promised I'd take care of her, and I let her down. I failed her. *I killed her.*

A sob breaks from my chest. I sit on the cold, hard ground with my head in my hands and bawl like a child. I feel someone place their hand on my shoulder and give it a gentle squeeze.

"You've got to go to her, Drew. She needs you at the hospital." I look up into my mother's sympathetic gaze. I don't deserve her pity. It's all my fault. I've failed her. Again.

The entire drive to the hospital, my mother takes pity on me and doesn't say a word. I look out the window into the dark abyss that matches my current state and don't even realize when her driver pulls up to the hospital entrance.

She says something, but I barely hear her. I'm jumping out of the car and running into the emergency room. Eyes scanning the room for a doctor or anyone who can tell me if she's okay.

"Drew," Harper calls from behind me, running in with panic etched across her face. "Where's Bailey?" she cries, tears streaming down her face. "Is she going to be okay?"

She runs into my arms, and I hold her while she sobs.

"Ms. Jameson?" a doctor asks, and Harper looks up, bobbing her head.

"How is she? Is she okay?" Harper asks the doctor now, and the doctor shakes her head.

Everything in me locks up.

"She was rushed back for emergency surgery. Her spleen was ruptured during impact and she has internal bleeding." She takes a breath. "This is a very serious injury."

"Will she be okay?" Harper whispers, and everything around me disappears while

I wait for the doctor to answer.

"Only time will tell," she says. "We'll keep you posted, but I suggest you stay close."

I don't move. I'm paralyzed in place, all my biggest fears playing out in my mind to further torment me. Harper steers me toward my seat, where I sit in shock. At some point, my mother joins me, but I don't so much as breathe.

Bailey could die. I could lose her. I sit like this for what feels like hours. The clock ticking on the wall threatens to undo me. Every second that goes by without news sends me further down the rabbit hole of misery.

"What if she doesn't make it, Mom?" I ask, breaking the deafening silence.

She turns in her seat, and I look over at her tear-filled face.

"We need to believe she will. She needs you to be strong for her, Drew."

"I caused this," I grate. "It's my fault."

"Whatever you did is done, Drew. But right now, you need to put your self-pity aside and put her first."

"I'm useless. I can't do anything." My voice rises, drawing unwanted attention from a few others sitting here waiting on news of their loved ones, but I don't give a fuck.

"I'm here, but there's nothing I can do." Her hand lands on my knee.

"You can pray, Drew." And I do. For the first time in probably my whole life, I walk to the chapel and fall to my knees.

I pray for Bailey. That she'll survive. That she'll be given a second chance to live a full, healthy life.

I pray for my sins, and for everyone I've ever hurt.

I pray for the chance to hold Bailey in my arms. Even if she chooses to walk away afterward.

"Drew, the doctor's waiting for you," my mom calls from the chapel door.

I say one last prayer for Bailey. *Please don't take her from me.*

chapter sixty-six

Bailey

"YOU WERE IN AN ACCIDENT. A RATHER SEVERE ONE," THE nurse says, checking my vitals and writing something on a notepad. "They had to cut you out of the car. You're lucky to be alive."

My eyes go wide, and I start to feel like I can't breathe. A machine starts to beep erratically.

"Calm down, Bailey. You're going to be okay," my mother says from my side.

"W-What happened to me?"

"Your spleen was ruptured, and you needed a blood transfusion." Harper's matter-of-fact words are just what I need at this moment. I need facts. *For once.*

I take a deep, cleansing breath. "I-I saw Daddy," I whisper, looking at my sister. "I dreamed of him. He held my hand while I was trapped in the car. He told me help was coming." A tear falls down her cheek, and she wipes it away, smiling.

"I have no doubt he was right there beside you, Bailey. You two always had such a special bond." This time it's my mother speaking. Her words are tender. Heartfelt.

I process this news, growing more grateful that I'm alive. I know how serious a spleen injury can be. I'm lucky to be alive.

Perhaps this entire event has been a wake-up call to my mother too? Only time will tell, but I decide to extend an olive branch. She is here, after all.

Reaching out, I lay my hand on top of hers. She smiles, sadly, and tears stream down her face. "I love you, Bailey."

"I love you too, Mom."

We sit in comfortable silence for a few minutes before I turn to the nurse still checking my vitals. "What happened to Reese?" I ask. Despite the entire accident being his fault, I still want to know he's all right. He wasn't in his right mind. It doesn't make it okay, but I don't want him to be dead.

"I'm not at liberty to talk about another patient," she says, finally managing to get the loud beeping to stop. A headache builds at my temples, and I close my eyes to ward it off.

"Can you just tell me if he's okay?"

"He's okay," Drew says, leaning against the doorway.

"You're not to be in here, sir." The nurse lasers him with a death glare.

"It's fine," Harper says. "We'll leave so you two can talk."

They both stand and exit the room, leaving me alone with the nurse and Drew.

"You upset her, and you're out of here," she warns before following my family. I need to tell this hospital she deserves a raise.

He takes a seat next to me but doesn't say a word and he doesn't touch me. Smart man.

"Tell me about Reese," I say, knowing he's the answer to my intel.

"He's stable. You experienced far worse injuries. He'll survive . . . if I don't kill him first."

I scoff. "I think you've hurt him enough."

Drew stiffens, catching my meaning. It isn't fair of me to bring up his part in Alexa's death. I can see the pain in his eyes. The regret.

"I want you to know that everything between us happened because I fell for you."

I chew on my cheek, not knowing if he believes what he's saying.

"I mean it, Bailey. At first, yes, I was drawn to you because you reminded me of her. But that's not why I fell for you," he says, eyes boring into mine. "That was all you. All Bailey Jameson. You might look like her, but that's where it starts and stops."

"Reese was talking to me like I was her. If he could be so easily confused, how am I supposed to believe that you weren't confusing us as well? That you weren't tangling your feelings for her with me. I just don't see how that's possible, Drew."

"I know it's hard to believe, and the fact I didn't tell you makes it look even worse, but I promise you, Bailey, you couldn't be more different. I cared about her greatly, but more as a life-long friend. She knew it, and so did I."

"Drew. Please stop. I can't do this with you."

He cuts me off, forging ahead. "Our relationship was out of convenience for both of us. If someone else would've come along and swept her off her feet, she'd have been gone."

"So you were more invested than she was? Is that what you're telling me?" I scoff. "I'm hardly seeing how that's supposed to make me feel better." I turn too suddenly, and pain radiates up my arm. "Ouch," I cry out, and Drew's eyes widen.

"Let me help you," he says, moving the wires so they don't pull on my IV.

"Thank you," I say.

His eyes are sad. I'm sure this isn't how he hoped our talk would go, but I'm hurt, both physically and mentally. He kept secrets from me—big secrets—and as much as I want to believe our relationship is based on true feelings, I can't help but feel like I'm the replacement Alexa.

"Stop," he commands. "Don't even think that way."

"How do you know what I'm thinking?" I snap.

"I know you, Bailey. I know everything about you because I'm in love with you."

I inhale at the intensity in his voice. "How do I know that, Drew? How do I know I'm not a fill-in? You lied to me."

He laughs, but it's not humorous. "You're not Alexa. You're the complete opposite," he starts. "You care about everyone else above yourself. You're selfless and kind." He grabs my hand. "That is what made me fall in love with you. I only kept it from you because of this. I never wanted you to doubt my love. It's not about what you look like, Bailey, but what's in here." He points at his heart. "I love you," he repeats.

"You loved her once."

He shakes his head. "Bailey. I. Love. You. It will always be you. One day, I'll make you my wife, and I'll spend a lifetime proving it."

My breath hitches at his declaration. Love is one thing, but marriage?

"Please tell me you want the same. Please tell me I haven't ruined everything," he begs.

I believe him. God help me, but looking into his soulful eyes, I see nothing but love shining back at me. The sincerity in his words touching me bone-deep. I love him. After almost dying, twice, I don't want to waste time with what-ifs. I have to take a leap of faith and trust that what I believe is truth. He loves me.

"I want the same, Drew. I want you. I love you."

His lips touch mine, and we lose ourselves in it. At this moment, it's just the two of us. The outside world can't touch us. For now, he's all I need.

chapter sixty-seven

Drew

I WALK INTO REESE'S ROOM, KNOWING THIS CAN'T BE AVOIDED. He needs to atone for what he put Bailey through. To hell with the property and all the ways in which he's fucked with me. This is about him almost killing an innocent girl.

He's asleep, and I contemplate waking him but think better of it. If Nurse Ratched is caring for him, she'll have my hide. When I'm about to leave, I hear his voice.

"Drew?" My name comes out raspy and weak.

I turn around to see Reese's eyes open, looking at me. He looks so small in that bed. Almost childlike. It doesn't escape me that he's alone. Nobody's here fussing over him.

That would've been Alexa. She was the only one who truly cared about her brother. She'd be here right now, and I know her absence is partially my fault. I need to learn that I can't take full responsibility for other people's actions. Their choices are their own, but I'm not there yet.

"How are you doing?" I step forward into the light and pause at the swelling and bruising around his eyes and up his neck.

Bailey's injuries were worse, but all of hers are internal or hidden by her clothes. At first glance, Reese's injuries physically look worse.

"I'm—" He looks embarrassed.

I remain quiet, needing him to speak.

"I'm so sorry." He inhales, wincing at whatever pain he must be feeling. "I-I lost my mind. I know it's no excuse, but my mind convinced me it was her. The drugs—" He trails off, sighing heavily. "Well, they fucked me up, man. You'll never know how sorry I am."

"You need help, Reese," I say, closing the distance and placing my hand on his shoulder.

"I know I do," he says, lowering his gaze to the bed. "The drugs help me forget. It's why I use." He looks at the ceiling for a long moment. "My life without Alexa is not one I want, Drew. She was the only person I cared about. She was the only person who cared about me."

I don't say a word. He obviously needs to get this out. Reese never saw a therapist after Alexa's death, which was a tragedy. His parents opposed it, saying he didn't need it. He'd survive. They are the lowest scum on this earth.

"She was the only person who really knew me. She was my only real family. The only one who gave a shit about me, and she's gone. How do I go on after losing that?"

I sigh, knowing that he truly feels that way. "She wouldn't want this. Alexa would never want you to repeat history. Your family did a number on her, too. Don't let them destroy you like they did her." I squeeze his shoulder. "We may not be able to choose our family, but we can choose to go our separate ways. There's nothing that says you're stuck with the hand you're dealt. Get up and walk the fuck away."

He nods. "I'm done with them. They couldn't even be bothered enough to visit. You're my only visitor."

I knew this was the case but hearing him say it only manages to churn my stomach. How could his parents be so damn cold?

"Thanks for coming, Drew. I know I'm probably the last person you want to see, but you being here means a lot."

"Listen, when you're released, you're going to be transported to a rehab facility in Arizona. It's the best in the nation. Everything is paid for. You go and get better. Understand?"

"Drew, you can't—"

"This is my final tribute to Alexa, Reese. She'd want you to get better. After this? I'm done. No more help. No more excuses. You get clean, or I write you off completely. Understand?"

He swallows hard, choking back the tears I can see welling in his eyes.

"I'll do better, Drew. For you."

I shake my head. "No. You get better and do better for you."

I squeeze his shoulder one final time before leaving Reese alone to think about what comes next. I can only hope he gets better.

I was given my redemption, and I feel he deserves his. Bailey is my happy ending, and I can only hope that one day, Reese finds his.

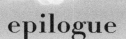

epilogue

Drew

I LOOK OVER AT MY SMILING WIFE.

Bailey looks radiant tonight. Her hair is swept up into an updo. At least I think that's what they fucking call it. And her navy-blue dress hits about an inch above her knees and scoops low on her open back. But it's my grandmother's ring on her finger that makes everything complete.

She's perfect, and she's mine.

It wasn't a smooth road to get here, but it was worth every bump and detour.

This weekend marks our fourth month as Mr. and Mrs. Lawson. I didn't think I'd ever want to hear those two words together in reference to me, but Bailey was a game changer.

She walks across the stage, head held high, and receives the diploma she's worked her ass off for. She didn't need it. I will always take care of her, but she insisted it was something she had to do for herself. I couldn't be prouder of the woman she is.

Bailey looks up, searching the room until her eyes land on me. She flashes me that knowing smile. I've been trying to get my hands up her dress all day. She looks too damn good, and she knows it. If she keeps it up, I'm going to fuck her right here.

After she's gotten her diploma, the rest of the ceremony

drags on. I bear it because this is important to her. But while her classmates get their recognition, I'm dreaming up all the ways I'm going to have her tonight.

When the ceremony has finally concluded, Bailey struts my way. All those dirty fantasies I'd concocted, coming back to my mind. When she gets close, I pull her into my arms.

"I want you."

"You have me," she says, ghosting her lips against mine.

"I'm so proud of you," I say, knowing she deserves to hear it. And I mean it wholeheartedly.

"Took me long enough."

I step back, hating how she still does that. She's constantly belittling herself, underselling all her hard work. It's something her therapist has been working on, and I've been helping push the change at home.

"But you did it. You went back to school. Got your degree, and then if I wasn't impressed enough, you got your master's. You are one kick-ass woman, beautiful."

She grins. "I couldn't have done it without you."

"Know what else you can't do without me?" I ask, waggling my brows suggestively, and she smacks my chest.

"You're such a Neanderthal." She laughs.

"But I'm all yours."

"Yes . . . that you are." She smiles.

"But seriously, we're going to do something after this."

Her brow lifts in question, but I want to drag out the suspense a little while longer.

I've been working on a surprise for her graduation. One that she and I have both played a part in, only she never realized I was ten steps ahead of everything she did. While she was picking out tables and color schemes for down the road, I was actually ordering it and having everything installed—with a lot of help from Carter, but I'm not allowing him to steal my thunder.

She got her Master's in Business Management, and I know she's going to rock the hell out of owning her very own restaurant. The deed's in her name. It's hers, and I can't wait to surprise her with it.

"What did you do, Mr. Lawson?"

I groan. "I love it when you call me that. It's so dirty, baby."

She chuckles. "Maybe we should get out of here so you can have your way with me."

She lifts up on her tiptoes and places a kiss on my lips.

"I love you," I whisper for her ears only.

"Always," she replies.

Life is good.

The End

acknowledgments

I want to thank my entire family. I love you all so much.

Thank you to my husband and my kids for always loving me. You guys are my heart!

Thank you to my Mom, Dad, Liz and Ralph for always believing in me, encouraging me and loving me!

Thank you to my in-laws for everything they do for me!

Thank you to all of my brothers and sisters!

Thank you to everyone that helped with Tempted.

Jenny Sims

Marla Esposito

Champagne Formats

Hang Le

Jill Glass

Jaime Ryter

Sarah Sentz

Viviana Izzo

Grey's Promotions

Special Thanks to Lulu! You're always there for me with amazing insight and I greatly appreciate all your feedback and friendship.

Suzi: You're always there to talk plot and find the holes, thank you!

Thank you to The Cover Lab for such a great image.

Thank you to Joe Arden, Andi Arndt, Kim Gilmour and Lyric for bringing Tempted to life on audio.

Thank you to Arden's Darlings for your support.

Thank you to my AMAZING ARC TEAM! You guys rock!

Thank you to my beta/test team.

Parker: You rock even if you send weird gifts . . .jk I adore you.

Leigh: Thank you for always being there for me. I love you!

Kelly: Thank you for all your input and proofing my audio.

Jessica. Thank you for your wonderful and extremely helpful feedback.

Jill: Thank you for all your help.

Melissa: Thanks for everything.

Harloe: Thanks for always being there.

Mia: Thanks for always talking shop ie plots and helping me write my blurbs.

Mary: Thank you for reading an early copy and helping come up with ideas.

I want to thank ALL my friends for putting up with me while I wrote this book. Thank you!

To all of my author friends who listen to me complain and let me ask for advice, thank you!

To the ladies in the Ava Harrison Support Group, I couldn't have done this without your support!

Please consider joining my Facebook reader group Ava Harrison Support Group

Thanks to all the bloggers! Thanks for your excitement and love of books!

Last but certainly not least…

Thank you to the readers!

Thank you so much for taking this journey with me.